PRAISE FROM BOTH SIDES OF THE ATLANTIC—

"Jamaica Inn is Daphne du Maurier's fourth novel, and it may be said to mark her veritable coming of age as a novelist..."

The New York Times

"There is more than horrors and thrills to be found in *Jamaica Inn*.... a good example of how readable craftsmanship can make a book."

Manchester Guardian

"...an exciting brew, reminiscent of Stevenson and some of Masefield, and just the thing for a late evening's reading...." *Saturday Review*

JAMAICA INN
was originally published by
Doubleday and Company, Inc.

Other books by Daphne du Maurier

Frenchman's Creek
Gerald: A Portrait
Hungry Hill
The Glass-Blowers
The Infernal World of Branwell Brontë
The King's General
Kiss Me Again, Stranger
The Loving Spirit
The Parasites
Rebecca
The Scapegoat

Published by Pocket Books, Inc.

Are there paperbound books you want but cannot find at your retail stores?

You can get any title that is in print in these famous series:
Pocket Book editions • Pocket *Cardinal* editions • Permabook editions
The Pocket Library • Washington Square Press • All Saints Press
Simply enclose retail price plus 10¢ per book
for mailing and handling costs.
Not responsible for orders containing cash.
Please send check or money order to:
Mail Service Department
Pocket Books, Inc.
1 West 39th Street
New York, N.Y. 10018

Free catalogue sent on request

JAMAICA INN

___

_____

_____

Daphne du Maurier

PUBLISHED BY **POCKET**  **BOOKS, INC.** NEW YORK

JAMAICA INN

Doubleday edition published April, 1936

A *Pocket Book* edition
1st printing.....September, 1946
9th printing..........July, 1965

This *Pocket Book* edition includes every word
contained in the original, higher-priced edition. It is printed
from brand-new plates made from completely reset, clear, easy-to-read
type. *Pocket Book* editions are published by Pocket Books, Inc., and
are printed and distributed in the U.S.A. by Affiliated Publishers, a
division of Pocket Books, Inc., 630 Fifth Avenue, New York, N.Y. 10020.
Trademark of Pocket Books, Inc., 630 Fifth Avenue,
New York, N.Y. 10020, registered in the United States
and other countries.

L

NOTE

JAMAICA INN *stands today, hospitable and kindly, a temperance house on the twenty-mile road between Bodmin and Launceston.*

In the following story of adventure I have pictured it as it might have been over a hundred and twenty years ago; and although existing place names figure in the pages, the characters and events described are entirely imaginary.

Daphne du maurier.

Bodinnick-by-Fowey.

Chapter 1

IT WAS a cold grey day in late November. The weather had
changed overnight, when a backing wind brought a granite
sky and a mizzling rain with it, and although it was now
only a little after two o'clock in the afternoon the pallor of
a winter evening seemed to have closed upon the hills,
cloaking them in mist. It would be dark by four. The air
was clammy cold, and for all the tightly closed windows it
penetrated the interior of the coach. The leather seats felt
damp to the hands, and there must have been a small crack
in the roof, because now and again little drips of rain fell
softly through, smudging the leather and leaving a dark
blue stain like a splodge of ink. The wind came in gusts, at
times shaking the coach as it travelled round the bend of
the road, and in the exposed places on the high ground it
blew with such force that the whole body of the coach
trembled and swayed, rocking between the high wheels like
a drunken man.

The driver, muffled in a greatcoat to his ears, bent almost
double in his seat in a faint endeavour to gain shelter from
his own shoulders, while the dispirited horses plodded sullenly to his command, too broken by the wind and the
rain to feel the whip that now and again cracked above
their heads, while it swung between the numb fingers of
the driver.

The wheels of the coach creaked and groaned as they
sank into the ruts on the road, and sometimes they flung up
the soft spattered mud against the windows, where it mingled with the constant driving rain, and whatever view

1

there might have been of the countryside was hopelessly obscured.

The few passengers huddled together for warmth, exclaiming in unison when the coach sank into a heavier rut than usual, and one old fellow, who had kept up a constant complaint ever since he had joined the coach at Truro, rose from his seat in a fury, and, fumbling with the window sash, let the window down with a crash, bringing a shower of rain in upon himself and his fellow passengers. He thrust his head out and shouted up to the driver, cursing him in a high petulant voice for a rogue and a murderer; that they would all be dead before they reached Bodmin if he persisted in driving at breakneck speed; they had no breath left in their bodies as it was, and he for one would never travel by coach again.

Whether the driver heard him or not was uncertain; it seemed more likely that the stream of reproaches was carried away in the wind, for the old fellow, after waiting a moment, put up the window again, having thoroughly chilled the interior of the coach, and, settling himself once more in his corner, wrapped his blanket about his knees and muttered in his beard.

His nearest neighbour, a jovial red-faced woman in a blue cloak, sighed heavily in sympathy, and, with a wink to anyone who might be looking and a jerk of her head towards the old man, she remarked for at least the twentieth time that it was the dirtiest night she ever remembered, and she had known some; that it was proper old weather and no mistaking it for summer this time; and, burrowing into the depths of a large basket, she brought out a great hunk of cake and plunged into it with strong white teeth.

Mary Yellan sat in the opposite corner, where the trickle of rain oozed through the crack in the roof. Sometimes a cold drip of moisture fell upon her shoulder, which she brushed away with impatient fingers.

She sat with her chin cupped in her hands, her eyes fixed on the window splashed with mud and rain, hoping with a sort of desperate interest that some ray of light would break the heavy blanket of sky, and but a momentary trace of that lost blue heaven that had mantled Helford yesterday shine for an instant as a forerunner of fortune.

Already, though barely forty miles by road from what had been her home for three-and-twenty years, the hope within her heart had tired, and that rather gallant courage which was so large a part of her, and had stood her in such stead during the long agony of her mother's illness and death, was now shaken by this first fall of rain and the nagging wind.

The country was alien to her, which was a defeat in itself. As she peered through the misty window of the coach she looked out upon a different world from the one she had known only a day's journey back. How remote now and hidden perhaps for ever were the shining waters of Helford, the green hills and the sloping valleys, the white cluster of cottages at the water's edge. It was a gentle rain that fell at Helford, a rain that pattered in the many trees and lost itself in the lush grass, formed into brooks and rivulets that emptied into the broad river, sank into the grateful soil which gave back flowers in payment.

This was a lashing, pitiless rain that stung the windows of the coach, and it soaked into a hard and barren soil. No trees here, save one or two that stretched bare branches to the four winds, bent and twisted from centuries of storm, and so blackened were they by time and tempest that, even if spring did breathe on such a place, no buds would dare to come to leaf for fear that the late frost should kill them. It was a scrubby land, without hedgerow or meadow; a country of stones, black heather, and stunted broom.

There would never be a gentle season here, thought Mary; either grim winter as it was today, or else the dry and parching heat of midsummer, with never a valley to give shade or shelter, but grass that turned yellow-brown before May was passed. The country had gone grey with the weather. Even the people on the road and in the villages changed in harmony with their background. At Helston, where she had taken the first coach, she had trodden familiar ground. So many childish memories clung about Helston. The weekly drive to market with her father in the

3

vanished days, and, when he was taken from them, the fortitude with which her mother held his place, driving backwards and forwards, winter and summer, as he had done, with her hens and her eggs and her butter at the back of the cart, while Mary sat at her side, clutching a basket as big as herself, her small chin resting on the handle. Folk were friendly in Helston; the name of Yellan was known and respected in the town, for the widow had had a hard fight against life when her husband died, and there were not many women who would have lived alone as she did with one child and a farm to tend, with never a thought of taking another man. There was a farmer at Manaccan who would have asked her had he dared, and another up the river at Gweek, but they could tell from her eyes she would have neither of them, but belonged in body and mind to the man who had gone. It was the hard work of the farm that told upon her in the end, for she would not spare herself, and, though she had driven and flogged her energy for the seventeen years of her widowhood, she could not stand up to the strain when the last test came, and her heart went from her.

Little by little her stock had decreased, and with times being bad—so she was told in Helston—and prices fallen to nothing, there was no money anywhere. Upcountry it was the same. There would be starvation in the farms before long. Then a sickness attacked the ground and killed the livestock in the villages round Helford. There was no name to it, and no cure could be discovered. It was a sickness that came over everything and destroyed, much as a late frost will out of season, coming with the new moon and then departing, leaving no trace of its passage save the little trail of dead things in its path. It was an anxious, weary time for Mary Yellan and her mother. One by one they saw the chickens and the ducklings they had reared sicken and die, and the young calf fell in the meadow where he stood. The most pitiful was the old mare who had served them twenty years, and upon whose broad and sturdy back Mary had first straddled her young legs. She died in the stall one morning, her faithful head in Mary's lap; and when a pit was dug for her under the apple tree in the orchard, and she was buried, and they knew she would no longer carry them to Helston market day, Mary's mother turned to her and said, "There's something of me gone in the grave with poor Nell, Mary. I don't know whether it's my faith or what it is, but my heart feels tired and I can't go on any more."

She went into the house and sat down in the kitchen, pale as a sheet, and ten years her age. Listless, she shrugged her shoulders when Mary said she would fetch the doctor. "It's too late, child," she said, "seventeen years too late." And she began to cry softly, who had never cried before.

Mary fetched the old doctor who lived at Mawgan and who had brought her into the world, and as he drove her back in his trap he shook his head at her. "I tell you what it is, Mary," he said; "your mother has spared neither her mind nor her body since your father died, and she has broken down at last. I don't like it. It's come at a bad time."

They drove along the twisting lane to the farmhouse at the top of the village. A neighbour met them at the gate, her face eager to impart bad news. "Your mother's worse," she cried. "She came out of the door just now, staring like a ghost, and she trembled all over, and fell down in the path. Mrs. Hoblyn has gone to her, and Will Searle; they've lifted her inside, poor soul. They say her eyes are shut."

Firmly the doctor pushed the little gaping crowd away from the door. Together he and the man Searle lifted the still figure from the floor and carried her upstairs to the bedroom.

"It's a stroke," said the doctor, "but she's breathing; her pulse is steady. This is what I've been afraid of—that she'd snap suddenly, like this. Why it's come just now after all these years is known only to the Lord and herself. You must prove yourself your parents' child now, Mary, and help her through this. You are the only one who can."

For six long months or more Mary nursed her mother in this her first and last illness, but with all the care she and the doctor gave her it was not the widow's will to recover. She had no wish to fight for her life.

It was as though she longed for release and prayed silently that it would come quickly. She said to Mary, "I don't want you to struggle as I have done. It's a breaking of the body and of the spirit. There's no call for you to stay on at Helford after I am gone. It's best for you to go to your aunt Patience up to Bodmin."

There was no use in Mary telling her mother that she would not die. It was fixed there in her mind, and there was no fighting it.

"I haven't any wish to leave the farm, Mother," she said. "I was born here and my father before me, and you were a Helford woman. This is where the Yellans belong to be. I'm not afraid of being poor, and the farm falling away. You worked here for seventeen years alone, so why shouldn't I do the same? I'm strong; I can do the work of a man; you know that."

"It's no life for a girl," said her mother. "I did it all these years because of your father, and because of you. Working for someone keeps a woman calm and contented, but it's another thing when you work for yourself. There's no heart in it then."

"I'd be no use in a town," said Mary. "I've never known anything but this life by the river, and I don't want to. Going into Helston is town enough for me. I'm best here, with the few chickens that's left to us, and the green stuff in the garden, and the old pig, and a bit of a boat on the river. What would I do up to Bodmin with my aunt Patience?"

"A girl can't live alone, Mary, without she goes queer in the head, or comes to evil. It's either one or the other. Have you forgotten poor Sue, who walked the churchyard at midnight with the full moon, and called upon the lover she had never had? And there was one maid, before you were born, left an orphan at sixteen. She ran away to Falmouth and went with the sailors.

"I'd not rest in my grave, nor your father neither, if we didn't leave you safe. You'll like your aunt Patience; she was always a great one for games and laughing, with a heart as large as life. You remember when she came here, twelve years back? She had ribbons in her bonnet and a silk petticoat. There was a fellow working at Trelowarren had an eye to her, but she thought herself too good for him."

Yes, Mary remembered Aunt Patience, with her curled fringe and large blue eyes, and how she laughed and chatted, and how she picked up her skirts and tiptoed through the mud in the yard. She was as pretty as a fairy.

"What sort of a man your uncle Joshua is I cannot say," said her mother, "for I've never set eyes on him nor known anyone what has. But when your aunt married him ten years ago last Michaelmas she wrote a pack of giddy nonsense you'd expect a girl to write, and not a woman over thirty."

"They'd think me rough," said Mary slowly. "I haven't the pretty manners they'd expect. We wouldn't have much to say to one another."

"They'll love you for yourself and not for any airs and graces. I want you to promise me this, child, that when I'm gone you'll write to your aunt Patience and tell her that it was my last and dearest wish that you should go to her."

"I promise," said Mary, but her heart was heavy and distressed at the thought of a future so insecure and changed, with all that she had known and loved gone from her, and not even the comfort of familiar trodden ground to help her through the bad days when they came.

Daily her mother weakened; daily the life ebbed from her. She lingered through harvesttime, and through the fruit picking, and through the first falling of the leaves. But when the mists came in the morning, and the frosts settled on the ground, and the swollen river ran in flood to meet the boisterous sea, and the waves thundered and broke on the little beaches of Helford, the widow turned restlessly in her bed, plucking at the sheets. She called Mary by her dead husband's name, and spoke of things that were gone and of people Mary had never known. For three days she lived in a little world of her own, and on the fourth day she died.

One by one Mary saw the things she had loved and understood pass into other hands. The livestock went at Helston market. The furniture was bought by neighbours, stick by stick. A man from Coverack took a fancy to the house and purchased it; with pipe in mouth he straddled the yard and pointed out the changes he would make, the trees he would cut down to clear his view; while Mary watched him in dumb loathing from her window as she packed her small belongings in her father's trunk.

This stranger from Coverack made her an interloper in her own home; she could see from his eye he wanted her to be gone, and she had no other thought now but to be away and out of it all, and her back turned for ever. Once more she read the letter from her aunt, written in a cramped hand, on plain paper. The writer said she was shocked at the blow that had befallen her niece; that she had had no idea her sister was ill, it was so many years now since she had been to Helford. And she went on: "There have been changes with us you would not know. I no longer live in Bodmin, but nearly twelve miles outside, on the road to Launceston. It's a wild and lonely spot, and if you were to come to us I should be glad of your company, wintertime. I have asked your uncle, and he does not object, he says, if you are quiet-spoken and not a talker, and will give help when needed. He cannot give you money, or feed you for nothing, as you will understand. He will expect your help in the bar, in return for your board and lodging. You see, your uncle is the landlord of Jamaica Inn."

Mary folded the letter and put it in her trunk. It was a strange message of welcome from the smiling Aunt Patience she remembered.

A cold, empty letter, giving no word of comfort, and admitting nothing, except that her niece must not ask for money. Aunt Patience, with her silk petticoat and delicate ways, the wife of an innkeeper! Mary decided that this was something her mother had not known. The letter was very different from the one penned by a happy bride ten years ago.

However, Mary had promised, and there was no returning on her word. Her home was sold; there was no place for her here. Whatever her welcome should be, her aunt was her own mother's sister, and that was the one thing to remember. The old life lay behind—the dear familiar farm and the shining Helford waters. Before her lay the future—and Jamaica Inn.

And so it was that Mary Yellan found herself northward bound from Helston in the creaking, swaying coach, through Truro town, at the head of the Fal, with its many roofs and spires, its broad cobbled streets, the blue sky overhead still speaking of the south, the people at the doors smiling and waving as the coach rattled past. But when Truro lay behind in the valley, the sky came overcast, and the country on either side of the highroad grew rough and untilled. Villages were scattered now, and there were few smiling faces at the cottage doors. Trees were sparse; hedges there were none. Then the wind blew, and the rain came with the wind. And so the coach rumbled into Bodmin, grey and forbidding like the hills that cradled it, and one by one the passengers gathered up their things in preparation for departure—all save Mary, who sat still in her corner. The driver, his face a stream of rain, looked in at the window.

"Are you going on to Launceston?" he said. "It'll be a wild drive tonight across the moors. You can stay in Bodmin, you know, and go on by coach in the morning. There'll be none in this coach going on but you."

"My friends will be expecting me," said Mary. "I'm not afraid of the drive. And I don't want to go as far as Launceston; will you please put me down at Jamaica Inn?"

The man looked at her curiously. "Jamaica Inn?" he said. "What would you be doing at Jamaica Inn? That's no place for a girl. You must have made a mistake, surely." He stared at her hard, not believing her.

"Oh, I've heard it's lonely enough," said Mary, "but I don't belong to a town anyway. It's quiet on Helford River, winter and summer, where I come from, and I never felt lonely there."

"I never said nothing about loneliness," answered the man. "Maybe you don't understand, being a stranger up here. It's

9

not the twenty-odd mile of moor I'm thinking of, though that'd scare most women. Here, wait a minute." He called over his shoulder to a woman who stood in the doorway of the Royal, lighting the lamp above the porch, for it was already dusk.

"Missus," he said, "come here an' reason with this young girl. I was told she was for Launceston, but she's asked me to put her down at Jamaica."

The woman came down the steps and peered into the coach.

"It's a wild, rough place up there," she said, "and if it's work you are looking for, you won't find it on the farms. They don't like strangers on the moors. You'd do better down here in Bodmin."

Mary smiled at her. "I shall be all right," she said. "I'm going to relatives. My uncle is landlord of Jamaica Inn."

There was a long silence. In the grey light of the coach Mary could see that the woman and the man were staring at her. She felt chilled suddenly, anxious; she wanted some word of reassurance from the woman, but it did not come. Then the woman drew back from the window. "I'm sorry," she said slowly. "It's none of my business, of course. Good night."

The driver began to whistle, rather red in the face, as one who wishes to rid himself of an awkward situation. Mary leant forward impulsively and touched his arm. "Would you tell me?" she said. "I shan't mind what you say. Is my uncle not liked? Is something the matter?"

The man looked very uncomfortable. He spoke gruffly and avoided her eyes. "Jamaica's got a bad name," he said; "queer tales get about; you know how it is. But I don't want to make any trouble. Maybe they're not true."

"What sort of tales?" asked Mary. "Do you mean there's much drunkenness there? Does my uncle encourage bad company?"

The man would not commit himself. "I don't want to make trouble," he repeated, "and I don't know anything. It's only what people say. Respectable folk don't go to Jamaica any more. That's all I know. In the old days we used to water the horses there, and feed them, and go in for a bit of a bite and drink. But we don't stop there any more. We whip the horses past and wait for nothing, not till we get to Five Lanes, and then we don't bide long."

"Why don't folk go there? What is their reason?" Mary persisted.

The man hesitated; it was as though he were searching for words.

"They're afraid," he said at last; and then he shook his head; he would say no more. Perhaps he felt he had been churlish and was sorry for her, for a moment later he looked in at the window again and spoke to her.

"Will you not take a cup of tea before we go?" he said. "It's a long drive before you, and it's cold on the moors."

Mary shook her head. Desire for food had left her, and though the tea would have warmed her, she did not wish to descend from the coach and walk into the Royal, where the woman would have stared at her, and people would murmur. Besides, there was a little nagging coward in her that whispered, "Stay in Bodmin, stay in Bodmin," and for all she knew she might have given way to it in the shelter of the Royal. She had promised her mother to go to Aunt Patience, and there must be no going back on her given word.

"We'd best be going then," said the driver. "You are the only traveller on the road tonight. Here's another rug for your knees. I'll whip the horses on when we've climbed the hill out of Bodmin, for it's no night for the road. I shan't be easy in my mind until I reach my bed in Launceston. There's not many of us likes to cross the moors in wintertime, not when the weather's dirty." He slammed the door and climbed to his seat.

The coach rumbled away down the street, past the safe and solid houses, the busy winking lights, the scattered people hurrying home for supper, their figures bowed against the wind and rain. Through the shuttered windows Mary could see chinks of friendly candlelight; there would be a fire within the grate, and a cloth spread on the table, a woman and children sitting down to their meal, while the man warmed his hands before the cheerful blaze. She thought of the smiling countrywoman who had been her fellow passenger; she wondered if she was now sitting at her own table, with her children by her side. How comfortable she had been, with her apple cheeks, her rough, worn hands! What a world of security in her deep voice! And Mary made a little story to herself of how she might have followed her from the coach, and prayed her company, and asked her for a home. Nor would she have been refused, she was certain of that. There would have been a smile for her, and a friendly hand, and a bed for her. She would have served the woman, and grown to love her, shared something of her life, become acquainted with her people.

Now the horses were climbing the steep hill out of the town, and, looking through the window at the back of the coach, Mary could see the lights of Bodmin fast disappearing, one by one, until the last glimmer winked and flickered and was gone. She was alone now with the wind and the rain, and twelve long miles of barren moor between her and her destination.

She wondered if this was how a ship felt when the security of harbour was left behind. No vessel could feel more desolate than she did, not even if the wind thundered in the rigging and the sea licked her decks.

It was dark in the coach now, for the torch gave forth a sickly yellow glare, and the draught from the crack in the roof sent the flame wandering hither and thither, to the danger of the leather, and Mary thought it best to extinguish it. She sat huddled in her corner, swaying from side to side as the coach was shaken, and it seemed to her that never before had she known there was malevolence in solitude. The very coach, which all the day had rocked her like a cradle, now held a note of menace in its creaks and groans. The wind tore at the roof, and the showers of rain, increasing in violence now there was no shelter from the hills, spat against the windows with new venom. On either side of the road the country stretched interminably into space. No trees, no lane, no cluster of cottages or hamlet,

12

but mile upon mile of bleak moorland, dark and untraversed, rolling like a desert land to some unseen horizon. No human being could live in this wasted country, thought Mary, and remain like other people; the very children would be born twisted, like the blackened shrubs of broom, bent by the force of a wind that never ceased, blow as it would from east and west, from north and south. Their minds would be twisted, too, their thoughts evil, dwelling as they must amidst marshland and granite, harsh heather and crumbling stone.

They would be born of strange stock who slept with this earth as a pillow, beneath this black sky. They would have something of the devil left in them still. On wound the road across the dark and silent land, with never a light to waver for an instant as a message of hope to the traveller within the coach. Perhaps there was no habitation in all the long one-and-twenty miles that stretched between the two towns of Bodmin and Launceston; perhaps there was not even a poor shepherd's hut on the desolate highway: nothing but the one grim landmark that was Jamaica Inn.

Mary lost count of time and space; the miles might have been a hundred and the hour midnight, for all she knew. She began to cling to the safety of the coach; at least it had some remnant of familiarity. She had known it since the early morning, and that was long ago. However great a nightmare was this eternal drive, there were at least the four close walls to protect her, the shabby leaking roof, and, within calling distance, the comfortable presence of the driver. At last it seemed to her that he was driving his horses to an even greater speed; she heard him shout to them, the cry of his voice blown past her window on the wind.

She lifted the sash and looked out. She was met with a blast of wind and rain that blinded her for the moment, and then, shaking clear her hair and pushing it from her eyes, she saw that the coach was topping the breast of a hill at a furious gallop, while on either side of the road was rough moorland, looming ink black in the mist and rain.

Ahead of her, on the crest, and to the left, was some sort of a building, standing back from the road. She could see

13

tall chimneys, murky dim in the darkness. There was no other house, no other cottage. If this was Jamaica, it stood alone in glory, foursquare to the winds. Mary gathered her cloak around her and fastened the clasp. The horses had been pulled to a standstill and stood sweating under the rain, the steam coming from them in a cloud.

The driver climbed down from his seat, pulling her box down with him. He seemed hurried, and he kept glancing over his shoulder towards the house.

"Here you are," he said; "across the yard there yonder. If you hammer on the door they'll let you in. I must be getting on or I'll not reach Launceston tonight." In a moment he was up on his seat again and picking up the reins. He shouted at his horses, whipping them in a fever of anxiety. The coach rumbled and shook, and in a moment it was away and down the road, disappearing as though it had never been, lost and swallowed up in the darkness.

Mary stood alone, with the trunk at her feet. She heard a sound of bolts being drawn in the dark house behind her, and the door was flung open. A great figure strode into the yard, swinging a lantern from side to side.

"Who is it?" came the shout. "What do you want here?"

Mary stepped forward and peered up into the man's face.

The light shone in her eyes, and she could see nothing. He swung the lantern to and fro before her, and suddenly he laughed and took hold of her arm, pulling her roughly inside the porch.

"Oh, it's you, is it?" he said. "So you've come to us after all? I'm your uncle, Joss Merlyn, and I bid you welcome to Jamaica Inn." He drew her into the shelter of the house, laughing again, and shut the door, and stood the lantern upon a table in the passage. And they looked upon each other face to face.

Chapter 2

HE WAS a great husk of a man, nearly seven feet high, with a creased black brow and a skin the colour of a gypsy. His thick dark hair fell over his eyes in a fringe and hung about his ears. He looked as if he had the strength of a horse, with immense powerful shoulders, long arms that reached almost to his knees, and large fists like hams. His frame was so big that in a sense his head was dwarfed and sunk between his shoulders, giving that half-stooping impression of a giant gorilla, with his black eyebrows and his mat of hair. But for all his long limbs and mighty frame there was nothing of the ape about his features, for his nose was hooked, curving to a mouth that might have been perfect once but was now sunken and fallen, and there was still something fine about his great dark eyes, in spite of the lines and pouches and the red blood flecks.

The best things left to him were his teeth, which were all good still, and very white, so that when he smiled they showed up clearly against the tan of his face, giving him the lean and hungry appearance of a wolf. And, though there should be a world of difference between the smile of a man and the bared fangs of a wolf, with Joss Merlyn they were one and the same.

"So you are Mary Yellan," he said at length, towering above her, his head bent to observe her more closely, "and you've come all this way to look after your uncle Joss. I call it very handsome of you."

He laughed again, mocking her, his laugh bellowing through the house, acting like a lash on the strung nerves of Mary.

"Where is my aunt Patience?" she asked, glancing around her in the dimly lit passage, cheerless with its cold stone flags and narrow rickety staircase. "Is she not expecting me, then?"

"'Where's my aunt Patience?'" mimicked the man. "Where's my dear auntie to kiss and daddle me, and make much of me? Can't you wait an instant without running to her? Haven't you a kiss for your uncle Joss?"

Mary drew back. The thought of kissing him revolted her. He was either mad or drunk, anyway. Probably both. She did not want to anger him, though; she was too frightened for that.

He saw the question pass through her mind, and he laughed again.

"Oh, no," he said, "I'm not going to touch you; you're safe as a church with me. I never did like dark women, my dear, and I've better things to do than to play cat's cradle with me own niece."

He jeered down at her contemptuously, treating her like a fool, tired of his joke. Then he lifted his head to the stairs.

"Patience," he roared, "what in hell are you doing? Here's the girl arrived, whimpering for you. She's sick of the sight of me already."

There was a little flutter at the head of the stairs, and a footstep dragged. Then the flicker of a candle, and an exclamation. Down the narrow stairs came a woman, shielding the light from her eyes. She wore a dingy mobcap on her thin grey hair, which hung in elflocks to her shoulders. She had turned the edges of her hair in a vain attempt to recapture ringlets, but the curl had gone. Her face had fallen away, and the skin was stretched tight across her cheekbones. Her eyes were large and staring, as though they asked perpetually a question, and she had a little nervous trick of working her mouth, now pursing the lips and now relaxing them. She wore a faded striped petticoat that had once been cherry coloured and was now a washed-out pink, and over her shoulders was flung a much-mended shawl. She had obviously just strung a new ribbon in her cap in some small attempt to brighten her dress, and it struck a false, in-

16

congruous note. It was bright scarlet and showed up in horrible contrast to the pallor of her face. Mary stared at her dumbly, stricken with sorrow. Was this poor tattered creature the bewitching Aunt Patience of her dreams, dressed now like a slattern, and twenty years her age?

The little woman came down the stairs and into the hall; she took Mary's hands in hers and peered into her face. "Have you really come?" she whispered. "It is my niece Mary Yellan, isn't it? My dead sister's child?"

Mary nodded, thanking God that her mother could not see her now. "Dear Aunt Patience," she said gently, "I'm glad to see you again. It's so many long years since you came to us at Helford."

The woman kept pawing her with her hands, stroking her clothes, feeling her, and suddenly she clung to her, burying her head against her shoulder, and she began to cry, loudly and fearfully, drawing her breath in gasps.

"Ah, stop that," growled her husband. "What sort of a welcome is this? What have you got to squark about, you damned fool? Can't you see the girl wants her supper? Get her out to the kitchen and give her some bacon and a drink."

He bent down and shouldered Mary's box as though it weighed less than a paper packet. "I'll take this to her room," he said, "and if you've not got a bite of supper on the table by the time I'm down again I'll give you something to cry about; and you too, if you like," he added, thrusting his face into Mary's and laying one great finger across her mouth. "Are you tame, or do you bite?" he said, and then he laughed once more, bellowing to the roof, and thundered up the narrow stairs with the box swaying on his shoulders.

Aunt Patience controlled herself. She made a tremendous effort and smiled, patting her thin locks into place in an old gesture that Mary half remembered, and then, blinking nervously and working her mouth, she led the way to yet another murky passage, and so into the kitchen, which was lit by three candles, while a low turf fire smouldered on the hearth.

"You mustn't mind your uncle Joss," she said, her manner changing suddenly, fawning almost, like a whimpering dog that has been trained by constant cruelty to implicit obedience, and who, in spite of kicks and curses, will fight like a tiger for its master. "Your uncle must be humoured, you know; he has his ways, and strangers don't understand him at first. He's a very good husband to me, and has been so since our wedding day."

She pattered on mechanically, going backwards and forwards across the flagged kitchen as she laid the table for supper, taking bread, cheese, and dripping from the big cupboard behind the panelling, while Mary crouched beside the fire in a hopeless attempt to warm her chilled fingers.

The kitchen was heavy with peat smoke. It crept up to the ceiling and into the corners, and hung about the air like a thin blue cloud. It stung Mary's eyes, and explored her nostrils, and lay upon her tongue.

"You'll soon come to like your uncle Joss, and fit into his ways," continued her aunt. "He's a very fine man, and a very brave one. He has a great name hereabouts, and is much respected. There's no one will say a word against Joss Merlyn. We have great company here at times. It's not always as quiet as this. It's a very busy highway, you know. The coaches pass every day. And the gentry are most civil to us, most civil. A neighbour was in only yesterday, and I made him a cake to take home. 'Mrs. Merlyn,' he said, 'you're the only woman in Cornwall can bake a cake.' Those were his very words. And even the squire himself—that's Squire Bassat, you know, from North Hill; he owns all the land hereabouts—he passed me on the road the other day— Tuesday it was—and he took off his hat. 'Good morning, madam,' he said, and he bowed to me from his horse. They say he was a great man for the women in his day. Then out comes Joss from the stable, where he had been mending the wheel of the trap. 'How's life, Mr. Bassat?' he says. 'As large as yourself, Joss,' answers the squire, and they both fell to laughing."

Mary murmured some reply to this little speech, but she was pained and worried to see how, when speaking, Aunt Patience avoided her eyes, and the very fluency of her words was in itself suspicious. She spoke much as a child does who tells herself a story and has a talent for invention. It hurt Mary to see her act this part, and she longed for her to be done with it, or be silent, for the flow of words was, in its way, more appalling than her tears had been. There was a footfall outside the door, and with a sinking heart Mary realized that Joss Merlyn had come downstairs again and had in all possibility listened to his wife's conversation.

Aunt Patience heard him too, for she turned pale and began to work her mouth. He came into the room and looked from one to the other.

"So the hens are clacking already?" he said, the smile and the laugh gone, his eyes narrow. "You'll soon stop your tears if you can talk. I heard you, you blathering fool—gobble, gobble, gobble, like a turkey hen. Do you think your precious niece believes a word you say? Why, you wouldn't take in a child, far less a bunch of petticoats like her."

He pulled a chair from the wall and crashed it against the table. He sat down heavily, the chair creaking beneath him, and, reaching for the loaf, cut himself off a great hunk of bread, which he slabbed with dripping. He crammed it into his mouth, the grease running down his chin, and beckoned Mary to the table. "You need food, I can see that," he said, and he proceeded to cut carefully a thin slice from the loaf, which he quartered in pieces and buttered for her, the whole business very delicately done and in striking contrast to his manner in serving himself—so much so that to Mary there was something almost horrifying in the change from rough brutality to fastidious care. It was as though there were some latent power in his fingers which turned them from bludgeons into deft and cunning servants. Had he cut her a chunk of bread and hurled it at her she would not have minded so much; it would have been in keeping with what she had seen of him. But this sudden coming to grace, this quick and exquisite moving of his hands, was a swift and rather sinister revelation, sinister because it was unexpected and not true to type. She thanked him quietly and began to eat.

Her aunt, who had not uttered since her husband entered

the room, was frying bacon over the fire. No one spoke. Mary was aware of Joss Merlyn watching her across the table, and behind her she could hear her aunt fumbling with ineffectual fingers at the hot handle of the frying pan. In a minute she had dropped it, uttering a little cry of distress. Mary rose from her place to help her, but Joss thundered at her to sit down.

"One fool is bad enough, without making a couple of them," he shouted. "Keep your seat and let your aunt clear up the mess. It won't be for the first time." He leant back in his chair and began to pick his teeth with his nails. "What'll you drink?" he asked her. "Brandy, wine, or ale? You may starve here, but you won't go thirsty. We don't get sore throats at Jamaica." And he laughed at her, and winked, and put out his tongue.

"I'll have a cup of tea if I may," said Mary. "I'm not used to drinking spirits, nor wine neither."

"Oh, you're not? Well, it's your loss, I'm glad to say. You can have your tea tonight, but, by God, you'll want some brandy in a month or two."

He reached across the table and took hold of her hand.

"You've a pretty enough paw for one who's worked on a farm," he said. "I was afraid it would be rough and red. If there's one thing that makes a man sick it's to have his ale poured out by an ugly hand. Not that my customers are overparticular, but then we've never had a barmaid before at Jamaica Inn." He gave her a mock bow and dropped her hand.

"Patience, my dear," he said, "here's the key. Go and fetch me a bottle of brandy, for the Lord's sake. I've a thirst on me that all the waters of Dozmary would not slake." His wife hurried across the room at his word and disappeared into the passage. Then he fell to picking his teeth again, whistling from time to time, while Mary ate her bread and butter and drank the tea that he placed before her. Already a splitting headache tightened her brow, and she was ready to drop. Her eyes watered from the peat smoke. But she was not too tired to watch her uncle, for already she had caught something of the nervousness of her aunt Patience

20

and felt that in some sense they were here like mice in a trap, unable to escape, with him playing with them like a monstrous cat.

In a few minutes his wife returned with the brandy, which she put in front of her husband, and while she finished her cooking of the bacon and served Mary and herself, he fell to drinking, staring moodily before him, kicking the leg of the table. Suddenly he thumped the table with his fist, shaking the plates and cups, while one platter crashed to the floor and broke.

"I tell you what it is, Mary Yellan," he shouted. "I'm master in this house, and I'll have you know it. You'll do as you're told, and help in the house and serve my customers, and I'll not lay a finger on you. But, by God, if you open your mouth and squark, I'll break you until you eat out of my hand the same as your aunt yonder."

Mary faced him across the table. She held her hands in her lap so that he should not see them tremble.

"I understand you," she said. "I'm not curious by nature, and I've never gossiped in my life. It doesn't matter to me what you do in the inn, or what company you keep. I'll do my work about the house and you'll have no cause to grumble. But if you hurt my aunt Patience in any way, I tell you this—I'll leave Jamaica Inn straight away, and I'll find the magistrate, and bring him here, and have the law on you; and then try and break me if you like."

Mary had turned very pale, and she knew that if he thundered at her now she would break down and cry, and he would have the mastery of her forever. The torrent of words had come from her in spite of herself, and, wrung with pity for the poor broken thing that was her aunt, she could not control them. Had she but known it, she had saved herself, for her little show of spirit impressed the man, and he leant back in his chair and relaxed.

"That's very pretty," he said; "very prettily put indeed. Now we know just what sort of lodger we have. Scratch her, and she shows her claws. All right, my dear; you and I are more akin than I thought. If we are going to play, we'll play together. I may have work for you at Jamaica one

21

Jamaica Inn

day, work that you've never done before. Man's work, Mary
Yellan, where you play with life and death." Mary heard
her aunt Patience give a little gasp beside her.

"Oh, Joss," she whispered. "Oh, Joss, please!"

There was so much urgency in her voice that Mary
stared at her in surprise. She saw her aunt lean forward and
motion her husband to be silent, and the very eagerness of
her chin and the agony in her eyes frightened Mary more
than anything that had happened that night. She felt eerie
suddenly, chilled, and rather sick. What had roused Aunt
Patience to such panic? What had Joss Merlyn been about to
say? She was aware of a fevered and rather terrible curiosity.
Her uncle waved his hand impatiently.

"Get up to bed, Patience," he said. "I'm tired of your
death's-head at my supper table. This girl and I understand
one another."

The woman rose at once and went to the door, with a
last ineffectual glance of despair over her shoulder. They
heard her patter up the stairs. Joss Merlyn and Mary were
alone. He pushed the empty brandy glass away from him
and folded his arms on the table.

"There's been one weakness in my life, and I'll tell you
what it is," he said. "It's drink. It's a curse, and I know it.
I can't stop myself. One day it'll be the end of me, and a
good job too. There's days go by and I don't touch more
than a drop, same as I've done tonight. And then I'll feel
the thirst come on me and I'll soak. Soak for hours. It's
power, and glory, and women, and the Kingdom of God,
all rolled into one. I feel a king then, Mary. I feel I've got
the strings of the world between my two fingers. It's heaven
and hell. I talk then, talk until every damned thing I've
ever done is spilt to the four winds. I shut myself in my
room and shout my secrets in my pillow. Your aunt turns
the key on me, and when I'm sober I hammer on the door
and she lets me out. There's no one knows that but she and I,
and now I've told you. I've told you because I'm already a
little drunk and I can't hold my tongue. But I'm not drunk
enough to lose my head. I'm not drunk enough to tell you
why I live in this God-forgotten spot, and why I'm the

landlord of Jamaica Inn." His voice was hoarse, and now he scarcely spoke above a whisper. The turf fire had sunk low in the hearth, and dark shadows stretched long fingers on the wall. The candles too had burnt down, and cast a monstrous shadow of Joss Merlyn on the ceiling. He smiled at her, and with a foolish drunken gesture he laid his finger against his nose.

"I've not told you that, Mary Yellan. Oh no, I've got some sense and cunning left. If you want to know any more you can ask your aunt. She'll pull you a tale. I heard her blathering tonight, telling you we kept fine company here, and the squire takes off his hat to her. It's lies, all lies. I'll tell you that much, for you'll come to know it anyway. Squire Bassat's too mortal scared to shove his nose in here. If he saw me in the road he'd cross his heart and spur his horse. And so would all the precious gentry. The coaches don't stop here now, nor the mails neither. I don't worry; I've customers enough. The wider berth the gentry give to me the better pleased I am. Oh, there's drinking here all right, and plenty of it too. There's some who come to Jamaica Saturday night, and there's some who turn the key of their door and sleep with their fingers in their ears. There are nights when every cottage on the moors is dark and silent, and the only lights for miles are the blazing windows of Jamaica Inn. They say the shouting and the singing can be heard as far down as the farms below Rough Tor. You'll be in the bar those nights, if you've a fancy for it, and you'll see what company I keep."

Mary sat very still, gripping the sides of her chair. She dared not move for fear of that swift changing of his mood which she had observed already, and which would turn him from this sudden intimate tone of confidence to a harsh and coarse brutality.

"They're all afraid of me," he went on; "the whole damned lot of 'em. Afraid of me, who's afraid of no man. I tell you, if I'd had education, if I'd had learning, I'd have walked the breadth of England beside King George himself. It's drink that's been against me, drink and my hot blood. It's

23

the curse of all of us, Mary. There's never been a Merlyn yet that died peaceful in his bed.

"My father was hanged at Exeter—he had a brawl with a fellow and killed him. My granddad had his ears cut for thieving; he was sent out to a convict settlement and died raving mad from a snake bite in the tropics. I'm the eldest of three brothers, all of us born under the shadow of Kilmar, away yonder above Twelve Men's Moor. You walk out over there across the East Moor till you come to Rushyford, and you'll see a great crag of granite like a devil's hand sticking up into the sky. That's Kilmar. If you'd been born under its shadow you'd take to drink, same as I did. My brother Matthew, he was drowned in Trewartha Marsh. We thought he'd gone for a sailor, and had no news of him, and then in the summer there was a drought, and no rain fell for seven months, and there was Matthew sticking up in the bog, with his hands above his head, and the curlews flying round him. My brother Jem, damn him, he was the baby. Hanging onto mother's skirts when Matt and I were grown men. I never did see eye to eye with Jem. Too smart he is, too sharp with his tongue. Oh, they'll catch him in time and hang him, same as they did my father."

He fell silent a moment, gazing at his empty glass. He picked it up and put it down again. "No," he said, "I've said enough. I'll have no more tonight. Go up to bed, Mary, before I wring your neck. Here's your candle. You'll find your room over the porch."

Mary took the candlestick without speaking and was about to pass him when he seized hold of her shoulder and twisted her round.

"There'll be nights sometimes when you'll hear wheels on the road," he said, "and those wheels will not pass on, but they'll stop outside Jamaica Inn. And you'll hear footsteps in the yard, and voices beneath your window. When that happens, you'll stay in your bed, Mary Yellan, and cover your head with the blankets. Do you understand?"

"Yes, Uncle."

"Very well. Now get out, and if you ever ask me a question again I'll break every bone in your body."

She went out of the room and into the dark passage, bumping against the settle in the hall, and so upstairs, feeling her way with her hands, judging her whereabouts by turning round and facing the stairs again. Her uncle had told her the room over the porch, and she crept across the dark landing, which was unlit, past two doors on either side—guest rooms, she imagined, waiting for those travellers who never came nowadays nor sought shelter beneath the roof of Jamaica Inn—and then stumbled against another door and turned the handle, and saw by the flickering flame of her candle that this was her room, for her trunk lay on the floor.

The walls were rough and unpapered, and the floor boards bare. A box turned upside down served as a dressing table, with a cracked looking-glass on top. There was no jug or basin; she supposed she would wash in the kitchen. The bed creaked when she leant upon it, and the two thin blankets felt damp to her hand. She decided she would not undress, but would lie down upon it in her travelling clothes, dusty as they were, with her cloak wrapped round her. She went to the window and looked out. The wind had dropped, but it was still raining—a thin wretched drizzle that trickled down the side of the house and smeared the dirt on the windowpane.

A noise came from the far end of the yard, a curious groaning sound like that of an animal in pain. It was too dark to see clearly, but she could make out a dark shape swinging gently to and fro. For one nightmare of a moment, her imagination on fire with the tales Joss Merlyn had told her, she thought it was a gibbet, and a dead man hanging. And then she realized it was the signboard of the inn, that somehow or other, through neglect, had become insecure upon its nails and now swung backwards, forwards, with the slightest breeze. Nothing but a poor battered board, that had once known prouder days in its first erection, but whose white lettering was now blurred and grey, and whose message was at the mercy of the four winds—Jamaica Inn. Mary pulled down the blind and crept to her bed. Her teeth were chattering, and her feet and hands

25

were numb. For a long while she sat huddled on the bed, a prey to despair. She wondered whether it was possible to break from the house and find her way back the twelve long miles to Bodmin. She wondered whether her weariness would prove too much for her, and if with an agony of fatigue she would drop by the roadside and fall asleep where she lay, only to be awakened by the morning light and to see the great form of Joss Merlyn towering above her.

She closed her eyes, and at once she saw his face smiling at her, and then the smile changing to a frown, and the frown breaking into a thousand creases as he shook with rage, and she saw his great mat of black hair, his hooked nose, and the long powerful fingers that held such deadly grace.

She felt caught here now, like a bird in a net, and however much she struggled she would never escape. If she wished to be free she must go now, climb from her window and run like a mad thing along the white road that stretched like a snake across the moors. Tomorrow it would be too late.

She waited until she heard his footsteps on the stairs. She heard him mutter to himself, and to her relief he turned aside and went along the other passage to the left of the staircase. In the distance a door closed, and there was silence. She decided that she would wait no longer. If she stayed even one night beneath this roof her nerve would go from her, and she would be lost. Lost, and mad, and broken, like Aunt Patience. She opened the door and stole into the passage. She tiptoed to the head of the stairs. She paused and listened. Her hand was on the banister and her foot on the top stair when she heard a sound from the other passage. It was somebody crying. It was someone whose breath came in little gasps and spasms, and who tried to muffle the sound in a pillow. It was Aunt Patience. Mary waited a moment, and then she turned back and went to her own room again and threw herself on her bed and closed her eyes. Whatever she would have to face in the future, and however frightened she would be, she would not leave Jamaica Inn now. She must stay with Aunt Patience. She was needed here. It might be that Aunt Patience would take comfort from her, and they would come to an understanding, and, in some way which she was now too tired to plan, Mary would act as a protector to Aunt Patience, and stand between her and Joss Merlyn. For seventeen years her mother had lived and worked alone and known greater hardships than Mary would ever know. She would not have run away because of a half-crazy man. She would not have feared a house that reeked of evil, however lonely it stood on its wind-blown hill, a solitary landmark defying man and storm. Mary's mother would have the courage to fight her enemies. Yes, and conquer them in the end. There would be no giving way for her.

And so Mary lay upon her hard bed, her mind teeming while she prayed for sleep, every sound a fresh stab to her nerves, from the scratching of a mouse in the wall behind her to the creaking of the sign in the yard. She counted the minutes and the hours of an eternal night, and when the first cock crew in a field behind the house she counted no more, but sighed, and slept like a dead thing.

Chapter 3

~~~~~~

MARY WOKE to a high wind from the west, and a thin watery sun. It was the rattling of the window that roused her from her sleep, and she judged from the broad daylight and the colour of the sky that she had slept late and that it must be past eight o'clock. Looking out at the window and across the yard, she saw that the stable door was open, and there were fresh hoofmarks in the mud outside. With a great sense of relief she realized that the landlord must have gone from home, and she would have Aunt Patience to herself, if only for a little time.

Hurriedly she unpacked her trunk, pulling out her thick skirt and coloured apron and the heavy shoes she had worn at the farm, and in ten minutes she was down in the kitchen and washing in the scullery at the back.

Aunt Patience came in from the chicken run behind the house with some new-laid eggs in her apron, which she produced with a little smile of mystery. "I thought you'd like one for your breakfast," she said. "I saw you were too tired to eat much last night. And I've saved you a spot of cream for your bread." Her manner was normal enough this morning, and in spite of the red rims round her eyes, which bespoke an anxious night, she was obviously making an effort to be cheerful. Mary decided it was only in the presence of her husband that she went to pieces like a frightened child, and when he was away she had that same child's aptitude for forgetting, and could seize pleasure from little situations such as this of making breakfast for Mary and boiling her an egg.

They both avoided any reference to the night before, and Joss's name was not mentioned. Where he had gone, and on what business, Mary neither asked nor cared; she was only too relieved to be rid of him.

Mary could see that her aunt was eager to speak of things unconnected with her present life; she seemed afraid of any questions, so Mary spared her and plunged into a description of the last years at Helford, the strain of the bad times, and her mother's illness and death.

Whether Aunt Patience took it in or not she could not tell; certainly she nodded from time to time, and pursed her lips, and shook her head, and uttered little ejaculations; but it seemed to Mary that years of fear and anxiety had taken away her powers of concentration, and that some underlying terror prevented her from giving her whole interest to any conversation.

During the morning there was the usual work of the house, and Mary was thus able to explore the inn more thoroughly.

It was a dark, rambling place, with long passages and unexpected rooms. There was a separate entrance to the bar, at the side of the house, and, though the room was empty now, there was something heavy in the atmosphere reminiscent of the last time it was full: a lingering taste of old tobacco, the sour smell of drink, and an impression of warm, unclean humanity packed one against the other on the dark-stained benches.

For all the unpleasant suggestion that it conjured, it was the one room in the inn that had vitality, and was not morne and drear. The other rooms appeared neglected or unused; even the parlour by the entrance porch had a solitary air, as though it were many months since an honest traveller had stepped upon the threshold and warmed his back before a glowing fire. The guest rooms upstairs were in an even worse state of repair. One was used for lumber, with boxes piled against the wall, and old horse blankets chewed and torn by families of rats or mice. In the room opposite, potatoes and turnips had been stored upon a broken-down bed.

Mary guessed that her own small room had been in much the same condition, and that she owed it to her aunt that it was now furnished at all. Into their room, along the further passage, she did not venture. Beneath it, down a passage that ran parallel to the one above, long and in the opposite direction from the kitchen, was another room, the door of which was locked. Mary went out into the yard to look at it through the window, but there was a board nailed up against the frame, and she could not see inside.

The house and outbuildings formed three sides of the little square that was the yard, in the centre of which was a grass bank and a drinking trough. Beyond this lay the road, a thin white ribbon that stretched on either hand to the horizon, surrounded on each side by moorland, brown and sodden from the heavy rains. Mary went out onto the road and looked about her, and as far as her eyes could see there was nothing but the black hills and the moors. The grey slate inn, with its tall chimneys, forbidding and uninhabited though it seemed, was the only dwelling place on the landscape. To the west of Jamaica high tors reared their heads; some were smooth like downland, and the grass shone yellow under the fitful winter sun; but others were sinister and austere, their peaks crowned with granite and great slabs of stone. Now and again the sun was obscured by cloud, and long shadows fled over the moors like fingers. Colour came in patches; sometimes the hills were purple, inkstained, and mottled, and then a feeble ray of sun would come from a wisp of cloud, and one hill would be golden brown while his neighbour still languished in the dark. The scene was never once the same, for it would be the glory of high noon to the east, with the moor as motionless as desert sand; and away to the westward arctic winter fell upon the hills, brought by a jagged cloud shaped like a highwayman's cloak, that scattered hail and snow and a sharp spittle rain onto the granite tors. The air was strong and sweet smelling, cold as mountain air, and strangely pure. It was a revelation to Mary, accustomed as she was to the warm and soft climate of Helford, with its high hedges and tall protecting trees. Even the east wind had been no hardship there, for the arm of the headland acted as a defence to those on land, and it was only the river that ran turbulent and green, the wave crests whipped with foam.

However grim and hateful was this new country, however barren and untilled, with Jamaica Inn standing alone upon the hill as a buffer to the four winds, there was a challenge in the air that spurred Mary Yellan to adventure. It stung her, bringing colour to her cheeks and a sparkle to her eyes; it played with her hair, blowing it about her face; and as she breathed deep she drew it through her nostrils and into her lungs, more quenching and sweeter than a draught of cider. She went to the water trough and put her hands under the spring. The water ran clear and icy cold. She drank some, and it was unlike any water she had drunk before, bitter, queer, with a lingering peat taste like the smoke from the turf fire in the kitchen.

It was deep and satisfying, for her thirst went from her.

She felt strong in her body and emboldened in spirit, and she went back into the house to find Aunt Patience, her appetite sharp for the dinner that she hoped awaited her. She fell to with a will upon stewed mutton and turnips, and, her hunger appeased now for the first time for four-and-twenty hours she felt her courage return to her, and she was ready to question her aunt and risk the consequences.

"Aunt Patience," she began, "why is my uncle the land-lord of Jamaica Inn?"

The sudden direct attack took the woman by surprise, and for a moment she stared at Mary without reply. Then she flushed scarlet and began to work her mouth. "Why," she faltered, "it's—it's a very prominent place here, on the road. You can see that. This is the main road from the south. The coaches pass here twice a week. They come from Truro, and Bodmin, and so on, to Launceston. You came yourself yesterday. There's always company on the road. Travellers, and private gentlemen, and sometimes sailors from Falmouth."

"Yes, Aunt Patience. But why don't they stop at Jamaica?"

"They do. They often ask for a drink in the bar. We've a good custom here."

"How can you say that when the parlour is never used, and the guest rooms are stored with lumber, fit only for rats and mice? I've seen them for myself. I've been to inns before, smaller ones than this by far. There was an inn at home, in the village. The landlord was a friend of ours. Many a time Mother and I had tea in the parlour; and upstairs, though there were only two rooms, they were furnished and fitted up in style for travellers."

Her aunt was silent for a moment, working her mouth and twisting her fingers in her lap. "Your uncle Joss doesn't encourage folks to stay," she said at length. "He says you never know who you are going to get. Why, in a lonely spot like this we might be murdered in our beds. There's all sorts on a road like this. It wouldn't be safe."

"Aunt Patience, you're talking nonsense. What is the use of an inn that cannot give an honest traveller a bed for the night? For what other purpose was it built? And how do you live, if you have no custom?"

"We have custom," returned the woman sullenly. "I've told you that. There's men come in from the farms and out-lying places. There are farms and cottages scattered over these moors for miles around, and folk come from there. There are evenings when the bar is full of them."

"The driver on the coach yesterday told me respectable

31

people did not come to Jamaica any more. He said they were afraid."

Aunt Patience changed colour. She was pale now, and her eyes roved from side to side. She swallowed, and ran her tongue over her lips.

"Your uncle Joss has a strong temper," she said; "you have seen that for yourself. He is easily roused; he will not have folk interfering with him."

"Aunt Patience, why should anyone interfere with a landlord of an inn who goes about his rightful business? However hot tempered a man may be, his temper doesn't scare people away. That's no excuse."

Her aunt was silent. She had come to the end of her resources and sat stubborn as a mule. She would not be drawn. Mary tried another question.

"Why did you come here in the first place? My mother knew nothing of this; we believed you to be in Bodmin; you wrote from there when you married."

"I met your uncle in Bodmin, but we never lived there," replied Aunt Patience slowly. "We lived near Padstow for a while, and then we came here. Your uncle bought the inn from Mr. Bassat. It had stood empty a number of years, I believe, and your uncle decided it would suit him. He wanted to settle down. He's travelled a lot in his time; he's been to more places than I can remember the names. I believe he was in America once."

"It seems a funny thing to come to this place to settle," said Mary. "He couldn't have chosen much worse, could he?"

"It's near his old home," said her aunt. "Your uncle was born only a few miles away, over on Twelve Men's Moor. His brother Jem lives there now in a bit of a cottage, when he's not roaming the country. He comes here sometimes, but your uncle Joss does not care for him much."

"Does Mr. Bassat ever visit the inn?"

"No."

"Why not, if he sold it to my uncle?"

Aunt Patience fidgeted with her fingers and worked her mouth.

"There was some misunderstanding," she replied. "Your uncle bought it through a friend. Mr. Bassat did not know who Uncle Joss was until we were settled in, and then he was not very pleased."

"Why did he mind?"

"He had not seen your uncle since he lived at Trewartha as a young man. Your uncle was wild as a lad; he got a name for acting rough. It wasn't his fault, Mary, it was his misfortune. The Merlyns all were wild. His young brother Jem is worse than ever he was, I am sure of that. But Mr. Bassat listened to a pack of lies about Uncle Joss, and was in a great way when he discovered that he'd sold Jamaica to him. There, that's all there is to it."

She leant back in her chair, exhausted from her cross-examination. Her eyes begged to be excused further questioning, and her face was pale and drawn. Mary saw she had suffered enough, but with the rather cruel audacity of youth she ventured one question more.

"Aunt Patience," she said, "I want you to look at me and answer me this, and then I won't worry you again: What has the barred room at the end of the passage to do with the wheels that stop outside Jamaica Inn by night?"

As soon as she had spoken she was sorry, and, like many a one before her who has spoken too hastily and too soon, she yearned for the words to be unsaid. It was too late, though, now. The damage had been done.

A strange expression crept upon the woman's face, and her great hollow eyes stared across the table in terror. Her mouth trembled, and her hand wandered to her throat. She looked fearful, haunted.

Mary pushed back her chair and knelt by her side. She put her arms round Aunt Patience, and held her close, and kissed her hair.

"I'm sorry," she said. "Don't be angry with me; I'm rude and impertinent. It's none of my business, and I've no right to question you, and I'm ashamed of myself. Please, please forget what I said."

Her aunt buried her face in her hands. She sat motionless and paid no attention to her niece. For some minutes they sat

33

there in silence, while Mary stroked her shoulder and kissed her hands.

Then Aunt Patience uncovered her face and looked down at her.

The fear had gone from her eyes, and she was calm. She took Mary's hands in hers and gazed into her face.

"Mary," she said, and her voice was hushed and low, scarcely above a whisper, "Mary, I can't answer your questions, for there's many I don't know the answer of myself. But because you are my niece, my own sister's child, I must give you a word of warning."

She glanced over her shoulder, as though she were afraid that Joss himself stood in the shadows behind the door.

"There's things that happen at Jamaica, Mary, that I've never dared to breathe. Bad things. Evil things. I can't ever tell you; I dare not even admit them to myself. Some of it in time you'll come to know. You can't avoid it, living here. Your uncle Joss mixes with strange men, who follow a strange trade. Sometimes they come by night, and from your window above the porch you will hear footsteps, and voices, and knocking at the door. Your uncle lets them in, and takes them along that passage to the room with the locked door. They go inside, and from my bedroom above I can hear the mutter of their voices through the long hours. Before dawn they are away, and no sign left that they have ever been. When they come, Mary, you will say nothing to me or to your uncle Joss. You must lie in bed, and put your fingers to your ears. You must never question me, nor him, nor anyone, for if you came to guess but half of what I know, your hair would go grey, Mary, as mine has done, and you would tremble in your speech and weep by night, and all that lovely careless youth of yours would die, Mary, as mine has died."

Then she rose from the table and pushed aside her chair, and Mary heard her climb the staircase with heavy, faltering feet, and go along the landing to her room, and close the door.

Mary sat on the floor beside the empty chair, and she saw through the kitchen window that the sun had already disappeared behind the furthest hill, and that before many hours had passed the grey malevolence of a November dusk would have fallen upon Jamaica once again.

Chapter 4

Joss MERLYN was away from home for nearly a week, and during that time Mary came to know something of the country.

Her presence was not required in the bar, for no one came to it when the landlord was from home, and, after giving her aunt a hand with the housework and in the kitchen, she was free to wander where she pleased. Patience Merlyn was no walker; she had no wish to stir beyond the chicken run at the back of the inn, and she had no sense of direction. She had a vague idea of the names of the tors, for she had heard them mentioned by her husband, but where they were, and how anyone found them, she did not know. So Mary would strike off on her own at midday, with nothing but the sun to guide her and a certain deep-grained common sense which was her natural inheritance as a countrywoman.

The moors were even wilder than she had at first supposed. Like an immense desert they rolled from east to west, with tracks here and there across the surface and great hills breaking the skyline.

Where was their final boundary she could not tell, except that once, away to the westward, after climbing the highest tor behind Jamaica, she caught the silver shimmer of the sea. It was a silent, desolate country though, vast and untouched by human hand; on the high tors the slabs of stone leant against one another in strange shapes and forms, massive sentinels who had stood there since the hand of God first fashioned them.

Some were shaped like giant furniture, with monstrous chairs and twisted tables; and sometimes the smaller crumbling stones lay on the summit of the hill like a giant himself, his huge, recumbent form darkening the heather and the coarse tufted grass. There were long stones that stood on end, balancing themselves in a queer miraculous way, as though they leant against the wind; and there were flat altar stones whose smooth and polished faces stared up towards the sky, awaiting a sacrifice that never came. Wild sheep dwelt on the high tors, and there were ravens too, and buzzards; the hills were homing places for all solitary things.

Black cattle grazed on the moors beneath, their careful feet treading the firm ground, and with inborn knowledge they avoided the tufted, tempting grass that was not grass at all, but soggy marsh that sighed and whispered. When the wind blew on the hills it whistled mournfully in the crevices of granite, and sometimes it shuddered like a man in pain.

Strange winds blew from nowhere; they crept along the surface of the grass, and the grass shivered; they breathed upon the little pools of rain in the hollowed stones, and the pools rippled. Sometimes the wind shouted and cried, and the cry echoed in the crevices, and moaned, and was lost again. There was a silence on the tors that belonged to another age; an age that is past and vanished as though it had never been, an age when man did not exist, but pagan footsteps trod upon the hills. And there was a stillness in the air, and a stranger, older peace, that was not the peace of God.

As Mary Yellan walked the moors, climbed the tors, and rested in the low dips beside the springs and streams, she thought about Joss Merlyn and what his boyhood must have been, and how he grew athwart like the stunted broom, with the bloom blown out of him by the north wind.

One day she crossed the East Moor, in the direction he had given her that first evening; and when she had gone some way and stood alone upon a ridge of down, surrounded on all sides by bleak moorland, she saw that the land descended to a deep and treacherous marsh, through which a brook burbled and sang. And rising beyond the marsh, away on the other side, pointing his great fingers to the sky, was a crag like a split hand coming sheer out of the moor, his surface moulded in granite as though sculptured, his slope a venomous grey.

So this was Kilmar Tor; and somewhere amongst that solid mass of stone, where the ridges hid the sun, Joss Merlyn had been born, and his brother lived today. Below her in the marsh, Matthew Merlyn had been drowned. In her fancy she saw him stride across the high ground, whistling a song, the murmur of the brook in his ears, and somehow evening came upon him before he was aware, and his footsteps faltered as he turned in his tracks. In her fancy she watched him pause, and think a moment, and curse softly, and then with a shrug of his shoulders he plunged down into the mist, his confidence returning; but before he had taken five steps he felt the ground sag under his feet, and he stumbled, and fell, and suddenly he was up above his knees in weed and slime. He reached out for a tuft of grass, and it sank beneath his weight. He kicked with his feet, and they would not answer him. He kicked once more, and one foot sucked itself free, but, as he plunged forward, reckless and panic stricken, he trod deeper water still, and now he floundered helplessly, beating the weed with his hands. She heard him scream in terror, and a curlew rose from the marsh in front of him, flapping his wings and whistling his mournful cry. When the curlew had flown from sight, disappearing behind a ridge of land, the marsh was still again; only a few grass stems shivered in the wind, and there was silence.

Mary turned her back upon Kilmar and began to run across the moor, stumbling amongst the heather and the stones, nor did she stop until the marsh had sunk beneath the level of the hill, and the crag itself was hidden. She had come further than she intended, and the way home was long. It seemed an eternity before the last hill was conquered and behind her, and the tall chimneys of Jamaica Inn stood out before her above the winding road. As she crossed the yard she noticed with sinking heart that the stable door was open and the pony was inside. Joss Merlyn had returned.

She opened the door as silently as possible, but it rubbed against the stone flags and grated in protest. The sound rang in the quiet passage, and in a minute the landlord appeared from the back, bending his head under the beam. His shirt sleeves were rolled above his elbow, and he had a glass in his hand, and a cloth. He was, it seemed, in high good humour, for he shouted boisterously at Mary, and waved the glass.

"Well," he roared, "don't drop your face a mile at the sight of me. Aren't you pleased to see me? Did you miss me much?"

Mary made an effort to smile and asked him if he had had a pleasant journey. "Pleasant be damned," he answered. "There was money in it, and that's all I care. I've not been staying in the palace with the King, if that's what you mean." He shouted with laughter at his joke, and his wife appeared behind his shoulders, simpering in harmony.

As soon as his laughter died away the smile faded from Aunt Patience's face, and the strained, haunted expression returned again, the fixed, almost idiot stare that she wore habitually in the presence of her husband.

Mary saw at once that the little freedom from care which her aunt had enjoyed during the past week was now no more, and she had again become the nervy, shattered creature of before.

Mary turned to go up the stairs to her room, when Joss called her. "Here," he said, "no skulking up there this evening. There'll be work for you in the bar, alongside of your uncle. Don't you know what day of the week it is?"

Mary paused to think. She was losing count of time. Was it Monday's coach she had taken? That made today Saturday. Saturday night. At once she realized what Joss Merlyn meant. Tonight there would be company at Jamaica Inn.

They came singly, the people of the moors, crossing the yard swiftly and silently, as though they had no wish to be seen. They lacked substance, in the dim light, and seemed no more than shadows as they skirted the wall and passed under the shelter of the porch to knock upon the door of the bar and gain admittance. Some carried lanterns, the fitful glare of which appeared to worry the bearers, for they attempted to screen the glow by covering it with their coats. One or two rode into the yard on ponies, whose hoofs rang sharply on the stones, and the clatter sounded strangely in the still night, followed as it was by the creaking of the stable door yawning on its hinges and the low mutter of voices as the men led their ponies to the stalls. Others were yet more furtive, bearing neither flare nor lantern, but flitting across the yard with hats pulled low and coats muffled to the chin, betraying by the very secrecy of their movements their desire to remain unseen. The reason for stealth was not apparent, for any passing traveller upon the road could see that tonight Jamaica Inn gave hospitality. The light streamed from the windows, usually so shuttered and barred, and, as the evening darkened and the hours went by, the sound of voices rose upon the air. There was singing at times, and shouting, and the rumble of laughter, showing that those visitors to the inn who came so furtively, as if in shame, had lost their fear when under cover of the house, and once packed close to their companions in the bar, with pipes alight and glasses filled, had thrown all caution aside.

They were a strange assortment gathered there, grouped around Joss Merlyn in the bar. Securely separated by the counter itself, and half screened by a barrier of bottles and glasses, Mary could look down upon the company and remain unobserved. They straddled the stools and sprawled upon the benches; they leant against the wall; they slouched beside the tables; and one or two, whose heads or stomachs were weaker than the rest, already lay full length upon the floor. They were dirty for the most part, ragged, ill kept, with matted hair and broken nails; tramps, vagrants, poachers, thieves, cattle stealers, and gypsies. There was a farmer who had lost his farm through bad management and dishonesty; a shepherd who had fired his master's rick; a horse dealer who had been hounded out of Devon. One fellow was a cobbler in Launceston, and under cover of his trade passed stolen goods; he who lay in a drunken stupor on the floor was once mate of a Padstow schooner and had run his ship ashore. The little man who sat in the far corner, biting his nails, was a Port Isaac fisherman, and rumour had it that he kept a store of gold rolled up in a stocking and hidden in the chimney of his cottage—but where the gold came from no one would say. There were men who lived near by, under the very shadow of the tors, who had known no other country but moorland, marsh and granite; one had come walking without a lantern from the Crowdy Marsh beyond Rough Tor, taking Brown Willy in his stride; another came from Cheesewring, and sat now with his face in a mug of ale, his boots on a table, side by side with the poor half-witted fellow who had stumbled up the lane from Dozmary. This last had a birthmark that ran the whole length of his face, blazing it purple, and he kept plucking at it with his hands, and pulling out his cheek, so that Mary, who stood in line with him, for all the bottles that divided them, turned sick and nearly faint at the sight of him; and what with the stale-drink smell, and the reek of tobacco, and the foul atmosphere of crowded unwashed bodies, she felt a physical disgust rise up in her, and she knew she would give way to it if she stayed there long. Luckily she did not have to move amongst them; her duty was to stand behind the bar, hidden as much as possible, and then do what washing and cleaning of glasses was required, refilling them from tap or bottle, while Joss Merlyn himself handed them to his customers or lifted the flap of the bar and strode out into the room, laughing at one, flinging a coarse word at another, patting someone on the shoulder, jerking his head at another. After the first hilarious outburst, the first curious stare, the shrug of the shoulder and the chuckle, the company gathered in the inn ignored Mary. They accepted her as niece of the landlord, a sort of serving-maid of Merlyn's wife, as she was introduced, and, though one or two of the younger men would have spoken to her and plagued her, they were wary of the eye of the landlord himself, fearing that any familiarity on their part might anger him, as he had probably brought her to Jamaica for his own amusement. So Mary was left undisturbed, greatly to her relief, though had she known the reason for their reticence she would have walked out of the bar that night in shame and loathing.

Her aunt did not appear before the company, though Mary was aware of her shadow behind the door at times, and a footstep in the passage, and once she caught sight of her frightened eyes peering through the crack in the door. The evening seemed interminable, and Mary longed for release. The air was so thick with smoke and breath that it was hard to see across the room, and to her weary, half-closed eyes, the faces of the men loomed shapeless and distorted, all hair and teeth, their mouths much too large for their bodies, while those who had drunk their fill and could take no more lay on the benches or the floor like dead men, their faces in their hands.

Those who remained sufficiently sober to stand had crowded round a dirty little blackguard from Redruth, who had established himself wit of the assembly. The mine where he had worked was now in ruins, and he had taken to the road as tinker, pedlar, bagman, and had stored up in consequence a string of loathsome songs, gleaned perhaps from the bowels of the black earth where he had once entombed himself, and with these jewels he now provided entertainment to the company at Jamaica Inn.

The laughter that greeted his sallies nearly shook the roof, topped, of course, by the bellow of the landlord himself, and to Mary there was something appalling in this ugly, screaming laughter, which in some strange way held not a note of mirth, but echoed down the dark stone passages and into the empty rooms above like a tortured thing. The pedlar was making bait of the wretched idiot from Dozmary, who, crazy from drink, had no control of himself and could not rise from the floor, where he squatted like an animal. They lifted him onto a table, and the pedlar made him repeat the words of his songs, complete with actions, amid the frenzy of laughter from the crowd; and the poor beast, excited by the applause that greeted him, jigged up and down on the table, whinnying delight, plucking at his spotted purple birthmark with a broken fingernail. Mary could bear it no longer. She touched her uncle on the shoulder, and he turned to her, his

41

face blotched with the heat of the room and streaming with perspiration.

"I can't stand this," she said. "You'll have to attend to your friends yourself. I'm going upstairs to my room."

He wiped the sweat from his forehead with his shirt sleeve and stared down at her. She was surprised to see that, although he had been drinking during the evening, he was himself sober, and even if he was the ringleader of this riotous, crazy company, he knew what he was doing. "Had enough of it, have you?" he said. "Think yourself a little bit too good for such as we? I'll tell you this, Mary: You've had an easy time behind the bar, and you ought to go down on your knees and thank me for it. Because you're my niece they've let you alone, my dear, but if you hadn't had that honour—by God, there wouldn't be much left of you now!" He shouted with laughter and pinched her cheek between his finger and thumb, hurting her. "Get out, then," he said; "it's close on midnight anyway, and I don't want you. You'll lock your door tonight, Mary, and pull down your blind. Your aunt's been in bed an hour with the blanket drawn over her head."

He lowered his voice; bending down to her ear and seizing her wrist, he doubled it behind her back, until she cried out in pain.

"All right," he said; "that's like a foretaste of punishment, and you know what to expect. Keep your mouth shut and I'll treat you like a lamb. It doesn't do to be curious at Jamaica Inn, and I'll have you remember that." He was not laughing now, but stared down at her, frowning, as though he would read her thoughts. "You're not a fool like your aunt," he said slowly, "that's the curse of it. You've got a clever little monkey face, and a ferreting monkey mind, and you're not easily scared. But I tell you this, Mary Yellan: I'll break that mind of yours if you let it go astray, and I'll break your body too. Now go upstairs to bed, and let's hear no more of you tonight."

He turned away from her and, frowning still, picked up a glass from the bar in front of him, turning it over and over in his hands, rubbing it slowly with a cloth. The contempt in her eyes must have irritated him, for his good humour had left him in a flash, and he flung aside the glass in a fit of ill temper, splitting it to fragments.

"Strip that damned idiot of his clothes," he thundered, "and send him back naked to his mother. Maybe the November air will cool that purple face of his and cure his dog tricks. We've had enough of him at Jamaica."

The pedlar and his group yelled in delight and, throwing the wretched half-wit on his back, began to tear off his coat and breeches, while the bewildered fellow flapped out at them with useless hands, bleating like a sheep.

Mary ran out of the room, slamming the door behind her, and as she went up the rickety stairs, her hands over her ears, she could not keep out that sound of laughter and wild song that echoed down the draughty passage, following her to her room, penetrating through the cracks on the floor boards.

She felt very sick and threw herself on her bed, her head in her hands. There was a babel of noise in the yard below, and yells of laughter, while a stream of light from a tossing lantern cast a beam up to her window. She got up and pulled down the blind, but not before she had seen the outline of a quivering, naked form bound across the yard with great loping strides, screaming like a hare and pursued by a handful of hooting, jeering men, with Joss Merlyn's giant figure in the lead cracking a horsewhip above his head.

Then Mary did as her uncle had told her. She undressed hurriedly and crept into bed, pulling the blanket over her head, stuffing her fingers in her ears, her only thought now to be deaf to the horror and the revelry below; but even with eyes shut and face pressed tight against the pillow, she could see the purple blotched face of the poor idiot man upturned towards his captors, and she could hear the thin echo of his cry as he stumbled into the ditch and fell.

She lay in that half-conscious state that waits on the borderland of sleep, when the events of the past day crowd into the mind and make a jumble of confusion. Images danced before her, and the heads of unknown people, and though at times she seemed to be wandering on the moor, with the great crag of Kilmar dwarfing the neighbouring hills, she was aware of the little path of light made by the moon on her bedroom floor, and the steady rattle of the window blind. There had been voices, and now there were none; somewhere far away on the highroad a horse galloped, and wheels rumbled, but now all was still. She slept; and then, without warning, she heard something snap in the peace of mind that had enfolded her, and she was awake suddenly, sitting up in bed, with the moonlight streaming on her face.

She listened, hearing nothing at first but the thumping of her own heart, but in a few minutes there came another sound, from beneath her room this time—the sound of heavy things being dragged along the stone flags in the passage downstairs, bumping against the walls.

She got out of bed and went to the window, pulling aside an inch of blind. Five waggons were drawn up in the yard outside. Three were covered, each drawn by a pair of horses, and the remaining two were open farm carts. One of the covered waggons stood directly beneath the porch, and the horses were steaming.

Gathered round the waggons were some of the men who had been drinking in the bar earlier in the evening; the cobbler from Launceston was standing under Mary's window, talking to the horse dealer; the sailor from Padstow had come to his senses and was patting the head of a horse; the pedlar who had tortured the poor idiot was climbing into one of the open carts and lifting something from the floor. And there were strangers in the yard whom Mary had never seen before. She could see their faces clearly because of the moonlight, the very brightness of which seemed to worry the men, for one of them pointed upwards and shook his head, while his companion shrugged his shoulders, and another man, who had an air of authority about him, waved his arm impatiently, as though urging them to make haste, and the three of them turned at once and passed under the porch into the inn. Meanwhile the heavy dragging sound continued, and Mary could trace the direction of it without difficulty from where she stood. Something was being taken along the passage to the room at the end, the room with the barred windows and the bolted door.

She began to understand. Packages were brought by the waggons and unloaded at Jamaica Inn. They were stored in the locked room. Because the horses were steaming, she knew they had come over a great distance—from the coast perhaps—and as soon as the waggons were unloaded they would take their departure, passing out into the night as swiftly and as silently as they had come.

The men in the yard worked quickly, against time. The contents of one covered waggon were not carried into the inn, but were transferred to one of the open farm carts drawn up beside the drinking well across the yard. The packages seemed to vary in size and description; some were large parcels, some were small, and others were long rolls wrapped round about in straw and paper. When the cart was filled, the driver, a stranger to Mary, climbed into the seat and drove away.

The remaining waggons were unloaded one by one, and the packages were either placed in the open carts and driven out of the yard or were borne by the men into the house. All was done in silence. Those men who had shouted and sung earlier that night were now sober and quiet, bent on the business in hand. Even the horses appeared to understand the need for silence, for they stood motionless.

Joss Merlyn came out of the porch, the pedlar at his side. Neither wore coat or hat, in spite of the cold air, and both had sleeves rolled to the elbows.

"Is that the lot?" the landlord called softly, and the driver of the last waggon nodded and held up his hand. The men began to climb into the carts. Some of those who had come to the inn on foot went with them, saving themselves a mile or two on their long trek home. They did not leave unrewarded; all carried burdens of a sort: boxes strapped over their shoulders, bundles under the arm; while the cobbler from Launceston had not only laden his pony with bursting saddlebags but had added to his own person as well, being several sizes larger round the waist than when he first arrived.

So the waggons and the carts departed from Jamaica, creaking out of the yard, one after the other in a strange funereal procession, some turning north and some south when they came out onto the highroad, until they had all gone and there was no one left standing in the yard but one man Mary had not seen before, the pedlar, and the landlord of Jamaica Inn himself.

Then they too turned and went back into the house, and the yard was empty. She heard them go along the passage in the direction of the bar, and then their footsteps died away and a door slammed.

There was no other sound except the husky wheezing of the clock in the hall and the sudden whirring note preparatory to the strike. It rang the hour—three o'clock—and then ticked on, choking and gasping like a dying man who cannot catch his breath.

Mary came away from the window and sat down upon the bed. The cold air blew in onto her shoulders, and she shivered and reached for her shawl.

The thought of sleep now was impossible. She was too wide awake, too alive in every nerve, and although the dislike and fear of her uncle was as strong as ever within her, a growing interest and curiosity held the mastery. She understood something of his business now. What she had witnessed here tonight was smuggling on the grand scale. There was no doubt that Jamaica Inn was ideally situated for his purpose, and he must have bought it for that reason alone. All that talk of returning to the home of his boyhood was nonsense, of course. The inn stood alone on the great highroad that ran north and south, and Mary could see that it must be easy enough for anyone with a capacity for organization to work a team of waggons from the coast to the Tamar bank, with the inn itself as halting place and general store.

Spies were needed about the countryside to make a success of the trade; hence the sailor from Padstow, the cobbler from Launceston, the gypsies and the tramps, the vile little pedlar.

And yet, allowing for his personality, his energy, the very fear which his enormous physical strength must engender in his companions, had Joss Merlyn the necessary brain and subtlety to lead such an enterprise? Did he plan every move and every departure, and had he been making preparations for tonight's work during the past week, when away from home?

It must be so; Mary could see no alternative, and, although her loathing for the landlord increased, she allowed herself a grudging respect for his management.

The whole business must be controlled, and the agents picked, for all their rough manners and wild appearance, otherwise the law could never have been evaded for so long. A magistrate who suspected smuggling would surely have suspected the inn before now, unless he were an agent himself. Mary frowned, her chin in her hand. If it were not for Aunt Patience she would walk out of the inn now, and find her way to the nearest town, and inform against Joss Merlyn. He would soon be in jail, and the rest of the rogues with him, and there would be an ending of the traffic. It was useless to reckon without Aunt Patience, however, and the fact that she still held a doglike devotion for her husband made the problem difficult and at the moment impossible.

Mary kept going over and over the question in her mind, and she was not yet satisfied that all was understood. Jamaica Inn was a nest of thieves and poachers, who, with her uncle as leader apparently, worked a profitable smuggling trade between the coast and Devon. So much was clear. But had she seen only part of the game, and was there still more for her to learn? She remembered the terror in Aunt Patience's eyes, and those words spoken in the hush of that first afternoon, when the shadows of early twilight crept across the kitchen floor: "There's things happen at Jamaica Inn, Mary, that I've never dared to breathe. Bad things. Evil things. . . . I dare not even admit them to myself." And she had climbed the staircase to her room, haunted and pale, dragging her feet like a creature old and tired.

Smuggling was dangerous; it was fraught with dishonesty; it was forbidden strictly by the law of the land; but was it evil? Mary could not decide. She needed advice, and there was no one she could ask. She was alone in a grim and rather hateful world, with little prospect of changing it for the better. Had she been a man, she would have gone downstairs and challenged Joss Merlyn to his face, and his friends with him. Yes, and fought them too, and drawn blood, if she were lucky. And then away on a horse from the stable, with Aunt Patience riding pillion, and so down to the south again, to the friendly Helford shore, setting up as a farmer in a small way up Mawgan way, or Gweek, with her aunt to keep house for her.

Well, there was little use in dreaming; the present situation must be faced, and courageously, too, if any good were to come of it.

Here she was on her bed, a girl of three-and-twenty, in a petticoat and a shawl, with no weapons but her own brain to oppose a fellow twice her age and eight times her strength, who, if he realized she had watched the scene tonight from her window, would encircle her neck with his hand and, pressing lightly with finger and thumb, put an end to her questioning.

Then Mary swore; a thing she had done only once before in her life, when chased by a bull at Manaccan, and then it had been for the same purpose as now—to give herself courage and a certain bold pretence.

"I'll not show fear before Joss Merlyn or any man," she said, "and, to prove it, I will go down now, in the dark passage, and take a look at them in the bar, and if he kills me it will be my own fault."

She dressed hurriedly and pulled on her stockings, leaving her shoes where they were, and then, opening the door, she stood and listened for a moment, hearing nothing but the slow choking tick of the clock in the hall.

She crept out into the passage and came to the stairs. By now she knew that the third step from the top creaked, and so did the last. She trod gently, one hand resting on the bannister and the other against the wall to lighten her weight, and so she came to the dim hall by the entrance door, empty except for one unsteady chair and the shadowed outline of the grandfather clock. Its husky breathing sounded loud beside her ear, and it jarred upon the silence like a living thing. The hall was as black as a pit, and, although she knew she stood alone there, the very solitude was threatening, the closed door to the unused parlour pregnant with suggestion.

The air was fusty and heavy, in strange contrast to the cold stone flags that struck chill to her stockinged feet. As she hesitated, gathering courage to continue, a sudden beam of light shone into the passage that ran at the back of the hall, and she heard voices. The door of the bar must have swung open, and someone come out, for she heard footsteps pass into the kitchen and in a few minutes return again, but whoever it was still left the door of the bar ajar, as the murmur of voices continued and the beam of light remained. Mary was tempted to climb the stairs again to her bedroom and seek safety in sleep, but at the same time there was a demon of curiosity within her that would not be stilled, and this part of her carried her through to the passage beyond, and so to crouch against the wall a few paces only from the door of the bar. Her hands and her forehead were wet now with perspiration, and at first she could hear nothing but the loud beating of her heart. The door was open enough for her to see the outline of the hinged bar itself, and the collection of bottles and glasses, while directly in front ran a narrow strip of floor. The splintered fragments of the glass her uncle had broken still lay where they had fallen, and beside them was a brown stain of ale, spilt by some unsteady hand. The men must be sitting on the benches against the further wall, for she could not see them; they had fallen to silence, and then suddenly a man's voice rang out, quavering and high, the voice of a stranger.

"No, and no again," he said. "I tell you for the final time, I'll not be a party to it. I'll break with you now and for ever, and put an end to the agreement. That's murder you'd have me do, Mr. Merlyn; there's no other name for it—it's common murder."

The voice was pitched high, trembling on the final note, as though the speaker were carried away by the force of his feelings and had lost command of his tongue. Someone—the landlord himself, no doubt—made reply in a low tone, and Mary could not catch his words, but his speech was broken by a cackle of laughter that she recognized as belonging to the pedlar. The quality of it was unmistakable—insulting and coarse.

He must have hinted a question, for the stranger spoke again swiftly in self-defence. "Swinging, is it?" he said. "I've risked swinging before, and I'm not afraid of my neck. No, I'm thinking of my conscience and of Almighty God; and though I'll face any man in a fair fight, and take punishment if need be, when it comes to the killing of innocent folk, and maybe women and children amongst them, that's going straight to hell, Joss Merlyn, and you know it as well as I do."

Mary heard the scraping of a chair, and the man rise to his feet, but at the same time someone thumped his fist on the table and swore, and her uncle lifted his voice for the first time.

"Not so fast, my friend," he said, "not so fast. You're soaked in this business up to your neck, and be damned to your blasted conscience! I tell you there's no going back on it now; it's too late; too late for you and for all of us. I've been doubtful of you from the first, with your gentleman's airs and your clean cuffs, and by God I've proved myself right. Harry, bolt the door over there and put the bar across it "

There was a sudden scuffle and a cry, and the sound of someone falling, and at the same time the table crashed to the floor, and the door to the yard was slammed. Once more the pedlar laughed, odious and obscene, and he began to whistle one of his songs "Shall we tickle him up like Silly Sam?" he said, breaking off in the middle. "He'd be a little body without his fine clothes. I could do with his watch and chain, too; poor men of the road like myself haven't the money to go buying watches. Tickle him up with the whip, Joss, and let's see the colour of his skin."

"Shut your mouth, Harry, and do as you're told," answered the landlord. "Stand where you are by the door and prick him with your knife if he tries to pass you. Now, look here, Mr. Lawyer-Clerk, or whatever you are in Truro town, you've made a fool of yourself tonight, but you're not going to make a fool of me. You'd like to walk out of that door, wouldn't you, and get on your horse, and be away to Bodmin? Yes, and by nine in the morning you'd have every magistrate in the country at Jamaica Inn, and a regiment of soldiers into the bargain. That's your fine idea, isn't it?"

Mary could hear the stranger breathe heavily, and he must have been hurt in the scuffle, for when his voice came it was jerky and contracted, as though he were in pain. "Do your devil's work if you must," he muttered. "I can't stop you, and I give you my word I'll not inform against you. But join you I will not, and there's my last word to you both."

There was a silence, and then Joss Merlyn spoke again. "Have a care," he said softly. "I heard another man say that once, and five minutes later he was treading the air. On the end of a rope it was, my friend, and his big toe missed the floor by half an inch. I asked him if he liked to be so near the ground, but he didn't answer. The rope forced the tongue out of his mouth, and he bit it clean in half. They said afterwards he had taken seven and three-quarter minutes to die."

Outside in the passage Mary felt her neck and her forehead go clammy with sweat, and her arms and legs were weighted suddenly, as though with lead. Little black specks flickered before her eyes, and with a growing sense of horror she realized that she was probably going to faint.

She had one thought in her mind, and that was to grope her way back to the deserted hall and reach the shadow of the clock; whatever happened, she must not fall here and be discovered. Mary backed away from the beam of light and felt along the wall with her hands. Her knees were shaking now, and she knew that at any moment they would give beneath her. Already a surge of sickness rose inside her, and her head was swimming.

Her uncle's voice came from very far away, as though he spoke with his hands against his mouth. "Leave me alone with him, Harry," he said; "there'll be no more work for you tonight at Jamaica. Take his horse and be off, and cast him loose the other side of Camelford. I'll settle this business by myself."

Somehow Mary found her way to the hall, and, hardly conscious of what she was doing, she turned the handle of the parlour door and stumbled inside. Then she crumpled in a heap on the floor, her head between her knees.

She must have fainted quite away for a minute or two, because the specks in front of her eyes grouped themselves into one tremendous whole, and her world went black; but the position in which she had fallen brought her to herself quicker than anything else could have done, and in a moment she was sitting up, propped on one elbow, listening to the clatter of a pony's hoofs in the yard outside. She heard a voice curse the animal to stand still—it was Harry the pedlar —and then he must have mounted and driven his heels into the pony's side, for the sound of the hoofs drew away and out of the yard and disappeared in the distance down the high-road, and so was lost beneath the slope of the hill. Her uncle was alone now in the bar with his victim, and Mary wondered whether it would be possible for her to find her way to the nearest dwelling place on the road to Dozmary and summon help. It meant a walk of two or three miles across a moorland track before the first shepherd's cottage was reached, and somewhere on that same track the poor idiot boy had flown, earlier in the evening, and was even now perhaps wailing and grimacing by the side of the ditch.

She knew nothing of the inhabitants of the cottage; possibly they belonged to her uncle's company, in which case she would be running straight into a trap. Aunt Patience, upstairs in bed, was useless to her, and if anything an encumbrance. It was a hopeless situation, and there seemed no way of escape for the stranger, whoever he should be, unless he himself came to some agreement with Joss Merlyn. If he had any cunning he might be able to overpower her uncle; now that the pedlar had gone they were evenly matched as far as numbers went, though her uncle's physical strength would tell heavily in his favour. Mary began to feel desperate. If only there were a gun somewhere, or a knife, she might be able to wound her uncle, or at least disarm him while the wretched man made his escape from the bar.

She felt careless now for her own safety; it was only a matter of time, anyway, before she was discovered, and there was little sense in crouching here in the empty parlour. That fainting attack had been a momentary affair, and she despised herself for her weakness. She got up from the floor, and, placing both hands on the latch for greater silence, she opened the door a few inches. There was not a sound in the hall but the ticking of the clock, and the beam of light in the back passage shone no more. The door of the bar must be shut. Perhaps at this moment the stranger was fighting for his life, struggling for breath in the great hands of Joss Merlyn, shaken backwards and forwards on the stone floor of the bar. She could hear nothing, though; whatever work there was behind that closed door happened in silence.

Mary was about to step out into the hall once more and creep past the stairs to the further passage, when a sound from above made her pause and lift her head. It was the creaking of a board. There was silence for a minute, and then it happened again: quiet footsteps pacing gently overhead. Aunt Patience slept in the further passage at the other end of the house, and Mary herself had heard Harry the pedlar ride away on his pony nearly ten minutes ago. Her uncle she knew to be in the bar with the stranger, and no one had climbed the stairs since she had descended them. There, the board creaked again, and the soft footsteps continued. Someone was in the empty guest room on the floor above.

Mary's heart began to thump in her side again, and her breath came quickly. Whoever was in hiding up above must have been there many hours. He must have lain in waiting there since the early evening; stood behind the door when she had gone to bed. Had he gone later she would have heard his footsteps on the stairs. Perhaps he had watched the arrival of the waggons from the window, as she had done, and had seen the idiot boy run screaming down the road to Dozmary. She had been separated from him by a thin partition of wall, and he must have heard her every movement—the falling onto her bed, and later her dressing, and her opening of her door.

Therefore he must wish to remain concealed, otherwise he would have stepped out onto the landing when she had done; had he been one of the company in the bar he would have spoken with her, surely; he would have questioned her movements. Who had admitted him? When could he have gone into the room? He must have hidden there so that he should remain unseen by the smugglers. Therefore he was not one of them; he was enemy to her uncle. The footfalls had ceased now, and, though she held her breath and listened intently, she could hear nothing. She had not been mistaken, though; she was convinced of that. Someone—an ally perhaps—was hiding in the guest room next to hers and could help her save the stranger in the bar. She had her foot on the lowest step of the stairs when the beam of light shone forth once more from the back passage, and she heard the door of the bar swing open. Her uncle was coming out into the hall. There was no time for Mary to climb the stairs before he turned the corner, so she was forced to step quickly back into the parlour and stand with her hand against the door. In the blackness of the hall he would never see that the door was not latched.

Trembling with excitement and fear, she waited in the parlour, and she heard the landlord pass across the hall and climb the stairs to the landing above. His footsteps came to a halt above her head, outside the guest room, and for a second or two he waited, as though he too listened for some alien sound. Then he tapped twice, very softly, on the door.

Once more the board creaked, and someone crossed the floor of the room above and the door was opened. Mary's heart sank within her, and her first despair returned. This could be no enemy to her uncle, after all. Probably Joss Merlyn had admitted him in the first place, early in the evening when she and Aunt Patience had been preparing the bar for the company, and he had lain in waiting there until all the men had departed. It was some personal friend of the landlord's, who had no wish to meddle in his evening's business and would not show himself even to the landlord's wife.

Her uncle had known him to be there all the time, and that was why he had sent the pedlar away. He did not wish the pedlar to see his friend. She thanked God then that she had not climbed the stairs and knocked on the door.

Supposing they went into her room to see if she was there and asleep? There would be little hope for her once her absence was discovered. She glanced behind her at the window. It was closed and barred. There was no road of escape. Now they were coming down the stairs; they stopped for an instant outside the parlour door. For one moment Mary thought they were coming inside. They were so close to her that she could have touched her uncle on the shoulder through the crack of the door. As it was, he spoke, and his voice whispered right against her ear.

"It's for you to say," he breathed; "it's your judgment now, not mine. I'll do it, or we'll do it between us. It's for you to say the word."

Screened as she was by the door, Mary could neither see nor hear her uncle's new companion, and whatever gesture or sign he made in return escaped her. They did not linger outside the parlour, but turned back along the hall to the further passage, and so down it to the bar beyond.

Then the door closed, and she heard them no more.

Her first instinct was to unbar the entrance and run out into the road, and so be away from them; but on reflection she realized that by doing this she would gain nothing; for all she knew, there might be other men—the pedlar himself perhaps, and the rest of them—posted at intervals along the highroad in the anticipation of trouble.

It seemed as though this new man, who had hidden all evening in the room above, could not have heard her leave her bedroom after all; had he done so he would by now have acquainted her uncle with the fact, and they would search for her; unless they dismissed her as being of no importance whatsoever in the general scheme of things. The man in the bar was their first concern; she could be attended to later.

She must have stood for ten minutes or more waiting for some sound or signal, but everything was still. Only the clock in the hall ticked on, wheezing slowly and impervious to action, a symbol of age and indifference. Once she fancied she heard a cry; but it was gone and lost in an instant and was so faint and far a thing that it might have been some strange conjuring of her imagination, whipped as it was by all she had seen since midnight.

Then Mary went out into the hall, and so through to the

dark passage. No crack of light came under the skirting of the door to the bar. The candles must have been extinguished. Were they sitting there inside the room, all three of them, in darkness? They made an ugly picture in her mind, a silent, sinister group, ruled by some purpose that she did not understand; but the very snuffing out of the light made the quietude more deadly.

She ventured as far as the door and laid her ear against the panel. There was not even the murmur of a voice, nor that unmistakable suggestion of living, breathing people. The old fusty drink smell that had clung to the passage all evening had cleared, and through the keyhole came a steady draught of air. Mary gave way to a sudden uncontrollable impulse, and, lifting the latch, she opened the door and stepped into the room.

There was nobody there. The door leading to the yard was open, and the room was filled with the fresh November air. It was this that caused the draught in the passage. The benches were empty, and the table that had crashed to the ground in the first scuffle still lay upon the floor, its three legs pointing to the ceiling.

The men had gone, though; they must have turned to the left outside the kitchen and walked straight onto the moor, for she would have heard them had they crossed the road. The air felt cold and sweet upon her face, and now that her uncle and the strangers had left it the room seemed harmless and impersonal once more. The horror was spent.

A last little ray of moonlight made a white circle on the floor, and into the circle moved a dark blob like a finger. It was the reflection of a shadow. Mary looked up to the ceiling and saw that a rope had been slung through a hook in the beam. It was the rope's end that made the blob in the white circle; and it kept moving backwards and forwards, blown by the draught from the open door.

Chapter 5

〜〜〜〜〜〜〜〜〜〜〜〜〜〜〜〜〜〜〜〜〜〜〜〜〜〜〜〜〜〜〜〜〜〜

As THE days passed, Mary Yellan settled down to life at Jamaica Inn with a sense of stubborn resolution. It was evident that she could not leave her aunt to face the winter alone, but perhaps, with the coming of spring, Patience Merlyn could be persuaded to see reason, and the pair of them would leave the moors for the peace and quietude of Helford valley.

This was at any rate Mary's hope, and meanwhile she must make the best of the grim six months that lay ahead, and if possible she was determined to have the better of her uncle in the long run and expose him and his confederates to the law. She would have shrugged her shoulders at smuggling alone, though the flagrant dishonesty of the trade disgusted her, but all she had seen so far went to prove that Joss Merlyn and his friends were not content with this only; they were desperate men, afraid of nothing and no one, and did not stop at murder. The events of that first Saturday night were never far from her mind, and the straggling rope's end hanging from the beam told its own tale. Mary had not a doubt that a stranger had been killed by her uncle and another man, and his body buried somewhere on the moors.

There was nothing to prove it, however, and, considered in the light of day, the very story seemed fantastic. She had returned to her room that night after the discovery of the rope, for the open door of the bar suggested that her uncle would be back at any moment, and, exhausted with all she had seen, she must have fallen asleep, for when she woke the sun was high, and she could hear Aunt Patience pattering about in the hall below.

No sign remained of the evening's work; the bar had been

swept and tidied, the furniture replaced and the broken glass taken away, and there was no rope hanging from the beam. The landlord himself spent the morning in the stable and the cowhouse, pitchforking filth into the yard and doing the work that a cowman should have done had he kept one; and when he came into the kitchen at midday, to wolf an enormous meal, he questioned Mary about the farm stock at Helford, and asked for her opinion on a calf that had fallen sick, nor did he make any reference to the events of the preceding night. He seemed in fair good humour and went so far as to forget to curse his wife, who hovered around him as usual, watching the expression in his eye like a dog who would please his master. Joss Merlyn behaved like a perfectly sober normal man, and it was impossible to believe that he had murdered a fellow being only a few hours before.

He might be guiltless of this, of course, and the blame rest upon his unknown companion, but at least Mary had seen him with her own eyes chase the naked idiot boy across the yard, and she had heard the boy scream as he felt the lash of the landlord's whip. She had seen him ringleader of that vile company in the bar; she had heard him threaten the stranger who opposed his will; and here he sat before her now, his mouth full of hot stew, shaking his head over a sick calf.

And she answered "Yes" and "No" in reply to her uncle, and drank down her tea, watching him over the brim of her cup, her eyes travelling from his great plate of steaming stew to his long powerful fingers, hideous in their strength and grace.

Two weeks went by and there was no repetition of Saturday night. Perhaps the last haul had satisfied the landlord and his companions, and they were content with that for the while, for Mary did not hear the waggons again, and, though she was sleeping soundly now, she was certain that the noise of wheels would have woken her. Her uncle appeared to have no objection to her wandering on the moors, and day by day she came to know more of the surrounding country, stumbling upon tracks she had not noticed at first and which kept her to the high ground, leading ultimately to the tors, while she learnt to avoid the low soggy grass with tufted tops that by their very harmless appearance invited inspection, only to reveal themselves as the border line of treacherous and dangerous marsh.

Though lonely, she was not actively unhappy, and these rambles in the grey light of early afternoon kept her healthy at least and went some way towards tempering the gloom and depression of the long dark evenings at Jamaica, when Aunt Patience sat with her hands in her lap, staring at the turf fire, and Joss Merlyn shut himself up alone in the bar or disappeared on the back of his pony to some unknown destination.

Companionship there was none, and no one came to the inn for rest or nourishment. The driver of the coach had spoken the truth when he told Mary they never stopped now at Jamaica, for she would stand out in the yard to watch the coaches pass twice in the week, and they were gone by in a moment, rumbling down the hill and climbing the further one towards Five Lanes without drawing rein or pausing for breath. Once Mary waved her hand as she recognized her driver, but he took no notice of her, only whipping his horses the harder, and she realized with a rather helpless sense of futility that so far as other people were concerned she must be considered in the same light as her uncle, and that even if she tried to walk to Bodmin or Launceston no one would receive her, and the doors would be shut in her face.

The future loomed very black at times, especially as Aunt Patience made little effort to be companionable; and though now and again she took hold of Mary's hand and patted it for a few minutes, telling her how glad she was to have her in the house, for the most part the poor woman existed in a dream, pottering about her household duties in a mechanical fashion and seldom uttering. When she did speak, it was to let forth a torrent of nonsense about the great man her husband might have been had not ill luck constantly followed him. Any normal conversation was practically impossible, and Mary came to humour her and talk gently as she would have done to a child, all of which was a strain on her nerves and on her patience.

So that it was in a mood of truculence, following upon a day of wind and rain that had made it impracticable to venture out of doors, that Mary one morning set herself to clean down the long stone passage that ran the full width of the back of the house. The hard work, if it strengthened her muscles, did not improve her temper, and by the time she had finished she was so disgusted with Jamaica Inn and its inhabitants that for very little she would have walked out into the patch of garden behind the kitchen, where her uncle was working, heedless of the rain upon his mat of hair, and thrown her bucket of dirty soapy water into his very face. The sight of her aunt, who with bent back poked at the dull peat fire with the end of a stick, defeated her, and Mary was about to start on the stone flags of the entrance hall when she heard a clatter of hoofs in the yard, and in a moment someone thundered on the closed door of the bar.

No one had approached Jamaica Inn before, and this summons was an event in itself. Mary went back to the kitchen to warn her aunt, but she had left the room, and, looking out of the window, Mary could see her pattering across the garden to her husband, who was loading turf from the stack into a barrow. They were both out of earshot, and neither could have heard the sound of this new arrival. Mary wiped her hands on her apron and went into the bar. The door must have been unlocked after all, for to her surprise there was a man sitting straddle-legged across a chair, with a glass in his hand filled to the brim with ale, which he had calmly poured out from the tap himself. For a few minutes they considered one another in silence.

Something about him was familiar, and Mary wondered where she had seen him before. The rather drooping lids, the curve of his mouth, and the outline of his jaw, even the bold and decidedly insolent stare with which he favoured her, were things known to her and definitely disliked.

The sight of him looking her up and down and drinking his ale at the same time irritated her beyond measure.

"What do you think you're doing?" she said sharply. "You haven't any right to walk in here and help yourself. Besides, the landlord doesn't encourage strangers." At any other mo-

60

ment she would have laughed to hear herself speak thus, as though in defence of her uncle, but scrubbing the stone flags had done away with her sense of humour, if only for the moment, and she felt she must vent her ill temper on the nearest victim.

The man finished his ale and held out the glass to be refilled.

"Since when have they kept a barmaid at Jamaica Inn?" he asked her, and, feeling in his pocket for a pipe, he lit it, puffing a great cloud of smoke into her face. His manner infuriated Mary, and she leant forward and pulled the pipe out of his hand, throwing it behind her onto the floor, where it smashed at once. He shrugged his shoulders and began to whistle, the very tunelessness adding fuel to her flame of irritation.

"Is this how they train you to serve customers?" he said, breaking off in the middle. "I don't think much of their choice. There are better-mannered maids in Launceston, where I was yesterday, and pretty as paint into the bargain. What have you been doing with yourself? Your hair is coming down at the back, and your face is none too clean."

Mary turned away and walked towards the door, but he called her back.

"Fill up my glass. That's what you're here for, isn't it?" he said. "I've ridden twelve miles since breakfast, and I'm thirsty."

"You may have ridden fifty miles for all I care," said Mary. "As you seem to know your way about here, you can fill your own glass. I'll tell Mr. Merlyn you are in the bar, and he can serve you himself if he has the mind."

"Oh, don't worry Joss; he'll be like a bear with a sore head at this time of day," came the answer. "Besides, he's never very anxious to see me. What's happened to his wife? Has he turned her out to make room for you? I call that hard on the poor woman. You'll never stay with him ten years, anyway."

"Mrs. Merlyn is in the garden, if you want to see her," said Mary. "You can walk out of the door and turn to the left, and you'll come to the patch of garden and the chicken

61

run. They were both of them down under, five minutes ago. You can't come through this way because I've just washed the passage, and I don't want to do it all over again."

"Oh, don't get excited; there's plenty of time," he replied. She could see he was still looking her up and down, wondering what to make of her, and the familiar, somewhat lazy insolence in his eyes maddened her.

"Do you want to speak to the landlord or not?" she asked at length. "Because I can't stand here all day awaiting your pleasure. If you don't want to see him, and you've finished your drink, you can put down your money on the counter and go away."

The man laughed, and his smile and the flash of his teeth struck a chord in her memory, but still she could not name the resemblance.

"Do you order Joss about in that way?" he said. "He must be a changed man if you do. What a creature of contradictions the fellow is, after all. I never thought he'd run a young woman alongside his other activities. What do you do with poor Patience of an evening? Do you turn her out on the floor, or do you sleep all three abreast?"

Mary flushed scarlet. "Joss Merlyn is my uncle by marriage," she said. "Aunt Patience was my mother's only sister. My name is Mary Yellan, if that means anything to you. Good morning. There's the door behind you."

She left the bar and walked into the kitchen, straight into the arms of the landlord himself. "Who in hell's name were you talking to in the bar?" he thundered. "I thought I'd warned you to keep your mouth shut?"

The loudness of his voice echoed in the passage. "All right," called the man from the bar, "don't beat her. She's broken my pipe and refused to serve me; that sounds like your training, doesn't it? Come in and let's have a look at you. I'm hoping this maid has done you some good."

Joss Merlyn frowned, and, pushing Mary aside, he stepped into the bar.

"Oh, it's you, Jem, is it?" he said. "What do you want at Jamaica today? I can't buy a horse from you, if that's what you're after. Things are going badly, and I'm as poor as a field mouse after a wet harvest." He closed the door, leaving Mary in the passage outside.

She went back to her bucket of water in the front hall, wiping the dirty mark from her face with her apron. So that was Jem Merlyn, her uncle's younger brother. Of course, she had seen the resemblance all the time, and, like a fool, had not been able to place it. He had reminded her of her uncle throughout the conversation, and she had not realized it. He had Joss Merlyn's eyes, without the blood-flecked lines and without the pouches, and he had Joss Merlyn's mouth, firm, though, where the landlord's was weak, and narrow where his lower lip sagged. He was what Joss Merlyn might have been eighteen, twenty years ago—but smaller in build and height, neater in person.

Mary splashed the water onto the stone flags and began to scrub furiously, her lips pressed tight together.

What a vile breed they were, then, these Merlyns, with their studied insolence and coarseness, their rough brutality of manner. This Jem had the same streak of cruelty as his brother; she could see it in the shape of his mouth. Aunt Patience had said he was the worst of the family. Although he was a head and shoulders smaller than Joss, and half the breadth, there was a certain strength about him that the elder brother did not possess. He looked hard and keen. The landlord sagged round the chin, and his shoulders weighed on him like a burden. It was as though his power had been wasted in some way and had run to seed. Drink did that to a man, Mary knew, and for the first time she was able to guess something of the wreck Joss Merlyn had become, in comparison to his former self. It was seeing his brother that had shown her. The landlord had betrayed himself. If the younger one had any sense in his head he would pull himself together before he travelled the same road. Perhaps he did not care, though; there must be a fatality about the Merlyn family that did away with striving forward, and making good in life, and resolution. Their record was too black. "There's no going against bad blood," her mother used to say, "it always comes out in the end. You may fight it as much as you like, but it will have the better of you. If

63

two generations live clean, that may clear the stream sometimes, but likely as not the third will break out and start it
going again." What a waste it all was, what a waste and a
pity! And here was poor Aunt Patience dragged in the current with the Merlyns, all her youth and gaiety gone before
her, leaving her—if the truth were faced—very little superior
to the idiot boy at Dozmary. And Aunt Patience might have
been a farmer's wife at Gweek, with sons of her own, and
a house and land, and all the little happy trivialities of a
normal happy life: gossip with the neighbours, and church
on Sundays, and driving into market once a week; fruit
picking, and harvesttime. Things she would have loved, things
that had foundation. She would have known placidity, and
they would be tranquil years that turned her hair in time
to grey—years of solid work and calm enjoyment. All this
promise she had thrown away, to live like a slattern with
a brute and a drunkard. Why were women such fools, so
shortsighted and unwise? wondered Mary; and she scrubbed
the last stone flag of the hall with venom, as though by her
very action she might cleanse the world and blot out the
indiscretions of her kind.

She had worked up her energy to a frenzy, and, turning
from the hall, proceeded to sweep the gloomy, dim parlour
that had not seen a broom for years. A cloud of dust met her
face, and she beat savagely at the wretched threadbare mat.
She was so absorbed in her disagreeable occupation that she
did not hear the stone flung at the window of the parlour,
and it was not until a shower of pebbles made a crack in
the glass that her concentration was disturbed, and, looking
out of the window, she saw Jem Merlyn standing in the
yard beside his pony.

Mary frowned at him and turned away, but he made
answer with another shower of pebbles, this time cracking
the glass in earnest, so that a small piece of the pane splintered onto the floor, with a stone beside it.

Mary unbolted the heavy entrance door and went out
into the porch.

"What do you want now?" she asked him, conscious suddenly of her loose hair and rumpled dirty apron.

He still looked down at her with curiosity, but the insolence had gone, and he had the grace to appear the smallest bit ashamed of himself.

"Forgive me if I was rude to you just now," he said. "Somehow I didn't expect to see a woman at Jamaica Inn—not a young girl like you, anyway. I thought Joss had found you in one of the towns and had brought you back here for his fancy lady."

Mary flushed again and bit her lip in annoyance. "There's nothing very fanciful about me," she said scornfully. "I'd look well in a town, wouldn't I, in my old apron and heavy shoes? I should have thought anyone with eyes in his head could see I was farm bred."

"Oh, I don't know," he said carelessly. "Put you in a fine gown and a pair of high-heeled shoes, and stick a comb in your hair, I daresay you'd pass for a lady even in a big place like Exeter."

"I'm meant to be flattered by that, I suppose," said Mary, "but, thanking you very much, I'd rather wear my old clothes and look like myself."

"You could do a lot worse than that, of course," he agreed; and, looking up, she saw that he was laughing at her. She turned to go back into the house.

"Come, don't go away," he said. "I know I deserve black looks for speaking to you as I did, but if you knew my brother as well as I do you'd understand me making the mistake. It looks strange, having a maid at Jamaica Inn. Why did you come here in the first place?"

Mary considered him from the shadow of the porch. He looked serious now, and his likeness to Joss had fled for the moment. She wished he were not a Merlyn.

"I came here to be with my aunt Patience," she said. "My mother died some weeks ago, and I have no other relative. I'll tell you one thing, Mr. Merlyn—I'm thankful my mother isn't alive to see her sister now."

"I don't suppose marriage with Joss is a bed of roses," said his brother. "He always had the temper of the devil himself, and he drinks like a fish. What did she marry him for? He's been the same as long as I can remember. He

65

used to thrash me when I was a lad, and he'd do the same today if he dared."

"I suppose she was misled by his bright eyes," said Mary scornfully. "Aunt Patience was always the butterfly down in Helford, Mother used to say. She wouldn't have the farmer who asked her, but took herself off upcountry, where she met your brother. That was the worst day in her life, anyway."

"You've not much opinion of the landlord, then," he said, mocking her.

"No, I have not," she replied. "He's a bully and a brute, and many worse things besides. He's turned my aunt from a laughing, happy woman into a miserable drudge, and I'll never forgive him for that as long as I live."

Jem whistled tunelessly and patted his horse's neck.

"We Merlyns have never been good to our women," he said. "I can remember my father beating my mother till she couldn't stand. She never left him, though, but stood by him all his life. When he was hanged at Exeter, she didn't speak to a soul for three months. Her hair went white with the shock. I can't remember my grandmother, but they say she fought side by side with Granddad once near Callington, when the soldiers came to take him, and she bit a fellow's finger right through to the bone. What she had to love in Granddad I can't say, for he never as much as asked for her after he'd been taken, and he left all his savings with another woman the other side of Tamar."

Mary was silent. The indifference in his voice appalled her. He spoke entirely without shame or regret, and she supposed that he had been born, like the rest of his family, lacking the quality of tenderness.

"How long do you mean to stay at Jamaica?" he asked abruptly. "It's waste for a maid like you, isn't it? There's not much company for you here."

"I can't help that," said Mary. "I'm not going away unless I take my aunt with me. I'd never leave her here alone, not after what I've seen."

Jem bent down to brush a piece of dirt from his pony's shoe.

"What have you learnt in your short time?" he questioned. "It's quiet enough here, in all conscience."

Mary was not easily led. For all she knew, her uncle had prompted his brother to speak to her, hoping in this way to obtain information. No, she was not quite such a fool as that. She shrugged her shoulders, dismissing the subject.

"I helped my uncle in the bar one Saturday night," she said, "and I did not think much of the company he kept."

"I don't suppose you did," said Jem. "The fellows who come to Jamaica have never been taught manners. They spend too much time in the county jail. I wonder what they thought of you? Made the same mistake as I did, I suppose, and are now spreading your fame far and wide about the countryside. You'll have Joss throwing dice for you next time, I daresay, and when he loses you'll find yourself riding pillion behind a dirty poacher from the other side of Rough Tor."

"There's not much likelihood of that," said Mary. "They'd have to knock me senseless before I rode pillion with anyone."

"Senseless or conscious, women are pretty much the same when you come down to it," said Jem. "The poachers on Bodmin Moor would never know the difference, anyway." And he laughed again and looked exactly like his brother.

"What do you do for a livelihood?" asked Mary, in sudden curiosity, for during their conversation she became aware that he spoke better than his brother.

"I'm a horse thief," he said pleasantly, "but there's not much money in it. My pockets are always empty. You ought to ride here. I've got a little pony that would suit you handsomely. He's over at Trewartha now. Why don't you come back with me and look at him?"

"Aren't you afraid of being caught?" said Mary.

"Thieving is an awkward thing to prove," he told her. "Supposing a pony strays from his pen, and his owner goes to look for him. Well, you've seen for yourself, these moors are alive with wild horses and cattle. It's not going to be so easy for that owner to find his pony. Say the pony had a long mane, and one white foot, and a diamond mark in his ear—that narrows the field down a bit, doesn't it? And off goes the owner to Launceston fair with his eyes wide open. But he doesn't find his pony. Mark you, the pony is there, right enough, and he's bought by some dealer and sold away upcountry. Only his mane is clipped, his four feet are all the same colour, and the mark in his ear is a slit, not a diamond. The owner didn't even look at him twice. That's simple enough, isn't it?"

"So simple that I can't understand why you don't ride past Jamaica in your own coach, with a powdered footman on the step," said Mary swiftly.

"Ah, well, there you are," he said, shaking his head. "I've never had the brain for figures. You'd be surprised to learn how quickly money slips through my fingers. Do you know, I had ten pounds in my pocket last week. I've only a shilling piece today. That's why I want you to buy that little pony."

Mary laughed, in spite of herself. He was so frank in his dishonesty that she had not the heart to be angry with him.

"I can't spend my small savings on horses," she said. "I'm laying aside for my old age, and if I ever get away from Jamaica I shall need every penny, you may depend on that."

Jem Merlyn looked at her gravely, and then, on a sudden impulse, he bent towards her, first glancing over her head into the porch beyond.

"Look here," he said, "I'm serious now; you can forget all the nonsense I've told you. Jamaica Inn is no place for a maid—nor for any woman, if it comes to that. My brother and I have never been friends, and I can say what I like about him. We go our own ways and be damned to one another. But there's no reason why you should be caught up in his dirty schemes. Why don't you run away? I'd see you on the road to Bodmin all right."

His tones were persuasive, and Mary could almost have trusted him. But she could not forget he was Joss Merlyn's brother, and as such might betray her. She dared not make a confidant of him—not yet, anyway. Time would show whose side he was on.

"I don't need any help," she said; "I can look after myself."

Jem threw his leg over the pony's back and stuck his feet into the leathers.

"All right," he said, "I won't worry you. My cottage is across the Withy Brook, if you ever want me. The other side of Trewartha Marsh, at the foot of Twelve Men's Moor. I shall be there until the spring, anyway. Good day to you." And he was off and away down the road before she had time to say a word in return.

Mary went slowly back into the house. She would have trusted him had his name been other than Merlyn. She was in urgent need of a friend; but she could not make a friend of the landlord's brother. He was no more than a common horse thief, a dishonest scoundrel, when all was said and done. He was little better than Harry the pedlar and the rest of them. Because he had a disarming smile and his voice was not unpleasing, she had been ready to believe in him, and he all the time perhaps laughing at her the other side of his face. There was bad blood in him; he broke the law every day of his life, and whatever way she looked at it there was no escaping from that one unredeemable fact —he was Joss Merlyn's brother. He had said there was no bond between them, but even that might be a lie to enlist her sympathy, while the whole of their conversation perhaps had been prompted by the landlord in the bar.

No, whatever happened, she must stand alone in this business and trust no one. The very walls of Jamaica Inn smelt of guilt and deceit, and to speak aloud in earshot of the building courted disaster.

It was dark in the house, and quiet once more. The landlord had returned to the peat stack at the bottom of the garden, and Aunt Patience was in her kitchen. The surprise of the visit had been a little excitement and a breaking up of the long, monotonous day. Jem Merlyn had brought something of the outer world with him, a world that was not entirely bounded by the moors and frowned upon by tors of granite; and now that he had departed the early brightness of the day went with him. The sky became overcast, and the inevitable rain came sweeping from the west, topping the hills in mist. The black heather bowed before the wind. The ill temper that had fastened upon Mary at the beginning of the morning had passed away, and in its place had stolen a numb indifference born of fatigue and despair. Interminably the days and weeks stretched themselves before her, with no other sight but the long white road to tempt her, the stone walls, and the everlasting hills.

She thought of Jem Merlyn riding away with a song on his lips, kicking his heels into his pony's side, and he would ride hatless, careless of the wind and the rain, choosing his own road.

She thought of the lane that led to Helford village, how it twisted and turned and wound suddenly to the water's edge, while the ducks paddled in the mud before the turn of the tide, and a man called to his cows from the field above. All those things were progressive, and part of life, and they went their way without a thought of her, but she was bound here by a promise that she must not break, and the very patter of Aunt Patience's feet as she passed to and fro in the kitchen was a reminder and a warning.

Mary watched the little stinging rain blur the glass of the parlour window, and as she sat there, alone, with her chin in her hand, the tears ran down her cheeks in company with the rain. She let them fall, too indifferent to wipe them away, while the draught from the door she had forgotten to close ruffled a long torn strip of paper on the wall. There had once been a rose pattern, but it was now faded and grey, and the walls themselves were stained deep brown where the damp had turned them. Mary turned away from the window; and the cold, dead atmosphere of Jamaica Inn closed in upon her.

Chapter 6

~~~~~~

THAT NIGHT the waggons came again. Mary woke to the
sound of the hall clock striking two, and almost at once
she was aware of footsteps beneath the porch, and she
heard a voice speak soft and low. She crept out of bed and
went over to the window. Yes, there they were; only two
carts this time, with one horse in harness, and less than
half a dozen men standing in the yard.

The waggons looked ghostly in the dim light, like hearses,
and the men themselves were phantom figures, having no
place in the world of day by day, but moving silently about
the yard like some weird pattern in a nightmare fantasy.
There was something horrible about them, something sinister
in the shrouded waggons themselves, coming as they did in
stealth by night. This night the impression they left upon
Mary was even more lasting and profound; for now she understood the significance of their trade.

They were desperate men who worked this road and
carried convoys to Jamaica Inn, and last time they brought
their waggons to the yard one of their number had been
murdered. Perhaps tonight yet another crime would be
committed, and the twisted length of rope dangle once
again from the beam below.

The scene in the yard held a fatal fascination, and Mary
could not leave the window. This time the waggons had
arrived empty and were loaded with the remainder of the
cargo deposited at the inn the time before. Mary guessed
that this was their method of working. The inn served as
a store for a few weeks at a time, and then, when opportunity
occurred, the waggons set forth once more, and the cargo

was carried to the Tamar bank and so distributed. The organization must be a big one to cover the ground in the time, and there would be agents scattered far and wide who kept the necessary watch on events. Perhaps there were hundreds implicated in the trade, from Penzance and St. Ives in the south to Launceston on the border of Devon. There had been little talk of smuggling in Helford, and when there had been, it was with a wink and a smile of indulgence, as though a pipe of baccy and a bottle of brandy from a ship in Falmouth port were an occasional harmless luxury and not a burden on any person's conscience.

This was different, though. This was a grim business, a stern and bloody business, and precious little smiling or winking went with it, from all that Mary had seen. If his conscience pricked a man, he received a rope round his neck in payment. There must be no weak link in the chain that stretched from the coast up to the border, and there was the explanation of the rope on the beam. The stranger had demurred, and the stranger had died. It was with a sudden sting of disappointment that Mary wondered whether the visit of Jem Merlyn to the Jamaica Inn this morning had significance. A strange coincidence that the waggons should follow in his train. He had come from Launceston, he said, and Launceston stood on the Tamar bank. Mary was angry with him and with herself. In spite of everything, her last thought before sleeping had been the possibility of his friendship. She would be a fool if she had hopes of it now. The two events ran together in an unmistakable fashion, and it was easy enough to read the purpose of it.

Jem might disagree with his brother, but they were both in the same trade. He had ridden to Jamaica to warn the landlord that he might expect the convoy in the evening. It was simple enough to understand. And then, having something of a heart, he had advised Mary to take herself to Bodmin. It was no place for a maid, he said. No one knew that better than he did himself, being one of the company. It was a wretched, damnable business in every way, without a ray of hope in any direction, and here she was in the midst of it all, with Aunt Patience like a child on her hands.

Now the two waggons were loaded, and the drivers climbed in the seats with their companions. The performance had not been a lengthy one tonight.

Mary could see the great head and shoulders of her uncle on a level with the porch, and he held a lantern in his hand, the light dimmed by a shutter. Then the carts rumbled out of the yard and turned to the left, as Mary had expected, and so in the direction of Launceston.

She came away from the window and climbed back into bed. Presently she heard her uncle's footsteps on the stairs, and he went along the further passage to his bedroom. There was no one hiding in the guest room tonight.

The next few days passed without incident, and the only vehicle on the road was the coach to Launceston, rumbling past Jamaica like a scared blackbeetle. There came a fine crisp morning with frost on the ground, and for once the sun shone in a cloudless sky. The tors stood out boldly against the hard blue heaven, and the moorland grass, usually soggy and brown, glistened stiff and white with the frost. The drinking well in the yard had a thin layer of ice. The mud had hardened where the cows had trodden, and the marks of their feet were preserved in formed ridges that would not yield until the next fall of rain. The light wind came singing from the northeast, and it was cold.

Mary, whose spirits always rose at the sight of the sun, had turned her morning into washing day, and, with sleeves rolled well above the elbows, plunged her arms into the tub, the hot soapy water, bubbling with froth, caressing her skin in exquisite contrast to the sharp stinging air.

She felt well in being, and she sang as she worked. Her uncle had ridden away on the moors somewhere, and a sense of freedom possessed her whenever he was gone. At the back here she was sheltered somewhat from the wind, the broad sturdy house acting as a screen, and as she wrung out her linen and spread it on the stunted gorse bush, she saw that the full force of the sun fell upon it, and it would be dry by noon.

An urgent tapping on the window made her look up, and

she saw Aunt Patience beckon to her, very white in the face and evidently frightened.

Mary wiped her hands on her apron and ran to the back door of the house. No sooner had she entered the kitchen than her aunt seized upon her with trembling hands and began to blabber incoherently.

"Quietly, quietly," said Mary. "I cannot understand what you're saying. Here, take this chair and sit down, and drink this glass of water, for mercy's sake. Now, what is it?"

The poor woman rocked backwards and forwards in her chair, her mouth working nervously, and she kept jerking her head towards the door.

"It's Mr. Bassat from North Hill," she whispered. "I saw him from the parlour window. He's come on horseback, and another gentleman with him. Oh, my dear, my dear, what are we going to do?"

Even as she spoke there was a loud knock at the entrance door and then a pause, followed by a thunder of blows.

Aunt Patience groaned aloud, biting the ends of her fingers and tearing at her nails. "Why has he come here?" she cried. "He's never been before. He's always kept away. He's heard something, I know he has. Oh, Mary, what are we going to do? What are we going to say?"

Mary thought quickly. She was in a very difficult position. If this was Mr. Bassat and he represented the law, it was her one chance of betraying her uncle. She could tell him of the waggons and all she had seen since her arrival. She looked down at the trembling woman at her side.

"Mary, Mary, for the sake of the dear Lord, tell me what I am to say?" pleaded Aunt Patience, and she took her niece's hand and held it to her heart.

The hammering on the door was incessant now.

"Listen to me," said Mary. "We shall have to let him in or he'll break down the door. Pull yourself together somehow. There's no need to say anything at all. Say Uncle Joss is away from home, and you know nothing. I'll come with you."

The woman looked at her with haggard, desperate eyes.

"Mary," she said, "if Mr. Bassat asks you what you know,

you won't answer him, will you? I can trust you, can't I? You'll not tell him of the waggons? If any danger came to Joss I'd kill myself, Mary."

There was no argument after that. Mary would lie herself into hell rather than let her aunt suffer. The situation must be faced, though, however ironical her position was to be.

"Come with me to the door," she said; "we'll not keep Mr. Bassat long. You needn't be afraid of me; I shall say nothing."

They went into the hall together, and Mary unbolted the heavy entrance door. There were two men outside the porch. One had dismounted, and it was he who had rained the blows on the door. The other was a big burly fellow, in a heavy topcoat and cape, seated on the back of a fine chestnut horse. His hat was pulled square over his eyes, but Mary could see that his face was heavily lined and weather-beaten, and she judged him to be somewhere about fifty years of age.

"You take your time here, don't you?" he called. "There doesn't seem to be much of a welcome for travellers. Is the landlord at home?"

Patience Merlyn poked at her niece with her hand, and Mary made answer.

"Mr. Merlyn is from home, sir," she said. "Are you in need of refreshment? I will serve you if you will go through to the bar."

"Damn refreshment!" he returned. "I know better than to come to Jamaica Inn for that. I want to speak to your master. Here, you, are you the landlord's wife? When do you expect him home?"

Aunt Patience made him a little curtsey. "If you please, Mr. Bassat," she said, speaking unnaturally loudly and clearly, like a child who has learnt a lesson, "my husband went out as soon as he had his breakfast, and whether he will be back before nightfall I really cannot say."

"H'mph," growled the squire, "that's a damned nuisance. I wanted a word or two with Mr. Joss Merlyn. Now look here, my good woman, your precious husband may have bought Jamaica Inn behind my back, in his blackguardly fashion and we'll not go into that again now, but one thing I won't stand for, and that's having all my land hereabouts made a byword for everything that's damnable and dishonest round the countryside."

"I'm sure, I don't know what you mean, Mr. Bassat," said Aunt Patience, working her mouth and twisting her hands in her dress. "We live very quietly here, indeed we do; my niece here will tell you the same."

"Oh, come, I'm not such a fool as that," answered the squire. "I've had my eyes on this place for a long while. A house doesn't get a bad name without reason, Mrs. Merlyn, and Jamaica Inn stinks from here to the coast. Don't you pretend to me. Here, Richards, hold my confounded horse, will you?"

The other man, who by his dress appeared to be a servant, held the bridle, and Mr. Bassat climbed heavily to the ground.

"While I'm here I may as well look round," he said, "and I'll tell you here and now that it's useless to refuse me. I'm a magistrate, and I have a warrant." He pushed his way past the two women, and so through to the little entrance hall. Aunt Patience made a movement as though to deter him, but Mary shook her head and frowned. "Let him go," she murmured. "If we try and stop him now we shall only anger him the more."

Mr. Bassat was looking about him in disgust. "Good God," he exclaimed, "the place smells like a tomb. What in the world have you done to it? Jamaica Inn was always roughcast and plain, and the fare homely, but this is a positive disgrace. Why, the place is as bare as a board; you haven't a stick of furniture."

He had thrown open the door of the parlour and pointed to the damp walls with his crop. "You'll have the roof about your ears if you don't stop that," he said. "I've never seen such a thing in my life. Go on, Mrs. Merlyn, lead the way upstairs." Pale and anxious, Patience Merlyn turned to the staircase, her eyes searching those of her niece for reassurement.

The rooms on the landing were thoroughly explored. The

squire peered into the dusty corners, lifted the old sacks, and prodded the potatoes, all the while uttering exclamations of anger and disgust. "Call this an inn, do you?" he said. "Why, you haven't even a bed fit to sleep a cat. The place is rotten, rotten right through. What's the idea, eh? Have you lost your tongue, Mrs. Merlyn?"

The poor woman was past replying; she kept shaking her head and working her mouth, and Mary knew that both she and her aunt were wondering what would happen when they came to the barred room in the passage below.

"The landlord's lady appears to be momentarily deaf and dumb," said the squire dryly. "What about you, young woman? Have you anything to say?"

"It's only lately I've come to stay here," replied Mary. "My mother died, and I'm here to look after my aunt. She's not very strong; you can see that for yourself. She's nervous and easily upset."

"I don't blame her, living in a place like this," said Mr. Bassat. "Well, there's nothing more to see up here, so you'll kindly take me downstairs again and show me the room that has barred windows. I noticed it from the yard, and I'd like to see inside."

Aunt Patience passed her tongue over her lips and looked at Mary. She was incapable of speech.

"I'm very sorry, sir," Mary replied, "but if you mean the old lumber room at the end of the passage, I'm afraid the door is locked. My uncle always keeps the key, and where he puts it I don't know."

The squire looked from one to the other in suspicion.

"What about you, Mrs. Merlyn? Don't you know where your husband keeps his keys?"

Aunt Patience shook her head. The squire snorted and turned on his heel. "Well, that's easily settled," he said. "We'll have the door down in no time." And he went out into the yard to call his servant. Mary patted her aunt's hand and drew her close.

"Try and not tremble so," she whispered fiercely. "Anyone can see you have something to hide. Your only chance

77

is to pretend you don't mind, and that he can see anything in the house for all you care."

In a few minutes Mr. Bassat returned with the man Richards, who, grinning all over his face at the thought of destruction, carried an old bar he had found in the stable, and which he evidently intended using as a battering-ram.

If it had not been for her aunt, Mary would have given herself to the scene with some enjoyment. For the first time she would be permitted a view of the barred room. The fact that her aunt, and herself too for that matter, would be implicated in any discovery that was made caused her mixed feelings, however, and for the first time she realized that it was going to be a very difficult task to prove their complete and thorough innocence. No one was likely to believe protestations, with Aunt Patience fighting blindly on the landlord's side.

It was with some excitement, then, that Mary watched Mr. Bassat and his servant seize the bar between them and ram it against the lock of the door. For a few minutes it withstood them, and the sound of the blows echoed through the house. Then there was a splitting of wood and a crash, and the door gave way before them. Aunt Patience uttered a little cry of distress, and the squire pushed past her into the room. Richards leant on the bar, wiping the sweat from his forehead, and Mary could see through to the room over his shoulder. It was dark, of course; the barred windows with their lining of sack kept the light from penetrating the room.

"Get me a candle, one of you," shouted the squire. "It's as black as a pit in here." The servant produced a stump of candle from his pocket, and a light was kindled. He handed the candle to the squire, who, lifting it high above his head, stepped into the centre of the room.

For a moment there was silence, as the squire turned, letting the light shine in every corner, and then, clicking his tongue in annoyance and disappointment, he faced the little group behind him.

"Nothing," he said; "absolutely nothing. The landlord has made a fool of me again."

Except for a pile of sacks in one corner the room was

completely empty. It was thick with dust, and there were cobwebs on the walls larger than a man's hand. There was no furniture of any sort, the hearth had been blocked up with stones, and the floor itself was flagged like the passage outside.

On the top of the sacks lay a length of twisted rope.

Then the squire shrugged his shoulders and turned once more into the passage.

"Well, Mr. Joss Merlyn has won this time," he said; "there's not enough evidence in that room to kill a cat. I'll admit myself beaten."

The two women followed him to the outer hall, and so to the porch, while the servant made his way to the stable to fetch the horses.

Mr. Bassat flicked his boot with his whip and stared moodily in front of him. "You've been lucky, Mrs. Merlyn," he said. "If I'd found what I expected to find in that blasted room of yours, this time tomorrow your husband would be in the county jail. As it is—" Once more he clicked his tongue in annoyance, and broke off in the middle of his sentence.

"Stir yourself, Richards, can't you?" he shouted. "I can't afford to waste any more of my morning. What the hell are you doing?"

The man appeared at the stable door, leading the two horses behind him.

"Now listen to me," said Mr. Bassat, pointing his crop at Mary. "This aunt of yours may have lost her tongue, and her senses with them, but you can understand plain English, I hope. Do you mean to tell me you know nothing of your uncle's business? Does nobody ever call here, by day or by night?"

Mary looked him straight in the eyes. "I've never seen anyone," she said.

"Have you ever looked into that barred room before today?"

"No, never in my life."

"Have you any idea why he should keep it locked up?"

"No, none at all."

79

"Have you ever heard wheels in the yard by night?"

"I'm a very heavy sleeper. Nothing ever wakes me."

"Where does your uncle go when he's away from home?"

"I don't know."

"Don't you think yourself it's very peculiar to keep an inn on the King's highway, and then bolt and bar your house to every passer-by?"

"My uncle is a very peculiar man."

"He is indeed. In fact, he's so damned peculiar that half the people in the countryside won't sleep easy in their beds until he's been hanged, like his father before him. You can tell him that from me."

"I will, Mr. Bassat."

"Aren't you afraid, living up here, without sound or sight of a neighbour, and only this half-crazy woman for companion?"

"The time passes."

"You've got a close tongue, haven't you, young woman? Well, I don't envy you your relatives. I'd rather see any daughter of mine in her grave than living at Jamaica Inn with a man like Joss Merlyn."

He turned away and climbed onto his horse, gathering the reins in his hands. "One other thing," he called from his saddle. "Have you seen anything of your uncle's younger brother, Jem Merlyn, of Trewartha?"

"No," said Mary steadily; "he never comes here."

"Oh, he doesn't? Well, that's all I want from you this morning. Good day to you both." And away they clattered from the yard, and so down the road and to the brow of the further hill.

Aunt Patience had already preceded Mary to the kitchen and was sitting on a chair in a state of collapse.

"Oh, pull yourself together," said Mary wearily. "Mr. Bassat has gone, none the wiser for his visit, and as cross as two sticks because of it. If he'd found the room reeking of brandy, then there would be something to cry about. As it is, you and Uncle Joss have scraped out of it very well."

She poured herself out a tumbler of water and drank it at one breath. Mary was in a fair way to losing her temper.

She had lied to save her uncle's skin, when every inch of her longed to proclaim his guilt. She had looked into the barred room, and its emptiness had hardly surprised her when she remembered the visitation of the waggons a few nights back; but to have been faced with that loathsome length of rope, which she recognized immediately as the one she had seen hanging from the beam, was almost more than she could bear. And because of her aunt she had to stand still and say nothing. It was damnable; there was no other word for it. Well, she was committed now, and there was no going back. For better, for worse, she had become one of the company at Jamaica Inn. As she drank down her second glass of water she reflected cynically that in the end she would probably hang beside her uncle. Not only had she lied to save him, she thought with rising anger, but she had lied to help his brother, Jem. Jem Merlyn owed her thanks as well. Why she had lied about him she did not know. He would probably never find out anyway, and, if he did, he would take it for granted.

Aunt Patience was still moaning and whimpering before the fire, and Mary was in no mood to comfort her. She felt she had done enough for her family for one day, and her nerves were on edge with the whole business. If she stayed in the kitchen a moment longer she would scream with irritation. She went back to the washtub in the patch of garden by the chicken run and plunged her hands savagely into the grey soapy water that was now stone-cold.

Joss Merlyn returned just before noon. Mary heard him step into the kitchen from the front of the house, and he was met at once with a babble of words from his wife. Mary stayed where she was by the washtub; she was determined to let Aunt Patience explain things in her own way, and, if he called to her for confirmation, there was time enough to go indoors.

She could hear nothing of what passed between them, but the voice of her aunt sounded shrill and high, and now and again her uncle interposed a question sharply. In a little while he beckoned Mary from the window, and she went inside. He was standing on the hearth, his legs straddled wide and his face as black as thunder.

"Come on!" he shouted. "Out with it. What's your side of the story? I get nothing but a string of words from your aunt; a magpie makes more sense than she. What in hell's been going on here? That's what I want to know."

Mary told him calmly, in a few well-chosen words, what had taken place during the morning. She omitted nothing —except the squire's question about his brother—and ended with Mr. Bassat's own words—that people would not sleep easy in their beds until Joss Merlyn was hanged, like his father before him.

The landlord listened in silence, and, when she had finished, he crashed his fist down on the kitchen table and swore, kicking one of the chairs to the other side of the room.

"The damned skulking bastard!" he roared. "He'd no more right to walk into my house than any other man. His talk of a magistrate's warrant was all bluff, you blithering fools; there's no such thing. By God, if I'd been here, I'd have sent him back to North Hill so as his own wife would never recognize him, and, if she did, she'd have no use for him again. Damn and blast his eyes! I'll teach Mr. Bassat who's got the run of this country, and have him sniffing round my legs, what's more. Scared you, did he? I'll burn his house round his ears if he plays his tricks again."

Joss Merlyn shouted at the top of his voice, and the noise was deafening. Mary did not fear him like this; the whole thing was bluster and show; it was when he lowered his voice and whispered that she knew him to be deadly. For all his thunder he was frightened; she could see that; and his confidence was rudely shaken.

"Get me something to eat," he said. "I must go out again, and there's no time to lose. Stop that yawling, Patience, or I'll smash your face in. You've done well today, Mary, and I'll not forget it."

His niece looked him in the eyes.

"You don't think I did it for you, do you?" she said.

"I don't care a damn why you did it, the result's the

same," he answered. "Not that a blind fool like Bassat would find anything anyway; he was born with his head in the wrong place. Cut me a hunk of bread, and quit talking, and sit down at the bottom of the table where you belong to be."

The two women took their seats in silence, and the meal passed without further disturbance. As soon as he had finished, the landlord rose to his feet and, without another word to either of them, made his way to the stable. Mary expected to hear him lead his pony out once more and ride off down the road, but in a minute or two he was back again, and, passing through the kitchen, he went down to the end of the garden and climbed the stile in the field. Mary watched him strike across the moor and ascend the steep incline that led to Tolborough Tor and Codda. For a moment she hesitated, debating the wisdom of the sudden plan in her head, and then the sound of her aunt's footsteps overhead appeared to decide her. She waited until she heard the door of the bedroom close, and then, throwing off her apron and seizing her thick shawl from its peg on the wall, she ran down the field after her uncle. When she reached the bottom she crouched beside the stone wall until his figure crossed the skyline and disappeared, and then she leapt up again and followed in his track, picking her way amongst the rough grass and stones. It was a mad and senseless venture, no doubt, but her mood was a reckless one, and she needed an outlet for it after her silence of the morning.

Her idea was to keep Joss Merlyn in view, remaining of course unseen, and in this way perhaps she would learn something of his secret mission. She had no doubt that the squire's visit to Jamaica had altered the landlord's plans, and that this sudden departure on foot across the heart of the West Moor was connected with it. It was not yet half past one, and an ideal afternoon for walking. Mary, with her stout shoes and short skirt to her ankles, cared little for the rough ground. It was dry enough underfoot—the frost had hardened the surface—and, accustomed as she was to the wet shingle of the Helford shore and the thick mud on the farmyard, this scramble over the moor seemed easy enough. Her earlier rambles had taught her some wisdom, and she kept to the high ground as much as possible, following as best she could the tracks taken by her uncle.

Her task was a difficult one, and after a few miles she began to realize it. She was forced to keep a good length between them in order to remain unseen, and the landlord walked at such a pace, and took such tremendous strides, that before long Mary saw she would be left behind. Codda Tor was passed, and he turned west now towards the low ground at the foot of Brown Willy, looking, for all his height, like a little black dot against the brown stretch of moor.

The prospect of climbing some thirteen hundred feet came as something of a shock to Mary, and she paused for a moment and wiped her streaming face. She let down her hair, for greater comfort, and let it blow about her face. Why the landlord of Jamaica Inn thought it necessary to climb the highest point on Bodmin Moor on a December afternoon she could not tell, but, having come so far, she was determined to have some satisfaction for her pains, and she set off again at a sharper pace.

The ground was now soggy beneath her feet, for here the early frost had thawed and turned to water, and the whole of the low-lying plain before her was soft and yellow from the winter rains. The damp oozed into her shoes with cold and clammy certainty, and the hem of her skirt was bespattered with bog and torn in places. Lifting it up higher, and hitching it round her waist with the ribbon from her hair, Mary plunged on in trail of her uncle, but he had already traversed the worst of the low ground with uncanny quickness born of long custom, and she could just make out his figure amongst the black heather and the great boulders at the foot of Brown Willy. Then he was hidden by a jutting crag of granite, and she saw him no more.

It was impossible to discover the path he had taken across the bog; he had been over and gone in a flash, and Mary followed as best she could, floundering at every step. She was a fool to attempt it, she knew that, but a sort of stubborn stupidity made her continue. Ignorant of the whereabouts of the track that had carried her uncle dryshod over the bog, Mary had sense enough to make a wide circuit to avoid the treacherous ground, and, by going quite two miles in the wrong direction, she was able to cross in comparative safety. She was now hopelessly left, without a prospect of finding her uncle again.

Nevertheless she set herself to climb Brown Willy, slipping and stumbling amongst the wet moss and the stones, scrambling up the great peaks of jagged granite that frustrated her at every turn, while now and again a hill sheep, startled by the sound of her, ran out from behind a boulder to gaze at her and stamp his feet. Clouds were bearing up from the west, casting changing shadows on the plains beneath, and the sun went in behind them.

It was very silent on the hills. Once a raven rose up at her feet and screamed; he went away flapping his great black wings, swooping to the earth below with harsh protesting cries.

When Mary reached the summit of the hill the evening clouds were banked high above her head and the world was grey. The distant horizon was blotted out in the gathering dusk, and thin white mist rose from the moors beneath. Approaching the tor from its steepest and most difficult side, as she had done, she had wasted nearly an hour out of her time, and darkness would soon be upon her. Her escapade had been to little purpose, for as far as her eyes could see there was no living thing within their range.

Joss Merlyn had long vanished; and for all she knew he might not have climbed the tor at all, but skirted its base amongst the rough heather and the smaller stones, and then made his way alone and unobserved, east or west as his business took him, to be swallowed up in the folds of the further hills.

Mary would never find him now. The best course was to descend the tor by the shortest possible way and in the speediest fashion, otherwise she would be faced with the prospect of a winter's night upon the moors, with dead-black heather for a pillow and no other shelter but frowning crags of granite. She knew herself now for a fool to have ventured so far on a December afternoon, for experience had proved to her that there were no long twilights on Bodmin Moor. When darkness came it was swift and sudden, without warning, and with an immediate blotting out of the sun. The mists were dangerous too, rising in a cloud from the damp ground and closing in about the marshes like a white barrier.

Discouraged and depressed, and all excitement gone from her, Mary scrambled down the steep face of the tor, one eye on the marshes below and the other for the darkness that threatened to overtake her. Directly below her there was a pool or well, said to be the source of the river Fowey that ran ultimately to the sea, and this must be avoided at all costs, for the ground around was boggy and treacherous and the well itself of an unknown depth.

She bore to her left to avoid it, but by the time she had reached the level of the plain below, with Brown Willy safely descended and lifting his mighty head in lonely splendour behind her, the mist and the darkness had settled on the moors, and all sense of direction was now lost to her.

Whatever happened she must keep her head, and not give way to her growing sense of panic. Apart from the mist the evening was fine, and not too cold, and there was no reason why she should not hit upon some track that would lead ultimately to habitation.

There was no danger from the marshes if she kept to the high ground, so, trussing up her skirt again and wrapping her shawl firmly round her shoulders, Mary walked steadily before her, feeling the ground with some care when in doubt, and avoiding those tufts of grass that felt soft and yielding to her feet. That the direction she was taking was unknown to her was obvious in the first few miles, for her way was barred suddenly by a stream that she had not passed on the outward journey. To travel by its side would only lead her once more to the low-lying ground and the marshes, so she plunged through it recklessly, soaking herself above the knee. Wet shoes and stockings did not worry her; she counted herself fortunate that the stream had not been deeper, which would have meant swimming for it, and a chilled body into the bargain. The ground now seemed to rise in front of her, which was all to the good, as the going was firm, and she struck boldly across the high downland for what seemed to be an interminable distance, coming at length to a rough track bearing ahead and slightly to the right. This at any rate had served for a cart's wheels at one time or other, and where a cart could go Mary could follow. The worst was past; and now that her real anxiety had gone she felt weak and desperately tired.

Her limbs were heavy, dragging things that scarcely belonged to her, and her eyes felt sunken away back in her head. She plodded on, her chin low and her hands at her side, thinking that the tall grey chimneys of Jamaica Inn would be, for the first time perhaps in their existence, a welcome and consoling sight. The track broadened now and was crossed in turn by another running left and right, and Mary stood uncertainly for a few moments, wondering which to take. It was then that she heard the sound of a horse, blowing as though he had been ridden hard, coming out of the darkness to the left of her.

His hoofs made a dull thudding sound on the turf. Mary waited in the middle of the track, her nerves ajingle with the suddenness of the approach, and presently the horse appeared out of the mist in front of her, a rider on his back, the pair of ghostly figures lacking reality in the dim light. The horseman swerved as he saw Mary and pulled up his horse to avoid her.

"Hullo," he cried, "who's there? Is anyone in trouble?"

He peered down at her from his saddle and exclaimed in surprise. "A woman!" he said. "What in the world are you doing out here?"

Mary seized hold of his rein and quietened the restive horse.

"Can you put me on the road?" she asked. "I'm miles from home and hopelessly lost."

"Steady there," he said to the horse. "Stand still, will you?

Where have you come from? Of course I will help you if I can."

His voice was low and gentle, and Mary could see he must be a person of quality.

"I live at Jamaica Inn," she said, and no sooner were the words out of her mouth than she regretted them. He would not help her now, of course; the very name was enough to make him whip on his horse and leave her to find her own way as best she could. She was a fool to have spoken.

For a moment the man was silent, which was only what she expected, but when he spoke again his voice had not changed, but was quiet and gentle as before.

"Jamaica Inn," he said. "You've come a long way out of your road, I'm afraid. You must have been walking in the opposite direction. You're the other side of Hendra Downs here, you know."

"That means nothing to me," she told him. "I've never been this way before; it was very stupid of me to venture so far on a winter's afternoon. I'd be grateful if you could show me to the right path, and, once on the highroad, it won't take me long to get home."

He considered her for a moment, and then he swung himself off the saddle to the ground. "You're exhausted," he said, "you aren't fit to walk another step; and, what's more, I'm not going to let you. We are not far from the village, and you shall ride there. Will you give me your foot, and I'll help you mount." In a minute she was up in the saddle, and he stood below her, the bridle in his hand. "That's better, isn't it?" he said. "You must have had a long and uncomfortable walk on the moors. Your shoes are soaking wet, and so is the hem of your gown. You shall come home with me, and dry those things and rest awhile, and have some supper, before I take you back myself to Jamaica Inn." He spoke with such solicitude, and yet with such calm authority, that Mary sighed with relief, throwing all responsibility aside for the time being, content to trust herself in his keeping. He arranged the reins to her satisfaction, and she saw his eyes for the first time looking up at her from beneath the brim of his hat. They were strange eyes, transparent like glass, and so

and you too. You don't understand. He's a desperate man, and he'd stop at nothing. No, if the worst comes to the worst I'll try and climb up the porch to my bedroom window, and get in that way. He must never know I have been here, or that I've met you even."

"Isn't your imagination running away with you a little?" said the vicar. "I know I must seem unsympathetic and cold, but this is the nineteenth century, you know, and men don't murder one another without reason. I believe I have as much right to drive you on the King's highway as your uncle himself. Having gone so far, don't you think you had better let me hear the rest of your story? What is your name, and how long have you been living at Jamaica Inn?"

Mary looked up at the pale eyes in the colourless face, the halo of cropped white hair, and she thought again how strange a freak of nature was this man, who might be twenty-one, who might be sixty, and who with his soft, persuasive voice would compel her to admit every secret her heart possessed, had he the mind to ask her. She could trust him; that at least was certain. Still she hesitated, turning the words over in her mind.

"Come," he said with a smile; "I have heard confession in my time. Not here in Altarnun, but in Ireland and in Spain. Your story will not sound as strange to me as you think. There are other worlds besides Jamaica Inn."

His speech made her feel humble and a little confused. It was as though he mocked her, for all his tact and kindness, and supposed her, in the back of his mind, to be hysterical and young. She plunged headlong into her story with jerky ill-framed sentences, beginning with that first Saturday night in the bar, and then working backwards to her arrival at the inn. Her tale sounded flat and unconvincing, even to herself who knew the truth of it, and her great fatigue made her labour in the telling of it, so that she was continually at a loss for words, and she kept pausing for reflection, and then going back on her story and repeating herself. He heard her to the end with patience, without comment or question, but all the while she felt his white eyes watching her, and he had a little trick of swallowing at intervals which she came instinctively to recognize and wait for. The fear she had sustained, the agony and the doubt, sounded to her ears, as she listened, like the worked-up invention of an over-stimulated mind, and the conversation in the bar between her uncle and the stranger had developed into an elaborate piece of nonsense. She sensed, rather than saw, the vicar's unbelief; and in a desperate attempt to tone down her now ridiculous and highly coloured story, her uncle, who had been the villain of it, became the usual hard-drinking bully of a countryman who beat his wife once a week, and the waggons themselves had no more menace than carriers' carts, travelling by night to expedite delivery.

The visit of the squire of North Hill early that day had some conviction, but the empty room struck another note of anticlimax, and the only part of the story that rang with any sense of reality was Mary's losing herself on the moors during the afternoon.

When she had finished, the vicar got up from his chair and began to pace about the room. He whistled softly under his breath and kept playing with a loose button on his coat that was hanging by a thread. Then he came to a standstill on the hearth, with his back to the fire, and looked down upon her—but Mary could read nothing from his eyes.

"I believe you, of course," he said, after a moment or so. "You haven't the face of a liar, and I doubt if you know the meaning of hysteria. But your story wouldn't go in a court of law—not as you've told it tonight, anyhow. It's too much of a fairy tale. And another thing—it's a scandal and an outrage, we all know that, but smuggling is rife all over the county, and half the magistrates do very well out of it. That shocks you, doesn't it? But I can assure you it's the truth. If the law was stricter there would be greater supervision, and your uncle's little nest there at Jamaica Inn would have been blotted out long ago. I have met Mr. Bassat once or twice, and I believe him to be an honest, genuine sort of fellow, but, between ourselves, a bit of a fool. He'd bluster and talk, but that's about all. He'll keep this morning's expedition very quiet, unless I'm much mistaken. Actually he had no business to walk into the inn and search the rooms, and if it becomes known that he did so, and found nothing for his pains, he'll become the laughingstock of the countryside. I can tell you one thing, though: his visit will have scared your uncle, and he'll lie low now for a time. There won't be any more waggons to Jamaica Inn for some while. I think you can be certain of that."

Mary listened to his reasoning with some misgiving. She had hoped he would be appalled, once admitting the truth of her story, but here he was, apparently quite unmoved, taking it all as a matter of course.

He must have seen the disappointment in her face, for he spoke again.

"I could see Mr. Bassat, if you like," he said, "and put your story to him. But unless he can catch your uncle at work, as it were, with the waggons in the yard, there's little chance of convicting him. That's what I must impress upon your mind. I'm afraid I sound very unhelpful, but the position is a difficult one from every point of view. And then again, you don't want your aunt to be implicated in the business, but I don't see how it can be avoided, if it comes to an arrest."

"What do you suggest I should do, then?" said Mary helplessly.

"If I were you I should play a waiting game," he replied. "Keep a close watch on your uncle, and when the waggons do come again you can report at once to me. We can then decide together what is best to be done. That is, if you will honour me again with your confidence."

"What about the stranger who disappeared?" said Mary. "He was murdered. I'm certain of that. Do you mean to say that nothing can ever be done about it?"

"I'm afraid not, unless his body is found, which is extremely unlikely," said the vicar. "It is quite possible that he was never killed at all, for that matter. Forgive me, but I think you allowed your imagination to run away with you over that. All you saw was a piece of rope, remember. If you had actually seen the man dead, or even wounded— well, that's a different tale altogether."

"I heard my uncle threaten him," persisted Mary. "Isn't that enough?"

"My dear child, people threaten one another every day in the year, but they don't hang for it. Now listen to me. I am your friend, and you can trust me. If you ever become worried or distressed in any way, I want you to come and tell me about it. You are not afraid of walking, judging by your performance this afternoon, and Altarnun is only a few miles by the highroad. If you come at any time and I'm not in, Hannah will be here, and she will look after you. Now that's a bargain between us, isn't it?"

"Thank you very much."

"Now put on your stockings again, and your shoes, while I go to the stable and get the trap. I'm going to drive you back to Jamaica Inn."

The thought of returning was hateful to Mary, but it had to be faced. The contrast between this peaceful room with the gently shaded candles, the warm log fire, the deep chair, and the cold grim passages of Jamaica Inn, with her own little cupboard of a room over the porch, must be avoided at all costs. There was one thing to bear in mind, and that was that she could come back here when she wished.

The night was fine; the dark clouds of the early evening had passed away, and the sky was ablaze with stars. Mary sat beside Francis Davey on the high seat of the dogcart, wrapped in a greatcoat with a top collar of velvet. This was not the same horse that he had been riding when she met him on the moor; this was a big grey cob who, fresh from his sojourn in the stable, went like the wind. It was a strange, exhilarating drive. The wind blew in Mary's face, stinging her eyes. The climb from Altarnun had been slow at first, for the hill was steep, but now they were upon the highroad, with their faces turned to Bodmin, the vicar pricked the cob with his whip, so that he laid his ears flat to his head and galloped like a mad thing.

His hoofs thundered on the hard white road, raising a cloud of dust, and Mary was flung against her companion. He made no effort to rein in his horse, and, glancing up at him, Mary saw that he was smiling. "Go on," he said, "go on; you can go faster than this"; and his voice was low and excited, as though he were talking to himself. The effect was unnatural, a little startling, and Mary was aware of a feeling of discomfiture, as though he had betaken himself to another world and had forgotten her existence.

Seated where she was, she could observe him for the first time in profile, and she saw how clear-cut were his features, how prominent the thin nose; perhaps it was the peculiarity of nature's creating him white in the beginning that made him different from any man she had ever seen before.

He looked like a bird. Crouched in his seat, with his black cape-coat blown out by the wind, his arms were like wings. He might be any age, and she could not place him at all. Then he smiled down at her and was human again.

"I love these moors," he said. "You have had a bad introduction to them, of course, so you can't understand me. If you knew them as well as I do, and had seen them in every mood, winter and summer, you would love them too. They have a fascination unlike any other part of the county. They go back a long way in time. Sometimes I think they are the survival of another age. The moors were the first things to be created; afterwards came the forests, and the valleys, and the sea. Climb Rough Tor one morning before sunrise and listen to the wind in the stones. You'll know what I mean then."

Mary kept thinking of the parson at her home. He was a cheerful little man with a long string of children exactly like himself, and his wife made damson cheese. He preached the same sermon always on Christmas Day, and his parishioners could have prompted him anywhere. She wondered what Francis Davey said in his church at Altarnun. Did he preach about Rough Tor, and the light on Dozmary pool? They had come to the dip in the road now, where a cluster of trees made a little valley for the river Fowey, and in front of them stretched the climb to the high, unsheltered ground. Already Mary could see the tall chimneys of Jamaica Inn outlined against the sky.

The drive was ended, and the exhilaration went from her.

The old dread and loathing for her uncle returned. The vicar stopped his horse just short of the yard, under the lee of the grass bank.

"There's no sign of anyone," he said quietly. "It's like a house of the dead. Would you like me to try the door?"

Mary shook her head. "It's bolted always," she whispered, "and the windows are barred. That's my room, over the porch. I can scramble up there, if you let me climb on your shoulder. I've managed worse places than that at home. My window is open at the top; once on the porch, it will be easy enough."

"You'll slip on those slates," he answered. "I won't let you do it. It's absurd. Is there no other way of getting in? What about the back?"

"The door of the bar will be bolted, and the kitchen too," said Mary. "We can slip round, if you like, and make certain."

She led the way round to the other side of the house, and then she turned to him suddenly, her finger to her lips. "There's a light in the kitchen," she whispered. "That means my uncle is there. Aunt Patience always goes up early. There are no curtains to the window; if we pass by he will see us." She leant back against the wall of the house. Her companion motioned her to be still.

"Very well," he said, "I will take care he does not see me. I am going to look in at the window."

She watched him to the side of the window, and he stood there for a few minutes gazing into the kitchen. Then he beckoned to her to follow, that same tense smile on his face she had noticed before. His face looked very pale against his black shovel hat. "There'll be no argument to-night with the landlord of Jamaica Inn," he said.

Mary followed the direction of his eyes and pressed forward to the window. The kitchen was lit by a single candle stuck sideways into a bottle. It had already burnt down halfway, and great blobs of grease clung to the side of it. The flame itself wavered and spluttered in the draught from the door, which was wide open to the garden. Joss Merlyn sprawled at the table in a drunken stupor, his great legs stretched out on either side of him, his hat on the back of his head. He stared before him at the guttering candle, his eyes glazed and fixed like a dead man's. Another bottle lay with its neck smashed on the table, and beside it an empty glass. The peat fire had smouldered itself to nothing.

Francis Davey pointed to the open door. "You can walk inside and go upstairs to bed," he said. "Your uncle will not even see you. Fasten the door after you, and blow out the candle. You don't want a fire on your hands. Good night to you, Mary Yellan. If you are ever in trouble and need me, I shall be waiting for you at Altarnun."

Then he turned the corner of the house and was gone.

Mary tiptoed into the kitchen and closed and fastened the door. She could have slammed it had she wished, it would not have roused her uncle.

He had gone to his kingdom of heaven, and the little world was lost to him. She blew out the light beside him and left him alone in the darkness.

Chapter 8

Joss MERLYN was drunk for five days. He was insensible most of the time and lay stretched out on a bed in the kitchen that Mary and her aunt had improvised between them. He slept with his mouth wide open, and the sound of his breathing could be heard from the bedrooms above. About five in the evening he would wake for half an hour or so, shouting for brandy and sobbing like a child. His wife went to him at once and soothed him and settled his pillow. She gave him a little weak brandy-and-water, talking to him gently as she would to a sick child, holding the glass to his lips; and he stared around him with glaring bloodshot eyes, muttering to himself, and shivering like a dog.

Aunt Patience became another woman, showing a calm coolness and a presence of mind that Mary had not believed her capable of possessing. She gave herself up entirely to this nursing of her husband. She was obliged to do everything for him, and Mary watched her change his blankets and his linen with a sick feeling of disgust in her own heart, for she could not have borne to go near him. Aunt Patience took it as a matter of course, and the oaths and screams with which he greeted her did not appear to frighten her. These were the only times when she had the controlling of him, and he would let her sponge his forehead with a towel and hot water without a protest. Then she would tuck the fresh blanket under him, and smooth his mat of hair, and in a few minutes he would be asleep again, his face purple and his mouth wide open, with his tongue protruding, snoring like a bull. It was impossible to live in the kitchen, and Mary and her aunt turned the little disused parlour into a dwelling room for themselves. For the first time Aunt Patience became something of a companion. She chatted happily of the old days in Helford, when she and Mary's mother had been girls together; she moved swiftly and lightly about the house, and sometimes Mary would hear her humming snatches of old hymns as she passed backwards and forwards to the kitchen. It seemed that every two months or so Joss Merlyn would have these bouts of drinking. The times used to be further apart, but now they were becoming more frequent, and Aunt Patience was never quite certain when they would occur. This present one had been caused by the visit of Squire Bassat to the inn —the landlord had been very angry and upset, she told Mary —and when he came back from the moors at six in the evening he went straight to the bar. She knew then what would happen.

Aunt Patience accepted without question her niece's explanation of losing herself on the moors. She told her she must beware of the bogs and left it at that. Mary was greatly relieved. She did not want to give details of the adventure, and she was determined to say nothing of her meeting with the vicar of Altarnun. Meanwhile Joss Merlyn lay in his stupor in the kitchen, and the two women spent five comparatively peaceful days.

The weather was cold and grey and did not tempt Mary from the house, but on the fifth morning the wind dropped and the sun shone, and, in spite of the adventure that had befallen her only a few days before, Mary decided to brave the moors again. The landlord was awake at nine and began to shout at the top of his voice, and what with the noise he made, and the smell from the kitchen that now pervaded the rest of the house, and the sight of Aunt Patience bustling downstairs with clean blankets over her arm, Mary was seized with a rush of disgust and a loathing for the whole business.

Feeling very ashamed of herself, she slipped out of the house, rolling a crust of bread in a handkerchief, and crossed the highroad to the moors. This time she made for the East Moor, striking out towards Kilmar, and with the whole day in front of her there was no fear of being lost. She kept thinking about Francis Davey, her strange vicar of Altarnun, and she realized how little he had told her of himself, while he had from her a life history in an evening. She thought what an odd figure he must have looked, painting his picture beside the waters of Dozmary, hatless, perhaps, his halo of white hair standing up around his head; and there would be gulls flying inland from the sea, skimming the surface of the lake. He would look like Elijah in the wilderness.

She wondered what had called him to priesthood, and whether he was loved by the people of Altarnun. It was nearly Christmas now, and home at Helford people would be decorating with holly and evergreen and mistletoe. There would be a great baking of pastry and cakes, and a fattening of turkeys and geese. The little parson, wearing a festive air, would beam upon his world, and on Christmas Eve he would ride up after tea to drink sloe gin at Trelowarren. Did Francis Davey decorate his church with holly and call down a blessing upon the people?

One thing was certain: there would be little gaiety at Jamaica Inn.

Mary had walked for an hour or more before she stopped

short in her tracks, her further progress barred by a stream
that divided and ran in opposite directions. The stream lay
in a valley between the hills and was encircled by marshes.
The country was not unknown to her, and, looking on beyond the smooth green face of the tor ahead, she saw the
great split hand of Kilmar pointing his fingers to the sky.
She was gazing at Trewartha Marsh once more, where she
had wandered that first Saturday, but this time her face
was turned to the southeast, and the hills looked different
in the brave sunshine. The brook burbled merrily over the
stones, and there was a fording gate across the shallow water.
The marsh stretched away to the left of her. The soft wind
blew the waving strands of grass, that shivered in company,
and sighed, and rustled; and planted amidst the pale in-
viting green were tufts of coarse brown-tipped grass with
yellow stocky strands.

These were the treacherous bog islands, suggesting solidity
by their breadth, but their weight was of thistledown, and
a man's foot planted upon them sank immediately, and the
little patches of slate-coloured water that rippled here and
there would churn into froth and turn black.

Mary turned her back on the marsh and forded the gate
over the stream. She kept to the high ground, with the
stream beneath her, and followed its course along the winding valley between the hills. There were few clouds today
to cast their shadows, and the moors rolled away beyond
her, sand coloured under the sun. A solitary curlew stood
pensively beside the stream, watching his reflection in the
water; and then his long beak darted with incredible swift-
ness into the reeds, stabbing at the soft mud, and, turning
his head, he tucked his legs under him and rose into the air,
calling his plaintive note and streaking for the south.

Something had disturbed him, and in a few minutes Mary
saw what it was. A handful of ponies had clattered down
the hill beyond and splashed into the stream to drink. They
clodhopped noisily amongst the stones, pushing into one
another, their tails whisking in the wind. They must have
come through a gate on the left, a little way ahead, that

stood wide open, propped by a jagged stone, and led to a rough farm track heavy with mud.

Mary leant against the gate and watched the ponies, and out of the tail of her eye she saw a man coming down the track, carrying a bucket in either hand. She was about to move and continue her walk round the bend of the hill when he waved a bucket in the air and shouted to her.

It was Jem Merlyn. There was no time to escape, and she stood where she was until he came to her. He wore a grimy shirt that had never seen a washtub, and a pair of dirty brown breeches, covered with horsehair and filth from an outhouse. He had neither hat nor coat, and there was a rough stubble of beard on his jaw. He laughed at her, showing his teeth, looking for all the world like his brother must have done twenty years ago.

"So you've found your way to me, have you?" he said. "I didn't expect you so soon or I'd have baked bread in your honour. I haven't washed for three days, and I've been living on potatoes. Here, take hold of this bucket."

He thrust one of the buckets in her hand before she had time to protest, and was down to the water after the ponies. "Come out of it!" he shouted. "Get back, will you, fouling my drinking water! Go on, you big black devil."

He hit the largest of the ponies on his hindquarters with the end of the bucket, and they stampeded up the hill out of the water, kicking their heels in the air. "My fault for not shutting the gate," he called to Mary. "Bring down that other bucket; the water's clear enough the other side of the brook."

She took it with her to the stream, and he filled them both, grinning at her over his shoulder. "What would you have done if you hadn't found me at home?" he said, wiping his face on his sleeve. Mary could not help smiling.

"I didn't even know you lived here," she said, "and I certainly never walked this way with the intention of finding you. I'd have turned left if I'd known."

"I don't believe you," he said. "You started out with the hope of sighting me, and it's no use pretending any different.

103

Well, you've come in good time to cook my dinner. There's a piece of mutton in the kitchen."

He led the way up the mud track, and, rounding the corner, they came to a small grey cottage built on the side of the hill. There were some rough outbuildings at the back, and a strip of land for potatoes. A thin stream of smoke rose from the squat chimney. "The fire's on, and it won't take you long to boil that scrap of mutton. I suppose you can cook?" he said.

Mary looked him up and down. "Do you always make use of folk this way?" she said.

"I don't often have the chance," he told her. "But you may as well stop while you're here. I've done all my own cooking since my mother died, and there's not been a woman in the cottage since. Come in, won't you?"

She followed him in, bending her head as he did under the low door.

The room was small and square, half the size of the kitchen at Jamaica, with a great open fireplace in the corner. The floor was filthy and littered with rubbish: potato scrapings, cabbage stalks, and crumbs of bread. There were odds and ends scattered all over the room, and ashes from the turf fire covered everything. Mary looked about her in dismay.

"Don't you ever do any cleaning?" she asked him. "You've got this kitchen like a pigsty. You ought to be ashamed of yourself. Leave me that bucket of water and find me a broom. I'll not eat my dinner in a place like this."

She set to work at once, all her instincts of cleanliness and order aroused by the dirt and squalor. In half an hour she had the kitchen scrubbed clean as a pin, the stone floor wet and shining, and all the rubbish cleared away. She had found crockery in the cupboard, and a strip of table-cloth, with which she proceeded to lay the table, and meanwhile the mutton boiled in the saucepan on the fire, surrounded by potato and turnip.

The smell was good, and Jem came in at the door, sniffing the air like a hungry dog. "I shall have to keep a woman," he said. "I can see that. Will you leave your aunt and come and look after me?"

"You'd have to pay me too much," said Mary. "You'd never have money enough for what I'd ask."

"Women are always mean," he said, sitting down at the table. "What they do with their money I don't know, for they never spend it. My mother was just the same. She used to keep hers hidden in an old stocking, and I never saw as much as saw the colour of it. Make haste with the dinner; I'm as empty as a worm."

"You're impatient, aren't you?" said Mary. "Not a word of thanks to me that's cooked it. Take your hands away—the plate's hot."

She put the steaming mutton down in front of him, and he smacked his lips. "They taught you something where you came from, anyway," he said. "I always say there's two things women ought to do by instinct, and cooking's one of 'em. Get me a jug of water, will you? You'll find the pitcher outside."

But Mary had filled a cup for him already, and she passed it to him in silence.

"We were all born here," said Jem, jerking his head to the ceiling, "up in the room overhead. But Joss and Matt were grown men when I was still a little lad, clinging to Mother's skirt. We never saw much of my father but when he was home we knew it all right. I remember him throwing a knife at Mother once—it cut her above her eye, and the blood ran down her face. I was scared and ran and hid in that corner by the fire. Mother said nothing; she just bathed her eye in some water, and then she gave my father his supper. She was a brave woman, I'll say that for her, though she spoke little and she never gave us much to eat. She made a bit of a pet of me when I was small on account of being the youngest, I suppose, and my brothers used to beat me when she wasn't looking. Not that they were as thick as you'd think—we were never much of a loving family—and I've seen Joss thrash Matt until he couldn't stand. Matt was a funny devil; he was quiet, more like my mother. He was drowned down in the marsh yonder. You could shout there until your lungs burst, no one would hear you except a bird or two and a stray pony. I've been nearly caught there myself in my time."

"How long has your mother been dead?" said Mary.

"Seven years this Christmas," he answered, helping himself to more boiled mutton. "What with my father hanged, and Matt drowned, and Joss gone off to America, and me growing up as wild as a hawk, she turned religious and used to pray here by the hour, calling on the Lord. I couldn't abide that, and I cleared off out of it. I shipped on a Padstow schooner for a time, but the sea didn't suit my stomach, and I came back home. I found Mother gone as thin as a skeleton. 'You ought to eat more,' I told her, but she wouldn't listen to me, so I went off again, and stayed in Plymouth for a while, picking up a shilling or two in my own way. I came back here to have my Christmas dinner, and I found the place deserted and the door locked up. I was mad. I hadn't eaten for twenty-four hours. I went back to North Hill, and they told me my mother had died. She'd been buried three weeks. I might just as well have stayed in Plymouth for all the dinner I got that Christmas. There's a piece of cheese in the cupboard behind you. Will you eat the half of it? There's maggots in it, but they won't hurt you."

Mary shook her head, and she let him get up and reach for it himself.

"What's the matter?" he said. "You look like a sick cow. Has the mutton turned sour on you already?"

Mary watched him return to his seat and spread the hunk of dry cheese onto a scrap of stale bread. "It will be a good thing when there's not a Merlyn left in Cornwall," she said. "It's better to have disease in a country than a family like yours. You and your brother were born twisted and evil. Do you never think of what your mother must have suffered?"

Jem looked at her in surprise, the bread and cheese halfway to his mouth.

"Mother was all right," he said. "She never complained. She was used to us. Why, she married my father at sixteen; she never had time to suffer. Joss was born the year after, and then Matt. Her time was taken up in rearing them, and by the time they were out of her hands she had to start all over again with me. I was an afterthought, I was. Father got drunk at Launceston fair, after selling three cows that didn't belong to him. If it wasn't for that I wouldn't be sitting here talking to you now. Pass that jug."

Mary had finished. She got up and began to clear away the plates in silence.

"How's the landlord of Jamaica Inn?" said Jem, tilting back on his chair and watching her dip the plates in water.

"Drunk, like his father before him," said Mary shortly.

"That'll be the ruin of Joss," said his brother seriously. "He soaks himself insensible and lies like a log for days. One day he'll kill himself with it. The damned fool! How long has it lasted this time?"

"Five days."

"Oh, that's nothing to Joss. He'd lay there for a week if you let him. Then he'll come to, staggering on his feet like a newborn calf, with a mouth as black as Trewartha Marsh. When he's rid himself of his surplus liquid, and the rest of the drink has soaked into him—that's when you want to watch him; he's dangerous then. You look out for yourself."

"He'll not touch me; I'll take good care of that," said Mary. "He's got other things to worry him. There's plenty to keep him busy."

"Don't be mysterious, nodding to yourself with your mouth pursed up. Has anything been happening at Jamaica?"

"It depends how you look at it," said Mary, watching him over the plate she was wiping. "We had Mr. Bassat from North Hill last week."

Jem brought his chair to the ground with a crash. "The devil you did," he said. "And what had the squire to say to you?"

"Uncle Joss was from home," said Mary, "and Mr. Bassat insisted on coming into the inn and going through the rooms. He broke down the door at the end of the passage, he and his servant between them, but the room was empty. He seemed disappointed, and very surprised, and he rode away in a fit of temper. He asked after you, as it happened, and I told him I'd never set eyes on you."

Jem whistled tunelessly, his expression blank as Mary told her tale, but when she came to the end of her sentence, and the mention of his name, his eyes narrowed, and then he laughed. "Why did you lie to him?" he asked.

"It seemed less trouble at the time," said Mary. "If I'd thought longer, no doubt I'd have told him the truth. You've got nothing to hide, have you?"

"Nothing much, except that black pony you saw by the brook belongs to him," said Jem carelessly. "He was dapple-grey last week, and worth a small fortune to the squire, who bred him himself. I'll make a few pounds with him at Launceston if I'm lucky. Come down and have a look at him."

They went out into the sun, Mary wiping her hands on her apron, and she stood for a few moments at the door of the cottage while Jem went off to the horses The cottage was built on the slope of the hill above the Withy Brook, whose course wound away in the valley and was lost in the further hills. Behind the house stretched a wide and level plain, rising to great tors on either hand, and this grassland —like a grazing place for cattle—with no boundary as far as the eye could reach except the craggy menace of Kilmar, must be the strip of country known as Twelve Men's Moor.

Mary pictured Joss Merlyn running out of the doorway here as a child, his mat of hair falling over his eyes in a fringe, with the gaunt, lonely figure of his mother standing behind him, her arms folded, watching him with a question in her eyes. A world of sorrow and silence, anger and bitterness too, must have passed beneath the roof of this small cottage.

There was a shout and a clatter of hoofs, and Jem rode up to her round the corner of the house, astride the black pony. "This is the fellow I wanted you to have," he said, "but you're so close with your money. He'd carry you well, too; the squire bred him for his wife. Are you sure you won't change your mind?"

Mary shook her head and laughed. "You'd have me tie

him up in the stable at Jamaica, I suppose," she said, "and when Mr. Bassat calls again he wouldn't be likely to recognize him, would he? Thanking you for your trouble, but I'd rather not risk it all the same. I've lied enough for your family, Jem Merlyn, for one lifetime." Jem pulled a long face and slid to the ground.

"You've refused the best bargain that you'll ever have offered to you," he said, "and I won't give you the chance again. He'll go to Launceston on Christmas Eve; the dealers there will swallow him up." He clapped his hands on the hindquarters of the pony. "Get on with you, then"; and the animal made a startled dash for the gap in the bank.

Jem broke off a piece of grass and began to chew it, glancing sideways at his companion. "What did Squire Bassat expect to see at Jamaica Inn?" he said.

Mary looked him straight in the eyes. "You ought to know that better than I do," she answered. Jem chewed his grass thoughtfully, spitting out little bits of it onto the ground.

"How much do you know?" he said suddenly, throwing the stalk away.

Mary shrugged her shoulders. "I didn't come here to answer questions," she said. "I had enough of that with Mr. Bassat."

"It was lucky for Joss the stuff had been shifted," said his brother quietly. "I told him last week he was sailing too close to the wind. It's only a matter of time before they catch him. And all he does in self-defence is to get drunk, the damned fool."

Mary said nothing. If Jem was trying to trap her by this exhibition of frankness he would be disappointed.

"You must have a good view from that little room over the porch," he said. "Do they wake you out of your beauty sleep?"

"How do you know that's my room?" Mary asked swiftly.

He looked taken aback at her question; she saw the surprise flash through his eyes. Then he laughed and picked another piece of grass from the bank.

"The window was wide open when I rode into the yard

109

the other morning," he said, "and there was a little bit of blind blowing in the wind. I've never seen a window open at Jamaica Inn before."

The excuse was plausible, but hardly good enough for Mary. A horrible suspicion came into her mind. Could it have been Jem who had hidden in the empty guest room that Saturday night? Something went cold inside her.

"Why are you so silent about it all?" he continued. "Do you think I'm going to go to my brother and say, 'Here, that niece of yours, she lets her tongue run away with her'? Damn it, Mary, you're not blind or deaf; even a child would smell a rat if he lived a month at Jamaica Inn."

"What are you trying to make me tell you?" said Mary. "And what does it matter to you how much I know? All I think about is getting my aunt away from the place as soon as possible. I told you that when you came to the inn. It may take a little time to persuade her, and I'll have to be patient. As for your brother, he can drink himself to death for all I care. His life is his own, and so is his business. It's nothing to do with me."

Jem whistled and kicked a loose stone with his foot.

"So smuggling doesn't appal you after all?" he said. "You'd let my brother line every room at Jamaica with kegs of brandy and rum, and you'd say nothing, is that it? But supposing he meddled in other things—supposing it was a question of life, and death, and perhaps murder—what then?"

He turned round and faced her, and she could see that this time he was not playing with her; his careless, laughing manner was gone, and his eyes were grave, but she could not read what lay behind them.

"I don't know what you mean," said Mary.

He looked at her for a long time without speaking. It was as though he debated some problem in his mind and could only find solution in the expression of her face. All his resemblance to his brother vanished. He was harder, older suddenly, and of a different breed.

"Perhaps not," he said at length, "but you'll come to know, if you stay long enough. Why does your aunt look

110

like a living ghost—can you tell me that? Ask her, next time the wind blows from the northwest."

And he began to whistle again softly, his hands in his pockets. Mary stared back at him in silence. He spoke in riddles, but whether it was to frighten her or not she could not say. Jem the horse stealer, with his careless, impecunious manner, she could understand and allow for, but this was a new departure. She was not sure whether she liked it as well.

He laughed shortly and shrugged his shoulders. "There'll be trouble between Joss and myself one day, and it's he that'll be sorry for it, not I," he said. And with that cryptic remark he turned on his heel and went off onto the moor after the pony. Mary watched him thoughtfully, her arms tucked into her shawl. So her first instinct had been right, and there was something behind the smuggling, after all. The stranger in the bar that night had talked of murder, and now Jem himself had echoed his words. She was not a fool, then, nor was she hysterical, whatever she was considered by the vicar of Altarnun.

What part Jem Merlyn played in all this it was hard to say, but that he was concerned in it somewhere she did not doubt for a moment.

And if he was the man who crept so stealthily down the stairs behind her uncle—why, he must know well enough that she had left her room that night, and was in hiding somewhere, and had listened to them. Then he, above all men, must remember the rope on the beam, and guess that she had seen it after he and the landlord had gone out onto the moor.

If Jem was the man, there would be reason enough for all his questions. "How much do you know?" he had asked her; but she had not told him.

The conversation had cast a shadow on her day. She wanted to be off now, and rid of him, and alone with her own thoughts. She began to walk slowly down the hill towards the Withy Brook. She had reached the gate at the bottom of the track when she heard his running footsteps behind her, and he flung himself first at the gate, looking like a half-bred gypsy with his growth of beard and his filthy breeches.

"Why are you going?" he said. "It's early yet; it won't be dark till after four. I'll walk back with you then as far as Rushyford Gate. What's the matter with you?" He took her chin in his hands and looked into her face. "I believe you're frightened of me," he said. "You think I've got barrels of brandy and rolls of tobacco in the little old bedrooms up above, and that I'm going to show them to you, and then cut your throat. That's it, isn't it? We're a desperate lot of fellows, we Merlyns, and Jem is the worst of the pack. Is that what you're thinking?"

She smiled back at him in spite of herself. "Something of the sort," she confessed, "but I'm not afraid of you; you needn't think that. I'd even like you if you didn't remind me so much of your brother."

"I can't help my face," he said, "and I'm much better looking than Joss, you must allow me that."

"Oh, you've conceit enough to make up for all the other qualities you lack," agreed Mary, "and I'll not deprive you of your handsome face. You may break as many hearts as you please. Now let me go; it's a long walk back to Jamaica Inn, and I don't fancy losing myself on the moors again."

"And when did you lose yourself before?" he asked.

Mary frowned slightly. The words had escaped her. "The other afternoon I was out on the West Moor," she said, "and the fog came on early. I wandered some time before I found my way back."

"You're a fool to go walking," he said. "There's places between Jamaica and Rough Tor that would swallow a herd of cattle, to say nothing of a slip of a thing like you. It's no pastime for a woman anyhow. What did you do it for?"

"I wanted to stretch my legs. I'd been shut in the house for days."

"Well, Mary Yellan, next time you want to stretch your legs you can stretch them in this direction. If you come through the gate you can't go wrong, not if you leave the

"I was walking on the moors," replied Mary. "I didn't think it mattered. Why should Uncle Joss ask for me?" She was aware of a little pang of nervousness, and she looked towards his bed in the corner of the kitchen. It was empty. "Where has he gone?" she said. "Is he better?"

"He wanted to sit in the parlour," said her aunt. "He said he was tired of the kitchen. He's been sitting there all afternoon at the window, looking out for you. You must humour him now, Mary, and speak fair to him, and not go against him. This is the bad time, when he's recovering—he will get a little stronger every day, and he'll be very self-willed, violent perhaps. You'll be careful what you say to him, won't you, Mary?"

This was the old Aunt Patience, with nervous hands and twitching mouth, who glanced over her shoulder as she talked. It was pitiable to see her, and Mary caught something of her agitation.

"Why should he want to see me?" she said. "He never has anything to say to me. What can he want?"

Aunt Patience blinked and worked her mouth. "It's only his fancy," she said. "He mutters and talks to himself; you mustn't pay any attention to what he says at times like these. He is not really himself. I'll go and tell him you're home." She went out of the room and along the passage to the parlour.

Mary crossed to the dresser and poured herself out a glass of water from the pitcher. Her throat was very dry. The glass trembled in her hands, and she cursed herself for a fool. She had been bold enough on the moors just now, and no sooner was she inside the inn than her courage must forsake her and leave her quaking and nervous as a child. Aunt Patience came back into the room.

"He's quiet for the moment," she whispered. "He's dozed off in the chair. He may sleep now for the evening. We'll have our supper early and get it finished. There's some cold pie for you here."

All hunger had gone from Mary, and she had to force her food. She drank two cups of scalding tea and then pushed her plate away. Neither of the women spoke. Aunt

115

Patience kept looking towards the door. When they had finished supper they cleared the things away silently. Mary threw some turf on the fire and crouched beside it. The bitter blue smoke rose in the air, stinging her eyes, but no warmth came to her from the smouldering turf.

Outside in the hall the clock struck six o'clock with a sudden whirring note. Mary held her breath as she counted the strokes. They broke upon the silence with deliberation; it seemed an eternity before the last note fell and echoed through the house and died away. The slow ticking of the clock continued. There was no sound from the parlour, and Mary breathed again. Aunt Patience sat at the table, threading a needle and cotton by candlelight. Her lips were pursed and her forehead puckered to a frown as she bent to her task.

The long evening passed; and still there was no call from the landlord in the parlour. Mary nodded her head, her eyes closed in spite of herself, and in that stupid, heavy state between sleeping and waking she heard her aunt move quietly from her chair and put her work away in the cupboard beside the dresser. In a dream she heard her whisper in her ear, "I'm going to bed. Your uncle won't wake now; he must have settled for the night. I shan't disturb him." Mary murmured something in reply, and half-consciously she heard the light patter of footsteps in the passage outside, and the creaking of the stairs.

On the landing above, a door closed softly. Mary felt the lethargy of sleep steal upon her, and her head sank lower into her hands. The slow ticking of the clock made a pattern in her mind, like footsteps dragging on a highroad . . . one . . . two . . . one . . . two . . . they followed one another; she was on the moors beside the running brook, and the burden that she carried was heavy, too heavy to bear. If she could lay it aside for a little while, and rest herself beside the bank, and sleep . . .

It was cold, though, much too cold. Her foot was wringing wet from the water. She must pull herself higher up the bank, out of the way. . . . The fire was out; there was no more fire. . . . Mary opened her eyes and saw that she was

116

lying on the floor beside the white ashes of the fire. The kitchen was very cold, and the light was dim. The candle had burnt low. She yawned and shivered and stretched her stiff arms. When she lifted her eyes she saw the door of the kitchen open very slowly, little by little, an inch at a time.

Mary sat without moving, her hands on the cold floor. She waited, and nothing happened. The door moved again, and then was flung wide, crashing against the wall behind it. Joss Merlyn stood on the threshold of the room, his arms outstretched, rocking on his two feet.

At first she thought he had not noticed her; his eyes were fixed on the wall in front of him, and he stood still where he was, without venturing further into the room. She crouched low, her head beneath the level of the table, hearing nothing but the steady thump of her heart. Slowly he turned in her direction and stared at her a moment or two without speaking. When his voice came, it was strained and hoarse, hardly above a whisper. "Who's there?" he said. "What are you doing? Why don't you speak?" His face was a grey mask, drained of its usual colour. His bloodshot eyes fastened themselves upon her without recognition. Mary did not move.

"Put away that knife," he whispered. "Put it away, I tell you."

She stretched her hand along the floor and touched the leg of a chair with the tips of her fingers. She could not hold onto it unless she moved. It was just out of reach. She waited, holding her breath. He stepped forward into the room, his head bent, his two hands feeling the air, and he crept slowly along the floor towards her.

Mary watched his hands until they were within a yard of her and she could feel his breath on her cheek.

"Uncle Joss," she said softly. "Uncle Joss—"

He crouched where he was, staring down at her, and then he leant forward and touched her hair and her lips. "Mary," he said, "is it you, Mary? Why don't you speak to me? Where have they gone? Have you seen them?"

"You've made a mistake, Uncle Joss," she said; "there is

117

no one here, only myself. Aunt Patience is upstairs. Are you ill? Can I help you?"

He looked about him in the half-light, searching the corners of the room.

"They can't scare me," he whispered. "Dead men don't harm the living. They're blotted out, like a candle. . . . That's it, isn't it, Mary?"

She nodded, watching his eyes. He pulled himself to a chair and sat down, his hands outstretched on the table. He sighed heavily and passed his tongue over his lips. "It's dreams," he said, "all dreams. The faces stand out like live things in the darkness, and I wake with the sweat pouring down my back. I'm thirsty, Mary; here's the key; go into the bar and fetch me some brandy." He fumbled in his pocket and produced a bunch of keys. She took them from him, her hand trembling, and slipped out of the room into the passage. She hesitated for a moment outside, wondering whether she should creep upstairs at once to her room, and lock the door, and leave him to rave alone in the kitchen. She began to tiptoe along the passage to the hall.

Suddenly he shouted to her from the kitchen. "Where are you going? I told you to fetch the brandy from the bar." She heard the chair scrape as he pushed it away from the table. She was too late. She opened the door of the bar and felt in the cupboard amongst the bottles. When she returned to the kitchen he was sprawling at the table, his head in his hands. At first she thought he was asleep again, but at the sound of her footstep he lifted his head, and stretched his arms, and leant back in the chair. She put the bottle and a glass on the table in front of him. He filled the glass half full, and held it between his two hands, watching her all the while over the rim of it.

"You're a good girl," he said. "I'm fond of you, Mary; you've got sense, and you've got pluck; you'd make a good companion to a man. They ought to have made you a boy." He rolled the brandy around on his tongue, smiling foolishly, and then he winked at her, and pointed his finger.

"They pay gold for this upcountry," he said; "the best that money can buy. King George himself hasn't better

118

brandy than this in his cellar. And what do I pay? Not one damned bloody sixpence. We drink free at Jamaica Inn."

He laughed and put out his tongue. "It's a hard game, Mary, but it's a man's game, for all that. I've risked my neck ten, twenty times. I've had the fellows thundering at my heels, with a pistol shot whistling through my hair. They can't catch me, Mary; I'm too cunning; I've been at the game too long. Before we came here I was at Padstow, working from the shore. We ran a lugger once a fortnight with the spring tides. There were five of us in it, besides myself. But there's no money working in a small way; you've got to do it big, and you've got to take your orders. There's over a hundred of us now, working inland to the border from the coast. By God, I've seen blood in my time, Mary, and I've seen men killed a score of times, but this game beats all of it—it's running side by side with death."

He beckoned her to his side, winking again, glancing first over his shoulder to the door. "Here," he whispered, "come close, down here by my side, where I can talk to you. You've got guts in you, I can see that; you're not scared like your aunt. We ought to be partners, you and I." He seized hold of Mary's arm and pulled her on the floor beside his chair. "It's this cursed drink that makes a fool of me," he said. "I'm as weak as a rat when it has hold of me, you can see that. And I have dreams, nightmares; I see things that never scare me when I'm sober. Damn it, Mary, I've killed men with my own hands, trampled them under water, beaten them with rocks and stones; and I've never thought no more about it; I've slept in my bed like a child. But when I'm drunk I see them in my dreams; I see their white-green faces staring at me, with their eyes eaten by fish; and some of them are torn, with the flesh hanging on their bones in ribbons, and some of them have seaweed in their hair. . . . There was a woman once, Mary; she was clinging to a raft, and she had a child in her arms; her hair was streaming down her back. The ship was close in on the rocks, you see, and the sea was as flat as your hand; they were all coming in alive, the whole bunch of 'em. Why, the water in places didn't come above your waist. She cried out to me to help her, Mary, and I smashed her face in with a stone; she fell back, her hands beating the raft. She let go of the child, and I hit her again; I watched them drown in four feet of water. We were scared then; we were afraid some of them would reach the shore. . . . For the first time we hadn't reckoned on the tide. In half an hour they'd be walking dry-shod on the sand. We had to pelt at 'em all with stones, Mary; we had to break their arms and legs; and they drowned there in front of us, like the woman and her child, with the water not up to their shoulders—they drowned because we smashed them with rocks and stones; they drowned because they couldn't stand. . . ."

His face was close to Mary, his red-flecked eyes staring into hers, and his breath on her cheek. "Did you never hear of wreckers before?" he whispered.

Outside in the passage the clock struck one o'clock, and the single note rang in the air like a summons. Neither of them moved. The room was very cold, for the fire had sunk away to nothing, and a little current of air blew in from the open door. The yellow flame of the candle bowed and flickered. He reached out to her and took her hand; it lay limp in his, like a dead hand. Perhaps he saw something of the frozen horror in her face, for he let her go and turned away his eyes. He stared straight before him at the empty glass, and he began to drum with his fingers on the table. Crouched on the floor beside him, Mary watched a fly crawl across his hand. She watched it pass through the short black hairs and over the thick veins to the knuckles, and it ran to the tips of the long slim fingers. She remembered the swift and sudden grace of those fingers when they cut bread for her that first evening, and how if they chose they could be delicate and light; she watched them drumming now on the table, and in her fancy she saw them curl round a block of jagged stone and fasten upon it; she saw the stone fly through the air. . . .

Once more he turned to her, his whisper hoarse, and he jerked his head towards the ticking of the clock. "The sound of it rings in my head sometimes," he said, "and when it struck one just now, it was like the tolling of a bell buoy in a bay. I've heard it come travelling down the air on the westerly wind: one-two-one-two, backwards and forwards the clapper goes against the bell, as though it tolled for dead men. I've heard it in my dreams, I heard it tonight. A mournful, weary sound, Mary, is a bell buoy out in the bay. It rubs on your nerves and you want to scream. When you work on the coast you have to pull out to them in a boat and muffle them; wrap the tongue in flannel. That deadens them. There's silence then. Maybe it's a misty night with patches of white fog on the water, and outside the bay there'll be a ship casting for scent like a hound. She listens for the buoy, and no sound comes to her. And she comes in then, driving through the fog—she comes straight in to us who are waiting for her, Mary—and we see her shudder suddenly, and strike, and then the surf has her."

He reached for the bottle of brandy and let a little liquid trickle slowly into the glass. He smelt it and rolled it on his tongue.

"Have you ever seen flies caught in a jar of treacle?" he said. "I've seen men like that; stuck in the rigging like a swarm of flies. They cling there for safety, shouting in terror at the sight of the surf. Just like flies they are, spread out on the yards, little black dots of men. I've seen the ship break up beneath them, and the masts and yards snap like thread, and there they'll be flung into the sea, to swim for their lives. But when they reach the shore they're dead men, Mary."

He wiped his mouth on the back of his hand and stared at her. "Dead men tell no tales, Mary," he said.

His face nodded at her, and narrowed suddenly, and was blotted out. No longer was she kneeling on the kitchen floor, her hands gripping the table; she was a child again, running beside her father on the cliffs beyond St. Keverne. He swung her up onto his shoulder, and there were other men running with them, who shouted and cried. Somebody pointed to the distant sea, and, clinging to her father's head, she saw a great white ship like a bird rolling helplessly in the trough of the sea, her masts broken short and her sails trailing in the water beside her. "What are they doing?" asked the child that had been herself; and nobody answered her; they stood

121

where they were, staring in horror at the ship that rolled and plunged. "God have mercy upon them," said her father; and the child Mary began to cry, calling for her mother, who came at once from amongst the crowd and took her in her arms, and walked away with her out of sight of the sea. There all memory snapped, and vanished, and there was no ending to the story; but when she grew to understanding, and was no longer a child, her mother would talk of the day they had gone to St. Keverne, when a great barque had sunk with all on board, her back broken on the dreaded Manacles. Mary shivered and sighed, and once more her uncle's face loomed before her in its frame of matted hair, and she was kneeling beside him again in the kitchen at Jamaica Inn. She felt deadly sick, and her hands and feet were icy cold. She longed only to stumble to her bed and bury her head in her hands, pulling the blanket and pillow over her for greater darkness. Perhaps if she pressed her hands against her eyes she would blot out his face and the pictures he had painted for her. Perhaps if she thrust her fingers in her ears she would muffle the sound of his voice and the thunder of the surf upon the shore. Here she could see the pale faces of drowned men, their arms above their heads; she could hear the screams of terror and the cries; she could hear the mournful clamour of the bell buoy as it swayed backwards and forwards in the sea. Mary shivered again.

She looked up at her uncle, and she saw that he had sloped forward in his chair, and his head had fallen on his chest. His mouth was wide open, and he snorted and spluttered as he slept. His long dark lashes swept his cheeks like a fringe. His arms rested on the table before him, and his hands were clasped as though in prayer.

Chapter 9

On Christmas Eve the sky was overcast and threatened rain. It had turned mild, too, in the night, and the mud in the yard was churned where the cows had trodden. The walls of Mary's bedroom felt damp to her hand, and there was a great yellow patch in one corner caused by the shrinking plaster.

Mary leant out of the window, and the soft wet wind blew upon her face. In an hour's time Jem Merlyn would be waiting for her on the moor, to take her to Launceston fair. Whether she met him or not depended upon herself, and she could not make up her mind. She had grown older in four days, and the face that looked back at her from the spotted, cracked mirror was drawn and tired.

There were dark rings beneath her eyes, and little hollows in her cheeks. Sleep came late to her at night, and she had no appetite for food. For the first time in her life she saw a resemblance between herself and her aunt Patience. They had the same pucker of the forehead, and the same mouth. If she pursed up her lips and worked them, biting the edges, it might be Aunt Patience who stood there, with the lank brown hair framing her face. The trick was an easy one to catch, as was the nervous twisting of the hands, and Mary turned away from the telltale mirror and began to pace up and down her cramped room. During the past few days she had kept as much as possible to the privacy of her own room, excusing herself on the score of a chill. Mary could not trust herself to speak to her aunt at present—not for any length of time. Her eyes would have betrayed her. They would look at one another with the same dumb horror, the same hidden anguish; and Aunt Patience would have understood. They shared a secret now, a secret that must never be spoken between them. Mary wondered how many years Aunt Patience had kept that knowledge to herself in an agony of silence. No one would ever know how greatly she had suffered. Wherever she would go in the future, the pain of that knowledge would go with her. It could never leave her alone. At last Mary was able to understand the pale, twitching face, the hands that plucked at the dress, the wide, staring eyes. The evidence screamed at her now that she knew.

At first she had felt sick, deadly sick; she had lain on her bed that night, praying for the mercy of sleep, and it had been denied her. There were faces in the darkness that she had not known; the worn and weary faces of drowned people. There was a child with broken wrists; and a woman whose long wet hair clung to her face; and the screaming, frightened faces of men who had never learnt to swim. Sometimes it seemed to her that her own mother and father were amongst them; they looked up at her with wide eyes and pallid lips, and they stretched out their hands. Perhaps this was what Aunt Patience suffered, alone in her room at night; the faces came to her too, and pleaded, and she pushed them away. She would not give them release. In her own way Aunt Patience was a murderer too. She had killed them by her silence. Her guilt was as great as Joss Merlyn's himself, for she was a woman and he was a monster. He was bound to her flesh, and she let him remain.

Now that it was the third day, and the first horror had passed, Mary felt indifferent, rather old, and very tired. Most of the feeling had gone from her. It seemed to her that she had always known now; that at the back of her mind she had been prepared. The first sight of Joss Merlyn, standing beneath the porch with a lantern in his hands, had been a warning; while the sound of the coach rattling away down the highroad and out of her hearing had rung like a farewell.

In the old days at Helford, there had been whispers of these things: little snatches of gossip overheard in the village lanes, a fragment of story, a denial, a shake of the head, but men did not talk much, and the stories were discouraged. Twenty, fifty years ago, perhaps, when her father had been young; but not now, not in the light of the new century. Once more she saw her uncle's face pressed close to hers, and she heard his whisper in her ear, "Did you never hear of wreckers before?" These were words that she had never heard breathed, but Aunt Patience had lived amongst them for ten years. . . . Mary did not consider her uncle any more. She had lost her fear of him. There was only loathing left in her heart, loathing and disgust. He had lost all hold on humanity. He was a beast that walked by night. Now that she had seen him drunk, and she knew him for what he was, he could not frighten her. Neither he nor the rest of his company. They were things of evil, rotting the countryside, and she would never rest until they were trodden underfoot, and cleared, and blotted out. Sentiment would not save them again.

There remained Aunt Patience—and Jem Merlyn. He broke into her thoughts against her will, and she did not want him. There was enough on her mind without reckoning with Jem. He was too like his brother. His eyes, and his mouth, and his smile. That was the danger of it. She could see her uncle in his walk, in the turn of his head; and she knew why Aunt Patience had made a fool of herself ten years ago. It would be easy enough to fall in love with Jem Merlyn. Men had not counted for much in her life up to the present; there had been too much to do on the farm at Helford to worry about them. There had been lads who had smiled at her in church and gone with her to picnics harvesttime; once a neighbour had kissed her behind a hayrick after a glass of cider. It was all very foolish, and she had avoided the man ever since; a harmless enough fellow, too, who forgot the incident five minutes later. Anyway, she would never marry; it was a long while since she had decided that. She would save money in some way and do a man's work on a farm. Once she got away from Jamaica Inn and could put it behind her, and make some sort of a home for Aunt Patience, she was not likely to have time on her hands to think of men. And there, in spite of herself, came Jem's face again,

125

with the growth of beard like a tramp, and his dirty shirt, and his bold offensive stare. He lacked tenderness; he was rude; and he had more than a streak of cruelty in him; he was a thief and a liar. He stood for everything she feared and hated and despised; but she knew she could love him. Nature cared nothing for prejudice. Men and women were like the animals on the farm at Helford, she supposed; there was a common law of attraction for all living things, some similarity of skin or touch, and they would go to one another. This was no choice made with the mind. Animals did not reason, neither did the birds in the air. Mary was no hypocrite; she was bred to the soil, and she had lived too long with birds and beasts, had watched them mate, and bear their young, and die. There was precious little romance in nature, and she would not look for it in her own life. She had seen the girls at home walk with the village lads; and there would be a holding of hands, and blushing and confusion, and long-drawn sighs, and a gazing at the moonlight on the water. Mary would see them wander down the grass lane at the back of the farm—Lovers' Lane they called it, though the older men had a better word for it than that— and the lad would have his arm round the waist of his girl, and she with her head on his shoulder. They would look at the stars and the moon, or the flaming sunset if it was summer weather, and Mary, coming out of the cowshed, wiped the sweat from her face with dripping hands, and thought of the newborn calf she had left beside its mother. She looked after the departing couple, and smiled, and shrugged her shoulders, and, going into the kitchen, she told her mother there would be a wedding in Helford before the month was past. And then the bells would ring, and the cake be cut, and the lad in his Sunday clothes would stand on the steps of the church with shining face and shuffling feet with his bride beside him dressed in muslin, her straight hair curled for the occasion; but before the year was out the moon and the stars could shine all night for all they cared, when the lad came home at evening tired from his work in the fields, and calling sharply that his supper was burnt, not fit for a dog, while the girl snapped back at him from the bedroom overhead, her figure sagging and her curls gone, pacing backward and forward with a bundle in her arms that mewed like a cat and would not sleep. There was no talk then of the moonlight on the water. No, Mary had no illusions about romance. Falling in love was a pretty name for it, that was all. Jem Merlyn was a man, and she was a woman, and whether it was his hands or his skin or his smile she did not know, but something inside her responded to him, and the very thought of him was an irritant and a stimulant at the same time. It nagged at her and would not let her be. She knew she would have to see him again.

Once more she looked up at the grey sky and the low-flying clouds. If she was going to Launceston, then it was time to make ready and be away. There would be no excuses to make; she had grown hard in the last four days. Aunt Patience could think what she liked. If she had any intuition, she must guess that Mary did not want to see her. And she would look at her husband, with his blood-shot eyes and his shaking hands, and she would understand. Once more, perhaps for the last time, the drink had loosened his tongue. His secret was spilt; and Mary held his future in her hands. She had not yet determined what use to make of her knowledge, but she would not save him again. Today she would go to Launceston with Jem Merlyn, and this time it was he who would answer her questions; he would show some humility too when he realized she was no longer afraid of them, but could destroy them when she chose. And tomorrow—well, tomorrow could take care of itself. There was always Francis Davey and his promise; there would be peace and shelter for her at the house in Altarnun.

This was a strange Christmastide, she pondered, as she strode across the East Moor with Hawk's Tor as her guide, and the hills rolling away from her on either side. Last year she had knelt beside her mother in church, and prayed that health and strength and courage should be given to them both. She had prayed for peace of mind and security; she had asked that her mother might be spared to her long, and that the farm should prosper. For answer came sickness, and poverty, and death. She was alone now, caught in a mesh of brutality and crime, living beneath a roof she loathed, amongst people she despised; and she was walking out across a barren, friendless moor to meet a horse thief and a murderer of men. She would offer no prayers to God this Christmas.

Mary waited on the high ground above Rushyford, and in the distance she saw the little cavalcade approach her: the pony, the jingle, and two horses tethered behind. The driver raised his whip in a signal of welcome. Mary felt the colour flame into her face and drain away. This weakness was a thing of torment to her, and she longed for it to be tangible and alive so that she could tear it from her and trample it underfoot. She thrust her hands into her shawl and waited, her forehead puckered in a frown. He whistled as he approached her and flung a small package at her feet. "A happy Christmas to you," he said. "I had a silver piece in my pocket yesterday and it burnt a hole. There's a new handkerchief for your head."

She had meant to be curt and silent on meeting him, but this introduction made it difficult for her. "That's very kind of you," she said. "I'm afraid you've wasted your money all the same."

"That doesn't worry me, I'm used to it," he told her, and he looked her up and down in the cool offensive way of his, and whistled a tuneless song. "You were early here," he said. "Were you afraid I'd be going without you?"

She climbed into the cart beside him and gathered the reins in her hands. "I like to have the feel of them again," she said, ignoring his remark. "Mother and I, we would drive into Helston once a week on market days. It all seems very long ago. I have a pain in my heart when I think of it, and how we used to laugh together, even when times were bad. You wouldn't understand that, of course. You've never cared for anything but yourself."

He folded his arms and watched her handle the reins.

"That pony would cross the moor blindfold," he told her. "Give him his head, can't you? He's never stumbled in his life. That's better. He's taking charge of you, remember, and you can leave him to it. What were you saying?"

Mary held the reins lightly in her hands and looked at the track ahead of her. "Nothing very much," she answered. "In a way I was talking to myself. So you're going to sell two ponies at the fair, then?"

"Double profit, Mary Yellan, and you shall have a new dress if you help me. Don't smile and shrug your shoulder. I hate ingratitude. What's the matter with you today? Your colour is gone, and you've no light in your eyes. Are you feeling sick, or have you a pain in your belly?"

"I've not been out of the house since I saw you last," she said. "I stayed up in my room with my thoughts. They didn't make cheerful company. I'm a deal older than I was four days ago."

"I'm sorry you've lost your looks," he went on. "I fancied jogging into Launceston with a pretty girl beside me, and fellows looking up as we passed and winking. You're drab today. Don't lie to me, Mary. I'm not as blind as you think. What's happened at Jamaica Inn?"

"Nothing's happened," she said. "My aunt patters about in the kitchen, and my uncle sits at the table with his head in his hands and a bottle of brandy in front of him. It's only myself that has changed."

"You've had no more visitors, have you?"

"None that I know of. Nobody's crossed the yard."

"Your mouth is set very firm, and there are smudges under your eyes. You're tired. I've seen a woman look like that before, but there was a reason for it. Her husband came back to her at Plymouth after four years at sea. You can't make that excuse. Have you been thinking about me by any chance?"

"Yes, I thought about you once," she said. "I wondered who would hang first, you or your brother. There's little in it, from what I can see."

"If Joss hangs, it will be his own fault," said Jem. "If ever a man puts a rope round his own neck, he does. He goes three quarters of the way to meet trouble. When it does get him it will serve him right, and there'll be no brandy bottle to save him then. He'll swing sober."

They jogged along in silence, Jem playing with the thong

of the whip, and Mary aware of his hands beside her. She glanced down at them out of the tail of her eye, and she saw they were long and slim; they had the same strength, the same grace, as his brother's. These attracted her; the others repelled her. She realized for the first time that aversion and attraction ran side by side; that the boundary line was thin between them. The thought was an unpleasant one, and she shrank from it. Supposing this had been Joss beside her ten, twenty years ago? She shuttered the comparison at the back of her mind, fearing the picture it conjured. She knew now why she hated her uncle.

His voice broke in upon her thoughts. "What are you looking at?" he said. She lifted her eyes to the scene in front of her. "I happened to notice your hands," she said briefly; "they are like your brother's. How far do we go across the moor? Isn't that the highroad winding away yonder?"

"We strike it lower down, and miss two or three miles of it. So you notice a man's hands, do you? I should never have believed it of you. You're a woman after all, then, and not a half-fledged farm boy. Are you going to tell me why you've sat in your room for four days without speaking, or do you want me to guess? Women love to be mysterious."

"There's no mystery in it. You asked me last time we met if I knew why my aunt looked like a living ghost. Those were your words, weren't they? Well, I know now, that's all."

Jem watched her with curious eyes, and then he whistled again.

"Drink's a funny thing," he said, after a moment or two. "I got drunk once, in Amsterdam, the time I ran away to sea. I remember hearing a church clock strike half past nine in the evening, and I was sitting on the floor with my arms round a pretty red-haired girl. The next thing I knew, it was seven in the following morning, and I was lying on my back in the gutter, without any boots or breeches. I often wonder what I did during those ten hours. I've thought and thought, but I'm damned if I can remember."

"That's very fortunate for you," said Mary. "Your brother

is not so lucky. When he gets drunk he finds his memory instead of losing it."

The pony slacked in his stride, and she flicked at him with the reins. "If he's alone he can talk to himself," she continued; "it wouldn't have much effect on the walls of Jamaica Inn. This time he was not alone, though. I happened to be there when he woke from his stupor. And he'd been dreaming."

"And when you heard one of his dreams, you shut yourself up in your bedroom for four days, is that it?" said Jem.

"That's as near as you'll ever get to it," she replied.

He leant over her suddenly and took the reins out of her hands.

"You don't look where you're going," he said. "I told you this pony never stumbled, but it doesn't mean you have to drive him into a block of granite the size of a cannon ball. Give him to me." She sank back in the jingle and allowed him to drive. It was true, she had lacked concentration, and deserved his reproach. The pony picked up his feet and broke into a trot.

"What are you going to do about it?" said Jem.

Mary shrugged her shoulders. "I haven't made up my mind," she said. "I have to consider Aunt Patience. You don't expect me to tell, do you?"

"Why not? I hold no brief for Joss."

"You're his brother, and that's enough for me. There are many gaps in the story, and you fit remarkably well into some of them."

"Do you think I'd waste my time working for my brother?"

"There'd be little waste of time, from what I've seen. There's profit enough and to spare in his business, and no payment in return for his goods. Dead men tell no tales, Jem Merlyn."

"No, but dead ships do, when they run ashore in a fair wind. It's lights a vessel looks for, Mary, when she's seeking harbour. Have you ever seen a moth flutter to a candle and singe his wings? A ship will do the same to a false light. It may happen once, twice, three times perhaps; but the fourth time a dead ship stinks to heaven, and the whole

131

country is up in arms and wants to know the reason why. My brother has lost his own rudder by now, and he's heading for the shore himself."

"Will you keep him company?"

"I? What have I to do with him? He can run his own head into the noose. I may have helped myself to baccy now and then, and I've run cargoes, but I'll tell you one thing, Mary Yellan, and you can believe it or not, as the mood takes you: I've never killed a man—yet."

He cracked the whip savagely over his pony's head, and the animal broke into a gallop. "There's a ford ahead of us, where that hedge runs away to the east. We cross the river and come out on the Launceston road half a mile on. Then we've seven miles or more before we reach the town. Are you getting tired?"

She shook her head. "There's bread and cheese in the basket under the seat," he said, "and an apple or two, and some pears. You'll be hungry directly. So you think I wreck ships, do you, and stand on the shore and watch men drown? And then put my hands into their pockets afterwards, when they're swollen with water? It makes a ˜retty picture."

Whether his anger was pretended or sincere she could not say, but his mouth was set firm, and there was a flaming spot of colour high on his cheekbone.

"You haven't denied it yet, have you?" she said.

He looked down at her with insolence, half contemptuous, half amused, and he laughed as though she were a child without knowledge. She hated him for it, and with a sudden intuition she knew the question that was forming itself, and her hands grew hot.

"If you believe it of me, why do you drive with me today to Launceston?" he said.

He was ready to mock her; an evasion or a stammered reply would be a triumph for him, and she steeled herself to gaiety.

"For the sake of your bright eyes, Jem Merlyn," she said. "I ride with you for no other reason," and she met his glance without a tremor.

He laughed at that, and shook his head, and fell to whistling again; and all at once there was ease between them, and a certain boyish familiarity. The very boldness of her words had disarmed him; he suspected nothing of the weakness that lay behind them, and for the moment they were companions without the strain of being man and woman.

They came now to the highroad, and the jingle rattled along behind the trotting pony, with the two stolen horses clattering in tow. The rain clouds swept across the sky, threatening and low, but as yet no drizzle fell from them, and the hills that rose in the distance from the moors were clear of mist. Mary thought of Francis Davey in Altarnun away to the left of her, and she wondered what he would say to her when she told him her story. He would not advise a waiting game again. Perhaps he would not thank her if she broke in upon his Christmas; and she pictured the silent vicarage, peaceful and still amongst the cluster of cottages that formed the village, and the tall church tower standing like a guardian above the roofs and chimneys.

There was a haven of rest for her in Altarnun—the very name spelt like a whisper—and the voice of Francis Davey would mean security and a forgetting of trouble. There was a strangeness about him that was disturbing and pleasant. That picture he had painted; and the way he had driven his horse; and how he had waited upon her with deft silence; and strange above all was the grey and sombre stillness of his room that bore no trace of his personality. He was a shadow of a man, and now she was not with him he lacked substance. He had not the male aggression of Jem beside her, he was without flesh and blood. He was no more than two white eyes and a voice in the darkness.

The pony shied suddenly at a gap in the hedge, and Jem's loud curse woke her with a jar from the privacy of her thoughts.

She threw a shot at a venture. "Are there churches hereabouts?" she asked him. "I've lived like a heathen these last months, and I hate the feeling."

133

"Get out of it, you blasted fool, you!" shouted Jem, stabbing at the pony's mouth. "Do you want to land us all in the ditch? Churches, do you say? How in the hell should I know about churches? I've only been inside one once, and then I was carried in my mother's arms and I came out Jeremiah. I can't tell you anything about them. They keep the gold plate locked up, I believe."

"There's a church at Altarnun, isn't there?" she said. "That's within walking distance of Jamaica Inn. I might go there tomorrow."

"Far better eat your Christmas dinner with me. I can't give you turkey, but I can always help myself to a goose from old Farmer Tuckett at North Hill. He's getting so blind he'd never know that she was missing."

"Do you know who has the living at Altarnun, Jem Merlyn?"

"No, I do not, Mary Yellan. I've never had any truck with parsons, and I'm never likely to. They're a funny breed of man altogether. There was a parson at North Hill when I was a boy; he was very shortsighted, and they say one Sunday he mislaid the sacramental wine and gave the parish brandy instead. The village heard in a body what was happening, and, do you know, that church was so packed, there was scarcely room to kneel; there were people standing up against the walls, waiting for their turn. The parson couldn't make it out at all; there'd never been so many in his church before, and he got up in the pulpit with his eyes shining behind his spectacles, and he preached a sermon about the flock returning to the fold. Brother Matthew it was told me the story; he went up twice to the altar rails and the parson never noticed. It was a great day in North Hill. Get out the bread and the cheese, Mary; my belly is sinking away to nothing."

Mary shook her head at him and sighed. "Have you ever been serious about anything in your life?" she said. "Do you respect nothing and nobody?"

"I respect my inside," he told her, "and it's calling out for food. There's the box, under my feet. You can eat the apple, if you're feeling religious. There's an apple comes in the Bible, I know that much."

It was a hilarious and rather heated cavalcade that clattered into Launceston at half past two in the afternoon. Mary had thrown trouble and responsibility to the winds, and, in spite of her firm resolution of the early morning, she had melted to Jem's mood and given herself to gaiety.

Away from the shadow of Jamaica Inn her natural youth and her spirits returned, and her companion noticed this in a flash and played upon them.

She laughed because she must, and because he made her; and there was an infection in the air caught from the sound and bustle of the town, a sense of excitement and well-being; a sense of Christmas. The streets were thronged with people, and the little shops were gay. Carriages, and carts, and coaches too, were huddled together in the cobbled square. There was colour, and life, and movement; the cheerful crowd jostled one another before the market stalls, turkeys and geese scratched at the wooden barrier that penned them, and a woman in a green cloak held apples above her head and smiled, the apples shining and red like her cheeks. The scene was familiar and dear; Helston had been like this, year after year at Christmastime; but there was a brighter, more abandoned spirit about Launceston; the crowd was greater and the voices mixed. There was space here, and a certain sophistication; Devonshire and England were across the river. Farmers from the next county rubbed shoulders with countrywomen from East Cornwall; and there were shopkeepers, and pastry cooks, and little apprentice boys who pushed in and out amongst the crowd with hot pasties and sausagemeat on trays. A lady in a feathered hat and a blue velvet cape stepped down from her coach and went into the warmth and light of the hospitable White Hart, followed by a gentleman in a padded greatcoat of powder-grey. He lifted his eyeglass to his eyes and strutted after her for all the world like a turkey cock himself.

This was a gay and happy world to Mary. The town was set on the bosom of a hill, with a castle framed in the centre, like a tale from old history. There were trees clustered here, and sloping fields, and water gleamed in the valley below. The moors were remote; they stretched away out of sight behind the town and were forgotten. Launceston had reality; these people were alive. Christmas came into its own again in the town and had a place amongst the cobbled streets, the laughing jostling crowd, and the watery sun struggled from his hiding place behind the grey banked clouds to join the festivity. Mary wore the handkerchief Jem had given her. She even unbent so far as to permit him to tie the ends under her chin. They had stabled the pony and jingle at the top of the town, and now Jem pushed his way through the crowd, leading his two stolen horses, Mary following at his heels. He led the way with confidence, making straight for the main square, where the whole of Launceston gathered and the booths and tents of the Christmas fair stood end to end. There was a place roped off from the fair for the buying and selling of livestock, and the ring was surrounded by farmers and countrymen, gentlemen too, and dealers from Devon and beyond. Mary's heart beat faster as they approached the ring; supposing there was someone from North Hill here, or a farmer from a neighbouring village, surely they would recognize the horses? Jem wore his hat at the back of his head, and he whistled. He looked back at her once and winked his eye. The crowd parted and made way for him. Mary stood on the outskirts, behind a fat market woman with a basket, and she saw Jem take his place amongst a group of men with ponies, and he nodded to one or two of them, and ran his eye over their ponies, bending as he did so to a flare to light his pipe. He looked cool and unperturbed. Presently a flashy-looking fellow with a square hat and cream breeches thrust his way through the crowd and crossed over to the horses. His voice was loud and important, and he kept hitting his boot with a crop, and then pointing to the ponies. From his tone, and his air of authority, Mary judged him to be a dealer. Soon he was joined by a little lynx-eyed man in a black coat, who now and again jogged his elbow and whispered in his ear.

Mary saw him stare hard at the black pony that had belonged to Squire Bassat; he went up to him and bent down and felt his legs. Then he whispered something in the ear of the loud-voiced man. Mary watched him nervously.

"Where did you get this pony?" said the dealer, tapping Jem on the shoulder. "He was never bred on the moors, not with that head and shoulders."

"He was foaled at Callington four years ago," said Jem carelessly, his pipe in the corner of his mouth. "I bought him as a yearling from old Tim Bray; you remember Tim? He sold up last year and went into Dorset. Tim always told me I'd get my money back on this pony. The dam was Irish bred, and won prizes for him upcountry. Have a look at him, won't you? But he's not going cheap, I'll tell you that."

He puffed at his pipe while the two men went over the pony carefully. The time seemed endless before they straightened themselves and stood back. "Had any trouble with his skin?" said the lynx-eyed man. "It feels very coarse on the surface, and sharp like bristles. There's a taint about him, too, I don't like. You haven't been doping him, have you?"

"There's nothing ailing with that pony," replied Jem. "The other one there, he fell away to nothing in the summer, but I've brought him back all right. I'd do better to keep him till the spring now, I believe, but he's costing me money. No, this black pony here, you can't fault him. I'll be frank with you over one thing, and it's only fair to admit it. Old Tim Bray never knew the mare was in foal—he was in Plymouth at the time, and his boy was looking after her—and when he found out he gave the boy a thrashing, but of course it was too late. He had to make the best of a bad job. It's my opinion the sire was a grey; look at the short hair there, close to the skin—that's grey, isn't it? Tim just missed a good bargain with this pony. Look at those shoulders; there's breeding for you. I tell you what, I'll take eighteen guineas for him." The lynx-eyed man shook his head, but the dealer hesitated.

"Make it fifteen and we might do business," he suggested.

"No, eighteen guineas is my sum, and not a penny less," said Jem.

The two men consulted together and appeared to disagree. Mary heard the word "fake," and Jem shot a glance at her over the heads of the crowd. A little murmur rose from the group of men beside him. Once more the lynx-eyed man bent and touched the legs of the black pony. "I'd advise another opinion on this pony," he said. "I'm not satisfied about him myself. Where's your mark?"

Jem showed him the narrow slit in the ear and the man examined it closely.

"You're a sharp customer, aren't you?" said Jem. "Anyone would think I'd stolen the horse. Anything wrong with the mark?"

"No, apparently not. But it's a good thing for you that Tim Bray has gone to Dorset. He'd never own this pony, whatever you like to say. I wouldn't touch him, Stevens, if I were you. You'll find yourself in trouble. Come away, man."

The loud-mouthed dealer looked regretfully at the black pony.

"He's a good looker," he said. "I don't care who bred him, or if his sire was piebald. What makes you so particular, Will?"

Once more the lynx-eyed man plucked at his sleeve and whispered in his ear. The dealer listened and pulled a face, and then he nodded. "All right," he said aloud: "I've no doubt that you're right. You've got an eye for trouble, haven't you? Perhaps we're better out of it. You can keep your pony," he added to Jem. "My partner doesn't fancy him. Take my advice and come down on your price. If you have him for long on your hands you'll be sorry." And he elbowed his way through the crowd, with the lynx-eyed man beside him, and they disappeared in the direction of the White Hart. Mary breathed a sigh of relief when she saw the last of them. She could make nothing of Jem's expression; his lips were framed in the inevitable whistle. People came and went; the shaggy moorland ponies were sold for two or three pounds apiece, and their late owners departed satisfied. No one came near the black pony again. He was looked at askance by the crowd. At a quarter to four Jem sold the other horse for six pounds to a cheerful, honest-looking farmer, after a long and very good-humoured argument. The farmer declared he would give five pounds, and Jem stuck out for seven. After twenty minutes riotous bargaining the sum of six pounds was agreed, and the farmer rode off on the back of his purchase with a grin from ear to ear. Mary began to flag on her feet. Twilight gathered in the market square, and the lamps were lit. The town wore an air of mystery. She was thinking of returning to the jingle when she heard a woman's voice behind her, and a high affected laugh. She turned and saw the blue cloak and the plumed hat of the woman who had stepped from the coach earlier in the afternoon. "Oh, look, James," she was saying. "Did you ever see such a delicious pony in your life? He holds his head just like poor Beauty did. The likeness would be quite striking, only this animal of course is black and has nothing of Beauty's breeding. What a nuisance Roger isn't here. I can't disturb him from his meeting. What do you think of him, James?"

Her companion put up his eyeglass and stared. "Damn it, Maria," he drawled, "I don't know a thing about horses. The pony you lost was a grey, wasn't it? This thing is ebony, positively ebony, my dear. Do you want to buy him?"

The woman gave a little trill of laughter. "It would be such a good Christmas present for the children," she said. "They've plagued poor Roger ever since Beauty disappeared. Ask the price, James, will you?"

The man strutted forward. "Here, my good fellow," he called to Jem, "do you want to sell that black pony of yours?"

Jem shook his head. "He's promised to a friend," he said. "I wouldn't like to go back on my word. Besides, this wouldn't carry you. He's been ridden by children."

"Oh, really. Oh, I see. Oh, thank you. Maria, this fellow says the pony is not for sale."

"Is he sure? What a shame! I'd set my heart on him. I'll pay him his price, tell him. Ask him again, James."

Once more the man put up his glass and drawled, "Look here, my man, this lady has taken a fancy to your pony.

139

She has just lost one, and she wants to replace him. Her children will be most disappointed if they hear about it. Damn your friend, you know. He must wait. What is your price?"

"Twenty-five guineas," said Jem promptly. "At least, that's what my friend was going to pay. I'm not anxious to sell him."

The lady in the plumed hat swept into the ring. "I'll give you thirty for him," she said. "I'm Mrs. Bassat from North Hill, and I want the pony as a Christmas present for my children. Please don't be obstinate. I have half the sum here in my purse, and this gentleman will give you the rest. Mr. Bassat is in Launceston now, and I want the pony to be a surprise to him as well as to my children. My groom shall fetch the pony immediately and ride him to North Hill before Mr. Bassat leaves the town. Here's the money."

Jem swept off his hat and bowed low. "Thank you, madam," he said. "I hope Mr. Bassat will be pleased with your bargain. You will find the pony exceedingly safe with children."

"Oh, I'm certain he will be delighted. Of course the pony is nothing like the one we had stolen. Beauty was a thoroughbred, and worth a great deal of money. This little animal is handsome enough and will please the children. Come along, James; it's getting quite dark, and I'm chilled to the bone."

She made her way from the ring towards the coach that waited in the square. The tall footman leapt forward to open the door. "I've just bought a pony for Master Robert and Master Henry," she said. "Will you find Richards and tell him he's to ride it back home? I want it to be a surprise to the squire." She stepped into the coach, her petticoats fluttering behind her, followed by her companion with the monocle.

Jem looked hastily over his shoulder and tapped a lad who stood behind him on the arm. "Here," he said, "would you like a five-shilling piece?" The lad nodded, his mouth agape. "Hang onto this pony, then, and, when the groom comes for him, hand him over for me, will you? I've just had word that my wife has given birth to twins and her life is in danger. I haven't a moment to lose. Here, take the bridle. A happy Christmas to you."

And he was off in a moment, walking hard across the square, his hands thrust deep in his breeches pockets. Mary followed, a discreet ten paces behind. Her face was scarlet, and she kept her eyes on the ground. The laughter bubbled up inside her, and she hid her mouth in her shawl. She was near to collapsing when they reached the further side of the square, out of sight of the coach and the group of people, and she stood with her hand to her side, catching her breath. Jem waited for her, his face as grave as a judge.

"Jem Merlyn, you deserve to be hanged," she said, when she had recovered herself. "To stand there as you did in the market square and sell that stolen pony back to Mrs. Bassat herself! You have the cheek of the devil, and the hairs in my head have gone grey from watching you."

He threw back his head and laughed, and she could not resist him. Their laughter echoed in the street until people turned to look at them, and they too caught the infection, and smiled, and broke into laughter; and Launceston itself seemed to rock in merriment as peal after peal of gaiety echoed in the street, mingling with the bustle and clatter of the fair; and with it all there was shouting, and calling, and a song from somewhere. The torches and the flares cast strange lights on the faces of people, and there was colour, and shadow, and the hum of voices, and a ripple of excitement in the air.

Jem caught at her hand and crumpled the fingers. "You're glad you came now, aren't you?" he said, and "Yes," she said recklessly, and she did not mind.

They plunged into the thick of the fair, with all the warmth and the suggestion of packed humanity about them. Jem bought Mary a crimson shawl and gold rings for her ears. They sucked oranges beneath a striped tent and had their fortunes told by a wrinkled gypsy woman. "Beware of a dark stranger," she said to Mary, and they looked at one another and laughed again.

"There's blood in your hand, young man," she told him.

"You'll kill a man one day"; and "What did I tell you in the jingle this morning?" said Jem. "I'm innocent as yet. Do you believe it now?" But she shook her head at him; she would not say. Little raindrops splashed onto their faces, and they did not care. The wind rose in gusts and billowed the fluttering tents, scattering paper and ribbons and silks; and a great striped booth shuddered an instant and crumpled, while apples and oranges rolled in the gutter. Flares streamed in the wind; the rain fell; and people ran hither and thither for shelter, laughing and calling to one another, the rain streaming from them.

Jem dragged Mary under cover of a doorway, his arms around her shoulders, and he turned her face against him and held her with his hands and kissed her. "Beware of the dark stranger," he said, and he laughed and kissed her again. The night clouds had come up with the rain, and it was black in an instant. The wind blew out the flares, the lanterns glowed dim and yellow, and all the bright colour of the fair was gone. The square was soon deserted; the striped tents and the booths gaped empty and forlorn. The soft rain came in gusts at the open doorway, and Jem stood with his back to the weather, making a screen for Mary. He untied the handkerchief she wore and played with her hair. She felt the tips of his fingers on her neck, travelling to her shoulders, and she put up her hands and pushed them away. "I've made a fool of myself long enough for one night, Jem Merlyn," she said. "It's time we thought of returning. Let me alone."

"You don't want to ride in an open jingle in this wind, do you?" he said. "It's coming from the coast, and we'll be blown under on the high ground. We'll have to spend the night together in Launceston."

"Very likely! Go and fetch the pony, Jem, while this shower lifts for the moment. I'll wait for you here."

"Don't be a Puritan, Mary. You'll be soaked to the skin on the Bodmin road. Pretend you're in love with me, can't you? You'd stay with me then."

"Are you talking to me like this because I'm the barmaid at Jamaica Inn?"

"Damn Jamaica Inn! I like the look of you, and the feel of you, and that's enough for any man. It ought to be enough for a woman too."

"I daresay it is, for some. I don't happen to be made that way."

"Do they make you different from other women, then, down on Helford River? Stay here with me tonight, Mary, and we can find out. You'd be like the rest by the time morning came, I'd take my oath on that."

"I haven't a doubt of it. That's why I'd rather risk a soaking in the jingle."

"God, you're as hard as flint, Mary Yellan. You'll be sorry for it when you're alone again."

"Better be sorry then than later."

"If I kissed you again would you change your mind?"

"I would not."

"I don't wonder my brother took to his bed and his bottle for a week, with you in the house. Did you sing psalms to him?"

"I daresay I did."

"I've never known a woman so perverse. I'll buy a ring for you if it would make you feel respectable. It's not often I have money enough in my pocket to make the offer."

"How many wives do you belong to have?"

"Six or seven scattered over Cornwall. I don't count the ones across the Tamar."

"That's a good number for one man. I'd wait awhile before I took on an eighth, if I were you."

"You're sharp, aren't you? You look like a monkey in that shawl of yours, with your bright eyes. All right, I'll fetch the jingle, and take you home to your aunt, but I'll kiss you first, whether you like it or not."

He took her face in his hands. "One for sorrow, two for joy," he said. "I'll give you the rest when you're in a more yielding frame of mind. It wouldn't do to finish the rhyme tonight. Stay where you're to; I'll not be long."

He bowed his head against the rain and strode across the street. She saw him disappear behind a line of stalls, and so around the corner.

She leant back once more within the shelter of the door. It would be desolate enough on the highroad, she knew that; this was a real driving rain, with a venomous wind behind it, and there would be little mercy from the moors. It required a certain amount of courage to stand those eleven miles in an open jingle. The thought of staying in Launceston with Jem Merlyn made her heart beat faster perhaps, and it was exciting to think upon it now he was gone and he could not see her face, but for all that she would not lose her head to please him. Once she departed from the line of conduct she had laid down for herself, there would be no returning. There would be no privacy of mind, no independence. She had given too much away as it was, and she would never be entirely free of him again. This weakness would be a drag on her and make the four walls of Jamaica Inn more hateful than they were already. It was better to bear solitude alone. Now the silence of the moors would be a torment because of his presence four miles distant from her. Mary wrapped her shawl around her and folded her arms. She wished that women were not the frail things of straw she believed them to be; then she could stay this night with Jem Merlyn and forget herself as he could forget, and both of them part with a laugh and a shrug of the shoulder in the morning. But she was a woman, and it was impossible. A few kisses had made a fool of her already. She thought of Aunt Patience, trailing like a ghost in the shadow of her master, and she shuddered. That would be Mary Yellan too, but for the grace of God and her own strength of will. A gust of wind tore at her skirt and another shower of rain blew in at the open doorway. It was colder now. Puddles ran on the cobbled stones, and the lights and the people had vanished. Launceston had lost its glamour. It would be a bleak and cheerless Christmas Day tomorrow.

Mary waited, stamping her feet and blowing upon her hands. Jem was taking his own time to fetch the jingle. He was annoyed with her, no doubt, for refusing to stay, and leaving her to become wet and chilled in the open doorway was to be his method of punishment. The long minutes passed, and still he did not come. If this was his system of revenge, the plan was without humour and lacked originality. Somewhere a clock struck eight. He had been gone over half an hour, and the place where the pony and jingle were stabled was only five minutes away. Mary was dispirited and tired. She had been on her legs since the early afternoon, and now that the high pitch of excitement had died away she wanted to rest. It would be difficult to recapture the careless, irresponsible mood of the last few hours. Jem had taken his gaiety with him.

At last Mary could stand it no longer, and she set off up the hill in search of him. The long street was deserted, save for a few stragglers, who hung about in the doubtful shelter of doorways as she had done. The rain was pitiless, and the wind came in gusts. There was nothing left now of the Christmas spirit.

In a few minutes she came to the stable where they had left the pony and jingle in the afternoon. The door was locked, and, peering through a crack, she saw that the shed was empty. Jem must have gone, then. She knocked at the little shop next door, in a fever of impatience, and after a while it was opened by the fellow who had admitted them to the shed earlier in the day.

He looked annoyed at being disturbed from the comfort of his fire, and at first did not recognize her, wild as she was in her wet shawl.

"What do you want?" he said. "We don't give food to strangers here."

"I haven't come for food," Mary replied. "I'm looking for my companion. We came here together with a pony and jingle, if you remember. I see the stable is empty. Have you seen him?"

The man muttered an apology. "You'll excuse me, I'm sure. Your friend has been gone twenty minutes or more. He seemed in a great hurry, and there was another man with him. I wouldn't be sure, but he looked like one of the servants from the White Hart. They turned back in that direction at any rate."

"He left no message, I suppose?"

"No, I'm sorry he did not. Maybe you'll find him at the White Hart. Do you know where it is?"

"Yes, thank you. I'll try there. Good night."

The man shut the door in her face, glad enough to be rid of her, and Mary retraced her steps in the direction of the town. What should Jem want with one of the servants from the White Hart? The man must have been mistaken. There was nothing for it but to find out the truth for herself. Once more she came to the cobbled square. The White Hart looked hospitable enough, with its lighted windows, but there was no sign of the pony and jingle. Mary's heart sank. Surely Jem had not taken the road without her? She hesitated for a moment, and then she went up to the door and passed inside. The hall seemed to be full of gentlemen, talking and laughing, and once again her country clothes and wet hair caused consternation, for a servant went up to her at once and bade her be gone. "I've come in search of a Mr. Jem Merlyn," said Mary firmly. "He came here with a pony and jingle and was seen with one of your servants. I'm sorry to trouble you, but I'm anxious to find him. Will you please make some enquiry?"

The man went off with an ill grace, while Mary waited by the entrance, turning her back on the little group of men who stood by the fire and stared. Amongst them she recognized the dealer and the little lynx-eyed man.

She was aware of a sudden sense of foreboding. In a few moments the servant returned with a tray of glasses, which he distributed amongst the company by the fire, and later he appeared again with cake and ham. He took no more notice of Mary, and only when she called to him for the third time did he come towards her. "I'm sorry," he said; "we've plenty here tonight without wasting our time over people from the fair. There's no man here by the name of Merlyn. I've asked outside, and nobody has heard of him."

Mary turned at once for the door, but the lynx-eyed man was there before her. "If it's the dark gypsy fellow who tried to sell my partner a pony this afternoon, I can tell you about him," he said, smiling wide, and showing a row of broken teeth. Laughter broke out from the group by the fire.

She looked from one to the other. "What have you to say?" she said.

"He was in the company of a gentleman barely ten minutes ago," returned the lynx-eyed man, still smiling, and looking her up and down, "and with the help of some of us he was persuaded to enter a carriage that was waiting at the door. He was inclined to resist us at first, but a look from the gentleman appeared to decide him. No doubt you know what became of the black pony? The price he was asking was undoubtedly high."

His remark brought forth a fresh burst of laughter from the group by the fire. Mary stared steadily at the little lynx-eyed man.

"Do you know where he went?" she asked.

He shrugged his shoulders and pulled a mock face of pity.

"His destination is unknown to me," he said, "and I regret to say that your companion left no message of farewell. However, it is Christmas Eve, the night is young yet, and you can see for yourself it's no weather to remain outside. If you care to wait here until your friend chooses to return, myself and the rest of these gentlemen will be delighted to entertain you."

He laid a limp hand on her shawl. "What a blackguard the fellow must be to desert you," he said smoothly. "Come in and rest, and forget him."

Mary turned her back on him without a word and passed out through the door once more. As it closed behind her she caught the echo of his laughter.

She stood in the deserted market square with the gusty wind and scattered showers of rain for company. So the worst had happened, and the theft of the pony had been discovered. There was no other explanation. Jem had gone. Stupidly she stared before her at the dark houses, wondering what was the punishment for theft. Did they hang men for that as well as murder? She felt ill in body, as though someone had beaten her, and her brain was in confusion. She could see nothing clearly, she could make no plans. She supposed that Jem was lost to her now anyway, and she would never see him again. The brief adventure was over. For the moment she was stunned, and, hardly knowing that she did so, she began to walk aimlessly across the square towards the castle hill. If she had consented to stay in Launceston this would never have happened. They would have gone from the shelter of the doorway and found a room in the town somewhere; she would have been beside him, and they would have loved one another.

And, even if he had been caught in the morning, they would have had those hours alone. Now that he was gone from her, mind and body cried out in bitterness and resentment, and she knew how much she had wanted him. It was her fault that he had been taken, and she could do nothing for him. No doubt they would hang him for this; he would die like his father before him. The castle wall frowned down upon her, and the rain ran in rivulets beside the road. There was no beauty left in Launceston any more; it was a grim, grey, hateful place, and every bend in the road hinted at disaster. She stumbled along with the mizzling rain driving in her face, caring little where she went and careless of the fact that eleven long miles lay between her and her bedroom at Jamaica Inn. If loving a man meant this pain and anguish and sickness, she wanted none of it. It did away with sanity and composure and made havoc of courage. She was a babbling child now when once she had been indifferent and strong. The steep hill rose before her. They had clattered down it in the afternoon; she remembered the gnarled tree trunk at the gap in the hedge. Jem had whistled, and she had sung snatches of song. Suddenly she came to her senses and faltered in her steps. It was madness to walk any further; the road stretched like a white ribbon in front of her, and two miles of it would bring exhaustion in this wind and rain.

She turned again on the slope of the hill, with the winking lights of the town beneath her. Someone perhaps would give her a bed for the night, or a blanket on the floor. She had no money; they would have to trust her for payment. The wind tore at her hair, and the small stunted trees bowed and curtseyed before it. It would be a wild, wet dawn to Christmas Day.

She went away down the road, driven like a leaf before the wind, and out of the darkness she saw a carriage crawling up the hill towards her. It looked like a beetle, stubby and black, and its progress was slow, with the full force of the weather against it. She watched it with dull eyes; the sight conveyed no message to her brain, except that somewhere on an unknown road Jem Merlyn travelled to his death perhaps by the same manner. The carriage had crept up to her and was passing by, before she ran towards it on an impulse and called to the driver wrapped in a greatcoat on the seat. "Are you taking the Bodmin road?" she cried. "Have you a passenger inside?" The driver shook his head and whipped on his horse, but before Mary could step aside an arm came out of the carriage window, and a hand was laid on her shoulder. "What does Mary Yellan do alone in Launceston on Christmas Eve?" said a voice from within.

The hand was firm, but the voice was gentle. A pale face stared at her from the dark interior of the carriage: white hair and white eyes beneath the black shovel hat. It was the vicar of Altarnun.

Chapter 10

SHE WATCHED his profile in the half-light; sharp it was and clear, the prominent thin nose thrust downward like the curved beak of a bird. His lips were narrow and colourless, pressed firm together, and he leant forward with his chin resting on a long ebony cane that he held between his knees.

For the moment she could see nothing of his eyes; they

were veiled by the short white lashes; and then he turned
in his seat and considered her, his lashes fluttering, and
the eyes that looked upon her were white also, transparent
and expressionless as glass.

"So we ride together for the second time," he said, and
his voice was soft and low, like the voice of a woman. "Once
more I have the good fortune to help you by the wayside.
You are wet through to the skin; you had better take off
your clothes." He stared at her with cold indifference, and she
struggled in some confusion with the pin that clasped her
shawl.

"There is a dry rug here that will serve you for the rest
of the journey," he continued. "As for your feet, they will
be better bare. This carriage is comparatively free from
draught."

Without a word she slipped out of her soaking shawl
and bodice and wrapped herself in the coarse hair blanket that he held out to her. Her hair fell from its band and
hung like a curtain about her bare shoulders. She felt like
a child that has been caught on an escapade, and now
sat with hands folded meekly together, obedient to the
master's word.

"Well?" he said, looking gravely upon her, and she
found herself at once stumbling into an explanation of her
day. As before at Altarnun, there was something about him
that made her untrue to herself, made her sound like a fool
and an ignorant country girl, for her story was poor telling,
and she came out of it badly—just another woman who had
cheapened herself at Launceston fair and had been left by
the man of her choice to find her way home alone. She was
ashamed to mention Jem by name, and she introduced him
lamely as a man who lived by breaking horses and whom
she had met once when wandering on the moor. And now
there had been some trouble in Launceston over the sale
of a pony, and she feared he had been caught in some dishonesty.

She wondered what Francis Davey must think of her,
riding to Launceston with a casual acquaintance and then
losing her companion in disgrace and running about the

town bedraggled and wet after nightfall, like a woman of the streets. He heard her to the end in silence, and she heard him swallow once or twice, a trick she remembered.

"So you have not been too lonely after all?" he said at length. "Jamaica Inn was not so isolated as you supposed?"

Mary flushed in the darkness, and, though he could not see her face, she knew that his eyes were upon her, and she felt guilty, as though she had done wrong and this were an accusation.

"What was the name of your companion?" he asked quietly; and she hesitated a moment, awkward and uncomfortable, her sense of guilt stronger than ever.

"He was my uncle's brother," she replied, aware of the reluctance in her voice, the admission dragging from her like a confession.

Whatever his opinion of her had been hitherto, he was unlikely to raise it after this. Barely a week had passed since she had called Joss Merlyn a murderer, and yet she had ridden from Jamaica Inn with his brother without compunction, a common barmaid who would see the fun of the fair.

"You think ill of me, of course," she went on hurriedly. "Mistrusting and loathing my uncle as I do, it was hardly in keeping to make a confidant of his brother. He is dishonest and a thief, I know that; he told me as much at the beginning; but beyond that . . ." Her words trailed off with some uncertainty. After all Jem had denied nothing; he had made little or no attempt to defend himself when she accused him. And now she ranged herself on his side, she defended him instead, without reason and against her sane judgment, bound to him already because of his hands upon her and a kiss in the dark.

"You mean the brother knows nothing of the landlord's trade by night?" continued the gentle voice at her side. "He is not of the company who brings the waggons to Jamaica Inn?"

Mary made a little gesture of despair. "I don't know," she said; "I have no proof. He admits nothing; he shrugs his shoulders. But he told me one thing: that he had never

151

killed a man. And I believed him. I still believe him. He said also that my uncle was running straight into the hands of the law, and they would catch him before long. He surely would not say that if he was one of the company."

She spoke now to reassure herself rather than the man at her side, and Jem's innocence became suddenly of vital importance.

"You told me before that you had some acquaintance with the squire," she said quickly. "Perhaps you have influence with him too. You could no doubt persuade him to deal mercifully with Jem Merlyn when the time comes. After all, he is young; he could start life afresh; it would be easy enough for you in your position."

His silence was an added humiliation, and, feeling those cold white eyes upon her, she knew what a little graceless fool he must think her, and how feminine. He must see that she was pleading for a man who had kissed her once, and that he despised her went without saying.

"My acquaintance with Mr. Bassat of North Hill is of the slightest," he told her gently. "Once or twice we have given one another good afternoon, and we have spoken of matters relating to our respective parishes. It is hardly likely that he should spare a thief because of me, especially if the thief is guilty and happens to be the brother of the landlord of Jamaica Inn."

Mary said nothing. Once again, this strange man of God had spoken words of logic and wisdom, and there was no argument in reply. But she was caught in the sudden fever of love that devastates reason and makes havoc of logic, therefore his words acted as an irritant and created fresh turmoil in her brain.

"You appear anxious for his safety," he said; and she wondered whether it was mockery she heard in his voice, or reproof, or understanding; but quick as a flash of lightning he continued: "And if your new friend was guilty of other things, of conspiring with his brother against the belongings and perhaps the lives of his fellow men, what then, Mary Yellan? Would you still seek to save him?" She felt his hand upon hers, cool and impersonal; and, because she was on edge after the excitement of the day, and was both frightened and frustrated in one, and loved a man against her judgment who was now lost to her through her own fault, she broke down and began to rave like a child deprived.

"I didn't bargain for this," she said fiercely. "I could face the brutality of my uncle, and the pathetic dumb stupidity of Aunt Patience; even the silence and the horror of Jamaica Inn itself could be borne without shrinking and running away. I don't mind being lonely. There's a certain grim satisfaction in this struggle with my uncle that emboldens me at times, and I feel I'll have the better of him in the long run, whatever he says or does. I'd planned to take my aunt away from him, and see justice done, and then, when it was all over, to find work on a farm somewhere and live a man's life, like I used to do. But now I can't look ahead any more; I can't make plans or think for myself; I go round and round in a trap, all because of a man I despise, who has nothing to do with my brain or my understanding. I don't want to love like a woman or feel like a woman, Mr. Davey; there's pain that way, and suffering, and misery that can last a lifetime. I didn't bargain for this; I don't want it."

She leant back, her face against the side of the carriage, worn out by her torrent of words and already ashamed of her outburst. She did not care what he thought of her now. He was a priest, and therefore detached from her little world of storm and passion. He could have no knowledge of these things. She felt sullen and unhappy.

"How old are you?" he asked abruptly.

"Twenty-three," she told him.

She heard him swallow in the darkness, and, taking his hand away from hers, he placed it once more upon the ebony stick and sat in silence.

The carriage had climbed away from the Launceston valley and the shelter of the hedges and was now upon the high ground leading to the open moorland, exposed to the full force of the wind and the rain. The wind was continuous, but the showers were intermittent, and now and again a wild star straggled furtively behind a low-sweeping cloud and hung for an instant like a pinprick of light. Then it would go, obscured and swept away by a black curtain of rain, and from the narrow window of the carriage nothing could be seen but the square dark patch of sky.

In the valley the rain had fallen with greater steadiness, and the wind, though persistent, had been moderate in strength and checked in its passage by the trees and the contour of the hill. Here on the high ground there was no such natural shelter; there was nothing but the moor on either side of the road, and, above, the great black vault of the sky; and there was a scream in the wind that had not been before.

Mary shivered and edged closer to her companion like a dog to his fellow. Still he said nothing, but she knew that he had turned and was looking down upon her, and for the first time she was aware of his proximity as a person; she could feel his breath on her forehead. She remembered that her wet shawl and bodice lay on the floor at her feet, and she was naked under her rough blanket. When he spoke again she realized how near he was to her, and his voice came as a shock, confusing suddenly, and unexpected.

"You are very young, Mary Yellan," he said softly: "you are nothing but a chicken with the broken shell still around you. You'll come through your little crisis. Women like you have no need to shed tears over a man encountered once or twice, and the first kiss is not a thing that is remembered. You will forget your friend with his stolen pony very soon. Come now, dry your eyes; you are not the first to bite your nails over a lost lover."

He made light of her problem and counted it as a thing of no account: that was her first reaction to his words. And then she wondered why he had not used the conventional phrases of comfort, said something about the blessing of prayer, the peace of God, and life everlasting. She remembered that last ride with him when he had whipped his horse into a fever of speed, and how he had crouched in his seat, with the reins in his hands; and he had whispered words under his breath she had not understood. Again she felt something of the same discomfort she had experienced then; a sensation of uneasiness that she connected instinctively with his freak hair and eyes, as though his physical departure from normality were a barrier between him and the rest of the world. In the animal kingdom a freak was a thing of abhorrence, at once hunted and destroyed, or driven out into the wilderness. No sooner had she thought of this than she reproached herself as narrow and un-Christian. He was a fellow creature and a priest of God; but as she murmured an apology to him for having made a fool of herself before him and talking like a common girl from the streets, she reached for her clothes and began to draw them on furtively under cover of the blanket.

"So I was right in my surmise, and all has been quiet at Jamaica Inn since I saw you last?" he said after a while, following some train of thought. "There have been no waggons to disturb your beauty sleep, and the landlord has played alone with his glass and his bottle?"

Mary, still fretful and anxious, with her mind on the man she had lost, brought herself back to reality with an effort. She had forgotten her uncle for nearly ten hours. At once she remembered the full horror of the past week and the new knowledge that had come to her. She thought of the interminable sleepless nights, the long days she had spent alone, and the staring bloodshot eyes of her uncle swung before her again, his drunken smile, his groping hands.

"Mr. Davey," she whispered, "have you ever heard of wreckers?"

She had never said the word aloud before; she had not considered it even, and now that she heard it from her own lips it sounded fearful and obscene, like a blasphemy. It was too dark in the carriage to see the effect upon his face, but she heard him swallow. His eyes were hidden from her under the black shovel hat, and she could see only the dim outline of his profile, the sharp chin, the prominent nose.

"Once, years ago, when I was hardly more than a child, I heard a neighbour speak of them," she said; "and then later, when I was old enough to understand, there were rumours of these things—snatches of gossip quickly suppressed. One of the men would bring back some wild tale after a visit to the north coast, and he would be silenced at once; such talk was forbidden by the older men; it was an outrage to decency.

"I believed none of these stories; I asked my mother, and she told me they were the horrible inventions of evil-minded people; such things did not and could not exist. She was wrong. I know now she was wrong, Mr. Davey. My uncle is one of them; he told me so himself."

Still her companion made no reply; he sat motionless, like a stone thing, and she went on again, never raising her voice above a whisper:

"They are in it, every one of them, from the coast to the Tamar bank; all those men I saw that first Saturday in the bar at the inn. The gypsies, poachers, sailors, the pedlar with the broken teeth. They've murdered women and children with their own hands; they've held them under the water; they've killed them with rocks and stones. Those are death waggons that travel the road by night, and the goods they carry are not smuggled casks alone, with brandy for some and tobacco for another, but the full cargoes of wrecked ships bought at the price of blood, the trust and the possession of murdered men. And that's why my uncle is feared and loathed by the timid people in the cottages and farms, and why all doors are barred against him, and why the coaches drive past his house in a cloud of dust. They suspect what they cannot prove. My aunt lives in mortal terror of discovery; and my uncle has only to lose himself in drink before a stranger and his secret is spilt to the four winds. There, Mr. Davey; now you know the truth about Jamaica Inn."

She leant back, breathless, against the side of the carriage, biting her lips and twisting her hands in an emotion she could not control, exhausted and shaken by the torrent of words that had escaped her; and somewhere in the dark places of her mind an image fought for recognition and found its way into the light, having no mercy on her feelings; and it was the face of Jem Merlyn, the man she loved, grown evil and distorted, merging horribly and finally into that of his brother.

The face beneath the black shovel hat turned towards her; she caught a sudden flicker of the white lashes, and the lips moved.

"So the landlord talks when he is drunk?" he said, and it seemed to Mary that his voice lacked something of its usual gentle quality; it rang sharper in tone, as though pitched on a higher note; but when she looked up at him his eyes stared back at her, cold and impersonal as ever.

"He talks, yes," she answered him. "When my uncle has lived on brandy for five days he'll bare his soul before the world. He told me so himself, the very first evening I arrived. He was not drunk then. But four days ago, when he had woken from his first stupor, and he came out to the kitchen after midnight, swaying on his two feet—he talked then. That's why I know. And that's perhaps why I've lost faith in humanity, and in God, and in myself; and why I acted like a fool today in Launceston."

The gale had increased in force during their conversation, and now with the bend in the road the carriage headed straight into the wind and was brought almost to a standstill. The vehicle rocked on its high wheels, and a sudden shower spattered against the windows like a handful of pebbles. There was no particle of shelter now; the moor on either hand was bare and unprotected, and the scurrying clouds flew fast over the land, tearing themselves asunder on the tors. There was a salt, wet tang in the wind that had come from the sea fifteen miles away.

Francis Davey leant forward in his seat. "We are approaching Five Lanes and the turning to Altarnun," he said; "the driver is bound to Bodmin and will take you to Jamaica Inn. I shall leave you at Five Lanes and walk down into the village. Am I the only man you have honoured with your confidence, or do I share it with the landlord's brother?"

Again Mary could not tell if there was irony or mockery in his voice. "Jem Merlyn knows," she said unwillingly. "We spoke of it this morning. He said little, though, and I

157

know he is not friendly with my uncle. Anyway, it doesn't matter now; Jem rides to custody for another crime."

"And suppose he could save his own skin by betraying his brother, what then, Mary Yellan? There is a consideration for you."

Mary started. This was a new possibility, and for a moment she clutched at the straw. But the vicar of Altarnun must have read her thoughts, for, glancing up at him for confirmation of her hopes, she saw him smile, the thin line of his mouth breaking for a moment out of passivity, as though his face were a mask and the mask had cracked. She looked away, uncomfortable, feeling like one who stumbles unawares upon a sight forbidden.

"That would be a relief to you and to him, no doubt," continued the vicar, "if he had never been involved. But there is always the doubt, isn't there? And neither you nor I know the answer to that question. A guilty man does not usually tie the rope around his own neck."

Mary made a helpless movement with her hands, and he must have seen the despair in her face, for his voice became gentle again that had been harsh hitherto, and he laid his hand on her knee. "Our bright days are done, and we are for the dark," he said softly. "If it were permitted to take our text from Shakespeare, there would be strange sermons preached in Cornwall tomorrow, Mary Yellan. Your uncle and his companions are not members of my congregation, however, and if they were they would not understand me. You shake your head at me. I speak in riddles. 'This man is no comforter,' you say; 'he is a freak with his white hair and eyes.' Don't turn away; I know what you think. I will tell you one thing for consolation, and you can make of it what you will. A week from now will bring the New Year. The false lights have flickered for the last time, and there will be no more wrecks; the candles will be blown."

"I don't understand you," said Mary. "How do you know this, and what has the New Year to do with it?"

He took his hand from her and began to fasten his coat preparatory to departure. He lifted the sash of the window and called to the driver to rein in his horse, and the cold

158

air rushed into the carriage with a sting of frozen rain. "I return tonight from a meeting in Launceston," he said, "which was but a sequel to many other similar meetings during the past few years. And those of us present were informed at last that His Majesty's Government were prepared to take certain steps during the coming year to patrol the coasts of His Majesty's country. There will be watchers on the cliffs instead of flares, and the paths known only at present to men like your uncle and his companions will be trodden by officers of the law.

"There will be a chain across England, Mary, that will be very hard to break. Now do you understand?" He opened the door of the carriage and stepped out into the road. He bared his head under the rain, and she saw the thick white hair frame his face like a halo. He smiled again to her and bowed, and he reached for her hand once more and held it a moment. "Your troubles are over," he said; "the waggon wheels will rust and the barred room at the end of the passage can be turned into a parlour. Your aunt will sleep in peace again, and your uncle will either drink himself to death and be a riddance to all of you, or he will turn Wesleyan and preach to travellers on the highroad. As for you, you will ride south again and find a lover. Sleep well tonight. Tomorrow is Christmas Day, and the bells at Altarnun will be ringing for peace and good will. I shall think of you." He waved his hand to the driver, and the carriage went on without him.

Mary leant out of the window to call to him, but he had turned to the right down one of the five lanes and was already lost to sight.

The carriage rattled on along the Bodmin road. There were still three miles to cover before the tall chimneys of Jamaica Inn broke upon the skyline, and those miles were the wildest and the most exposed of all the long one-and-twenty that stretched between the two towns.

Mary wished now that she had gone with Francis Davey. She would not hear the wind in Altarnun, and the rain would fall silently in the sheltered lane. Tomorrow she could have knelt in the church and prayed for the first time since leaving Helford. If what he said was true, then there would be cause for rejoicing after all, and there would be some sense in giving thanks. The day of the wrecker was over; he would be broken by the new law, he and his kind; they would be blotted out and razed from the countryside as the pirates had been twenty, thirty years ago; and there would be no memory of them any more, no record left to poison the minds of those who should come after. A new generation would be born who had never heard their name. Ships would come to England without fear; there would be no harvest with the tide. Coves that had sounded once with the crunch of footsteps on shingle and the whispered voices of men would be silent again, and the scream that broke upon the silence would be the scream of a gull. Beneath the placid surface of the sea, on the ocean bed, lay skulls without a name, green coins that had once been gold, and the old bones of ships: they would be forgotten for ever more. The terror they had known died with them. It was the dawn of a new age, when men and women would travel without fear, and the land would belong to them. Here, on this stretch of moor, farmers would till their plot of soil and stack the sods of turf to dry under the sun as they did today, but the shadow that had been upon them would have vanished. Perhaps the grass would grow and the heather bloom again where Jamaica Inn had stood.

She sat in the corner of the carriage, with the vision of the new world before her; and through the open window, travelling down upon the wind, she heard a shot ring out in the silence of the night, and a distant shout, and a cry. The voices of men came out of the darkness, and the padding of feet upon the road. She leant out of the window, the rain blowing in on her face, and she heard the driver of the carriage call out in fear as his horse shied and stumbled. The road rose steeply from the valley, winding away to the top of the hill, and there in the distance were the lean chimneys of Jamaica Inn crowning the skyline like a gallows. Down the road came a company of men, led by one who leapt like a hare and tossed a lantern before him as he ran.

hours' time. We'll waste no more of it here. Get your horse, Harry, and put him in the traces here; the carriage will carry half a dozen of us. And bring the pony and the farm cart from the stable; he's had no work for a week. Come on, you lazy drunken devils, don't you want to feel gold and silver run through your hands? I've lain like a hog for seven crazy days, and by God, I feel like a child tonight and I want the coast again. Who'll take the road with me through Camelford?"

A shout rose from a dozen voices, and hands were thrust into the air. One fellow burst into a snatch of song, waving a bottle over his head, reeling on his feet as he stood; then he staggered and fell, crumpling onto his face in the ditch. The pedlar kicked him as he lay, and he did not stir; and, snatching the bridle of the horse, he dragged the animal forward, urging him with blows and cries to the steep hill, while the wheels of the carriage passed over the body of the fallen man, who, kicking for an instant like a wounded hare, struggled from the mud with a scream of terror and pain, and then lay still.

The men turned with the carriage and followed it, the sound of their running feet pattering along the highroad, and Joss Merlyn stood for a moment looking down upon Mary with a foolish drunken smile; then on a sudden impulse he caught her in his arms and pulled her towards the carriage, wrenching the door once more. He threw her onto the seat in the corner, and then, leaning out of the window, he yelled to the pedlar to whip the horse up the hill.

His cry was echoed by the men who ran beside him, and some of them leapt onto the step and clung to the window, while others mounted the driver's empty seat and rained at the horse with sticks and a shower of stones.

The animal quivered, sweating with fear; and he topped the hill at a gallop, with half a dozen madmen clinging to the reins and screaming at his heels.

Jamaica Inn was ablaze with light; the doors were open, and the windows were unbarred. The house gaped out of the night like a live thing.

The landlord placed his hand over Mary's mouth and forced her back against the side of the carriage. "You'd inform against me, would you?" he said. "You'd run to the law and have me swinging on a rope's end like a cat? All right, then, you shall have your chance. You shall stand on the shore, Mary, with the wind and the sea in your face, and you shall watch for the dawn and the coming in of the tide. You know what that means, don't you? You know where I'm going to take you?"

She stared back at him in horror; the colour drained from her face, and she tried to speak to him, but his hands forbade her.

"You think you're not afraid of me, don't you?" he said. "You sneer at me with your pretty white face and your monkey eyes. Yes, I'm drunk; I'm drunk as a king, and heaven and earth can smash for all I care. Tonight we shall ride in glory, every man jack of us, maybe for the last time; and you shall come with us, Mary; to the coast. . . ."

He turned away from her, shouting to his companions, and the horse, startled by his cry, started forward again in his stride, dragging the carriage behind him; and the lights of Jamaica Inn vanished in the darkness.

Chapter 11

IT WAS a nightmare journey of two hours or more to the coast, and Mary, bruised and shaken by her rough handling, lay exhausted in the corner of the carriage, caring little what became of her. Harry the pedlar and two other men had climbed in beside her uncle, and the air became foul at once with the stink of tobacco and stale drink and the smell of their bodies.

The landlord had worked himself and his companions into a state of wild excitement, and the presence of a woman amongst them brought a vicious tang to their enjoyment, her weakness and distress acting pleasurably upon them.

At first they talked at her and for her, laughing and singing to win her notice, Harry the pedlar bursting into his lewd songs, which rang with immoderate force in such close quarters and brought howls of appreciation from his audience, stimulating them to greater excitement.

They watched for the effect upon her face, hoping that she would show some sign of shame or discomfort, but Mary was too tired now for any word or song to penetrate her. She heard their voices through a haze of exhaustion; she was aware of her uncle's elbow thrust in her side, bringing another dull ache to add to her pains, and with throbbing head and smarting eyes she saw a sea of grinning faces through the smoke. What they said or did hardly mattered to her any more, and the longing for sleep and forgetfulness became a torment.

When they saw how lifeless she was, and dull, her presence lost its flavour; even the songs lost sting, and Joss Merlyn fumbled in his pocket and produced a pack of cards. They turned from her at once to this new interest, and, in the momentary lull that blessed her, Mary shrank closer in her corner, away from the hot, animal smell of her uncle, and, closing her eyes, she resigned herself to the movement of the swaying, jolting carriage. Her fatigue was such that full consciousness was no longer part of her; she was swinging in a trance land across the border. She was aware of pain, and the rocking carriage wheels, and in the far distance a murmur of voices; but these things moved away from her and not with her; she could not identify them with her own existence. Darkness came upon her like a boon from heaven, and she felt herself slip away into it; and so was lost. Time had nothing to do with her then. It was the cessation of movement that dragged her back to the world; the sudden stillness, and the cold damp air blowing upon her face through the open carriage window.

She was alone in her corner. The men had gone, taking

their light with them. She sat motionless at first, fearing to bring them back and uncertain what had befallen her; and then, when she leant forward to the window, the pain and stiffness in her body were intolerable. A weal of pain ran across her shoulders where the cold had numbed her, and her bodice was still damp from the rain that had soaked her early in the evening. She waited a moment and then leant forward again. It was still blowing hard, but the driving rain had ceased, and only a thin cold mizzle pattered against the window. The carriage had been abandoned in a narrow gullyway with high banks on either side, and the horse had been taken from the traces. The gully appeared to descend sharply, the path becoming rough and broken. Mary could not see more than a few yards in front of her. The night had thickened considerably, and in the gullyway it was black like a pit. There were no stars now in the sky, and the sharp wind of the moors had become a boisterous thing of noise and bluster, trailing a wet fog for company. Mary put her hand out of the window and touched the bank. Her fingers came upon loose sand and stems of grass, sodden through with the rain. She tried the handle of the door, but it was locked. Then she listened intently. Her eyes strained to pierce the darkness ahead of her, down the sharp descent of the gullyway, and borne up to her on the wind came a sound at once sullen and familiar, a sound that for the first time in her life she could not welcome, but must recognize with a leap of her heart and a shiver of foreboding.

It was the sound of the sea. The gully was a pathway to the shore.

She knew now why a softness had crept upon the air, and why the mizzle of rain fell on her hand lightly, with a tang of salt. The high banks gave a false feeling of shelter in contrast to the bleak wilderness of the moors, but once away from their deceptive shadow the illusion would be lost and the tearing gale cry louder than before. There could be no stillness where the sea broke upon the rockbound shore. She heard it again now, and continually; a murmur and a sigh as the spent water gave itself to the strand and withdrew reluctantly, and then a pause as the sea gathered itself for a renewal of effort—a momentary fragment in time—and then once more the thunder and the crash of fulfilment, the roar of surf upon shingle and the screaming scatter of stones as they followed the drag of the sea. Mary shuddered; somewhere in the darkness below, her uncle and his companions waited for the tide. If she could have heard some sound of them, the waiting in the empty carriage would have been more bearable. The wild shouting, the laughter, and the singing with which they had fortified themselves for the journey would have been a relief, however loathsome; but this deadly quietude was sinister. Business had sobered them, and they had found work for their hands. Now that her senses were her own again, and her first fatigue cast aside, Mary found inactivity impossible. She considered the size of the window. The door was locked, as she knew, but with straining and wriggling she might yet attempt to squeeze her body through the narrow frame.

The endeavour was worth the risk. Whatever happened tonight, her own life could be counted of little value; her uncle and his companions could find her and kill her if they wished. This country was known to them, and not to her. They could trace her in a moment if they wanted, like a pack of hounds. She worked and strained at the window, leaning backwards through the gap, the effort made even more difficult because of her stiff shoulder and her back. The roof of the carriage was slippery and wet, giving no grip to her fingers, but she struggled and pushed through the gap, and then, with a sickening squeeze and pressure, her hips were through, the frame of the window scraping the flesh and turning her faint. She lost foothold and balance, and fell backwards through the window to the ground below.

The drop was nothing; but the fall shook her, and she felt a little trickle of blood run down her side where the window had caught her. She gave herself a moment to recover, and then she dragged herself to her feet and began to creep uncertainly up the lane, in the dark shelter of the bank. She had not yet formed a plan in her head, but, with her back turned away from the gully and the sea, she would be putting distance between herself and her late companions. There was little doubt that they had descended to the shore. This lane, winding upwards and to the left, would take her at least to the high ground of the cliffs, where in spite of the darkness she would be able to make something of the land. Somewhere there would be a road—the carriage itself must have travelled by one; and if there was a road there would be dwelling houses before long; there would be honest men and women to whom she could tell her tale, and who would rouse the countryside when they heard her story.

She felt her way along the narrow ditch, stumbling now and again over the stones, her hair blowing into her eyes and troubling her, and, coming suddenly round the sharp corner of the bank, she put up her hands to screw back the loose strands from her eyes, and because of this she did not see the humped figure of a man kneeling in the ditch with his back towards her, his eyes watchful of the winding lane ahead. She came against him, knocking the breath from her body, and he, taken by surprise, fell with her, crying out in mingled terror and rage, smashing at her with his clenched fist.

They fought on the ground, she straining away from him, her hands tearing at his face, but in a moment he was too strong for her, and, rolling her over on her side, he twisted his hands in her hair, pulling at the roots, until the pain forced her to stillness. He leant on her, breathing heavily, for the fall had winded him, and then he peered closely at her, his gaping mouth showing yellow broken teeth.

It was Harry the pedlar. Mary lay motionless; the first move should come from him; and meanwhile she cursed herself for a fool in blundering up the lane the way she had, with never a thought of the outpost that even a child at play would have placed in his position.

He expected her to cry or struggle, but when she did neither he shifted his weight to his elbow and smiled at her slyly, jerking his head in the direction of the shore. "Didn't think to see me, did you?" he said. "Thought I was down on the shore with the landlord and the rest, baiting the pots. And so you woke up from your beauty sleep and took a walk up the lane. And now you're here I'll make you very welcome." He grinned at her, touching her cheek with a black fingernail. "It's been cold and damp in the ditch," he said, "but that's no odds now. They'll be hours down there yet. I can see you've turned against Joss, by the way you spoke to him tonight. He's no right to keep you up at Jamaica like a bird in a cage, with no pretty things to wear. I doubt if he's given you as much as a brooch for your bodice, has he? Don't you mind about that. I'll give you lace for your neck, and bangles for your wrist, and soft silk for your skin. Let's look now. . . ."

He nodded at her, reassuring her, smiling still, smirking and sly, and she felt his furtive hand fasten itself upon her. She moved swiftly, lashing out at him, and her fist caught him underneath the chin, shutting his mouth like a trap, with his tongue caught between his teeth. He squealed like a rabbit, and she struck him again, but this time he grabbed at her and lurched sideways upon her, all pretense of gentle persuasion gone, his strength horrible, his face drained of all colour. He was fighting now for possession, and she knew it, and, aware that his strength was greater than hers and must prevail in the end, she lay limp suddenly, to deceive him, giving him the advantage for the moment. He grunted in triumph, relaxing his weight, which was what she intended, and as he moved his position and lowered his head she jabbed at him swiftly with the full force of her knee, at the same time thrusting her fingers in his eyes. He doubled up at once, rolling onto his side in agony, and in a second she had struggled from under him and pulled herself to her feet, kicking at him once more as he rocked defenceless, his hands clasped to his belly. She grabbed in the ditch for a stone to fling at him, finding nothing but loose earth and sand, and she dug handfuls of this, scattering it in his face and in his eyes, so that he was blinded momentarily and could make no return. Then she turned again and began to run like a hunted thing up the twisting lane, her mouth open, her hands outstretched, tripping and stumbling over the ruts in the path; and when she heard his shout behind her once more, and the padding of his feet, a sense of panic swamped her reason and she started to climb up the high bank that bordered the lane, her foot slipping at every step in the soft earth, until with the very madness of effort born in terror she reached the top, and crawled, sobbing, through a gap in the thorn hedge that bordered the bank. Her face and her hands were bleeding, but she had no thought for this and ran along the cliff away from the lane, over tussocks of grass and humped uneven ground, all sense of direction gone from her, her one idea to escape from the thing that was Harry the pedlar.

A wall of fog closed in upon her, obscuring the distant line of hedge for which she had been making, and she stopped at once in her headlong rush, aware of the danger of sea mist, and how in its deception it might bring her back to the lane again. She fell at once upon hands and knees, and crawled slowly forward, her eyes low to the ground, following a narrow sandy track that wound in the direction she wished to take. Her progress was slow, but instinct told her that the distance was increasing between her and the pedlar, which was the only thing that mattered. She had no reckoning of time; it was three, perhaps four, in the morning, and the darkness would give no sign of breaking for many hours to come. Once more the rain came down through the curtain of mist, and it seemed as though she could hear the sea on every side of her and there were no escape from it; the breakers were muffled no longer; they were louder and clearer than before. She realized that the wind had been no guide to direction, for even now, with it behind her, it might have shifted a point or two, and with her ignorance of the coastline she had not turned east, as she had meant to do, but was even now upon the brink of a sagging cliff path that, judging by the sound of the sea, was taking her straight to the shore. The breakers, though she could not see them because of the fog, were somewhere beyond her in the darkness, and to her dismay she sensed they were on a level with her, and not beneath her. This meant that the cliffs here descended abruptly to the shore, and, instead of a long and tortuous path to a cove that she had pictured from the abandoned carriage, the gullyway must have been only a few yards from the sea itself. The banks of the gully had muffled the sound of the breakers. Even as she decided this, there was a gap in the mist ahead of her, showing a patch of sky. She crawled on uncertainly, the path widening and the fog clearing, and the wind veered in her face once more; and there she knelt amongst driftwood and seaweed and loose shingle, on a narrow strand, with the land sloping up on either side of her, while not fifty yards away, and directly in front of her, were the high combing seas breaking upon the shore.

After a while, when her eyes had accustomed themselves to the shadows, she made them out, huddled against a jagged rock that broke up the expanse of the beach: a little knot of men, grouped together for warmth and shelter, silently peering ahead of them into the darkness. Their very stillness made them the more menacing who had not been still before; and the attitude of stealth, the poise of their bodies, crouched as they were against the rock, the tense watchfulness of their heads turned one and all to the incoming sea, was a sight at once fearful and pregnant with danger.

Had they shouted and sung, called to one another, and made the night hideous with their clamour, their heavy boots resounding on the crunching shingle, it would have been in keeping with their character and with what she expected; but there was something ominous in this silence, which suggested that the crisis of the night had come upon them. A little jutting piece of rock stood between Mary and the bare exposed beach, and beyond this she dared not venture for fear of betraying herself. She crawled as far as the rock and lay down on the shingle behind it, while ahead of her, directly in her line of vision when she moved her head, stood her uncle and his companions, with their backs turned to her.

She waited. They did not move. There was no sound. Only the sea broke in its inevitable monotony upon the shore, sweeping the strand and returning again, the line of breakers showing thin and white against the black night.

The mist began to lift very slowly, disclosing the narrow outline of the bay. Rocks became more prominent, and the cliffs took on solidity. The expanse of water widened, opening from a gulf to a bare line of shore that stretched away interminably. To the right, in the distance, where the highest part of the cliff sloped to the sea, Mary made out a faint pinprick of light. At first she thought it a star, piercing the last curtain of dissolving mist, but reason told her that no star was white, nor ever swayed with the wind on the surface of a cliff. She watched it intently, and it moved again; it was like a small white eye in the darkness. It danced and curtseyed, storm tossed, as though kindled and carried by the wind itself, a living flare that would not be blown. The group of men on the shingle below heeded it not; their eyes were turned to the dark sea beyond the breakers.

And suddenly Mary was aware of the reason for their indifference, and the small white eye that had seemed at first a thing of friendliness and comfort, winking bravely alone in the wild night, became a symbol of horror.

The star was a false light placed there by her uncle and his companions. The pinprick gleam was evil now, and the curtsey to the wind became a mockery. In her imagination the light burnt fiercer, extending its beam to dominate the cliff, and the colour was white no more, but old and yellow like a scab. Someone watched by the light so that it should not be extinguished. She saw a dark figure pass in front of it, obscuring the gleam for a moment, and then it burnt clear again. The figure became a blot against the grey face of the cliff, moving quickly in the direction of the shore. Whoever it was climbed down the slope to his companions on the shingle. His action was hurried, as though time pressed him, and he was careless in the manner of his coming for the loose earth and stones slid away from under him, scattering down onto the beach below. The sound startled the men beneath, and for the first time since Mary had watched them they withdrew their attention from the incoming tide and looked up to him. Mary saw him put his hands to his mouth and shout, but his words were caught up in the wind and did not come to her. They reached the little group of men waiting on the shingle, who broke up at once in some excitement, some of them starting halfway up the cliff to meet him; but when he shouted again and pointed to the sea, they ran down towards the breakers, their stealth and silence gone for the moment, the sound of their footsteps heavy on the shingle, their voices topping one another above the crash of the sea. Then one of them —her uncle it was; she recognized his great loping stride and massive shoulders—held up his hand for silence; and they waited, all of them, standing upon the shingle with the waves breaking beyond their feet; spread out in a thin line they were, like crows, their black forms outlined against the white beach. Mary watched with them; and out of the mist and darkness came another pinprick of light in answer to the first. This new light did not dance and waver as the one on the cliff had done; it dipped low and was hidden, like a traveller weary of his burden, and then it would rise again, pointing high to the sky, a hand flung into the night in a last and desperate attempt to break the wall of mist that hitherto had defied penetration. The new light drew nearer to the first. The one compelled the other. Soon they would merge and become two white eyes in the darkness. And still the men crouched motionless upon the narrow strand, waiting for the lights to close with one another.

The second light dipped again; and now Mary could see the shadowed outline of a hull, the black spars like fingers spreading above it, while a white surging sea combed beneath the hull, and hissed, and withdrew again. Closer drew the mast light to the flare upon the cliff, fascinated and held, like a moth coming to a candle.

Mary could bear no more. She scrambled to her feet and ran down upon the beach, shouting and crying, waving her hands above her head, pitting her voice against the wind and the sea, which tossed it back to her in mockery. Someone caught hold of her and forced her down upon the beach. Hands stifled her. She was trodden upon and kicked. Her cries died away, smothered by the coarse sacking that choked her, and her arms were dragged behind her back and knotted together, the rough cord searing her flesh.

They left her then, with her face in the shingle, the breakers sweeping towards her not twenty yards away; and as she lay there helpless, the breath knocked from her and her scream of warning strangled in her throat, she heard the cry that had been hers become the cry of others, and fill the air with sound. The cry rose above the searing smash of the sea and was seized and carried by the wind itself; and with the cry came the tearing splinter of wood, the horrible impact of a massive live thing finding resistance, the shuddering groan of twisting, breaking timber.

Drawn by a magnet, the sea hissed away from the strand, and a breaker running high above its fellows flung itself with a crash of thunder upon the lurching ship. Mary saw the black mass that had been a vessel roll slowly upon its side, like a great flat turtle; the masts and spars were threads of cotton, crumpled and fallen. Clinging to the slippery, sloping surface of the turtle were little black dots that would not be thrown; that stuck themselves fast to the splintering wood like limpets; and, when the heaving, shuddering mass beneath them broke monstrously in two, cleaving the air, they fell one by one into the white tongues of the sea, little black dots without life or substance.

A deadly sickness came upon Mary, and she closed her eyes, her face pressed into the shingle. The silence and the stealth were gone; the men who had waited during the cold hours waited no more. They ran like madmen hither and thither upon the beach, yelling and screaming, demented and inhuman. They waded waist deep into the breakers, careless of danger, all caution spent; snatching at the bobbing, sodden wreckage borne in on the surging tide.

They were animals, fighting and snarling over lengths of splintered wood; they stripped, some of them, and ran naked in the cold December night, the better to fight their way into the sea and plunge their hands amongst the spoil that the breakers tossed to them. They chattered and squabbled like monkeys, tearing things from one another; and one of them kindled a fire in the corner by the cliff, the flame burning strong and fierce in spite of the mizzling rain. The spoils of the sea were dragged up the beach and heaped beside it. The fire cast a ghastly light upon the beach, throwing a yellow brightness that had been black before, and casting long shadows down the beach where the men ran backwards and forwards, industrious and horrible.

When the first body was washed ashore, mercifully spent and gone, they clustered around it, diving amongst the remains with questing, groping hands, picking it clean as a bone; and, when they had stripped it bare, tearing even at the smashed fingers in search of rings, they abandoned it again, leaving it to loll upon its back in the scum where the tide had been.

Whatever had been the practice hitherto, there was no method in their work tonight. They robbed haphazard, each man for himself; crazy they were and drunk, mazed with this success they had not planned—dogs snapping at the heel of their master whose venture had proved a triumph, whose power this was, whose glory. They followed him where he ran naked amongst the breakers, the water streaming from the hair on his body, a giant above them all.

The tide turned, the water receded, and a new chill came upon the air. The light that swung above them on the cliff, still dancing in the wind, like an old mocking man whose joke has long been played, turned pallid now and dim. A grey colour came upon the water and was answered by the sky. At first the men did not notice the change; they were delirious still, intent upon their prey. And then Joss Merlyn himself lifted his great head and sniffed the air, turning about him as he stood, watching the clear contour of the cliffs as the darkness slipped away; and he shouted suddenly, calling the men to silence, pointing to the sky that was leaden now and pale.

They hesitated, glancing once more at the wreckage that surged and fell in the trough of the sea, unclaimed as yet and waiting to be salved; and then they turned with one accord and began to run up the beach towards the entrance of the gully, silent once more, without words or gesture, their faces grey and scared in the broadening light. They had outstayed their time. Success had made them careless. The dawn had broken upon them unawares, and by lingering overlong they had risked the accusation which daylight would bring to them. The world was waking up around them; night, that had been their ally, covered them no more.

It was Joss Merlyn who pulled the sacking away from her mouth and jerked Mary to her feet. Seeing that her weakness had become part of her now, and could not be withstood, for she could neither stand alone nor help herself in any way, he cursed her furiously, glancing behind him at the cliffs that every minute became harder, more distinct; and then he bent down to her, for she had stumbled to the ground again, and threw her over his shoulder as he would a sack. Her head lolled without support, her arms lifeless, and she felt his hands pressing into her scarred side, bruising it once again, rubbing the numb flesh that had lain upon the shingle. He ran with her up the strand to the entrance of the gully; and his companions caught up already in a mesh of panic, flung the remnants of spoil they had snatched from the beach upon the backs of the three horses tethered there. Their movements were feverish and clumsy, and they worked without direction, as though unhinged, lacking all sense of order; while the landlord, sober now from necessity and strangely ineffectual, cursed and bullied them to no avail. The carriage, stuck in the bank halfway up the gully, resisted their efforts to extract it, and this sudden reverse to their fortune increased the panic and stampede. Some of them began to scatter up the lane, forgetting everything in a blind concentration on personal safety. Dawn was their enemy, and more easily withstood alone, in the comparative security of ditch and hedge, than in the company of five or six upon the road. Suspicion would lie in numbers here on the coast, where every face was known and strangers were remarkable; but a poacher, or tramp, or gypsy could make his way alone, finding his own cover and his own path. These deserters were cursed by those who remained, struggling with the carriage, and now, through stupidity and panic, the vehicle was wrenched from the bank in so rough a manner that it overturned, falling upon one side and smashing a wheel.

This final disaster let loose pandemonium in the gullyway. There was a wild rush to the remaining farm cart that had been left further up the lane, and to the already over-burdened horses. Someone, still obedient to the leader and with a sense of necessity, put fire to the broken carriage, whose presence in the lane screamed danger to them all, and the riot that followed—fight between man and man for the possession of the farm cart that might yet carry them away inland—was a hideous scrap of tooth and nail, of teeth smashed by stones, of eyes cut open by broken glass.

Those who carried pistols now had the advantage, and the landlord, with his remaining ally Harry the pedlar by his side, stood with his back to the cart and let fly amongst the rabble, who, in the sudden terror of pursuit that would follow with the day, looked upon him now as an enemy, a false leader who had brought them to destruction. The first shot went wide and stubbed the soft bank opposite; but it gave one of the opponents a chance to cut the landlord's eye open with a jagged flint. Joss Merlyn marked his assailant with his second shot, spattering him in mid-stomach, and while the fellow doubled up in the mud amongst his companions, mortally wounded and screaming like a hare, Harry the pedlar caught another in the throat, the bullet ripping the windpipe, the blood spouting jets like a fountain.

It was the blood that won the cart for the landlord; for the remaining rebels, hysterical and lost at the sight of their dying fellows, turned as one man and scuttled like crabs up the twisting lane, intent only on putting a safe distance between themselves and their late leader. The landlord leant against the cart with smoking, murderous pistol, the blood running freely from the cut on his eye. Now that they were alone, he and the pedlar wasted little time. What wreckage had been salved and brought to the gully they threw upon the cart beside Mary—miscellaneous odds and ends, useless and unprofitable, the main store still down on the beach and washed by the tide. They dared not risk the fetching of it, for that would be the work of a dozen men, and already the light of day had followed the early dawn and made clear the countryside. There was not a moment to spare.

The two men who had been shot sprawled in the lane beside the cart. Whether they still breathed or not was not a matter to be discussed; their bodies bore witness, and must be destroyed. It was Harry the pedlar who dragged them to the fire. It burnt well; much of the carriage was already consumed, while one red wheel stuck out above the charred and splintered wood.

Joss Merlyn led the remaining horse to the traces, and without a word the two men climbed into the cart and jerked the horse to action.

Lying on her back in the cart, Mary watched the low clouds pass across the sky. Darkness had gone; the morning was damp and grey. She could still hear the sound of the sea, more distant and less insistent, a sea that had spent its full fury and now let itself be carried by the tide.

The wind had dropped too; the tall stems of grass on the banks above the gully were still, and a silence had come upon the coast. There was a smell in the air of damp earth and turnips, of a mist that had lain overnight upon the land. The clouds became one with the grey sky. Once again a thin mizzle of rain fell upon Mary's face and upon her upturned hands.

The wheels of the cart crunched the uneven lane, and, turning right, came out upon a smoother surface of gravel that was a road, running northwards between low hedges. From far away, across many fields and scattered plough-lands, came the merry peal of bells, odd and discordant, in the morning air.

She remembered suddenly that it was Christmas Day.

Chapter 12

THE SQUARE pane of glass was familiar to her. It was larger
than the carriage window and had a ledge before it, and
there was a crack across the pane that she remembered well.
She kept her eyes upon it, struggling with memory, and she
wondered why she no longer felt the rain on her face and
the steady current of wind. There was no movement under
her, and her first thought was that the carriage had come
to a standstill, thrust against the bank in the gullyway once
more, and that circumstance and fate would compel her to
react in frightful repetition the things she had already per-
formed. When she climbed through the window she would
fall and bruise herself, and, heading yet again up the twisting lane, would come upon Harry the pedlar, squatting in
his ditch; but this time she would not have the strength to
withstand him. Down on the shingle strand the men waited
for the tide, and the great black turtle of a ship rolled
flat and monstrous in the trough of the sea. Mary moaned
and turned her head restlessly from side to side; out of
the tail of her eye she saw the brown discoloured wall beside her, and the rusty nailhead where a text had once been
hung.

She was lying in her bedroom at Jamaica Inn.

The sight of this room she hated, however cold it was
and drear, was at least protection from the wind and the
rain and from the hands of Harry the pedlar. Nor could
she hear the sea. The roar of surf would not disturb her
again. If Death came now, he would be an ally; existence
was not a thing she welcomed any more. Life had been
crushed from her, anyway, and the body lying on the bed

did not belong to her. She had no wish to live. Shock had made a dummy of her and taken away her strength; tears of self-pity welled into her eyes.

Now there was a face bending down to her, and she shrank back against the pillow, her hands thrust outward and protesting; for the puffy mouth and broken teeth of the pedlar were ever in her mind.

Her hands were held gently, though, and the eyes that peered at her, red rimmed like her own from weeping, were tremulous and blue.

It was Aunt Patience. They clung to one another, seeking comfort in proximity; and after Mary had wept awhile, easing herself of sorrow and allowing the tide of emotion to carry her to the limit, nature took command of her again and she was strengthened, something of the old courage and force coming back to her again.

"You know what has happened?" she asked, and Aunt Patience held her hands tightly, so that they could not be withdrawn, the blue eyes begging dumbly for forgiveness, like an animal punished through no fault of his own.

"How long have I lain here?" Mary questioned, and she was told that this was the second day. For a moment or two Mary was silent, considering the information, new to her and sudden; two days was a long time to one who but a few moments ago had watched the dawn break on the coast.

Much could happen in that time, and she had been on her bed here, helpless.

"You should have woken me," she said roughly, pushing away the hands that clung to her. "I'm not a child, to be mothered and pampered because of a few bruises. There's work for me to do; you don't understand."

Aunt Patience stroked her, the caress timid and ineffectual.

"You could not move," she whimpered. "Your poor body was bleeding and broken. I bathed you while you were still unconscious; I thought at first they had injured you terribly, but thank the dear God no real harm has come to you. Your bruises will heal, and your long sleep has rested you."

"You know who did it, don't you? You know where they took me?"

Bitterness had made her cruel. She knew that the words acted like a lash, and she could not stop herself. She began to talk about the men on the shore. Now it was the elder woman's turn to whimper, and when Mary saw the thin mouth working, the vapid blue eyes stare back at her in terror, she became sickened of herself and could not continue. She sat up in bed and swung her legs to the floor, her head swimming with the effort, her temples throbbing.

"What are you going to do?" Aunt Patience pulled at her nervously, but her niece shook her aside and began to drag on her clothes.

"I have business of my own," she said curtly.

"Your uncle is below. He will not let you leave the inn."

"I'm not afraid of him."

"Mary, for your sake, for my sake, do not anger him again. You know what you have suffered already. Ever since he returned with you he has sat below, white and terrible, a gun across his knees; the doors of the inn are barred. I know you have seen and endured horrible, unspeakable things; but, Mary, don't you understand if you go down now he may hurt you again—he may even kill you? . . . I have never seen him like this. I can't answer for his mood. Don't go down, Mary. I beg you on my knees not to go down."

She began to drag on the floor, clutching at Mary's skirt, clasping at her hands and kissing them. The sight was miserable, unnerving.

"Aunt Patience, I have gone through enough out of loyalty to you. You can't expect me to stand any more. Whatever Uncle Joss may have been to you once, he is inhuman now. All your tears won't save him from justice; you must realize that. He's a brute, half mad with brandy and blood. Men were murdered by him on the shore; don't you understand? Men were drowned in the sea. I can see nothing else. I shall think of nothing else to my dying day."

Her voice rose, dangerously high; hysteria was not far away. She was still too weak for consecutive thought, and saw herself running out upon the highroad, crying loudly for the help that would surely be forthcoming.

Aunt Patience prayed too late for silence; the warning finger was unheeded. The door opened, and the landlord of Jamaica Inn stood on the threshold of the room. He stooped his head under the beam and stared at them. He looked haggard and grey; the cut above his eye was still a vivid scarlet. He was filthy and unwashed, and there were black shadows beneath his eyes.

"I thought I heard voices in the yard," he said. "I went to a chink in the shutters, downstairs in the parlour, but I saw no one. Did you hear anything, from this room?"

Nobody answered. Aunt Patience shook her head, the little nervous smile that she conjured for his presence trailing uneasily across her face without her knowledge. He sat down on the bed, his hands plucking at the clothes, his restless eyes roaming from the window to the door.

"He'll come," he said; "he's bound to come. I've cut my own throat; I've gone against him. He warned me once, and I laughed at him; I didn't listen. I wanted to play the game on my own. We're as good as dead, all three of us sitting here—you, Patience, and Mary, and I.

"We're finished, I tell you; the game is up. Why did you let me drink? Why didn't you break every blasted bottle in the house, and turn the key on me, and let me lie? I'd not have hurt you; I'd not have touched a hair of your heads, either of you. Now it's too late. The end has come."

He looked from one to the other of them, his bloodshot eyes hollow, his massive shoulders humped to his neck. They stared back at him without understanding, dumbfounded and awed at the expression on his face they had not seen before.

"What do you mean?" said Mary at length. "Who are you afraid of? Who warned you?"

He shook his head, and his hands strayed to his mouth, the fingers restless. "No," he said slowly, "I'm not drunk now, Mary Yellan; my secrets are still my own. But I'll tell you one thing—and there's no escape for you; you're in it now as much as Patience there—we have enemies on either side of us now. We have the law on one hand, and on the other—" He checked himself, the old cunning in his eyes once more as he glanced at Mary.

"You'd like to know, wouldn't you?" he said. "You'd like to sneak out of the house with the name on your lips and betray me. You'd like to see me hanged. All right, I don't blame you for it; I've hurt you enough to make you remember to the rest of your days, haven't I? But I saved you too, didn't I? Have you thought what that rabble would have done to you had I not been there?" He laughed and spat on the floor, something of his usual self returning to him. "You can put one good mark against me for that alone," he said. "Nobody touched you that night but myself, and I've not spoilt your pretty face. Cuts and bruises mend, don't they? Why, you poor weak thing, you know as well as I do I could have had you your first week at Jamaica Inn if I'd wanted you. You're a woman after all. Yes, by heaven, and you'd be lying at my feet now, like your Aunt Patience, crushed and contented and clinging, another God-damn bloody fool. Let's get out of here. The room stinks of damp and decay."

He shambled to his feet, dragging her after him into the passage, and, when they came onto the landing, he thrust her against the wall, beneath the candle stuck in the bracket, so that the light fell upon her bruised, cut face. He took her chin in his hands and held her for a moment, smoothing the scratches with delicate, light fingers. She stared back at him in loathing and disgust, the gentle, graceful hands reminding her of all she had lost and renounced; and, when he bent his hated face lower, indifferent of Patience, who stood beside him, and his mouth, so like his brother's, hovered an instant on hers, the illusion was horrible and complete; and she shuddered and closed her eyes. He blew out the light; they followed him down the stairs without a word, their footsteps pattering sharply through the empty house.

He led the way into the kitchen, where even there the door was bolted and the window barred. Two candles were on the table to light the room.

Then he turned and faced the two women, and, reaching

183

for a chair, he straddled his legs across it and considered them, fumbling in his pocket for his pipe meanwhile and filling it.

"We've got to think out a plan of campaign," he said; "we've been sitting here for nigh on two days now, like rats in a trap, waiting to be caught. And I've had enough, I tell you. I never could play that sort of game; it gives me the horrors. If there's going to be a scrap, then, by Almighty God, let's have it in the open." He puffed awhile at his pipe, staring moodily at the floor, tapping his foot on the stone flags.

"Harry's loyal enough," he continued, "but he'd split and have the house about our ears if he thought there'd be profit for himself. As for the rest—they're scattered over the countryside, whining, their tails between their legs, like a blasted pack of curs. This has scared 'em forever. Yes, and it's scared me too, you can know that. I'm sober now, all right; I can see the damn-fool unholy mess I've landed in, and we'll be lucky, all of us, if we get out of it without swinging. You, Mary, can laugh if you like, with your white, contemptuous face; it'll be as bad for you as for Patience and I. You're in it too, up to the neck; you'll not escape. Why didn't you turn the key on me, I say? Why didn't you stop me from drinking?"

His wife stole over to him and plucked at his jacket, passing her tongue over her lips in preparation for speech.

"Well, what is it?" he said fiercely.

"Why can't we creep away now, before it's too late?" she whispered. "The trap's in the stable; we'll be in Launceston and across to Devon in a few hours. We could travel by night; we could make for the eastern counties."

"You damned idiot!" he shouted. "Don't you realize there are people on the road between here and Launceston who think I'm the devil himself—who are only waiting their chance to fasten every crime in Cornwall on my head and get me? The whole country knows by now what happened on the coast on Christmas Eve, and if they see us bolting they'll have the proof. God, don't you think I haven't itched to get away and save my skin? Yes, and by doing so have every man in the country point his finger at us. We'd look fine, wouldn't we, riding in the trap on top of our goods and chattels, like farmers on market day, waving good-bye in Launceston square? No, we've got one chance, one single chance in a million. We've got to lie quiet; we've got to lie mum. If we sit here tight at Jamaica Inn they may start scratching their heads and rubbing their noses. They've got to look for proof, mind you. They've got to get the sworn proof before they lay hands on us. And unless one of that blasted rabble turns informer they won't get the proof.

"Oh yes, the ship's there, with her back broken on the rocks, and there's chunks of stuff lying on the beach—piles of it—ready to take away, put there by someone, they'll say. They'll ind two bodies, charred to cinders, and a heap of ashes. 'What's this?' they'll say. 'There's been a fire; there's been a scrap.' It'll look dirty, it'll look bad for many of us, but where's your proof? Answer me that. I spent my Christmas Eve like a respectable man, in the bosom of my family, playing cat's cradle and snapdragon with my niece." He put his tongue in his cheek and winked.

"You've forgotten one thing, haven't you?" said Mary.

"No, my dear, I have not. The driver of that carriage was shot, and he fell in the ditch, not a quarter of a mile down the road outside. You were hoping we'd left the body there, weren't you? Maybe it will shock you, Mary, but the body travelled with us to the coast, and it lies now, if I remember rightly, beneath a ten-foot bank of shingle. Of course, someone is going to miss him; I'm prepared for that; but as they'll never find his carriage it doesn't make much odds. Maybe he was tired of his wife and has driven to Penzance. They're welcome to look for him there. And now that we've both come to our senses again, you can tell me what you were doing in that carriage, Mary, and where you had been. If you don't answer me, you know me well enough by now. I can find a way of making you talk."

Mary glanced at her aunt. The woman was shivering like a frightened dog, her blue eyes fixed upon her husband's face. Mary thought rapidly. It was easy enough to lie; time was the all-important factor now and must be reckoned with and cherished if she and her aunt Patience were to come out of this alive. She must play upon it and give her uncle rope enough to hang himself. His confidence would go against him in the end. She had one hope of salvation, and he was near, not five miles away, waiting in Altarnun for a signal from her.

"I'll tell you my day, and you can believe it or not," she said; "it doesn't matter much to me what you think. I walked to Launceston on Christmas Eve and went to the fair. I was tired by eight o'clock, and when it came to rain and blow I was wet through and fit for nothing. I hired that carriage, and I told the man I wanted him to take me to Bodmin. I thought if I said the Jamaica Inn he would have refused the journey. There, I've nothing more to tell you than that."

"Were you alone in Launceston?"

"Of course I was alone."

"And you spoke to no one?"

"I bought a handkerchief from a woman at a stall."

Joss Merlyn spat on the floor. "All right," he said. "Whatever I did to you now, you'd tell the same story, wouldn't you? You've got the advantage for once, because I can't prove if you're lying or not. Not many maids your age would spend the day alone in Launceston, I can tell you that. Nor would they drive home by themselves. If your story's true, then our prospects improve. They'll never trace that driver here. God damn it, I shall feel like another drink in a moment."

He tilted back his chair and pulled at his pipe.

"You shall drive in your own coach yet, Patience," he said, "and wear feathers in your bonnet, and a velvet cloak. I'm not beaten yet. I'll see the whole band of 'em in hell first. You wait; we'll start afresh again, we'll live like fighting cocks. Maybe I'll turn sober and go to church on Sundays. And you, Mary, you shall hold my hand in my old age and spoon me my food."

He threw back his head and laughed; but his laugh broke short in the middle, his mouth shut like a trap, and he crashed his chair down on the floor again and stood up in the middle of the room, his body turned sideways, his face as white as a sheet. "Listen," he whispered hoarsely; "listen. . . ."

They followed the direction of his eyes, fastened as they were upon the chink of light that came through the narrow gap in the shutters.

Something was scraping gently at the kitchen window . . . tapping lightly, softly, scratching furtively at the pane of glass.

It was like the sound made by a branch of ivy when it has broken loose from the trunk and, bending downwards, teases a window or a porch, disturbed and restless with every breath of wind. But there was no ivy on the slate walls of Jamaica Inn, and the shutters were bare.

The scraping continued, persuasive and undaunted, tap . . . tap . . . like the drumming of a beak; tap . . . tap . . . like the four fingers of a hand

There was no other sound in the kitchen except the frightened breathing of Aunt Patience, whose hand crept out across the table to her niece. Mary watched the landlord as he stood motionless on the kitchen floor, his figure shadowed monstrously on the ceiling, and she saw his lips blue through the dark stubble of his beard. Then he bent forward, crouching on tiptoe like a cat, and, sliding his hand along the floor, his fingers fastened themselves upon his gun that stood against the further chair, never once taking his eyes from the chink of light between the shutters.

Mary swallowed, her throat dry as dust; whether the thing behind the window was friend or enemy to herself made the suspense more poignant, but in spite of her hopes the thumping of her heart told her that fear was infectious, as were the beads of perspiration on her uncle's face. Her hands wandered to her mouth, trembling and clammy.

For a moment he waited beside the closed shutters, and then he sprang forward, tearing at the hinge and pulling them apart, the grey light of afternoon slanting at once into the room. A man stood outside the window, his livid face pressed against the pane, his broken teeth gaping in an evil grin.

It was Harry the pedlar. . . . Joss Merlyn swore and threw

open the window. "God damn you, come inside, can't you?" he shouted. "Do you want a bullet in your guts, you blasted fool? You've had me here standing like a deaf-mute for five minutes, with my gun trained on your belly. Unbolt the door, Mary; don't lean against the wall there like a ghost. There's nerves enough in this house without you turning sour." Like all men who have been badly scared, he threw the blame of his own panic upon the shoulders of another and now blustered to reassure himself. Mary crossed slowly to the door. The sight of the pedlar brought back a vivid memory of her struggle in the lane, and reaction came swift upon her. Her nausea and disgust returned in force, and she could not look upon him. She opened the door without a word, screening herself behind it, and when he came into the kitchen she turned at once and went to the dull fire, piling the turf upon the embers mechanically, her back towards him. "Well, have you brought news?" questioned the landlord.

The pedlar smacked his lips in reply and jerked his thumb over his shoulder.

"The country's gone up in smoke," he said. "Every cluttering tongue in Cornwall, from the Tamar to St. Ives. I was in Bodmin this forenoon; the town was ringing with it, and they're hot mad for blood and justice too. Last night I slept at Camelford, every man jack in the place shaking his fist in the air and blabbing to his neighbour. There'll only be one end to this storm, Joss, and you know the name for it, don't you?"

He made a gesture with his hands across his throat.

"We've got to run for it," he said; "it's our only chance. The roads are poison, and Bodmin and Launceston worst of all. I'll keep to the moors, and get into Devon above Gunnislake; it'll take me longer, I know that, but what's the odds if you save your skin? Have you got a bite of bread in the house, missus? I've not touched food since yesterday forenoon."

He threw his question at the landlord's wife, but his glance fell upon Mary. Patience Merlyn fumbled in the cupboard for bread and cheese, her mouth working nervously, her movements clumsy, her mind anywhere but on her mission. As she laid the table she looked beseechingly at her husband.

"You hear what he says," she pleaded. "It's madness to stop here; we must go now, at once, before it's too late. You know what this means to the people; they will have no mercy on you; they'll kill you without trial. For God's sake, listen to him, Joss. You know I don't care for myself; it's for you. . . ."

"Shut your mouth, can't you?" thundered her husband. "I've never asked your counsel yet, and I don't ask it now. I can face what's coming to me alone, without you bleating beside me like a sheep. So you'll throw your hand in too, Harry, will you? Run with your tail between your legs because a lot of clerks and Wesleyans are howling to Jesus for your blood? Have they proved it on us? Tell me that. Or has your liver conscience gone against you?"

"Damn my conscience, Joss; it's common sense I'm thinking of. This part of the country has come unhealthy, and I'll go from it while I can. As to proof, we've sailed close enough to the wind these last months to be proof enough, haven't we? I've stuck to you, haven't I? Come out here today, risking my neck, to give you warning. I'm not saying anything against you, Joss, but it was your damned stupidity brought us into this mess, wasn't it? You got us mad drunk like yourself and led us to the shore, on a crazy harebrained venture that none of us had planned. We took a chance in a million, and the chance came off—too damned bloody well. Because we were drunk we lost our heads, left the stuff and a hundred tracks scattered on the shore. And whose fault was it? Why, yours, I say." He smashed his fist on the table, his yellow, impudent face thrust close to the landlord, a sneer on his cracked lips.

Joss Merlyn considered him for a moment, and when he spoke his voice was dangerous and low. "So you accuse me, do you, Harry?" he said. "You're like the rest of your kind, wriggling like a snake when the luck of the game turns against you. You've done well out of me, haven't you? Had gold to burn you never had before; lived like a prince all these months, instead of at the bottom of a mine, where

189

you belong. And supposing we'd kept our heads the other night, and cleared in order before dawn, as we've done a hundred times before? You'd be sucking up to me now to fill your pockets, wouldn't you? You'd be fawning on me with the rest of the sniffing curs, begging your share of the spoil, calling me God Almighty; you'd lick my boots and lie down in the dust. Run, then, if you like; run to the Tamar bank with your tail between your legs, and be damned to you! I'll take the world on alone."

The pedlar forced a laugh and shrugged his shoulders. "We can talk, can't we, without cutting each other's throats? I've not gone against you; I'm on your side still. We were all mad drunk on Christmas Eve, I know that; let's leave it alone then: what's done is done. Our lot is scattered, and we needn't reckon with them. They'll be too scared to show their heads and worry us. That leaves you and I, Joss. We've been in this business, the pair of us, deeper than most, I know that, and the more we help each other, the better it'll be for us both. Now then, that's why I'm here, to talk it over and see where we stand." He laughed again, showing his soft gums, and began to beat a tattoo on the table with his squat black fingers.

The landlord watched him coolly and reached once more for his pipe.

"Just what would you be driving at, Harry?" he said, leaning against the table and filling his pipe afresh.

The pedlar sucked his teeth and grinned. "I'm not driving at anything," he said. "I want to make things easier for all of us. We've got to quit, that's evident, unless we want to swing. But it's like this, Joss; I don't see the fun in quitting empty-handed, for all that. There's a mint of stuff we dumped along in the room yonder two days ago, from the shore. That's right, isn't it? And by rights it belongs to all of us who worked for it on Christmas Eve. But there's none of 'em left to claim it but you and I. I'm not saying there's much of value there—it's junk mostly, no doubt—but I don't see why some of it shouldn't help us into Devon, do you?"

The landlord blew a cloud of smoke into his face. "So you didn't came back to Jamaica Inn because of my sweet

190

smile alone, then?" he said. "I was thinking you were fond of me, Harry, and wanted to hold my hand."

The pedlar grinned again and shifted on his chair. "All right," he said; "we're friends, aren't we? There's no harm done in plain speaking. The stuff's there, and it'll take two men to shift it. The women here can't do it. What's against you and I striking a bargain, and be done with it?"

The landlord puffed thoughtfully at his pipe. "You're teeming with ideas, all strung out as pretty as the fancy trinkets on your tray, my friend. And supposing the stuff isn't there, after all? Supposing I've disposed of it already? I've been here kicking my heels for two days, you know, and the coaches pass my door. What then, Harry boy?"

The grin faded from the face of the pedlar, and he thrust out his jaw.

"What's the joke?" he snarled. "Do you play a double game up here at Jamaica Inn? You'll find it hasn't paid you, if you have. You've been mighty silent sometimes, Joss Merlyn, when cargoes were run and when we had the waggons on the road. I've seen things sometimes I haven't understood, and heard things too. You've made a brilliant job of this trade, month in, month out; too brilliant, some of us thought, for the small profit we made out of it, who took most of the risks. And we didn't ask you how you did it, did we? Listen here, Joss Merlyn: do you take your orders from one above you?"

The landlord was on him like a flash. He caught the pedlar on the point of the chin with his clenched fist, and the man went over backwards onto his head, the chair beneath him striking the stone flags with a crash. He recovered instantly and scrambled to his knees, but the landlord towered above him, the muzzle of his gun pointed at the pedlar's throat.

"Move, and you're a dead man," he said softly.

Harry the pedlar looked up at his assailant, his little mean eyes half closed, his puffy face yellow. The fall had winded him, and he breathed shortly. At the first sign of a struggle Aunt Patience had flattened herself against the wall, terror stricken, her eyes searching those of her niece

191

in vain appeal. Mary watched her uncle closely; she had no clue this time to his state of mind. He lowered his gun and pushed at the pedlar with his foot.

"Now we can talk reason, you and I," he said. He leant once more against the table, his gun across his arm, while the pedlar sprawled, half kneeling, half crouching, on the floor.

"I'm the leader in this game and always have been," said the landlord slowly. "I've worked it from the beginning three years ago, when we ran cargoes from little twelve-ton luggers to Padstow and thought ourselves lucky when we were sevenpence-halfpenny in pocket. I've worked it until the trade was the biggest thing in the country, from Hartland to Hayle. I take orders? My God, I'd like to see the man who dared to try me. Well, it's over now. We've run our course, and the day is done. The game is up, for all of us. You didn't come here tonight to warn me; you came to see what you could get out of the smash. The inn was barred, and your little mean heart rejoiced. You scraped at the window there because you knew from experience that the hasp of the shutter is loose and easy to force. You didn't think to find me here, did you? You thought it would be Patience here, or Mary; and you would scare them easy, wouldn't you, and reach for my gun, where it hangs handy on the wall, as you've often seen? And then to hell with the landlord of Jamaica Inn. You little rat, Harry, do you think I didn't see it in your eye when I flung back the shutter and saw your face at the window? Do you think I never heard your gasp of surprise, nor watched your sudden yellow grin?"

The pedlar passed his tongue over his lips and swallowed. He threw a glance towards Mary, motionless by the fire, the round button of his eye watchful, like a cornered rat's. He wondered if she would throw in the dice against him. But she said nothing. She waited for her uncle.

"Very well," he said; "we'll strike a bargain, you and I, as you suggested. We'll come to handsome terms. I've changed my mind after all, my loving friend, and with your help we'll take the road to Devon. There's stuff in this place worth taking, as you reminded me, nor can I load alone. Tomorrow is Sunday, and a blessed day of rest. Not even the wrecking of fifty ships will drag the people of this country from their knees. There'll be blinds down, and sermons, and long faces, and prayers offered for poor sailormen who come by misadventure by the devil's hand; but they'll not go seeking the devil on the Sabbath.

"Twenty-four hours we have, Harry, my boy, and tomorrow night, when you've broken your back spading turf and turnips over my property in the farm cart, and kissed me good-bye, and Patience too, and maybe Mary there as well —why then you can go down on your knees and thank Joss Merlyn for letting you go free with your life, instead of squatting on your scut in a ditch, where you belong to be, with a bullet in your black heart."

He raised his gun again, edging the cold muzzle close to the man's throat. The pedlar whimpered, showing the whites of his eyes. The landlord laughed.

"You're a pretty marksman in your way, Harry," he said. "Isn't that the spot you touched on Ned Santo the other night? You laid his windpipe bare, and the blood whistled out in a stream. He was a good boy, was Ned, but hasty with his tongue. That's where you got him, wasn't it?"

Closer the muzzle pressed against the pedlar's throat. "If I made a mistake now, Harry, your windpipe would come clean, just like poor Ned's. You don't want me to make a mistake, do you?"

The pedlar could not speak. His eyes rolled up in a squint, and his hand opened wide, the four fingers spread square, as though clamped to the floor.

The landlord shifted his gun, and, bending down, he jerked the pedlar to his feet. "Come on," he said; "do you think I'm going to play with you all night? A jest is a jest for five minutes; after that it becomes a burden on the flesh. Open the kitchen door and turn to the right and walk down the passage until I tell you to stop. You can't escape through the entrance to the bar; every door and window in this place is barred. Your hands have been itching to explore the wreckage we brought from the shore, haven't they, Harry? You shall spend the night in the storeroom amongst it all. Do you know, Patience, my dear, I believe this is the first time we've offered hospitality at Jamaica Inn. I don't count Mary there; she's part of the household." He laughed, in high good humour, his mood switched round now like a weathercock, and, butting his gun into the pedlar's back, he prodded him out of the kitchen and down the dark flagged passage to the store. The door, that had been battered in rough-and-ready manner by Squire Bassat and his servant, had been reinforced with new planking and post, and was now as strong as, if not stronger than, before. Joss Merlyn had not been entirely idle during the past week.

After he had turned the key on his friend, with a parting injunction not to feed the rats, whose numbers had increased, the landlord returned to the kitchen, a rumble of laughter in his chest.

"I thought Harry would turn sour," he said. "I've seen it coming in his eyes for weeks, long before this mess landed on us. He'll fight on the winning side, but he'll bite your hand when the luck turns. He's jealous; he's yellow-green with it, rotten through and through. He's jealous of me. They're all jealous of me. They knew I had brains and hated me for it. What are you staring at me for, Mary? You'd better get your supper and go to bed. You have a long journey before you tomorrow night, and I warn you here and now it won't be an easy one."

Mary looked at him across the table. The fact that she would not be going with him did not concern her for the moment; he might think as he liked about it. Tired as she was, for the strain of all she had seen and done weighed heavily upon her, her mind was seething with plans.

Sometime, somehow, before tomorrow night, she must go to Altarnun. Once there, her responsibility was over. Action would be taken by others. It would be hard for Aunt Patience, hard for herself at first, perhaps; she knew nothing of the jingle and complexities of the law; but at least justice would win. It would be easy enough to clear her own name and her aunt's. The thought of her uncle, who sat before her now, his mouth full of stale bread and cheese, standing as he would with his hands bound behind him, powerless for the first time and forever, was something that afforded her exquisite pleasure, and she turned the picture over and over in her mind, improving upon it. Aunt Patience would recover in time; and the years would drain away from her, bringing her peace at last, and quietude. Mary wondered how the capture would be effected when the moment came. Perhaps they would set out upon the journey as he had arranged, and as they turned out upon the road, he laughing in his assurance, they would be surrounded by a band of men, strong in number and in arms, and as he struggled against them hopelessly, borne to the ground by force, she would lean down to him and smile. "I thought you had brains, Uncle," she would say to him, and he would know.

She dragged her eyes away from him and turned to the dresser for her candle. "I'll have no supper tonight," she said.

Aunt Patience made a little murmur of distress, lifting her eyes from the plain slab of bread on the plate before her, but Joss Merlyn kicked at her for silence. "Let her stay sulky if she has the mind, can't you?" he said. "What does it matter to you if she eats or not? Starvation is good for women and beasts; it brings 'em to heel. She'll be humble enough in the morning. Wait, Mary; you shall sleep sounder still if I turn the key on you. I want no prowlers in the passage."

His eyes strayed to the gun against the wall and half-consciously back to the shutter, which still gaped open before the kitchen window.

"Fasten that window, Patience," he said thoughtfully, "and put the bar across the shutter. When you have finished your supper, you too can go to bed. I shall not leave the kitchen tonight."

His wife looked up at him in fear, struck by the tone of his voice, and would have spoken, but he cut her short. "Haven't you learnt by now not to question me?" he shouted. She rose at once and went to the window. Mary, her candle alight, waited by the door. "All right," he said. "Why are you standing there? I told you to go." Mary went out into the dark passage, her candle throwing her shadow behind her as she walked. No sound came from the store at the end of the passage, and she thought of the pedlar lying there in the darkness, watching and waiting for the day. The thought of him was abhorrent to her; like a rat he was, imprisoned amongst his fellows, and she suddenly pictured him with rat's claws scratching and gnawing at the framework of the door, scraping his way to freedom in the silence of the night.

She shuddered, strangely thankful that her uncle had decided to make a prisoner of her as well. The house was treacherous tonight, her very footsteps sounding hollow on the flags, and there were echoes that came unbidden from the walls. Even the kitchen, the one room in the house to possess some measure of warmth and normality, gaped back at her as she left it, yellow and sinister in the candlelight. Was her uncle going to sit there, then, the candles extinguished, his gun across his knee, waiting for something? . . . for someone? . . . He crossed into the hall as she mounted the stairs, and he followed her along the landing to the bedroom over the porch.

"Give me your key," he said, and she handed it to him without a word. He lingered for a moment, looking down at her, and then he bent low and laid his fingers on her mouth.

"I've a soft spot for you, Mary," he said; "you've got spirit still, and pluck, for all the knocks I've given you. I've seen it in your eyes tonight. If I'd been a younger man I'd have courted you, Mary—aye, and won you, too, and ridden away with you to glory. You know that, don't you?"

She said nothing. She stared back at him as he stood beyond the door, and her hand that held the candlestick trembled slightly without her knowledge.

He lowered his voice to a whisper. "There's danger for me ahead," he said. "Never mind the law; I can bluff my way to freedom if it comes to that. The whole of Cornwall can come running at my heels for all I care. It's other game I have to watch for—footsteps, Mary, that come in the night and go again, and a hand that would strike me down."

His face looked lean and old in the half-light, and there was a flicker of meaning in his eyes that leapt like a flame to tell her, and then dulled again. "We'll put the Tamar between us and Jamaica Inn," he said; and then he smiled, the curve of his mouth painfully familiar to her and known, like an echo from the past. He shut the door upon her and turned the key.

She heard him tramp down the stairs and so down into the passage, and he turned the corner to the kitchen and was gone.

She went then to her bed and sat down upon it, her hands in her lap; and, for some reason forever unexplained, thrust away from her later and forgotten, side by side with the little old sins of childhood and those dreams never acknowledged to the sturdy day, she put her fingers to her lips as he had done, and let them stray thence to her cheek and back again.

And she began to cry, softly and secretly, the tears tasting bitter as they fell upon her hand.

Chapter 13

SHE HAD fallen asleep where she lay, without undressing, and her first conscious thought was that the storm had come again, bringing with it the rain which streamed against her window. She opened her eyes and saw that the night was still, without a tremor of wind from without or the patter of rain. Her senses were alert at once, and she waited for a repetition of the sound that had woken her. It came again in an instant—a shower of earth flung against the pane of glass from the yard outside. She swung her legs to the floor and listened, weighing in her mind the possibility of danger.

If this was a warning signal, the method was a crude one, and better ignored. Someone with little idea of the geography of the inn might have mistaken her window for the landlord's. Her uncle waited below with his gun across his knee in preparation for a visitor; perhaps the visitor had come and was now standing in the yard. . . . Curiosity gained the better of her in the end, and she crept softly to the window, holding herself in the shadow of the jutting wall. The night was black still, and there were shadows everywhere, but low in the sky a thin line of cloud foretold the dawn.

She had not been mistaken, though; the earth on the floor was real enough, and so was the figure standing directly beneath the porch: the figure of a man. She crouched by the window, waiting for his further movement. He bent again to the ground, fumbling in the barren flower bed outside the parlour window, and then he raised his hand and threw the little clod of earth at her window, spattering the pane with pebbles and soft mud.

This time she saw his face, and the wonder of it made her cry out in surprise, forgetting the caution to which she had trained herself.

It was Jem Merlyn standing below her in the yard. She leant forward at once, opening her window, and would have called to him, but he lifted his hand for silence. He came close against the wall, skirting the porch which would have hidden her from him, and he cupped his hands to his mouth and whispered up to her, "Come down to the door here, and unbolt it for me."

She shook her head at him. "I cannot do that. I am locked here in my room," she told him. He stared at her, nonplussed and evidently puzzled, and he looked back at the house as though it might offer some solution of its own. He ran his hands along the slates, testing them, feeling for rusted nails used long ago for creepers, that might afford him foothold of a sort. The low tiles of the porch

were within his reach, but they had no gripping surface; he
would swing his legs from the ground to no purpose.

"Fetch me the blanket from your bed," he called softly.

She guessed at once his meaning and tied one end of
her blanket to the foot of her bed, throwing the other out
of the window, where it dragged limply above his head.
This time he had holding power, and, swinging himself to
the low roof of the jutting porch, he was able to wedge his
body between it and the walls of the house, his feet gripping the slates, and in this manner haul himself up the porch
on a level with her window.

He swung his legs over, and straddled the porch, his
face close to hers now, the blanket hanging loosely beside
him. Mary struggled with the framework of the window,
but her efforts were useless. The window opened only a
foot or so; he could not enter the room without smashing
the glass.

"I shall have to talk to you here," he said. "Come closer,
where I can see you." She knelt on the floor of her room,
her face at the window gap, and they stared at one another
for a moment without speaking. He looked worn, and his
eyes were hollow, like the eyes of one who has not slept
and has endured fatigue. There were lines about his mouth
she had not noticed before, nor did he smile.

"I owe you an apology," he said at length. "I deserted
you without excuse at Launceston on Christmas Eve. You
can forgive me or not, as you feel; but the reason for it—
that I can't give you. I'm sorry."

This attitude of harshness did not suit him; he appeared
to have changed much, and the change was unwelcome to
her.

"I was anxious for your safety," she said. "I traced you
to the White Hart, and there I was told you had entered
a carriage with some gentleman; nothing beyond that, no
message, no word of explanation. Those men were there,
standing before the fire, the horse dealer who spoke with
you in the market square. They were horrible men, curious, and I mistrusted them. I wondered if the theft of the
199

pony had been discovered. I was wretched and worried. I blame you for nothing. Your business is your own."

She was hurt by his manner. She had expected anything but this. When she saw him first, in the yard outside her window, she thought of him only as the man she loved, who had come now to her in the night, seeking her presence. His coolness damped her flame, and she withdrew inside herself at once, trusting that he had not seen the blank disappointment in her face.

He did not even ask how she returned that night, and his indifference stunned her. "Why are you locked in your room?" he questioned.

She shrugged her shoulders, and her voice was flat and dull when she replied:

"My uncle does not care for eavesdroppers. He fears I should wander in the passage and stumble upon his secrets. You appear to have the same dislike of intrusion. To ask you why you are here tonight would be an offence, I suppose?"

"Oh, be as bitter as you like; I deserve it," he flashed suddenly. "I know what you think of me. One day I may be able to explain, if you're not out of my reach by then. Be a man for the moment, and send your hurt pride and your curiosity to hell. I'm treading delicate ground, Mary, and one false step will finish me. Where is my brother?"

"He told us he would spend the night in the kitchen. He is afraid of something or someone; the windows and doors are barred, and he has his gun."

Jem laughed harshly. "I don't doubt he's afraid. He'll be more frightened still before many hours are passed, I can tell you that. I came here to see him, but if he sits there with a gun across his knee I can postpone my visit until tomorrow, when the shadows are gone."

"Tomorrow may be too late."

"What do you mean?"

"He intends to leave Jamaica Inn at nightfall."

"Are you telling me the truth?"

"Why should I lie to you now?"

Jem was silent. The news had evidently come as a sur-

prise to him, and he was turning it over in his mind. Mary
watched him, tortured by doubt and indecision; she was
thrown back now upon her old suspicion of him. He was
the visitor expected by her uncle, and therefore hated by
him and feared. He was the man who held the threads of
her uncle's life between his hands. The sneering face of the
pedlar returned to her again, and his words, that so provoked
the landlord to a flame of fury: "Listen here, Joss Merlyn:
do you take your orders from one above you?" The man
whose wits made service of the landlord's strength, the man
who had hidden in the empty room.

She thought again of the laughing, carefree Jem who
had driven her to Launceston, who had swung hands with
her in the market square, who had kissed her and held her.
Now he was grave and silent, his face in shadow. The idea
of dual personality troubled her, and frightened her as well.
He was like a stranger to her tonight, obsessed by some
grim purpose she could not understand. Warning him of the
landlord's intended flight had been a false move on her part;
it might confound the issue of her plans. Whatever Jem had
done or intended to do, whether he was false and treacherous
and a murderer of men, she loved him, in the weakness of
her flesh, and owed him warning.

"You'd best have a care for yourself when you see your
brother," she said. "His mood is dangerous; whoever inter-
feres with his plans now risks his life. I tell you this for
your own safety."

"I have no fear of Joss, nor ever had."

"Perhaps not; but what if he is afraid of you?"

To this he said nothing, but, leaning forward suddenly,
he looked into her face and touched the scratch that ran
from her forehead to her chin.

"Who did this?" he said sharply, turning from the scratch
to the bruise on her cheek. She hesitated a moment and
then answered him:

"I got them Christmas Eve."

The gleam in his eye told her at once that he understood,
and had knowledge of the evening, and because of it was
here now at Jamaica Inn.

"You were there with them, on the shore?" he whispered.

She nodded, watching him carefully, wary of speech, and for answer he cursed aloud, and, reaching forward, smashed the pane of glass with his fist, careless of the splitting sound of glass and the blood that spouted immediately from his hand. The gap in the window was wide enough now for entrance, and he had climbed into the room and was beside her before she realized what he had done. He lifted her in his arms and carried her to the bed, and laid her down upon it; and, fumbling in the darkness for a candle, he found it at length and lit it, and came back to the bed and knelt beside it, throwing the light upon her face. He traced the bruises with his finger down her neck, and when she winced with the pain he drew in his breath quickly, and again she heard him swear. "I might have spared you this," he said; and then, blowing out the light, he sat down beside her on the bed and reached for her hand, which he held a moment, tight, and then gave back to her.

"God Almighty, why did you go with them?" he said.

"They were crazy with drink. I don't think they knew what they were doing. I could no more have stood against them than a child. There were a dozen of them or more, and my uncle . . . he led them. He and the pedlar. If you know about it, why do you ask me? Don't make me remember. I don't want to remember."

"How much have they hurt you?"

"Bruises, scratches—you can see for yourself. I tried to escape, and I grazed my side. They caught me again, of course. They bound my hands and feet down on the shore, and tied sacking over my mouth so that I could not scream. I saw the ship come through the mist, and I could do nothing —alone there in the wind and the rain. I had to watch them die."

She broke off, her voice trembling, and she turned on her side, her face in her hands. He made no move towards her; he sat there silently on the bed beside her, and she felt him far from her, wrapped in secrecy.

She was lonelier then than before.

"Was it my brother who hurt you most?" he said presently.

She sighed wearily. It was all too late and did not matter now.

"I've told you he was drunk," she said. "You know, better than I perhaps, what he can do then."

"Yes, I know." He paused a moment, and then once again he took her hand.

"He shall die for this," he said.

"His death will not bring back the men he killed."

"I'm not thinking of them now."

"If you're thinking of me, don't waste your sympathy. I can revenge myself in my own way. I've learnt one thing at least—to rely on myself."

"Women are frail things, Mary, for all their courage. You are best out of this business now. The issue lies with me."

She did not answer him. Her plans were her own, and he did not enter into them.

"What do you intend to do?" he asked.

"I have not made up my mind," she lied.

"If he leaves tomorrow night, you have little time to decide," he said.

"He expects me to go with him, and Aunt Patience as well."

"And you?"

"That will depend upon tomorrow."

Whatever she felt for him, she would not hazard her plans into his keeping. He was still an unknown quantity, and above all else an enemy to justice. It came to her then that by betraying her uncle she might also betray him.

"If I ask you to do something, how would you answer me?" she said.

He smiled then for the first time, mocking and indulgent, as he had done in Launceston, and her heart leapt to him at once, encouraged at the change.

"How can I tell?" he said.

"I want you to go away from here."

"I'm going now."

"No, I mean away from the moors, away from Jamaica Inn. I want you to tell me you won't return here again. I can stand up against your brother; I'm in no danger from him now. I don't want you to come here tomorrow. Please promise me you'll go away."

"What have you got in your mind?"

"Something which has no concern with you, but might bring you to danger. I can't say any more. I would rather you trusted me."

"Trust you? Good God, of course I trust you. It's you who won't trust me, you damned little fool." He laughed silently, and bent down to her, putting his arms round her, and he kissed her then as he had kissed her in Launceston, but deliberately now, with anger and exasperation.

"Play your own game by yourself, then, and leave me to play mine," he told her. "If you must be a boy, I can't stop you, but for the sake of your face, which I have kissed, and shall kiss again, keep away from danger. You don't want to kill yourself, do you? I have to leave you now; it will be daylight within the hour. And if both our plans miscarry, what then? Would you mind if you never saw me again? No, of course you would not care."

"I have not said so. You hardly understand."

"Women think differently to men; they travel separate paths. That's why I have no liking for them; they make for trouble and confusion. It was pleasure enough to take you to Launceston, Mary, but when it comes to life and death, like my business now, God knows I wish you a hundred miles away, or sitting primly, your sewing in your lap, in a trim parlour somewhere, where you belong to be."

"That's never been my life, nor ever will."

"Why not? You'll wed a farmer one day, or small tradesman, and live respectably among your neighbours. Don't tell them you lived once at Jamaica Inn and had love made to you by a horse thief. They'd shut their doors against you. Good-bye, and here's prosperity to you."

He rose from the bed and went towards the window, climbing through the gap he had broken in the pane; and, swinging his legs over the porch, with one hand on the blanket, he lowered himself to the ground.

She watched him from the window, instinctively waving him farewell, but he had turned and gone without looking back at her, slipping across the yard like a shadow. Slowly she pulled up the blanket and replaced it on the bed. Morning would soon be here; she would not sleep again.

She sat on her bed, waiting until her door should be unlocked; and she made her plans for the evening to come. She must not draw suspicion upon herself during the long day; she must act passively, sullenly perhaps, as though feeling had at last been stifled in her, and she was prepared to undertake the proposed journey with the landlord and Aunt Patience.

Then, later, she would make some excuse—fatigue perhaps, a desire to rest in her room before the strain of the night journey—and then would come the most dangerous moment of her day. She would have to leave Jamaica Inn secretly and unobserved, and run like a hare to Altarnun. This time Francis Davey would understand; time would be against them, and he must act accordingly. She would then return to the inn, with his approval, and trust that her absence had remained unnoticed. This was the gamble. If the landlord went to her room and found her gone, her life would be worth nothing. She must be prepared for that. No excuse would save her then. But if he believed her to be sleeping still, then the game would continue. They would make preparations for the journey; they might even climb into the cart and come out upon the road; after that her responsibility would end. Their fate would be in the hands of the vicar of Altarnun. Beyond this she could not think, nor had she any great desire to look ahead.

So Mary waited for the day; and, when it came, the long hours stretched interminably before her; every minute was an hour, and an hour a particle of eternity itself. The atmosphere of strain was apparent amongst them all. In silence, haggardly, they waited for the night. Little progress could be made during the light of day; intrusion was always possible. Aunt Patience wandered from the kitchen to her room, her footsteps pattering incessantly in the passage and on the stairs, as she made helpless and ineffectual preparations. She would make bundles of what poor clothes remained to her, and then undo them again, when the memory of some forgotten garment jogged her wandering mind. She pottered in the kitchen aimlessly, opening the cupboards, looking into drawers, and she fingered her pots and pans with restless fingers, incapable of deciding which to take and which to leave behind. Mary helped her as best she could, but the unreality of her task made it the more difficult; she knew, while her aunt did not, that all this labour was in vain.

Her heart misgave her at times, when she allowed her thoughts to dwell upon the future. How would Aunt Patience act? How would she look when they came to take her husband from her? She was a child and must be tended as a child. Again she pattered from the kitchen, climbing the stairs to her room, and Mary would hear her drag her box on the floor, pace up and down, up and down, as she wrapped a single candlestick in a shawl and put it side by side with a cracked teapot and a faded muslin cap, only to unwrap them again and discard them for treasures more ancient.

Joss Merlyn would watch her moodily, cursing her in irritation now and again as she dropped something on the floor or caught her foot and stumbled. His mood had changed again overnight. His watch in the kitchen had not improved his temper, and the very fact that the hours had been undisturbed and his visitor had not come upon him made him if possible more restless than before. He roamed about the house, nervy and abstracted, muttering to himself at times, peering from the windows as though he expected to see someone come upon him unawares. His nerves reacted upon his wife and Mary. Aunt Patience watched him anxiously, and she too turned her eyes to the window and would listen, her mouth working, her hands twisting and untwisting her apron.

No sound came from the pedlar in the barred room, nor did the landlord go to him or mention him by name;

and this silence was sinister in itself, strange and unnatural. Had the pedlar shouted obscenities, or thundered on the door, it would have been more in keeping with his character; but he lay there in the darkness without sound or movement, and for all her loathing of him Mary shuddered at the possibility of his death.

At the midday meal they sat round the table in the kitchen, eating silently, furtively almost, and the landlord, who usually had the appetite of an ox, drummed moodily with his fingers on the table, the cold meat on his plate untouched. Once Mary lifted her eyes and saw him staring at her beneath shaggy brows. The wild fear ran through her mind that he suspected her and had some knowledge of her plans. She had counted upon his high humour of the preceding night and had been prepared to fall in with it if necessary, answer banter with banter, setting up no opposition to his will. He sat sullen, though, wrapped in gloom, and this was a mood she had experienced before, and, she knew now, led to danger. At length she took courage in both hands and asked him what time he intended to leave Jamaica Inn.

"When I am prepared," he told her shortly and would say no more.

She schooled herself to continue, though, and when she had helped to clear the meal away and, at her own suggestion, adding deceit upon deceit, had impressed upon her aunt the necessity of packing a basket of provisions against the journey, she turned to her uncle and spoke again.

"If we are to travel tonight," she said, "would it not be better if Aunt Patience and myself rested now during the afternoon, and so could start out fresh upon the journey? There will be no sleep for any of us tonight. Aunt Patience has been upon her feet since daybreak, and I too, for that matter. We do little good, as far as I can see, waiting here for the dusk to fall." She kept her voice as casual as possible, but the tight band across her heart was a sign that she waited his answer with misgiving, and she could not look into his eyes. He debated the matter a moment, and to control her anxiety she turned away and pretended to fumble in the cupboard.

"You may rest if you will," he said at length. "There'll be work for you both, later. You are right when you say there will be no sleep for you tonight. Go then; I shall be well rid of you for the time."

The first step had been achieved, and Mary lingered awhile with her pretended work in the cupboard, fearing that haste to leave the kitchen should be judged suspicious. Her aunt, who acted always like a dummy to suggestion, followed her meekly upstairs when the time came, and padded along the further passage to her own room as an obedient child would do.

Mary entered her own little room above the porch and closed the door, turning the key. Her heart beat fast at the prospect of adventure, and she could hardly tell whether excitement or fear had the mastery. It was close on four miles to Altarnun by the road, and she could walk the distance in an hour. If she left Jamaica Inn at four o'clock, when the light was failing, she would be back again soon after six; and the landlord would hardly come to rouse her before seven. She had three hours, then, in which to play her part, and she had already determined upon her method of departure. She would climb out onto the porch and fall to the ground, as Jem had done this morning. The drop was an easy one, and she would escape with little more than a scratch and a jar to her nerves. At any rate, it would be safer to do this than to risk coming upon her uncle in the passage below. The heavy entrance door would never open noiselessly, and to go through the bar would mean passing the open kitchen.

She put on her warmest dress and fastened her old shawl across her shoulders with trembling, hot hands. It was the enforced delay that irked her most. Once she was upon the road, the purpose of the walk would bring courage, and the very movement of her limbs would be a stimulant.

She sat by the window, looking out upon the bare yard and the highroad where no one ever passed, waiting for the clock in the hall below to strike four. When it sounded at last, the strokes rang out in the silence like an alarm, pounding her nerves; and, unlocking the door, she listened for a moment, hearing footsteps echo the strokes, and whispers in the air.

It was imagination, of course; nothing moved. The clock ticked on into the next hour. Every second was precious to her now, and she must waste no time to be gone. She shut the door, locking it again, and went to the window. She crawled through the gap, as Jem had done, her hands on the sill, and in a moment she was astride the porch, looking down upon the ground.

The distance seemed greater, now that she crouched above it, and she had no blanket to control her fall and let her swing, as he had done. The tiles of the porch were slippery and gave no grip to hands or feet. She turned, clinging desperately to the security of the window sill, that seemed desirable suddenly, and a thing well known; then she shut her eyes and launched herself into the air. Her feet found the ground almost immediately—the jump was nothing, as she had already foreseen—but the tiles had grazed her hands and arms and brought back to her again a vivid memory of her last fall, from the carriage in the gullyway beside the shore.

She looked up at Jamaica Inn, sinister and grey in the approaching dusk, the windows barred; she thought of the horrors the house had witnessed, the secrets now embedded in its walls, side by side with the other old memories of feasting and firelight and laughter before her uncle cast his shadow upon it; and she turned away from it, as one turns instinctively from a house of the dead, and went out upon the road.

The evening was fine—that at least favoured her—and she strode out towards her destination with her eyes fixed upon the long white road that lay ahead. Dusk came as she walked, bringing shadows across the moors that lay on either side of her. Away to the left the high tors, shrouded at first in mist, were gathered to the darkness. It was very still. There was no wind. Later there would be a moon. She wondered if her uncle had reckoned with this force of nature that would shine upon his plans. For herself it would not matter. Tonight she had no fear of the moors; they did not concern her. Her business was with the road. The moors lost their significance when unnoticed and untrodden; they loomed beyond her and away from her.

She came at length to the Five Lanes, where the roads branched, and she turned to her left, down the steep hill of Altarnun. Excitement rose high within her now as she passed the twinkling cottage lights and smelt the friendly smoke of chimneys. Here were neighbourly sounds that had long been lost to her: the barking of a dog, the rustle of trees, the clank of a pail as a man drew water from a well. There were open doors, and voices from within. Chickens clucked beyond a hedge, and a woman called shrilly to a child who answered with a cry. A cart lumbered past her into the shadows, and the driver gave her good evening. Here was a drowsy movement, a placidity and a peace; here were all the old village smells she knew and understood. She passed them by; and she went to the vicarage beside the church. There were no lights here. The house was shrouded and silent. The trees closed in upon it, and once again she was vividly aware of her first impression that this was a house that lived in its own past, and slept now, with no knowledge of the present. She hammered upon the door, and she heard the blows echo through the empty house. She looked in through the windows, and her eyes met nothing but the soft and negative darkness.

Then, cursing her stupidity, she turned back again towards the church. Francis Davey would be there, of course. It was Sunday. She hesitated a moment, uncertain of her movements, and then the gate opened and a woman came out into the road, carrying flowers.

She stared hard at Mary, knowing her a stranger, and would have passed her by with a good night had not Mary turned and followed her.

"Forgive me," she said; "I see you have come from the church. Can you tell me if Mr. Davey himself is there?"

"No, he is not," said the woman; and then, after a moment, "Were you wishing to see him?"

"Very urgently," said Mary. "I have been to his house, and I can get no answer. Can you help me?"

The woman looked at her curiously and then shook her head.

"I am sorry," she said. "The vicar is from home. He went away today to preach at another parish, many miles from here. He is not expected back in Altarnun tonight."

Chapter 14

AT FIRST Mary stared at the woman in disbelief. "Away from home?" she repeated. "But that is impossible. Surely you are mistaken?"

Her confidence had been such that she rejected instinctively this sudden and fatal blow to her plans. The woman looked offended; she saw no reason why this stranger should doubt her word. "The vicar left Altarnun yesterday afternoon," she said. "He rode away after dinner. I ought to know, for I keep house for him."

She must have seen something of the agony of disappointment in Mary's face, for she relented and spoke with kindness. "If there is any message you would like me to give him when he does return—" she began, but Mary shook her head hopelessly, spirit and courage gone from her in a moment with the news.

"It will be too late," she said in despair. "This is a matter of life and death. With Mr. Davey gone, I don't know where I can turn."

Once more a gleam of curiosity came into the woman's eyes. "Has someone been taken sick?" she enquired. "I could point you out where our doctor lives, if that would help you. Where have you come from tonight?"

Mary did not answer. She was thinking desperately of some way out of the situation. To come to Altarnun and then return again without help to Jamaica Inn was impossible. She could not place confidence in the village people, nor would they believe her tale. She must find someone in authority—someone who knew something of Joss Merlyn and Jamaica Inn.

"Who is the nearest magistrate?" she said at length.

The woman puckered her brow and considered the question. "There's no one close by us here in Altarnun," she said doubtfully. "Why, the nearest would be Squire Bassat over to North Hill, and that must be over four miles from here—maybe more, maybe less. I cannot say for certain, for I have never been there. You surely would not walk out there tonight?"

"I must," said Mary; "there is nothing else for me to do. I must lose no time either. Forgive me for being so mysterious, but I am in great trouble, and only your vicar or a magistrate can help me. Can you tell me if the road to North Hill is hard to find?"

"No, that's easy enough. You go two miles along the Launceston road, and then turn right by the turnpike; but it's scarcely a walk for a maid like you after nightfall, and I'd never go myself. There's rough folk on the moors at times, and you cannot trust them. We dare not venture from our homes these days, with robbery on the highroad even, and violence, too."

"Thank you for your sympathy; I am very grateful to you," said Mary, "but I have lived all my life in lonely places, and I am not afraid."

"You must please yourself," answered the woman, "but you'd best stay here and wait for the vicar, if you can."

"That is impossible," said Mary, "but when he does return, could you tell him perhaps that . . . Wait, though; if you have pen and paper I will write him a note of explanation; that would be better still."

"Come into my cottage here, and you may write what you will. When you have gone, I can take the note to his house

at once, and leave it on his table, where he will see it as
soon as he comes home."

Mary followed the woman to the cottage and waited
impatiently while she searched her kitchen for a pen. The
time was slipping away fast, and the added journey to
North Hill had upset every former calculation.

She could hardly return to Jamaica Inn once she had
seen Mr. Bassat and still hope her absence had remained
unnoticed. Her uncle would take warning from her flight
and leave the inn before the intended time. In which case
her mission would have been in vain. . . . Now the woman returned with paper and quill, and Mary wrote desperately, never pausing to choose her words:

*I came here to ask your help, and you were gone. By
now you will have heard with horror, as everyone in the
country must have done, of the wreck upon the coast on
Christmas Eve. It was my uncle's doing, he and the company from Jamaica Inn; that you will have guessed already.
He knows that suspicion will fall on him before long, and
because of this he plans to leave the inn tonight, and cross
the Tamar into Devon. Finding you absent, I go now with
all possible haste to Mr. Bassat at North Hill, to tell everything to him, and warn him of the escape, so that he can
send at once to Jamaica Inn to seize my uncle before it is
too late. I am giving this note to your housekeeper, who
will, I trust, lay it where your eyes will fall upon it directly
you return. In haste, then,*

MARY YELLAN.

This she folded and gave to the woman by her side,
thanking her and assuring her that she had no fear of the
road; and so set out again upon a walk of four miles or more
to North Hill. She climbed the hill from Altarnun with a
heavy heart and a wretched sense of isolation.

She had placed such faith in Francis Davey that it was
hard to realize even yet that by his absence he had failed
her. He had not known, of course, that she needed him,
and, even if he had, perhaps his plans would have come

213

before her troubles. It was disheartening and bitter to leave the lights of Altarnun behind her, with nothing as yet accomplished. At this moment, perhaps, her uncle was thundering upon her bedroom door, calling her to answer. He would wait a moment and then force the door. He would find her gone, and the smashed window would tell him the manner of her going. Whether this would play havoc with his plans was a matter for conjecture. She could not know. Aunt Patience was her concern, and the thought of her setting out upon the journey like a shivering dog tethered to its master made Mary run along the bare white road with fists clenched and chin thrust in the air.

She came at last to the turnpike and turned down the narrow twisting lane as the woman in Altarnun had told her. High hedges screened the country on either side, and the dark moor was thrust away and hidden from her eyes. The road twisted and turned, as the lanes in Helford used to do, and this change of scene, coming so suddenly after the bleak highroad, put faith in her once more. She cheered herself by painting a picture of the Bassat family as kindly and courteous, like the Vyvyans at Trelowarren, who would listen to her with sympathy and understanding. She had not seen the squire at his best before; he had come upon Jamaica Inn in high ill humour, and she thought now with regret of the part she had played in his deception. As for his lady, she must know now that a horse thief had made a fool of her in Launceston market square, and it was lucky for Mary that she had not stood at Jem's side when the pony was sold back to his rightful owner. She continued with her fantasy of the Bassats, but the little incidents came back to her in spite of it, and at the bottom of her heart she looked upon the approaching interview with trepidation.

The contour of the land had changed again, and hills rose away from her, forested and dark, and somewhere beyond her ran a stream singing and breaking over stones. The moorland was no more. The moon came now, topping the further trees, and she walked in confidence with the light blazing a path for her, leading her downwards to the valley, where the trees closed in friendliness upon her. She came at last to lodge gates and the entrance to a drive, while beyond her the lane continued to a village.

That must be North Hill, and this the manor house belonging to the squire. She went down the avenue to the house, and away in the distance a church clock struck seven. She had been about three hours already from Jamaica Inn. Her nervousness returned as she rounded upon the house, large and forbidding in the darkness, with the moon not yet risen high enough to shine kindly upon it. She swung the great bell, and the sound was met at once by the furious baying of hounds. She waited, and presently she heard footsteps from within, and the door was opened by a manservant. He called sharply at the dogs, who thrust their noses at the door and sniffed at Mary's feet. She felt inferior and small and was conscious of her old dress and shawl before this man who waited for her to speak. "I have come to see Mr. Bassat on very urgent business," she told him. "He would not know my name, but if he could speak to me for a few minutes I would explain. The matter is of desperate importance, otherwise I would not disturb him at such an hour, and on a Sunday night."

"Mr. Bassat left for Launceston this morning," answered the man. "He was called away hurriedly, and he has not yet returned."

This time Mary could not control herself, and a cry of despair escaped her.

"I have come some way," she said, in an agony of feeling, as though by her very distress she could bring the squire to her side. "If I do not see him within the hour something terrible will happen, and a great criminal escape the hands of the law. You look at me blankly, but I am speaking the truth. If only there was someone I could turn to—"

"Mrs. Bassat is at home," said the man, stung with curiosity. "Perhaps she will see you, if your business is as urgent as you say. Follow me, will you, to the library. Never mind the dogs; they will not hurt you."

Mary crossed the hall in a dream, knowing only that her plan had failed again, through chance alone, and that she was powerless now to help herself.

The wide library, with its blazing fire, seemed unreal to her, and, accustomed as she was to the darkness, she blinked at the flood of light that met her eyes. A woman whom she recognized immediately as the fine lady from Launceston market square was sitting in a chair before the fire, reading aloud to two children, and she looked up in surprise when Mary was shown into the room.

The servant began his explanation in some excitement. "This young woman has very grave news for the squire, madam," he said. "I thought it best to show her in to you directly."

Mrs. Bassat rose to her feet at once, dropping the book from her lap.

"It isn't one of the horses, is it?" she said. "Richards told me Solomon had been coughing and that Diamond would not take his food. With this undergroom anything may happen."

Mary shook her head. "Your household is not in trouble," she said gravely. "I bring news of another kind. If I could speak to you alone—"

Mrs. Bassat appeared relieved that her horses were not affected, and she spoke quickly to her children, who ran from the room, followed by the manservant.

"What can I do for you?" she said graciously. "You look pale and frightened. Won't you sit down?"

Mary shook her head impatiently. "Thank you, but I must know when Mr. Bassat is returning home."

"I have no idea," replied his lady. "He was obliged to leave this morning at a moment's notice, and, to tell you the truth, I am seriously concerned about him. If this dreadful innkeeper shows fight, as he is certain to do, Mr. Bassat may be wounded, in spite of the soldiers."

"What do you mean?" said Mary swiftly.

"Why, the squire has set out upon a highly dangerous mission. Your face is new to me, and I conclude you are not from North Hill, otherwise you would have heard of this man Merlyn who keeps an inn upon the Bodmin road. The squire has suspected him for some while of terrible crimes, but it was not until this morning that the full proof came into his hands. He departed at once for Launceston to summon help, and, from what he told me before he went, he intends to surround the inn tonight and seize the inhabitants. He will go well armed, of course, and with a large body of men, but I shall not rest until he returns."

Something in Mary's face must have warned her, for she turned very pale and backed towards the fire, reaching out for the heavy bellpull that hung on the wall. "You are the girl he spoke about," she said quickly, "the girl from the inn, the niece of the landlord. Stay where you are; don't move, or I'll summon my servants. You are the girl. I know it; he described you to me. What do you want with me?"

Mary put out her hand, her face as white as the woman's by the fire.

"I won't hurt you," she said. "Please do not ring. Let me explain. Yes, I am the girl from Jamaica Inn." Mrs. Bassat did not trust her. She watched Mary with troubled eyes and kept her hand upon the bell rope.

"I have no money here," she said. "I can do nothing for you. If you have come to North Hill to plead for your uncle, it is too late."

"You misunderstand me," said Mary quietly. "And the landlord of Jamaica Inn is a relative to me by marriage only. Why I have been living there does not matter now, and the story would take too long in the telling. I fear and detest him more than you or anyone in the country, and with reason. I came here to warn Mr. Bassat that the landlord intended to leave the inn tonight, and so escape justice. I have definite proof of his guilt, which I did not believe Mr. Bassat to possess. You tell me that he has already gone, and perhaps even now is at Jamaica Inn. Therefore I have wasted my time in coming here."

She sat down then, her hands in her lap, and stared blankly at the fire. She had come to the end of her resources, and for the moment she could not look ahead. All that her weary mind could tell her was that her labour of the evening had been purposeless and in vain. She need never have left her bedroom at Jamaica Inn. Mr. Bassat would have

217

come in any case. And now, by her secret meddling, she had blundered into the very mistake she had wished to avoid. She had stayed away too long; and by now her uncle would have guessed the truth and in all probability made his escape. Squire Bassat and his men would ride to a deserted inn.

She lifted her eyes once more to the lady of the house. "I have done a very senseless thing in coming here," she said hopelessly. "I thought it clever, and I have only succeeded in making a fool of myself and of everyone else. My uncle will discover my room is empty and guess at once that I have betrayed him. He will leave Jamaica Inn before Mr. Bassat arrives."

The squire's lady let go of the bell rope now and came towards her.

"You speak sincerely, and you have an honest face," she said kindly. "I am sorry if I misjudged you at first, but Jamaica Inn has a terrible name, and I believe anyone would have done the same had they been confronted suddenly with the landlord's niece. You have been placed in a fearful position, and I think you very brave to come here tonight, all those lonely miles, to warn my husband. I should have gone mad with fear. The question is this: what would you have me do now? I am willing to help you in any way you think best."

"There is nothing we can do," said Mary, shaking her head. "I must wait here, I suppose, until Mr. Bassat returns. He won't be overpleased to see me when he hears how I have blundered. God knows I deserve every reproach. . . ."

"I will speak for you," replied Mrs. Bassat. "You could not possibly know my husband had already been informed, and I will soon smooth him down if he needs it. Be thankful you are here in safety meanwhile."

"How did the squire learn the truth so suddenly?" asked Mary.

"I have not the slightest idea; he was sent for very suddenly this morning, as I have told you already, and he only gave me the barest details before his horse was saddled and he was gone. Now, won't you rest yourself, and forget for the time the whole hateful business? You are probably famished for want of food." Once more she approached the fireplace, and this time she pulled the bell rope three or four times. For all her worry and distress, Mary could not help seeing the irony of the situation. Here was the lady of the house offering hospitality, who a moment ago had threatened her with seizure by the same servants who would now bring her food. She thought also of the scene in the market square when this same lady, in velvet cloak and feathered hat, had paid a high price for her own pony, and she wondered whether the trickery had been discovered. If Mary's own part in the deception should come to light, Mrs. Bassat would hardly be so lavish with her hospitality.

Meanwhile the servant appeared, his inquisitive nose in the air, and was told by his mistress to bring a tray of supper for Mary, and the dogs, who had followed him into the room, came now to make friends with the stranger, wagging their tails and pushing their soft noses into her hands, accepting her as a member of the household. Her presence in the manor house at North Hill was still without reality, and, though Mary tried, she could not throw aside anxiety and relax. She felt she had no right to be sitting here before a glowing fire, when outside, in the darkness, life and death fought hand to hand before Jamaica Inn. She ate mechanically, forcing herself to swallow the food she needed, aware of the prattle of her hostess at her side, who in the mistaken kindness of her heart believed that incessant conversation about nothing at all was the only method of alleviating worry. The chatter, had she but realized, increased it, and when Mary had finished her supper and sat once more with her hands on her lap, staring at the fire, Mrs. Bassat, searching in her mind for suitable distraction, fetched an album of her own water colours and proceeded to turn the pages for the benefit of her guest.

When the clock on the mantelpiece chimed eight o'clock in piercing tones, Mary could bear it no longer. This dragging inactivity was worse than danger and pursuit. "Forgive me," she said, rising to her feet; "you have been so kind, and I can never thank you enough; but I am anxious, desperately anxious. I can think of nothing but my poor aunt, who at this moment may be suffering the tortures of hell. I must know what is happening at Jamaica Inn, if I walk back there myself tonight."

Mrs. Bassat dropped her album in a flutter of distress. "Of course you are anxious. I have seen it all along, and tried to take your mind off it. How terrible it is! I am as concerned as you are, for my husband's sake. But you cannot possibly walk back there now, alone. Why, it would be after midnight before you arrived, and heaven knows what might not happen to you on the way. I will order the trap, and Richards shall go with you. He is most trustworthy and dependable, and can be armed in case of need. If there is fighting in progress, you would see it from the bottom of the hill, and would not approach until it was over. I would come with you myself, but my health is delicate at the moment—and—"

"Of course you will do nothing of the kind," said Mary swiftly. "I am used to danger and the road by night, and you are not. I shall be putting you to very great trouble in harnessing your horse at this hour and rousing your groom. I assure you I'm no longer tired, and I can walk."

But Mrs. Bassat had already pulled the bell. "Have word sent to Richards to bring the trap around immediately," she said to the astonished servant. "I will give him further orders when he arrives. Tell him there must be as little delay as possible." She then fitted Mary out with a heavy cloak and hood, thick rug and foot warmer, protesting all the while that only her state of health prevented her from making the journey, too, for which Mary was utterly thankful, Mrs. Bassat being hardly the ideal companion for so improvident and dangerous an escapade.

In a quarter of an hour the trap drove up to the door, with Richards in charge, Mary recognizing him at once as the servant who had ridden with Mr. Bassat originally to Jamaica Inn. His reluctance at leaving his fireside on a Sunday night was soon overcome when he learnt his mission, and with two large pistols stuck in his belt, and orders to fire at anyone who threatened the trap, he assumed at once an air of truculence and authority hitherto unknown to him. Mary climbed in beside him, the dogs baying a chorus of farewell, and it was only when the drive twisted and the house was out of sight that Mary realized she had set out on what was probably to be a foolhardy and dangerous expedition.

Anything might have happened during the five hours she had been absent from Jamaica Inn, and even with the trap she could scarcely hope to arrive there before half past ten. She could make no plans, and her action depended upon the moment when it came. With the moon now high in the sky and the soft air blowing upon her she felt emboldened to face disaster when it came, and this ride to the scene of action, however dangerous, was better than sitting like a helpless child listening to the prattle of Mrs. Bassat. This man Richards was armed, and she herself would use a gun if necessary. He was burning with curiosity, of course, but she gave short answers to his questions and did not encourage him.

The drive was silent then, for the most part, with no other sound but the steady clopping of the horse's hoofs upon the road, and now and again an owl hooted from the still trees. The rustle of hedgerow and the creeping country whispers were left behind when the trap came out upon the Bodmin road, and once again the dark moor stretched out on either side, lapping the road like a desert. The ribbon of the highway shone white under the moon. It wound and was lost in the fold of the further hill, bare and untrodden. There were no travellers but themselves upon the road tonight. On Christmas Eve, when Mary had ridden here, the wind had lashed venomously at the carriage wheels, and the rain hammered the windows: now the air was still cold and strangely still, and the moor itself lay placid and silver in the moonlight. The dark tors held their sleeping faces to the sky, the granite features softened and smoothed by the light that bathed them. Theirs was a peaceful mood, and the old gods slept undisturbed.

221

Briskly the horse and trap covered the weary miles that Mary had walked alone. She recognized each bend in the road now, and how at times the moor encroached upon it, with high tufts of grass or twisted stem of broom.

There, beyond her in the valley, would be the lights of Altarnun, and already the Five Lanes branched out from the road like fingers from a hand.

The wild stretch to Jamaica lay before them. Even when the night was still the wind played here, bare and open as it was to every compass point, and tonight it hummed from Rough Tor in the west, keen as a knife and cold, gathering the marsh smells as it came, over the bitter turf and the running streams. There was still no sign of man or beast upon the road, which rose and dipped again across the moor, and, though Mary strained her eyes and her ears, she could hear nothing. On such a night the slightest sound would be magnified, and the approach of Mr. Bassat's party, numbering, as they would, a dozen men or so, said Richards, would easily be heard two miles or more away.

"We shall find them there before us, as likely as not," he told Mary, "and the landlord, with his hands bound, breathing fire at the squire. It will be a good thing for the neighbourhood when he's put out of harm's way, and he would have been before now, if the squire could have had his way. It's a pity we were not here sooner; there'll have been some sport in taking him, I reckon."

"Little sport if Mr. Bassat finds that his bird has flown," said Mary quietly. "Joss Merlyn knows these moors like the back of his hand, and he'll not linger once he has the start of an hour, or less than that."

"My master was bred here, same as the landlord," said Richards; "if it comes to a chase across country, I'd lay odds on the squire every time. He's hunted here, man and boy, for nearly fifty years, I should say, and where a fox will go the squire will follow. But they'll catch this one before he starts to run, if I'm not mistaken." Mary let him continue; his occasional jerky statements did not worry her as the kindly prattle of his mistress had done, and his broad back and honest rugged face gave her some confidence in this night of strain.

They were approaching the dip in the road and the narrow bridge that spanned the river Fowey; Mary could hear the ripple and play of the stream as it ran swiftly over the stones. The steep hill to Jamaica rose in front of them, white beneath the moon, and as the dark chimneys appeared above the crest, Richards fell silent, fumbling with the pistols in his belt, and he cleared his throat with a nervous jerk of his head. Mary's heart beat fast now, and she held tight to the side of the trap. The horse bent to the climb, his head low, and it seemed to Mary that the clop of his hoofs rang too loudly on the surface of the road, and she wished they had been more silent.

As they drew near to the summit of the hill, Richards turned and whispered in her ear, "Would it be best for you to wait here, in the trap, by the side of the road, and I go forward and see if they are there?"

Mary shook her head. "Better for me to go," she said, "and you follow a pace or two behind, or stay here and wait until I call. From the silence, it seems as though the squire and his party are not yet come, after all, and that the landlord has escaped. Should he be there, however—my uncle, I mean—I can risk an encounter with him, when you could not. Give me a pistol; I shall have little to fear from him then."

"I hardly think it right for you to go alone," said the man doubtfully. "You may walk right into him, and I hear no sound from you again. It's strange, as you say, this silence. I'd expected shouting and fighting, and my master's voice topping it all. It's almost unnatural, in a way. They must have been detained in Launceston. I half fancy there'd be more wisdom if we turned aside down that track there and waited for them to come."

"I've waited long enough tonight, and gone half mad with it," said Mary. "I'd rather come upon my uncle face to face than lie here in the ditch, seeing and hearing nothing. It's my aunt I'm thinking of. She's as innocent as a child in all this business, and I want to care for her if I can. Give me a pistol and let me go. I can tread like a cat, and I'll not run my head into a noose, I promise you." She threw off the heavy cloak and hood that had protected her from the cold night air, and seized hold of the pistol that he handed down to her reluctantly. "Don't follow me unless I call or give some signal," she said. "Should you hear a shot fired, then perhaps it would be as well to come after me. But come warily, for all that. There's no need for both of us to run like fools into danger. For my part, I believe my uncle to have gone."

She hoped now that he had, and by driving into Devon made an end to the whole business. The country would be rid of him, and in the cheapest possible way. He might, even as he had said, start life again, or, more likely still, dig himself in somewhere five hundred miles from Cornwall and drink himself to death. She had no interest now in his capture; she wanted it finished and thrust aside; she wanted above all to lead her own life and forget him, and to put the world between her and Jamaica Inn. Revenge was an empty thing. To see him bound and helpless, surrounded by the squire and his men, would be of little satisfaction. She had spoken to Richards with confidence, but for all that she dreaded an encounter with her uncle, armed as she was; and the thought of coming upon him suddenly in the passage of the inn, with his hands ready to strike, and his bloodshot eyes staring down upon her, made her pause in her stride, before the yard, and glance back to the dark shadow in the ditch that was Richards and the trap. Then she levelled her pistol, her finger upon the trigger, and looked round the corner of the stone wall to the yard.

It was empty. The stable door was shut. The inn was as dark and silent as when she had left it nearly seven hours before, and the windows and the door were barred. She looked up to her window, and the pane of glass gaped empty and wide, unchanged since she had climbed from it that afternoon.

There were no wheel marks in the yard, no preparations for departure. She crept across to the stable and laid her ear against the door. She waited a moment, and then she heard the pony move restlessly in his stall; she heard his hoofs clink on the cobbles.

Then they had not gone, and her uncle was still at Jamaica Inn.

Her heart sank; and she wondered if she should return to Richards and the trap, and wait, as he had suggested, until Squire Bassat and his men arrived. She glanced once more at the shuttered house. Surely, if her uncle intended to leave, he would have gone before now. The cart alone would take an hour to load, and it must be nearly eleven o'clock. He might have altered his plans and decided to go on foot, but then Aunt Patience could never accompany him. Mary hesitated; the situation had become odd now, and unreal.

She stood by the porch and listened. She even tried the handle of the door. It was locked, of course. She ventured a little way round the corner of the house, past the entrance to the bar, and so to the patch of garden behind the kitchen. She trod softly now, keeping herself in shadow, and she came to where a chink of candlelight would show through the gap in the kitchen shutter. There was no light. She stepped close now to the shutter and laid her eye against the slit. The kitchen was black as a pit. She laid her hand on the knob of the door and slowly turned it. It gave, to her astonishment, and the door opened. This easy entrance, entirely unforeseen, shocked her for a moment, and she was afraid to enter.

Supposing her uncle sat on his chair, waiting for her, his gun across his knee? She had her own pistol, but it gave her no confidence.

Very slowly she laid her face to the gap made by the door. No sound came to her. Out of the tail of her eye she could see the ashes of the fire, but the glow was almost gone. She knew then that nobody was there. Some instinct told her that the kitchen had been empty for hours. She pushed the door wide and went inside. The room struck cold and damp. She waited until her eyes had become accustomed to the darkness, and she could make out the shape of the kitchen table and the chair beside it. There was a candle on the table, and she thrust it into the feeble glow of the fire, where it took light and flickered. When it burnt strong enough, she held it high above her head and looked about her. The kitchen was still strewn with the preparations for departure. There was a bundle belonging to Aunt Patience on the chair, and a heap of blankets lay on the floor ready to be rolled. In the corner of the room, where it always stood, was her uncle's gun. They had decided, then, to wait for another day, and were now abed and asleep in the room upstairs.

The door to the passage was wide open, and the silence became more oppressive than before, strangely and horribly still.

Something was not as it had been; some sound was lacking that must account for the silence. Then Mary realized that she could not hear the clock. The ticking had stopped.

She stepped into the passage and listened again. She was right; the house was silent because the clock had stopped. She went forward slowly, with the candle in one hand and the pistol levelled in the other.

She turned the corner, where the long dark passage branched into the hall, and she saw that the clock, which stood always against the wall beside the door into the parlour, had toppled forward and fallen upon its face. The glass was splintered in fragments on the stone flags, and the wood was split. The wall gaped bare where it had stood, very naked now and strange, with the paper marked a deep yellow in contrast to the faded pattern of the wall. The clock had fallen across the narrow hall, and it was not until she came to the foot of the stairs that Mary saw what was beyond.

The landlord of Jamaica Inn lay on his face amongst the wreckage.

The fallen clock had hidden him at first, for he sprawled in the shadow, one arm flung high above his head and the other fastened upon the broken splintered door. Because his legs were stretched out on either side of him, one foot jamming the wainscoting, he looked even larger in death

than he did before, his great frame blocking the entrance
from wall to wall.

There was blood on the stone floor; and blood between
his shoulders, dark now and nearly dry, where the knife
had found him.

When he was stabbed from behind he must have stretched
out his hands and stumbled, dragging at the clock; and
when he fell upon his face the clock crashed with him to
the ground, and he died there, clutching at the door.

Chapter 15

IT WAS A long while before Mary moved away from the
stairs. Something of her own strength had ebbed away,
leaving her powerless, like the figure on the floor. Her eyes
dwelt upon little immaterial things: the fragments of glass
from the smashed clock face that were bloodstained too,
and the discoloured patch of wall where the clock had
stood.

A spider settled on her uncle's hand; and it seemed
strange to her that the hand stayed motionless and did not
seek to rid itself of the spider. Her uncle would have
shaken it free. Then it crawled from his hand and ran up
his arm, working its way beyond the shoulder. When it
came to the wound it hesitated and then made a circuit,
returning to it again in curiosity, and there was a lack of
fear in its rapidity that was somehow horrible and desecrating
to death. The spider knew that the landlord could not harm
him. Mary knew this, too, but she had not lost her fear, like
the spider.

It was the silence that frightened her most. Now that the
clock no longer ticked, her nerves strained for the sound

of it; the slow wheezing choke had been familiar and a symbol of normality.

The light of her candle played upon the walls, but it did not reach to the top of the stairs, where the darkness gaped at her like a gulf.

She knew she could never climb those stairs again, nor tread that empty landing. Whatever lay beyond her and above must rest there undisturbed. Death had come upon the house tonight, and its brooding spirit still hovered in the air. She felt now that this was what Jamaica Inn had always waited for and feared. The damp walls, the creaking boards, the whispers in the air, and the footsteps that had no name: these were the warnings of a house that had felt itself long threatened.

Mary shivered; and she knew that the quality of this silence had origin in far-off buried and forgotten things.

She dreaded panic, above all things; the scream that forced itself to the lips, the wild stumble of groping feet and hands that beat the air for passage She was afraid that it might come to her, destroying reason; and, now that the first shock of discovery had lessened, she knew that it might force its way upon her, close in and stifle her. Her fingers might lose their sense of grip and touch, and the candle fall from her hands. Then she would be alone and covered by the darkness. The tearing desire to run seized hold of her, and she conquered it. She backed away from the hall towards the passage, the candle flickering in the draught of air, and when she came to the kitchen and saw the door still open to the patch of garden, her calm deserted her, and she ran blindly through the door to the cold free air outside, a sob in her throat, her outstretched hands grazing the stone wall as she turned the corner of the house. She ran like a thing pursued across the yard and came to the open road, where the familiar stalwart figure of the squire's groom confronted her. He put out his hands to save her, and she groped at his belt, feeling for security, her teeth chattering now in the full shock of reaction.

"He's dead," she said; "he's dead there on the floor. I saw him"; and, try as she did, she could not stop this

said; "I've only seen the suffering there's been, and the cruelty, and the pain. When my uncle came to Jamaica Inn he must have cast his shadow over the good things, and they died." Their voices had sunk to a whisper, and they glanced half-consciously over their shoulders to the tall chimneys that stood out against the sky, clear-cut and grey, beneath the moon. They were both thinking of one thing, and neither had the courage to mention it first; the groom from delicacy and tact, Mary from fear alone. Then at last she spoke, her voice husky and low:

"Something has happened to my aunt as well; I know that; I know she is dead. That's why I was afraid to go upstairs. She is lying there in the darkness, on the landing above. Whoever killed my uncle will have killed her too."

The groom cleared his throat. "She may have run out onto the moor," he said, "she may have run for help along the road—"

"No," whispered Mary, "she would never have done that. She would be with him now, down in the hall there, crouching by his side. She is dead. I know she is dead. If I had not left her, this would never have happened."

The man was silent. He could not help her. After all, she was a stranger to him, and what had passed beneath the roof of the inn while she had lived there was no concern of his. The responsibility of the evening lay heavy enough upon his shoulders, and he wished that his master would come. Fighting and shouting he understood; there was sense in that; but if there had really been a murder, as she said, and the landlord lying dead there, and his wife too—why, they could do no good in staying here like fugitives themselves, crouching in the ditch, but were better off and away, and so down the road to sight and sound of human habitation.

"I came here by the orders of my mistress," he began awkwardly; "but she said the squire would be here. Seeing as he is not—"

Mary held up a warning hand. "Listen," she said sharply. "Can you hear something?"

They strained their ears to the north. The faint clop of

horses was unmistakable, coming from beyond the valley, over the brow of the further hill.

"It's them," said Richards excitedly; "it's the squire; he's coming at last. Watch now; we'll see them go down the road into the valley."

They waited, and when a minute had passed, the first horseman appeared like a black smudge against the hard white road, followed by another, and another. They strung out in a line, and closed again, travelling at a gallop; while the cob who waited patiently beside the ditch pricked his ears and turned an enquiring head. The clatter drew near, and Richards in his relief ran out upon the road to greet them, shouting and waving his arms.

The leader swerved and drew rein, calling out in surprise at the sight of the groom. "What the devil do you do here?" he shouted, for it was the squire himself, and he held up his hand to warn his followers behind.

"The landlord is dead, murdered," cried the groom. "I have his niece here with me in the trap. It was Mrs. Bassat herself who sent me out here, sir. This young woman had best tell you the story in her own words."

He held the horse while his master dismounted, answering as well as he could the rapid questions put to him by the squire, and the little band of men gathered around him too, pressing for news; some of them dismounting also, and stamping their feet on the ground, blowing upon their hands for warmth.

"If the fellow has been murdered, as you say, then, by God, it serves him right," said Mr. Bassat; "but I'd rather have clapped irons on him myself for all that. You can't pay scores against a dead man. Go on into the yard, the rest of you, while I see if I can get some sense out of the girl yonder."

Richards, relieved of responsibility, was surrounded at once and treated as something of a hero who had not only discovered the murder but had tackled the author of it single-handed; until he reluctantly admitted that his part in the adventure had been small. The squire, whose mind worked slowly, did not realize what Mary was doing in the trap, and considered her as his groom's prisoner.

He heard with astonishment how she had walked the long miles to North Hill in the hopes of finding him, and, not content with that, must return again to Jamaica Inn. "This is altogether beyond me," he said gruffly. "I believed you to be in conspiracy with your uncle against the law. Why did you lie to me, then, when I came here earlier in the month? You told me you knew nothing."

"I lied because of my aunt," said Mary wearily. "Whatever I said to you then was for her sake only, nor did I know as much then as I do now. I am willing to explain everything in a court of law should it be necessary; but if I tried to tell you now you would not understand."

"Nor have I the time to listen," replied the squire. "You did a brave thing in walking all that way to North Hill to warn me, and I shall remember it in your favour; but all this trouble could have been avoided, and the terrible crime of Christmas Eve prevented, had you been frank with me before.

"However, all that for later. My groom tells me that you have found your uncle murdered, but beyond that you know nothing of the crime. Had you been a man you should go with me now to the inn, but I will spare you that. I can see you have endured enough." He raised his voice and shouted for the servant. "Take the trap up to the yard and stay beside it with the young woman while we break into the inn"; and, turning to Mary: "I must ask you to wait in the yard, if your courage permits you; you are the only one amongst us who knows anything of the matter, and you were the last to see your uncle alive." Mary nodded her head. She was nothing more now than a passive instrument of the law and must do as she was bidden. He had at least spared her the ordeal of going once more into the empty inn and looking upon the body of her uncle. The yard, that had lain in shadow when she came, was now the scene of activity; horses stamped on the cobblestones, and there was the shaking, ringing sound of bit and bridle, and there were the footsteps and the voices of the men, topped by the squire's gruff word of command.

He led the way round to the back, at Mary's direction,

and presently the bleak and silent house lost its shuttered air. The window in the bar was flung open, and the windows of the parlour; some of the men went upstairs and explored the empty guest rooms above, for these windows were unbarred also and opened to the air. Only the heavy entrance door remained shut; and Mary knew that the landlord's body lay stretched across the threshold.

Someone called sharply from the house and was answered by a murmur of voices and a question from the squire. The sounds came plainly now through the open parlour window to the yard outside. Richards glanced across at Mary, and he saw by the pallor of her face that she had heard.

A man who stood by the horses, and who had not gone with the others inside the inn, shouted to the groom. "Do you hear what they say?" he said in some excitement. "There's another body there, on the landing upstairs."

Richards said nothing. Mary drew her cloak further around her shoulders and pulled the hood across her face. They waited in silence. Presently the squire himself came out into the yard and crossed to the trap.

"I'm sorry," he said. "I have bad news for you. Perhaps you expected it."

"Yes," said Mary.

"I don't think she suffered at all. She must have died at once. She was lying just inside the bedroom at the end of the passage. Stabbed, like your uncle. She could have known nothing. Believe me, I am very sorry. I wish I could have spared you this." He stood by her, awkward and distressed, and repeated again that she could not have suffered, that she had not known, but was killed instantly; and then, seeing that Mary were better left alone, and he could not help her, he stamped back across the yard to the inn.

Mary sat motionless, shrouded in her cloak; and she prayed in her own way that Aunt Patience would forgive her and find peace now, wherever she should be, and that the dragging chains of life would fall away from her, leaving her free. She prayed also that Aunt Patience would understand what she had tried to do; and above all that her

234

mother would be there, and she would not be alone. These
were the only thoughts that brought her a measure of consolation, and she knew if she went over in her mind again
the story of the last few hours she would come to the one
and only accusation: had she not left Jamaica Inn, Aunt
Patience might not have died.

Once again, though, there came a murmur of excitement
from the house, and this time there was shouting, and
the sound of running feet, and several voices raised in unison;
so that Richards ran to the open parlour window, forgetting
his trust in the excitement of the moment, and thrust his
leg over the sill. There was a crash of splintering wood, and
the shutters were torn away from the window of the barred
room, which no one, apparently, had entered up to now.
The men were tearing away the barricade of wood, and
someone held a flare to light the room; Mary could see the
flame dance in the draught of air.

Then the light vanished, and the voices died away, and
she could hear the sound of footsteps tramping to the back
of the house; and then round the corner to the yard they
came, six or seven of them, led by the squire, holding amongst
them something that squirmed and wriggled and fought
for release, with hoarse bewildered cries. "They've got him!
It's the murderer!" shouted Richards, calling to Mary; and
she turned, brushing aside the hood that covered her face,
and looked down upon the group of men who came to the
trap. The captive stared up at her, blinking at the light
they flashed in his eyes, his clothes cobweb covered, his
face unshaven and black: and it was Harry the pedlar.

"Who is he?" they shouted. "Do you know him?" And the
squire came round in front of the trap and bade them bring
the man close, so that she could see him. "What do you know
of this fellow?" he said to Mary. "We found him in the
barred room yonder lying on some sacks, and he denies all
knowledge of the crime."

"He was of the company," said Mary slowly, "and he
came to the inn last night and quarreled with my uncle. My
uncle had the better of him and locked him up in the barred
room, threatening him with death. He had every reason

235

to kill my uncle, and no one could have done it but he. He is lying to you."

"But the door was locked upon him; it took three of us or more to break it down from the outside," said the squire. "This fellow had never been from the room at all. Look at his clothes; look at his eyes, dazzled still by the light. He's not your murderer."

The pedlar glanced furtively from one to the other of his guards, his small mean eyes darting to right and left, and Mary knew at once that what the squire had said was no more than the truth; Harry the pedlar could not have committed the crime. He had lain in the barred room since the landlord put him there, over twenty-four hours ago. He had lain there in the dark, waiting for release, and during the long hours someone had come to Jamaica Inn and gone again, his work completed, in the silence of the night.

"Whoever did it knew nothing of this rascal, locked in the room yonder," continued the squire, "and he's no use to us as a witness, as far as I can see, for he heard and saw nothing. But we'll have him in jail for all that, and hang him too, if he deserves it, which I'll be bound he does. But he shall turn King's evidence first and give us the names of his companions. One of them has killed the landlord for revenge, you may depend on that, and we'll track him down if we set every hound in Cornwall on his heels. Take this fellow to the stable, some of you, and hold him there; the rest come back to the inn with me."

They dragged the pedlar away, who, realizing that some crime had been discovered and suspicion might possibly rest upon him, found his tongue at last and began to blab his innocence, whining for mercy and swearing by the Trinity, until someone cuffed him to silence and threatened him with the rope, there and then, above the stable door. This silenced him, and he fell to muttering blasphemies beneath his breath, turning his rat's eyes now and again to Mary, who sat above him in the trap, a few yards away.

She waited there, her chin in her hands and the hood fallen away from her face, and she neither heard his blasphemies nor saw his furtive narrow eyes, for she remembered other eyes that had looked upon her in the morning, and another voice that had spoken calm and cold, saying of his brother, "He shall die for this."

There was the sentence, flung carelessly, on the way to Launceston fair: "I have never killed a man yet"; and there was the gypsy woman in the market square: "There's blood on your hand; you'll kill a man one day." All the little things she would forget rose up again and clamoured against him: his hatred of his brother, his streak of callous cruelty, his lack of tenderness, his tainted Merlyn blood.

That, before all things, would betray him first. Like to like. One of a kind. He had gone to Jamaica Inn as he had promised, and his brother had died, as he had sworn. The whole truth stared up at her in ugliness and horror, and she wished now that she had stayed, and he had killed her too. He was a thief, and like a thief in the night he had come and was gone again. She knew that the evidence could be built against him piece by piece, with herself as witness; it would be a fence around him from which there would be no escape. She had only to go now to the squire and say, "I know who it is that has done this thing," and they would listen to her, all of them; they would crowd around her like a pack of hounds panting for the chase, and the trail would lead them to him, past Rushyford, and through Trewartha Marsh, to Twelve Men's Moor. He slept there now perhaps, forgetful of his crime and caring not at all, stretched on his bed in the lonely cottage where he and his brother had been born. When morning came he would be gone, whistling perhaps, throwing his legs across a horse, and so away and out of Cornwall forever, a murderer like his father before him.

In her fancy she heard the clop of his horse upon the road, far distant in the quiet night, beating a tempo of farewell; but fancy became reason, and reason became certainty, and the sound she heard was not the dream thing of her imagination but the live tapping of a horse upon the highway.

She turned her head and listened, nerves strung now to

the limit; and the hands that held the cloak around her were clammy and cold with sweat.

The sound of the horse drew nearer still. He was trotting at a steady, even pace, neither hurried nor slow, and the rhythmic jogging tune that he played on the road had echo in her throbbing heart.

She was not alone now as she listened. The men who guarded the pedlar murmured to one another in low tones and looked towards the road, and the groom Richards, who was with them, hesitated a moment and then went swiftly to the inn to call the squire. The beat of the horse's hoofs rang loud now as he climbed the hill, sounding like a challenge to the night so silent and still, and as he topped the summit and rounded the wall into view the squire came out of the inn, followed by his man.

"Stop!" he called. "In the name of the King. I must ask your business on the road tonight."

The horseman drew rein and turned into the yard. The black riding cape gave no clue to his identity, but when he bowed and bared his head, the thick halo of hair shone white under the moon, and the voice that spoke in answer to the squire was gentle and sweet.

"Mr. Bassat of North Hill, I believe," he said, and he leant forward in his saddle, with a note in his hand. "I have a message here from Mary Yellan of Jamaica Inn, who asks my help in trouble; but I see by the company assembled here that I have come too late. You remember me, of course; we have met before. I am the vicar of Altarnun."

Chapter 16

MARY SAT alone in the living room at the vicarage and watched the smouldering turf fire. She had slept long and was now rested and refreshed; but the peace for which she craved had not yet come to her.

They had been kind to her and patient; too kind perhaps, coming so sudden and unexpected after the long strain; and Mr. Bassat himself, with clumsy, well-meaning hands, patted her on the shoulder as he would a hurt child and said to her in his gruff kind way, "Now you must sleep, and forget all you have gone through, and remember it's behind you now and over. I can promise you that we shall find the man who killed your aunt soon, very soon, and he shall hang at the next Assizes. And when you are a little recovered from the shock of these last few months, you shall say what you would like to do, and where you would like to go."

She had no will of her own; they could make decisions for her; and, when Francis Davey offered his home for shelter, she accepted meekly and without feeling, conscious that her listless word of thanks savoured of ingratitude. Once more she knew the humility of being born a woman, when the breaking down of strength and spirit was taken as natural and unquestioned.

Were she a man, now, she would receive rough treatment, or indifference at the best, and be requested to ride at once perhaps to Bodmin or to Launceston to bear witness, with an understanding that she should find her own lodging and betake herself to the world's end if she wished when all questions had been asked. And she would depart, when

239

they had finished with her, and go on a ship somewhere, working her passage before the mast; or tramp the road with one silver penny in her pocket and her heart and soul at liberty. Here she was, with tears ready to the surface and an aching head, being hurried from the scene of action with smooth words and gestures, a nuisance and a factor of delay, like every woman and every child after tragedy.

The vicar had driven her himself in the trap—with the squire's groom following behind on his horse—and he at least had the gift of silence, for he questioned her not at all, nor murmured sympathy to be both wasted and ignored, but drove swiftly to Altarnun and arrived there as his church clock struck one.

He roused his housekeeper from the cottage near by, the same woman that Mary had spoken with in the afternoon, and bade her come with him to the vicarage to prepare a room for his guest, which she did at once, without chattering or exclaiming in wonder, bringing the aired linen from her own home to lay on the bed. She kindled a fire in the grate and warmed a rough woollen nightdress before it, while Mary shed her clothes, and when the bed was ready for her, and the smooth sheets turned back, Mary allowed herself to be led to it as a child is led to a cradle.

She would have closed her eyes at once but for an arm suddenly around her shoulders and a voice in her ear, "Drink this," persuasive and cool, and Francis Davey himself stood beside the bed, with a glass in his hand and his strange eyes looking into hers, pale and expressionless.

"You will sleep now," he said, and she knew from the bitter taste that he had put some powder in the hot drink which he had brewed for her, and that he had done this in understanding of her restless, tortured mind.

The last that she remembered was his hand upon her forehead and those still white eyes that told her to forget; and then she slept, as he had bidden her.

It was nearly four in the afternoon before she woke, and the fourteen hours of sleep had done the work that he intended, turning the edge of sorrow and blunting her to pain. The sharp grief for Aunt Patience had softened, and the bitterness too. Reason told her that she could not put the blame upon herself: she had done only what her conscience had commanded her to do. Justice had come first. Her dull wit had not foreseen the tragedy; there lay the fault. There remained regret, and regret could not bring Aunt Patience back again.

These were her thoughts on rising; but when she was dressed, and had gone below to the living room, to find the fire burning and the curtains drawn, and the vicar abroad upon some business, the old nagging sense of insecurity returned to her, and it seemed to her that responsibility for the disaster lay on her shoulders alone. Jem's face was ever present with her as she had seen it last, drawn and haggard in the false grey light, and there had been a purpose in his eyes then, and in the very set of his mouth, that she had wilfully ignored. He had been the unknown factor from the beginning to the end, from that first morning when he had come to the bar in Jamaica Inn, and deliberately she had shut her eyes to the truth. She was a woman, and for no reason in heaven or earth she loved him. He had kissed her, and she was bound to him for ever. She felt herself fallen and degraded, weakened in mind and body, who had been strong before; and her pride had gone with her independence.

One word to the vicar when he returned, and a message to the squire, and Aunt Patience would be avenged. Jem would die with a rope round his neck as his father had done; and she would return to Helford, seeking the threads of her old life, that lay twisted even now and buried in the soil.

She got up from the chair beside the fire and began to walk the length of the room, with some idea that she wrestled now with her ultimate problem, but even as she did so she knew that her very action was a lie, a poor trick to appease her conscience, and that the word would never be given.

Jem was safe from her, and he would ride away with a song on his lips and a laugh at her expense, forgetful of her, and of his brother, and of God; while she dragged through the years, sullen and bitter, the stain of silence marking her, coming in the end to ridicule as a soured spinster who had been kissed once in her life and could not forget it.

Cynicism and sentimentality were two extremes to be avoided, and as Mary prowled about the room, her mind as restless as her body, she felt as though Francis Davey himself were watching her, his cold eyes probing her soul. The room held something of him after all, now that he was not here, and she could imagine him standing in the corner by the easel, his brush in his hand, staring out of the window at things that were dead and gone.

There were canvases with their faces to the wall close to the easel, and Mary turned them to the light in curiosity. Here was an interior of a church—his church, she supposed—painted in the twilight of midsummer it would seem, with the nave in shadow. There was a strange green afterglow upon the arches, stretching to the roof, and this light was something sudden and unexpected that lingered in her memory after she had laid the picture aside, so that she returned to it and considered it once more.

It might be that this green afterglow was a faithful reproduction, and peculiar to his church at Altarnun, but, for all that, it cast a haunting and uncanny light upon the picture, and Mary knew that had she a home she would not care for it to hang upon her walls.

She could not have put her feeling of discomfort into words, but it was as though some spirit, having no knowledge of the church itself, had groped its way into the interior and breathed an alien atmosphere upon the shadowed nave. As she turned the paintings, one by one, she saw that they were all tainted in the same manner and to the same degree; what might have been a striking study of the moor beneath Brown Willy on a spring day, with the high clouds banked up behind the tor, had been marred by the dark colour and the very contour of the clouds that dwarfed the picture and overwhelmed the scene, with this same green light predominating all.

She wondered, for the first time, whether by being born

albino, and a freak of nature, his colour sense was therefore in any way impaired, and his sight itself neither
normal nor true. This might be the explanation, but, even
so, her feeling of discomfort remained after she had replaced
the canvases with their faces to the wall. She continued
her inspection of the room, which told her little, it being
sparsely furnished anyway, and free of ornaments and
books. Even his desk was bare of correspondence and looked
seldom used. She drummed with her fingers on the polished
surface, wondering if he sat here to write his sermons, and
suddenly and unpardonably she opened the narrow drawer
beneath the desk. It was empty; and at once she was ashamed.
She was about to shut it when she noticed that the paper
with which the drawer was laid had one corner turned, and
there was some sketch drawn upon the other side. She took
hold of the paper and glanced at the drawing. Once again
it represented the interior of a church, but this time the
congregation was assembled in the pews, and the vicar
himself in the pulpit. At first Mary saw nothing unusual in
the sketch; it was a subject natural enough for a vicar to
choose who had skill with his pen; but when she looked
closer she realized what he had done.

This was not a drawing at all, but a caricature, grotesque
as it was horrible. The people of the congregation were
bonneted and shawled, and in their best clothes as for
Sunday, but he had drawn sheep's heads upon their shoulders instead of human faces. The animal jaws gaped foolishly
at the preacher, with silly vacant solemnity, and their hoofs
were folded in prayer. The features of each sheep had been
touched upon with care, as though representing a living
soul, but the expression on every one of them was the
same—that of an idiot who neither knew nor cared. The
preacher, with his black gown and halo of hair, was Francis
Davey; but he had given himself a wolf's face, and the
wolf was laughing at the flock beneath him.

The thing was a mockery, blasphemous and terrible. Mary
covered it quickly and replaced the paper in the drawer,
with the white sheet uppermost; then she shut the drawer
and went away from the desk and sat once more in the chair

beside the fire. She had stumbled upon a secret, and she would rather that the secret stayed concealed. This was something that concerned her not at all, but rested between the draughtsman and his God.

When she heard his footstep on the path outside, she rose hurriedly and moved the light away from her chair so that she would be in shadow when he came into the room and he could not read her face.

Her chair had its back to the door, and she sat there, waiting for him; but he was so long in coming that she turned at last to listen for his step, and then she saw him, standing behind her chair, having entered the room noiselessly from the hall. She started in surprise, and he came forward then into the light, making apology for his appearance.

"Forgive me," he said; "you did not expect me so soon, and I have blundered into your dreams."

She shook her head and stammered an excuse, and then he asked at once after her health, and how she had slept, stripping himself of his greatcoat as he spoke and standing before the fire in his black clerical dress.

"Have you eaten today?" he asked, and, when she told him she had not, he took out his watch and noted the time—a few minutes before six—which he compared with the clock upon his desk. "You have supped with me before, Mary Yellan, and you shall sup with me again," he said; "but this time, if you do not mind and if you are rested enough, you shall lay the table and fetch the tray from the kitchen. Hannah will have left it prepared, and we will not trouble her again. For my part, I have writing to do; that is, if you have no objection."

She assured him that she was rested and would like nothing better than to make herself useful, and he nodded his head then and said, "At a quarter to seven," turning his back on her; and she gathered she was dismissed.

She made her way to the kitchen, put something out of countenance at his abrupt arrival, and she was glad that he had given her an added half-hour to herself, for she had been ill prepared for conversation when he found her. Perhaps supper would be a brief affair, and, once over, he would turn to his desk again and leave her to her thoughts. She wished she had not opened the drawer. The memory of the caricature lingered with her unpleasantly. She felt much as a child does who acquires knowledge forbidden by his parents and then hangs his head, guilty and ashamed, fearful that his tongue will betray him. She would have been more comfortable could she have taken her meal alone here in the kitchen and been treated by him as a handmaid rather than a guest. As it was, her position was not defined, for his courtesy and his commands were curiously mingled. She made play then of getting the supper, at home amongst the familiar kitchen smells, and awaited reluctantly the summons of the clock. The church itself chimed the three quarters and gave her no excuse, so she carried the tray to the living room, hoping that nothing of her inner feeling showed upon her face.

He was standing with his back to the fire, and he had pulled the table in readiness before it. Although she did not look at him, she felt his scrutiny upon her, and her movements were clumsy. She was aware, too, that he had made some alteration to the room, and out of the tail of her eye she saw that he had taken down his easel, and the canvases were no longer stacked against the wall. The desk, for the first time, was in disorder, with papers and correspondence piled upon it, and he had been burning letters too, for the yellow, blackened scraps lay amongst the ashes under the turf.

They sat down together at the table, and he helped her to the cold pie.

"Is curiosity dead in Mary Yellan that she does not ask me what I have done with my day?" he said at length, mocking her gently and bringing the flush of guilt to her face at once.

"It is no business of mine where you have been," she answered.

"You are wrong there," he said, "and it is your business. I have meddled in your affairs the livelong day. You asked for my help, did you not?"

Mary was ashamed and hardly knew what to reply. "I have not thanked you yet for coming so promptly to Jamaica

245

Inn," she said, "nor for my bed last night and my sleep today. You think me ungrateful."

"I never said that. I wondered only at your patience. It had not struck two when I bade you sleep this morning, and it is now seven in the evening. Long hours; and things do not stand still by themselves."

"Did you not sleep, then, after you left me?"

"I slept until eight. And then I breakfasted and was away again. My grey horse was lame, and I could not use him, so progress was slow with the cob. He jogged like a snail to Jamaica Inn, and from Jamaica Inn to North Hill."

"You have been to North Hill?"

"Mr. Bassat entertained me to luncheon. There were eight or ten of us present, I daresay, and each one of us shouting his opinion to the deaf ear of his neighbour. It was a lengthy meal, and I was glad when we came to the end of it. However, we were all of one accord that the murderer of your uncle will not remain at liberty for long."

"Does Mr. Bassat suspect anyone?" Mary's tone was guarded, and she kept her eyes on her plate. The food tasted like sawdust in her mouth.

"Mr. Bassat is ready to suspect himself. He has questioned every inhabitant within a radius of ten miles, and the number of strange persons who were abroad last night is legion. It will take a week or more to have the truth from every one of them; but no matter. Mr. Bassat is not deterred."

"What have they done with—with my aunt?"

"They were taken, both of them, to North Hill this morning and are to be buried there. All that has been arranged, and you need not concern yourself. As for the rest—well, we shall see."

"And the pedlar? They have not let him go?"

"No, he is safe under lock and key, screaming curses to the air. I do not care for the pedlar. Neither, I think, do you."

Mary laid aside the fork she had lifted to her lips and put down the meat again untasted.

"How do you mean?" she said, on the defensive.

"I repeat, you do not care for the pedlar. I can well

246

understand it, for a more unpleasant and disagreeable fellow I have never clapped eyes on. I gather from Richards, groom to Mr. Bassat, that you suspected the pedlar of the murder and said as much to Mr. Bassat himself. Hence my conclusion that you do not care for him. It is a pity for all of us that the barred room proves him innocent. He would have made an excellent scapegoat and saved a deal of trouble."

The vicar continued to make an excellent supper, but Mary was only playing with her food, and when he offered her a second helping she refused.

"What has the pedlar done to incur your displeasure to such an extent?" he enquired, harping upon the subject with persistence.

"He attacked me once."

"I thought as much. He is true to a particular type. You resisted him, of course?"

"I believe I hurt him. He did not touch me again."

"No, I do not suppose he did. When did this happen?"

"On Christmas Eve."

"After I left you at Five Lanes?"

"Yes."

"I am beginning to understand. You did not return, then, to the inn that night? You fell in with the landlord and his friends upon the road?"

"Yes."

"And they took you with them to the shore to add to their sport?"

"Please, Mr. Davey, do not ask me any more. I would rather not speak of that night, neither here nor in the future, nor ever again. There are some things that are best buried deep."

"You shall not speak of it, Mary Yellan. I blame myself for having allowed you to continue your journey alone. Looking at you now, with your clear eye and skin, and the way you carry your head, and, above all, the set of your chin, you bear little trace of what you endured. The word of a parish priest may not go for much—but you have shown remarkable fortitude. I admire you."

She looked up at him, and then away again, and fell to crumbling a piece of bread in her hand.

"When I consider the pedlar," he continued, after a while, helping himself generously to stewed damsons, "I feel it very remiss of the murderer not to have looked into the barred room. It may have been that he was pressed for time, but a minute or two could hardly have affected the issue, and he would most certainly have made the whole affair more thorough."

"In what way, Mr. Davey?"

"Why, by putting paid to the pedlar's account."

"You mean, he might have killed him too?"

"Precisely. The pedlar is no ornament to the world while he lives, and dead he would at least make food for worms. That is my opinion. What is more, had the murderer known that the pedlar had attacked you, he would have had a motive strong enough to kill twice over."

Mary cut herself a slice of cake she did not want and forced it between her lips. By making a pretence of eating she gave herself countenance. The hand shook, though, that held the knife, and she made a poor job of her slice.

"I don't see," she said, "what I have to do in the matter."

"You have too modest an opinion of yourself," he replied.

They continued to eat in silence, Mary with lowered head and eyes firm fixed upon her plate. Instinct told her that he played her as an angler plays the fish upon his line. At last she could wait no longer, but must blurt him a question: "So Mr. Bassat and the rest of you have made little headway, after all, and the murderer is still at large?"

"Oh, but we have not moved as slowly as that. Some progress has been made. The pedlar, for instance, in a hopeless attempt to save his own skin, has turned King's evidence to the best of his ability, but he has not helped us much. We have had from him a bald account of the work done on the coast on Christmas Eve—in which, he says, he took no part—and also some patching together of the long months that have gone before. We heard of the waggons that came to Jamaica Inn by night among other things, and we were given the names of his companions. Those he knew, that is to say. The organization appears to have been far larger than was hitherto supposed."

Mary said nothing. She shook her head when he offered her the damsons.

"In fact," continued the vicar, "he went so far as to suggest that the landlord of Jamaica Inn was their leader in name only, and that your uncle had his orders from one above him. That, of course, puts a new complexion on the matter. The gentlemen became excited and a little disturbed. What have you to say of the pedlar's theory?"

"It is possible, of course."

"I believe you once made the same suggestion to me?"

"I may have done. I forget."

"If this is so, it would seem that the unknown leader and the murderer must be one and the same person. Don't you agree?"

"Why, yes, I suppose so."

"That should narrow the field considerably. We may disregard the general rabble of the company and look for someone with a brain and a personality. Did you ever see such a person at Jamaica Inn?"

"No, never."

"He must have gone to and fro in stealth, possibly in the silence of the night when you and your aunt were abed and asleep. He would not have come by the highroad, because you would have heard the clatter of his horse's hoofs. But there is always the possibility that he came on foot, is there not?"

"Yes, there is always that possibility, as you say."

"In which case the man must know the moors, or at least have local knowledge. One of the gentlemen suggested that he lived near by—within walking or riding distance, that is to say. And that is why Mr. Bassat intends to question every inhabitant in the radius of ten miles, as I explained to you at the beginning of supper. So you see the net will close around the murderer, and if he tarries long he will be caught. We are all convinced of that. Have you finished already? You have eaten very little."

"I am not hungry."

"I am sorry for that. Hannah will think her cold pie was not appreciated. Did I tell you I saw an acquaintance of yours today?"

"No, you did not. I have no friends but yourself."

"Thank you, Mary Yellan. That is a pretty compliment, and I shall treasure it accordingly. But you are not being strictly truthful, you know. You have an acquaintance; you told me so yourself."

"I don't know who you mean, Mr. Davey."

"Come now. Did not the landlord's brother take you to Launceston fair?"

Mary gripped her hands under the table and dug her nails into her flesh.

"The landlord's brother?" she repeated, playing for time. "I have not seen him since then. I believed him to be away."

"No, he has been in the district since Christmas. He told me so himself. As a matter of fact, it had come to his ears that I had given you shelter, and he came up to me with a message for you. 'Tell her how sorry I am.' That is what he said. I presume he referred to your aunt."

"Was that all he said?"

"I believe he would have said more, but Mr. Bassat interrupted us."

"Mr. Bassat? Mr. Bassat was there when he spoke to you?"

"Why, of course. There were several of the gentlemen in the room. It was just before I came away from North Hill this evening, when the discussion was closed for the day."

"Why was Jem Merlyn present at the discussion?"

"He had a right, I suppose, as brother of the deceased. He did not appear much moved by his loss, but perhaps they did not agree."

"Did—did Mr. Bassat and the gentlemen question him?"

"There was a considerable amount of talk amongst them the whole day. Young Merlyn appears to possess intelligence. His answers were most astute. He must have a far better brain than his brother ever had. You told me he lived somewhat precariously, I remember. He stole horses, I believe."

Mary nodded. Her fingers traced a pattern on the table-cloth.

"He seems to have done that when there was nothing better to do," said the vicar, "but when a chance came for him to use his intelligence he took it, and small blame to him, I suppose. No doubt he was well paid."

The gentle voice wore away at her nerves, pinpricking them with every word, and she knew now that he had defeated her, and she could no longer keep up the pretence of indifference. She lifted her face to him, her eyes heavy with the agony of restraint, and she spread out her hands in supplication.

"What will they do to him, Mr. Davey?" she said. "What will they do to him?"

The pale, expressionless eyes stared back at her, and for the first time she saw a shadow pass across them, and a flicker of surprise.

"Do?" he said, obviously puzzled. "Why should they do anything? I suppose he has made his peace with Mr. Bassat and has nothing more to fear. They will hardly throw old sins in his face after the service he has done them."

"I don't understand you. What service has he done?"

"Your mind works slowly tonight, Mary Yellan, and I appear to talk in riddles. Did you not know that it was Jem Merlyn who informed against his brother?"

She stared at him stupidly, her brain clogged and refusing to work. She repeated the words after him like a child who learns a lesson.

"Jem Merlyn informed against his brother?"

The vicar pushed away his plate and began to set the things in order on the tray. "Why, certainly," he said; "so Mr. Bassat gave me to understand. It appears that it was the squire himself who fell in with your friend at Launceston on Christmas Eve and carried him off to North Hill as an experiment. 'You've stolen my horse,' said he, 'and you're as big a rogue as your brother. I've the power to clap you in jail tomorrow and you wouldn't set eyes on a horse for a dozen years or more. But you can go free if you bring me

251

proof that your brother at Jamaica Inn is the man I believe him to be.'

"Your young friend asked for time; and when the time was up he shook his head. 'No,' said he; 'you must catch him yourself if you want him. I'm damned if I'll have truck with the law.' But the squire pushed a proclamation under his nose. 'Look there, Jem,' he said, 'and see what you think of that. There's been the bloodiest wreck on Christmas Eve since the *Lady of Gloucester* went ashore above Padstow last winter. Now will you change your mind?' As to the rest of the story, the squire said little in my hearing—people were coming and going all the time, you must remember—but I gather your friend slipped his chain and ran for it in the night, and then came back again yesterday morning, when they thought to have seen the last of him, and went straight to the squire as he came out of church and said, as cool as you please, 'Very well, Mr. Bassat, you shall have your proof.' And that is why I remarked to you just now that Jem Merlyn had a better brain than his brother."

The vicar had cleared the table and set the tray in the corner, but he continued to stretch his legs before the fire and take his ease in the narrow high-backed chair. Mary took no account of his movements. She stared before her into space, her whole mind split, as it were, by his information, the evidence she had so fearfully and so painfully built against the man she loved collapsing into nothing like a pack of cards.

"Mr. Davey," she said slowly, "I believe I am the biggest fool that ever came out of Cornwall."

"I believe you are, Mary Yellan," said the vicar.

His dry tone, so cutting after the gentle voice she knew, was a rebuke in itself, and she accepted it with humility.

"Whatever happens," she continued, "I can face the future now, bravely and without shame."

"I am glad of that," he said.

She shook her hair back from her face and smiled for the first time since he had known her. The anxiety and the dread had gone from her at last.

"What else did Jem Merlyn say and do?" she asked.

The vicar glanced at his watch and replaced it with a sigh.

"I wish I had the time to tell you," he said, "but it is nearly eight already. The hours go by too fast for both of us. I think we have talked enough about Jem Merlyn for the present."

"Tell me one thing—was he at North Hill when you left?"

"He was. In fact, it was his last remark that hurried me home."

"What did he say to you?"

"He did not address himself to me. He announced his intention of riding over tonight to visit the blacksmith at Warleggan."

"Mr. Davey, you are playing with me now."

"I most certainly am not. Warleggan is a long trek from North Hill, but I daresay he can find his way in the dark."

"What has it to do with you if he visits the blacksmith?"

"He will show the nail he picked up in the heather, down in the field below Jamaica Inn. The nail comes from a horse's shoe; the job was carelessly done, of course. The nail was a new one, and Jem Merlyn, being a stealer of horses, knows the work of every blacksmith on the moors. 'Look here,' he said to the squire. 'I found it this morning in the field behind the inn. Now you have had your discussions and want me no more, I'll ride to Warleggan, with your leave, and throw this in Tom Jory's face as bad workmanship.'"

"Well, and what then?" said Mary.

"Yesterday was Sunday, was it not? And on Sunday no blacksmith plies his trade unless he has great respect for his customer. Only one traveller passed Tom Jory's smithy yesterday and begged a new nail for his lame horse, and the time was, I suppose, somewhere near seven o'clock in the evening. After which the traveller continued his journey by way of Jamaica Inn."

"How do you know this?" said Mary.

"Because the traveller was the vicar of Altarnun," he said.

Chapter 17

A SILENCE had fallen upon the room. Although the fire burnt steady as ever, there was a chill in the air that had not been there before. Each waited for the other to speak, and Mary heard Francis Davey swallow once. At length she looked into his face and saw what she expected: the pale, steadfast eyes staring at her across the table, cold no longer, but burning in the white mask of his face like living things at last. She knew now what he would have her know, but still she said nothing; she clung to ignorance as a source of protection, playing for time as the only ally in her favour.

His eyes compelled her to speak, and she continued to warm her hands at the fire, forcing a smile. "You are pleased to be mysterious tonight, Mr. Davey."

He did not answer at once; she heard him swallow again, and then he leant forward in his chair, with an abrupt change of subject.

"You lost your confidence in me today before I came," he said. "You went to my desk and found the drawing; you were disturbed. No, I did not see you; I am no keyhole watcher; but I saw that the paper had been moved. You said to yourself, as you have said before, 'What manner of man is this vicar of Altarnun?' and when you heard my footsteps on the path you crouched in your chair there, before the fire, rather than look upon my face. Don't shrink from me, Mary Yellan; there is no longer any need for pretence between us, and we can be frank with one another, you and I."

Mary turned to him and then away again; there was a message in his eyes she feared to read. "I am very sorry I went to your desk," she said; "such an action was unforgivable, and I don't yet know how I came to it. As for the drawing, I am ignorant of such things, and whether it be good or bad I cannot say."

"Never mind if it be good or bad, the point was that it frightened you?"

"Yes, Mr. Davey, it did."

"You said to yourself again, 'This man is a freak of nature, and his world is not my world.' You were right there, Mary Yellan. I live in the past, when men were not so humble as they are today. Oh, not your heroes of history in doublet and hose and narrow-pointed shoes—they were never my friends—but long ago in the beginning of time, when the rivers and the sea were one, and the old gods walked the hills."

He rose from his chair and stood before the fire, a lean black figure with white hair and eyes, and his voice was gentle now, as she had known it first.

"Were you a student, you would understand," he said, "but you are a woman, living already in the nineteenth century, and because of this my language is strange to you. Yes, I am a freak in nature and a freak in time. I do not belong here, and I was born with a grudge against the age, and a grudge against mankind. Peace is very hard to find in the nineteenth century. The silence is gone, even on the hills. I thought to find it in the Christian Church, but the dogma sickened me, and the whole foundation is built upon a fairy tale. Christ himself is a figurehead, a puppet thing created by man himself.

"However, we can talk of these things later, when the heat and turmoil of pursuit are not upon us. We have eternity before us. One thing at least, we have no traps or baggage, but can travel light, as they travelled of old."

Mary looked up at him, her hands gripping the sides of her chair.

"I don't understand you, Mr. Davey."

"Why, yes, you understand me very well. You know by now that I killed the landlord of Jamaica Inn, and his wife, too; nor would the pedlar have lived had I known of his existence. You have pieced the story together in your

255

own mind while I talked to you just now. You know that it was I who directed every move made by your uncle and that he was a leader in name alone. I have sat here at night, with him in your chair there and the map of Cornwall spread out on the table before us. Joss Merlyn, the terror of the countryside, twisting his hat in his hands and touching his forelock when I spoke to him. He was like a child in the game, powerless without my orders, a poor blustering bully that hardly knew his right hand from his left. His vanity was like a bond between us, and the greater his notoriety amongst his companions the better was he pleased. We were successful, and he served me well; no other man knew the secret of our partnership.

"You were the block, Mary Yellan, against which we stubbed our toes. With your wide enquiring eyes and your gallant inquisitive head, you came amongst us, and I knew that the end was near. In any case, we had played the game to its limit, and the time had come to make an end. How you pestered me with your courage and your conscience, and how I admired you for it! Of course you must hear me in the empty guest room at the inn, and must creep down to the kitchen and see the rope upon the beam: that was your first challenge.

"And then you steal out upon the moor after your uncle, who had tryst with me on Rough Tor, and, losing him in the darkness, stumble upon myself and make me confidant. Well, I became your friend, did I not, and gave you good advice? Which, believe me, could not have been bettered by a magistrate himself. Your uncle knew nothing of our strange alliance, nor would he have understood. He brought his own death upon himself by disobedience. I knew something of your determination, and that you would betray him at the first excuse. Therefore he should give you none, and time alone would quiet your suspicions. But your uncle must drink himself to madness on Christmas Eve, and, blundering like a savage and a fool, set the whole country in a blaze. I knew then he had betrayed himself and with the rope around his neck would play his last card and name me master. Therefore he had to die, Mary Yellan, and your aunt, who was his shadow; and, had you been at Jamaica Inn last night when I passed by, you too— No, you would not have died."

He leant down to her, and, taking her two hands, he pulled her to her feet, so that she stood level with him, looking in his eyes.

"No," he repeated, "you would not have died. You would have come with me then as you will come tonight."

She stared back at him, watching his eyes. They told her nothing—they were clear and cold as they had been before—but his grip upon her wrists was firm and held no promise of release.

"You are wrong," she said; "you would have killed me then as you will kill me now. I am not coming with you, Mr. Davey."

"Death to dishonour?" he said, smiling, the thin line breaking the mask of his face. "I face you with no such problem. You have gained your knowledge of the world from old books, Mary, where the bad man wears a tail beneath his cloak and breathes fire through his nostrils. You have proved yourself a dangerous opponent, and I prefer you by my side; there, that is a tribute. You are young, and you have a certain grace which I should hate to destroy. Besides, in time we will take up the threads of our first friendship, which has gone astray tonight."

"You are right to treat me as a child and a fool, Mr. Davey," said Mary. "I have been both since I stumbled against your horse that evening. Any friendship we may have shared was a mockery and a dishonour, and you gave me counsel with the blood of an innocent man scarce dry upon your hands. My uncle at least was honest; drunk or sober, he blurted his crimes to the four winds, and dreamt of them by night—to his terror. But you—you wear the garments of a priest of God to shield you from suspicion; you hide behind the Cross. You talk to me of friendship—"

"Your revolt and your disgust please me the more, Mary Yellan," he replied. "There is a dash of fire about you that the women of old possessed. Your companionship is not a thing to be thrown aside. Come, let us leave religion out

257

of our discussion. When you know me better we will return to it, and I will tell you how I sought refuge from myself in Christianity and found it to be built upon hatred, and jealousy, and greed—all the man-made attributes of civilization, while the old pagan barbarism was naked and clean.

"I have had my soul sickened. . . . Poor Mary, with your feet fast in the nineteenth century and your bewildered faun face looking up to mine, who admit myself a freak of nature and a shame upon your little world. Are you ready? Your cloak hangs in the hall, and I am waiting."

She backed to the wall, her eyes upon the clock; but he still held her wrists and tightened his grip upon them.

"Understand me," he said gently, "the house is empty, you know that, and the pitiful vulgarity of screams would be heard by no one. The good Hannah is in her cottage by her own fireside, the other side of the church. I am stronger than you would suppose. A poor white ferret looks frail enough and misleads you, doesn't he?—but your uncle knew my strength. I don't want to hurt you, Mary Yellan, or spoil that trace of beauty you possess, for the sake of quiet; but I shall have to do that if you withstand me. Come, where is that spirit of adventure which you have made your own? Where is your courage, and your gallantry?"

She saw by the clock that he must have overstepped already his margin of time and had little in reserve. He concealed his impatience well, but it was there, in the flicker of his eye and the tightening of his lips. It was half past eight, and by now Jem would have spoken with the blacksmith at Warleggan. Twelve miles lay between them perhaps, but no more. And Jem was not the fool that Mary herself had been. She thought rapidly, weighing the chances of failure and success. If she went now with Francis Davey she would be a drag upon him, and a brake on his speed; that was inevitable, and he must have gambled upon it. The chase would follow hard upon his heels, and her presence would betray him in the end. Should she refuse to go, why then there would be a knife in her heart at best, for he would not encumber himself with a wounded companion, for all his flattery.

Gallant he had called her, and possessed with the spirit of adventure. Well, he should see what distance her courage took her, and that she could gamble with her life as well as he. If he were insane—and this she believed him to be—why, then his insanity would bring about his destruction; if he were not mad, she would be that same stumbling block she had been to him from the beginning, with her girl's wits matched against his brains. She had the right upon her side, and faith in God, and he was an outcast in a hell of his own creation.

She smiled then and looked into his eyes, having made her decision.

"I'll come with you, Mr. Davey," she said, "but you'll find me a thorn in the flesh and a stone in your path. You will regret it in the end."

"Come as enemy or friend, that does not matter to me," he told her. "You shall be the millstone round my neck, and I'll like you the better for it. You'll soon cast your mannerisms aside, and all your poor trappings of civilization that you sucked into your system as a child. I'll teach you to live, Mary Yellan, as men and women have not lived for four thousand years or more."

"You'll find me no companion in your road, Mr. Davey."

"Roads? Who spoke of roads? We go by the moors and the hills, and tread granite and heather as the Druids did before us."

She could have laughed in his face, but he turned to the door and held it open for her, and she bowed to him, mocking, as she went into the passage. She was filled with the wild spirit of adventure, and she had no fear of him, and no fear of the night. Nothing mattered now, because the man she loved was free and had no stain of blood upon him. She could love him without shame, and cry it aloud had she the mind; she knew what he had done for her, and that he would come to her again. In fancy she heard him ride upon the road in their pursuit, and she heard his challenge and his triumphant cry.

She followed Francis Davey to the stable where the

horses were saddled, and this was a sight for which she was ill prepared.

"Do you not mean to take the trap?" she said.

"Are you not great enough encumbrance already, without further baggage?" he replied. "No, Mary, we must travel light and free. You can ride; every woman born on a farm can ride; and I shall hold your rein. Speed I cannot promise you, alas, for the cob has been worked today and will begrudge us more; as for the grey, he is lame, as you know, and will make poor mileage for us. Ah, Restless, this departure is half your fault, did you but know it; when you cast your nail in the heather you betrayed your master. You must carry a woman on your back as penance."

The night was dark, with a raw dampness in the air and a chill wind. The sky was overcast with low-flying cloud, and the moon was blotted out. There would be no light upon the way, and the horses would travel unseen. It seemed as though the first cast were against Mary, and the night itself favoured the vicar of Altarnun. She climbed into the saddle, wondering whether a shout and a wild cry for help would rouse the sleeping village, but even as the thought flashed through her mind she felt his hand upon her foot, placing it in the stirrup, and, looking down upon him, she saw the gleam of steel beneath his cape, and he lifted his head and smiled.

"That were a fool's trick, Mary," he said. "They go to bed early in Altarnun, and by the time they were astir and rubbing their eyes I should be away on the moor yonder, and you—you would be lying on your face, with the long wet grass for pillow, and your youth and beauty spoilt. Come now; if your hands and feet are cold, the ride will warm them, and Restless will carry you well."

She said nothing, but took the reins in her hands. She had gone too far now in her game of chance and must play it to the finish.

He mounted the bay cob, with the grey attached to him by a leading rein, and they set out upon their fantastic journey like two pilgrims.

As they passed the silent church, shadowed and enclosed,

and left it behind them, the vicar flourished his black shovel hat and bared his head.

"You should have heard me preach," he said softly. "They sat there in the stalls like sheep, even as I drew them, with their mouths agape and their souls asleep. The church was a roof above their heads, with four walls of stone, and because it had been blessed at the beginning by human hands they thought it holy. They do not know that beneath the foundation stone lie the bones of their pagan ancestors, and the old granite altars where sacrifice was held long before Christ died upon His cross. I have stood in the church at midnight, Mary, and listened to the silence; there is a murmur in the air and a whisper of unrest that is bred deep in the soil and has no knowledge of the church and Altarnun."

His words found echo in her mind and carried her away, back to the dark passage at Jamaica Inn. She remembered how she had stood there with her uncle dead upon the ground, and there was a sense of horror and fear about the walls that was born of an old cause. His death was nothing, was only a repetition of what had been before, long ago in time, when the hill where Jamaica stood today was bare but for heather and stone. She remembered how she had shivered, as though touched by a cold, inhuman hand; and she shivered now, looking at Francis Davey with his white hair and eyes: eyes that had looked upon the past.

They came to the fringe of moor and the rough track leading to the ford, and then beyond this and across the stream to the great black heart of the moor, where there were no tracks and no paths, but only the coarse tufted grass and the dead heather. Ever and again the horses stumbled on the stones, or sank in the soft ground bordering the marshes, but Francis Davey found his way like a hawk in the air, hovering an instant and brooding upon the grass beneath him, then swerving again and plunging to the hard ground.

The tors rose up around them and hid the world behind, and the two horses were lost between the tumbling hills. Side by side they picked their path through the dead bracken with short, uncanny stride.

Mary's hopes began to falter, and she looked over her shoulder at the black hills that dwarfed her. The miles stretched between her and Warleggan, and already North Hill belonged to another world. There was an old magic in these moors that made them inaccessible, spacing them to eternity. Francis Davey knew their secret and cut through the darkness like a blind man in his home.

"Where are we bound?" she said at length, and he turned to her, smiling beneath his shovel hat, and pointed to the north.

"The time will come when officers of the law will walk the coasts of Cornwall," he said. "I told you that on our last journey, when you rode with me from Launceston. But tonight and tomorrow we shall meet no such interference; only the gulls and the wild birds haunt the cliffs from Boscastle to Hartland. The Atlantic has been my friend before; savage perhaps and more ruthless than I intended, but my friend nevertheless. You have heard of ships, Mary Yellan, I believe, though of late you would not speak of them; and a ship it will be that shall carry us from Cornwall."

"So we are to leave England, are we, Mr. Davey?"

"What else would you suggest? After today the vicar of Altarnun must cast himself adrift from Holy Church and become a fugitive again. You shall see Spain, Mary, and Africa, and learn something of the sun; you shall feel desert sand under your feet, if you will. I care little where we go; you shall make the choice. Why do you smile and shake your head?"

"I smile because everything you say is fantastic, Mr. Davey, and impossible. You know as well as I do that I shall run from you at the first chance, and at the first village perhaps. I came with you tonight because you would have killed me otherwise, but in daylight, within sight and sound of men and women, you will be as powerless as I am now."

"As you will, Mary Yellan. I am prepared for the risk. You forget, in your happy confidence, that the north coast of Cornwall bears no relation to the south. You come from Helford, you told me, where the pleasant lanes wind by the side of the river, and where your villages touch one another string upon string, and there are cottages upon the road. This north coast is hardly so hospitable, as you will find. It is as lonely and untravelled as these moors themselves, and never a man's face shall you look upon but mine until we come to the haven that I have in mind."

"Let me grant you that, then," said Mary, with a bluster born of fear; "let me grant even that the sea is reached, and we upon your waiting ship, with the coast behind us. Name any country as you please, Africa or Spain, and do you think that I should follow you there and not expose you, a murderer of men?"

"You will have forgotten it by then, Mary Yellan."

"Forgotten that you killed my mother's sister?"

"Yes, and more besides. Forgotten the moors, and Jamaica Inn, and your own little blundering feet that stumbled across my path. Forgotten your tears on the highroad from Launceston, and the young man who caused them."

"You are pleased to be personal, Mr. Davey."

"I am pleased to have touched you on the raw. Oh, don't bite your lip and frown. I can guess your thoughts. I told you before, I have heard confessions in my day, and I know the dreams of women better than you do yourself. There I have the advantage of the landlord's brother."

He smiled again, the thin line breaking in his face, and she turned away so that she could not see the eyes that degraded her.

They rode on in silence, and after a while it seemed to Mary that the darkness of the night became intensified and the air closer, nor could she see the hills around her as she had before. The horses picked their way delicately, and now and again stopped in their tracks and snorted, as though in fear, uncertain of their steps. The ground was soggy now and treacherous, and, though Mary could no longer see the land on either side, she knew by the feel of the soft, yielding grass that they were encompassed by marshes.

This accounted for the horses' fear, and she glanced at her companion to discover his mood. He leant forward in his saddle, straining his eyes to the darkness that every moment became thicker and harder to penetrate, and she saw by his tense profile and his thin mouth tight closed like a trap that he was concentrating every nerve upon their passage, fraught suddenly with a new danger. The nervousness of her horse communicated itself to the rider, and Mary thought of these same marshes as she had seen them in the broad light of day, the brown tufted grass swaying to the wind, and, beyond, the tall, thin reeds quivering and rustling at the merest breath, crowded together and moving as one force, while beneath them the black water waited in silence. She knew how the people of the moors themselves could go astray and falter in their step, so that he who walked with confidence one moment could stumble the next, and sink without warning. Francis Davey knew the moors, but even he was not infallible and might lose his way.

A brook burbled and made song; a brook could be heard running over stones for a mile or more; but the water of the marshes made no sound. The first slip could be the last. Her nerves were strung to expectation, and half-consciously she made preparations to fling herself from the saddle should her horse stagger suddenly and with a sickening plunge grope like a blind thing in the strangling weeds. She heard her companion swallow, and the little trick put an edge upon her fear. He peered to right and left, his hat in his hand to better his sight, and already the moisture glistened in his hair and clung to his garments. Mary watched the damp mist rise from the low ground. She smelt the sour and rotting tang of reeds. And then, in front of them, barring their further progress, rolled a great bank of fog out of the night, a white wall that stifled every scent and sound.

Francis Davey drew rein, and the two horses obeyed him instantly, trembling and snorting, the steam from their flanks merging with the mist.

They waited awhile, for a moorland fog can roll away as suddenly as it comes, but this time there was no thin clearing of the air and no dissolving threads. It hung about them like a spider's web.

Then Francis Davey turned to Mary; like a ghost he looked beside her, with the fog on his lashes and his hair, and his white mask face inscrutable as ever.

"The gods have gone against me after all," he said. "I know these fogs of old, and this one will not lift for several hours. To continue now amongst the marshes would be worse madness than to return. We must wait for the dawn."

She said nothing, her first hopes returning to her again; but even as the thought came to her she remembered that fog baffled pursuit and was an enemy to the hunter as well as the hunted.

"Where are we?" she asked, and as she spoke he took her rein once more and urged the horses to the left, away from the low ground, until the yielding grass gave place to firmer heather and loose stones, while the white fog moved with them step by step.

"There will be rest for you after all, Mary Yellan," he said, "and a cave for your shelter and granite for your bed. Tomorrow may bring the world to you again, but tonight you shall sleep on Rough Tor."

The horses bent to the strain, and they climbed slowly and ponderously out of the mist to the black hills beyond.

Later Mary sat shrouded in her cloak like a phantom figure, with her back against a hollow stone. Her knees were drawn to her chin, with her arms clasped tight around them, but, even so, the raw air found its way between the folds of her cloak and lapped her skin. The great jagged summit of the tor lifted its face to the sky like a crown above the mist, and below them the clouds hung solid and unchanged, a massive wall defying penetration.

The air was pure here, and crystal clear, disdaining knowledge of the world below, where living things must grope and stumble in the mist. There was a wind here that whispered in the stones and stirred the heather; there was a breath, keen as a knife and cold, that blew upon the surface of the altar slabs and echoed in the caves. These sounds mingled with one another and became like a little clamour in the air.

Then they would droop again, and fall away, and an old dead silence come upon the place. The horses stood against a boulder for shelter, their heads together for company, but even they were restless and uneasy, turning now and again towards their master. He sat apart, a few yards distant from his companion, and sometimes she felt his eyes upon her in consideration, weighing the chances of success. She was ever watchful, ever ready for attack; and when he moved suddenly, or turned upon his slab of stone, her hands unclasped themselves from her knees and waited, her fists clenched.

He had bade her sleep, but sleep would never come to her tonight.

Should it creep to her insidiously, she would fight against it, beat it away with her hands and strive to overcome it, even as she must overcome her enemy. She knew that sleep might take her suddenly, before she was aware; and later she would wake with the touch of his cold hands upon her throat and his pale face above her. She would see the short white hair frame his face like a halo, and the still, expressionless eyes glow with a light that she had known before. This was his kingdom here, alone in the silence, with the great twisted peaks of granite to shield him and the white mist below to shroud him. Once she heard him clear his throat as though to speak; and she thought how far removed they were from any sphere of life, two beings flung together in eternity, and that this was a nightmare, with no day to follow it, so that soon she must lose herself and merge into his shadow.

He said nothing; and out of the silence came the whisper of the wind again. It rose and fell, making a moan upon the stones. This was a new wind, with a sob and cry behind it, a wind that came from nowhere, bound from no shore. It rose from the stones themselves, and from the earth beneath the stones; it sang in the hollow caves and in the crevices of rock, at first a sigh and then a lamentation. It played upon the air like a chorus from the dead.

Mary drew her cloak around her and pulled the hood about her ears to muffle the sound, but even as she did so the wind increased, tugging at her hair, and a little ripple of draught ran screaming to the cave behind her.

There was no source to the disturbance; for below the tor the heavy fog clung to the ground, obstinate as ever, with never a breath of air to roll away the clouds. Here on the summit the wind fretted and wept, whispering of fear, sobbing old memories of bloodshed and despair, and there was a wild, lost note that echoed in the granite high above Mary's head, on the very peak of Rough Tor, as though the gods themselves stood there with their great heads lifted to the sky. In her fancy she could hear the whisper of a thousand voices and the tramping of a thousand feet, and she could see the stones turning to men beside her. Their faces were inhuman, older than time, carved and rugged like the granite; and they spoke in a tongue she could not understand, and their hands and feet were curved like the claws of a bird.

They turned their stone eyes upon her and looked through her and beyond, heeding her not, and she knew she was like a leaf in the wind, tossed hither and thither to no ultimate purpose, while they lived and endured, monsters of antiquity.

They came towards her, shoulder to shoulder, neither seeing nor hearing her, but moving like blind things to her destruction; and she cried suddenly and started to her feet, every nerve in her body throbbing and alive.

The wind dropped and was no more than a breath upon her hair; the slabs of granite stood beyond her, dark and immobile, as they had done before, and Francis Davey watched her, his chin upon his hands.

"You fell asleep," he said; and she told him no, doubting her own statement, her mind still grappling with the dream that was no dream.

"You are tired, yet you persist in watching for the dawn," he said. "It is barely midnight now, and there are long hours to wait. Give way to nature, Mary Yellan, and relax. Do you think I want to harm you?"

"I think nothing, but I cannot sleep."

"You are chilled, crouched there in your cloak with a stone behind your head. I am little better myself, but there is no draught here from a crevice in the rock. We would do well if we gave our warmth to one another."

"No, I am not cold."

267

"I make the suggestion because I understand something of the night," he said; "the coldest hour comes before the dawn. You are unwise to sit alone. Come and lean against me, back to back, and sleep then if you will. I have neither the mind nor the desire to touch you."

She shook her head in reply and pressed her hands together beneath her cloak. She could not see his face, for he sat in shadow, with his profile turned to her, but she knew that he was smiling in the darkness and mocked her for her fear. She was cold, as he had said, and her body craved for warmth, but she would not go to him for protection. Her hands were numb now, and her feet had lost all feeling, and it was as though the granite had become part of her and held her close. Her brain kept falling on and off into a dream, and he walked into it, a giant, fantastic figure with white hair and eyes, who touched her throat and whispered in her ear. She came to a new world, peopled with his kind, who barred her progress with outstretched arms; and then she would wake again, stung to reality by the chill wind on her face, and nothing had changed, neither the darkness nor the mist, nor the night itself, and only sixty seconds gone in time.

Sometimes she walked with him in Spain, and he picked her monstrous flowers with purple heads, smiling on her the while; and when she would have thrown them from her they clung about her skirt like tendrils, creeping to her neck, fastening upon her with poisonous, deadly grip.

Or she would ride beside him in a coach, squat and black like a beetle, and the walls closed in upon them both, squeezing them together, pressing the life and breath from their bodies until they were flat, and broken, and destroyed, and lay against one another, poised into eternity, like two slabs of granite.

She woke from this last dream to certainty, feeling his hand upon her mouth, and this time it was no hallucination of her wandering mind, but grim reality. She would have struggled with him, but he held her fast, speaking harshly in her ear and bidding her be still.

He forced her hands behind her back and bound them,

268

neither hastily nor brutally, but with cool and calm deliberation, using his own belt. The strapping was efficient but not painful, and he ran his finger under the belt to satisfy himself that it would not chafe her skin.

She watched him helplessly, feeling his eyes with her own, as though by doing so she might anticipate a message from his brain.

Then he took a handkerchief from the pocket of his coat and folded it and placed it in her mouth, knotting it behind her head, so that speech or cry was now impossible, and she must lie there, waiting for the next move in the game. When he had done this he helped her to her feet, for her legs were free and she could walk, and he led her a little way beyond the granite boulders to the slope of the hill. "I have to do this, Mary, for both our sakes," he said. "When we set forth last night upon this expedition I reckoned without the mist. If I lose now, it will be because of it. Listen to this, and you will understand why I have bound you, and why your silence may save us yet."

He stood on the edge of the hill, holding her arm, and pointing downwards to the white mist below. "Listen," he said again. "Your ears may be sharper than mine."

She knew now she must have slept longer than she thought, for the darkness had broken above their heads and morning had come. The clouds were low, and straggled across the sky as though interwoven with the mist, while to the east a faint glow heralded the pale, reluctant sun.

The fog was with them still and hid the moors below like a white blanket. She followed the direction of his hand and could see nothing but mist and the soaking stems of heather. Then she listened, as he had bidden her, and far away, from beneath the mist, there came a sound between a cry and a call, like a summons in the air. It was too faint at first to distinguish, and the tone was strangely pitched, unlike a human voice, unlike the shouting of men. It came nearer, rending the air with some excitement, and Francis Davey turned to Mary, the fog still white on his lashes and his hair.

"Do you know what it is?" he said.

269

She stared back at him and shook her head, nor could she have told him had speech been possible. She had never heard the sound before. He smiled then, a slow grim smile that cut into his face like a wound.

"I heard once, and I had forgotten it, that the squire of North Hill keeps bloodhounds in his kennels. It is a pity for both of us, Mary, that I did not remember."

She understood; and with a sudden comprehension of that distant eager clamour she looked up at her companion, horror in her eyes, and from him to the two horses, standing patiently as ever by the slabs of stone.

"Yes," he said, following her glance, "we must let them loose and drive them down to the moors below They can serve us no longer now and would only bring the pack upon us. Poor Restless, you would betray me once again."

She watched him, sick at heart, as he released the horses and led them to the steep slope of the hill. Then he bent to the ground, gathering stones in his hands, and rained blow after blow upon their flanks, so that they slipped and stumbled amongst the wet bracken on the hillside; and then, when his onslaught continued and their instinct jogged them into action, they fled, snorting with terror, down the steep slope of the tor, dislodging boulders and earth in their descent, and so plunged out of sight into the white mists below. The baying of the hounds came nearer now, deep-pitched and persistent, and Francis Davey ran to Mary, stripping himself of his long black coat that hung about his knees and throwing his hat into the heather.

"Come," he said. "Friend or enemy, we share a common danger now."

They scrambled up the hill amongst the boulders and the slabs of granite, he with his arm about her, for her bound hands made progress difficult; and they waded in and out of crevice and rock, knee deep in soaking bracken and black heather, climbing ever higher and higher to the great peak of Rough Tor. Here, on the very summit, the granite was monstrously shaped, tortured and twisted into the semblance of a roof, and Mary lay beneath the great stone slab, breathless, and bleeding from her scratches, while he climbed above her, gaining foothold in the hollows of the stone. He reached down to her, and, though she shook her head and made sign that she could climb no further, he bent and dragged her to her feet again, cutting at the belt that bound her and tearing the handkerchief from her mouth.

"Save yourself, then, if you can," he shouted, his eyes burning in his pale face, his white halo of hair blowing in the wind. She clung to a table of stone some ten feet from the ground, panting and exhausted, while he climbed above her and beyond, his lean black figure like a leech on the smooth surface of the rock. The baying of the hounds was unearthly and inhuman, coming as it did from the blanket of fog below, and the chorus was joined now by the cries and the shouting of men, a turmoil of excitement that filled the air with sound and was the more terrible because it was unseen. The clouds moved swiftly across the sky, and the yellow glow of the sun swam into view above a breath of mist. The mist parted and dissolved. It rose from the ground in a twisting column of smoke, to be caught up in the passing clouds, and the land that it had covered for so long stared up at the sky pallid and newborn. Mary looked down upon the sloping hillside; and there were little dots of men standing knee deep in the heather, the light of the sun shining upon them, while the yelping hounds, crimson-brown against the grey stone, ran before them like rats amongst the boulders.

They came fast upon the trail, fifty men or more, shouting and pointing to the great tablets of stone; and, as they drew near, the clamour of the hounds echoed in the crevices and whined in the caves.

The clouds dissolved as the mist had done, and a patch of sky, larger than a man's hand, showed blue above their heads.

Somebody shouted again, and a man who knelt in the heather, scarcely fifty yards from Mary, lifted his gun to his shoulder and fired.

The shot spat against the granite boulder without touching her, and when he rose to his feet she saw that the man was Jem, and he had not seen her.

He fired again, and this time the shot whistled close to her ear, and she felt the breath of its passing upon her face.

The hounds were worming in and out amidst the bracken, and one of them leapt at the jutting rock beneath her, his great muzzle snuffling the stone. Then Jem fired once more; and, looking beyond her, Mary saw the tall black figure of Francis Davey outlined against the sky, standing upon a wide slab like an altar, high above her head. He stood for a moment poised like a statue, his hair blowing in the wind; and then he flung out his arms as a bird throws his wings for flight, and drooped suddenly and fell; down from his granite peak to the wet dank heather and the little crumbling stones.

Chapter 18

IT WAS a hard, bright day in early January. The ruts and holes in the highroad, which were generally inches thick in mud or water, were covered with a thin layer of ice, and the wheel tracks were hoary with frost.

This same frost had laid a white hand upon the moors themselves, and they stretched to the horizon pale and indefinite in colour, a poor contrast to the clear blue sky above. The texture of the ground was crisp, and the short grass crunched beneath the foot like shingle. In a country of lane and hedgerow the sun would have shone warmly, with a make-belief of spring, but here the air was sharp and cutting to the cheek, and everywhere upon the land was the rough, glazed touch of winter. Mary walked alone on Twelve Men's Moor, with the keen wind slapping her face, and she wondered why it was that Kilmar, to the left of her, had lost its menace and was now no more than a black scarred hill under the sky. It might be that anxiety had blinded her to beauty, and she had made confusion in her mind with man and nature; the austerity of the moors had been strangely interwoven with the fear and hatred of her uncle and Jamaica Inn. The moors were bleak still, and the hills were friendless, but their old malevolence had vanished, and she could walk upon them with indifference.

She was at liberty now to go where she would, and her thoughts turned to Helford and the green valleys of the south. She had a queer, sick longing for home in her heart and the sight of warm, familiar faces.

The broad river ran from the sea, and the water lapped the beaches. She remembered with pain every scent and sound that had belonged to her so long, and how the creeks branched away from the parent river like wayward children, to lose themselves in the trees and the narrow whispering streams.

The woods gave sanctuary to the weary, and there was music in the cool rustle of the leaves in summer, and shelter beneath the naked branches even in winter. She was hungry for birds and for their flight amongst the trees. She yearned for the homely murmurs of a farm: the cluck of hens, the clarion screech of a cock, and the flustered rasp of geese. She wanted to smell again the rich, warm dung in the sheds and feel the warm breath of cows upon her hands, heavy footsteps treading the yard, and the clank of pails beside the well. She wanted to lean against a gate and look upon a village lane, give good night to a passing friend, and see the blue smoke curl from the chimneys. There would be voices she would know, rough and gentle in her ear, and a laugh somewhere from a kitchen window. She would concern herself with the business of her farm; rise early and draw water from the well, move amongst her little flock with confidence and ease, bend her back to labour and count the strain a joy and an antidote to pain. All seasons would be welcome for the harvest they should bring, and there would be peace and contentment in her mind. She belonged to the soil and would return to it again, rooted to the earth as her forefathers had been. Helford had given her birth, and when she died she would be part of it once more.

Loneliness was a thing of poor account and came not into her consideration. A worker paid no heed to solitude, but slept when his day was done. She had determined upon her course, and the way seemed fair and good to follow. She would not linger any more as she had done during the week, faint and indecisive, but make known her project to the Bassats when she returned for the midday meal. They were kind and full of suggestions—overfull, perhaps, with their entreaties that she should stay amongst them, for the winter at least—and, rather than she should feel a burden upon them, had put to her, with kindly tact, that they would employ her even in some position in the household—have a care, perhaps, for the children, be companion to Mrs. Bassat herself.

To these conversations she had lent a meek and an unwilling ear, committing nothing, studiously polite, and continually thanking them for what they had already done.

The squire, bluff and good-humoured, twitted her at dinner for her silence. "Come, Mary, smiles and thanks are well enough in their way, but you must make up your mind. You are too young to live alone, you know, and I'll tell you to your face you're too pretty. There's a home for you here at North Hill, you know that, and my wife joins with me in begging you to stay. Plenty to do, you know, plenty to do. There are flowers to be cut for the house, and letters to write, and the children to scold. Why, you'd have your hands full, I promise you." And in the library Mrs. Bassat would say much the same, laying a friendly hand on Mary's knee. "We love to have you in the house; why do you not continue here indefinitely? The children adore you, and Henry told me yesterday you should have his pony if you but said the word! And that is a high tribute from him, I can assure you. We would give you a pleasant, carefree time, with no worries or cares, and you would be a companion to me when Mr. Bassat is away. Do you still fret after your home at Helford?"

Then Mary smiled and thanked her once again, but she could not put into words how much the memory of Helford meant to her.

They guessed that the strain of the past months still had its hand upon her, and in their kindness strove to make amends; but the Bassats kept open house at North Hill, and the neighbours for many miles around called, with, naturally enough, one topic of conversation on their lips. Fifty and a hundred times must Squire Bassat tell his tale, and the names of Altarnun and Jamaica became loathsome to Mary's ear, who would be rid of them for ever.

Here was another reason for departure: she had become too much an object of curiosity and discussion, and the Bassats, with a little show of pride, would point her as a heroine to their friends.

She strove in gratitude to do her best, but she was never at her ease amongst them. They were not her kind. They were another race, another class. She had respect for them, and liking, and good will, but she could not love them.

In the kindness of their hearts they would have her enter into conversation when company was present, and strove that she should not sit aside; while she longed the while for the silence of her own bedroom or the homely kitchen of Richards the groom, whose apple-cheeked wife would make her welcome.

And the squire, flogging his humour, would turn to her for advice, laughing heartily at every word he said. "There'll be the living vacant at Altarnun. Will you turn parson, Mary? I warrant you'd make a better one than the last"; and she must smile at this for his sake, wondering that he should be so dull as not to guess the bitter memories his words aroused.

"Well, there'll be no more smuggling at Jamaica Inn," he would say, "and, if I could have my way, no drinking either. I'll sweep the place clean of all those cobwebs, and not a poacher nor a gypsy will dare show his face within the walls when I have done with it. I'll put an honest fellow there who's never smelt brandy in his life, and he shall wear an apron round his waist, and write the word 'Welcome' above the door. And do you know who shall call upon him first? Why, Mary, you and I." And he would burst into a shout of laughter, slapping his thigh, while Mary forced a smile in answer, rather than his joke should fail.

She thought of these things as she walked alone on Twelve Men's Moor, and she knew she must go away from North Hill very soon, for these people were not her people, and only amongst the woods and streams of her own Helford valley would she know peace and contentment again.

There was a cart coming towards her from Kilmar, making tracks in the white frost like a hare. It was the one moving thing upon the silent plain. She watched it in suspicion, for there were no cottages on this moor except Trewartha, away in the valley by the Withy Brook, and Trewartha, she knew, stood empty. Nor had she seen its owner since he had fired at her on Rough Tor. "He's an ungrateful rascal, like the rest of his breed," said the squire. "But for me he'd be in jail now, with a long sentence to serve to break his spirit. I forced his hand and he had to knuckle under. I grant he did well after that and was the means of tracing you, Mary, and that black-coated scoundrel; but he's never as much as thanked me for clearing his name in the business, and has taken himself to the world's end now, for all I know. There's never been a Merlyn yet that came to any good, and he'll go the way of the rest of them." So Trewartha stood empty, and the horses were gone wild with their fellows and roamed free upon the moors, and their master had ridden away with a song on his lips, as she had known he would.

The cart came nearer to the slope of the hill, and Mary shielded her eyes from the sun to watch its progress. The horse bent to the strain, and she saw that it laboured beneath a strange load of pots and pans and mattresses and sticks. Someone was making for the country with his home upon his back. Even then she did not tumble to the truth, and it was not until the cart was below her and the driver, walking by the side, looked up to her and waved that she recognized him. She went down towards the cart with a fine show of indifference and turned at once to the horse to pat him and speak to him, while Jem kicked a stone under the wheel and wedged it there for safety.

"Are you better?" he called from behind the cart. "I heard you were sick and had taken to your bed."

"You must have heard wrong," said Mary. "I've been about the house there at North Hill and walking in the grounds; there's never been much the matter with me except a hatred for my neighbourhood."

"There was a rumour you were to settle there and be companion to Mrs. Bassat. That's more like the truth, I suppose. Well, you'll lead a soft enough life with them, I daresay. No doubt they're kindly people when you know them."

"They've been kinder to me than anyone else in Cornwall since my mother died; that's the only thing that matters to me. But I'm not staying at North Hill for all that."

"Oh, you're not?"

"No; I'm going back home to Helford."

"What will you do there?"

"I shall try and start the farm again, or at least work my way to it, for I haven't the money yet. But I've friends there, and friends in Helston too, that will help me at the beginning."

"Where will you live?"

"There's not a cottage in the village I couldn't call home if I wanted to. We're neighbourly in the south, you know."

"I've never had neighbours, so I cannot contradict you, but I've had the feeling always it would be like living in a box, to live in a village. You poke your nose over your gate into another man's garden, and if his potatoes are larger than your own there's a talking upon it, and argument; and you know if you cook a rabbit for your supper he'll have the sniff of it in his kitchen. Damn it, Mary, that's no life for anyone."

She laughed at him, for his nose was wrinkled in disgust, and then she ran her eye over his laden cart and the confusion he had there.

"What are you doing with that?" she asked him.

"I've got a hatred for my neighbourhood the same as you," he said. "I want to get away from the smell of peat and bog, and the sight of Kilmar yonder, with his ugly face frowning upon me from dusk till dawn. Here's my home,

277

Mary, all I've ever had of it, here in the cart, and I'll take it with me and set it up wherever my fancy takes me. I've been a rover since a boy; never any ties, nor roots, nor fancies for a length of time; and I daresay I'll die a rover, too. It's the only life in the world for me."

"There's no peace, Jem, in wandering, and no quiet. Heaven knows that existence itself is a long enough journey, without adding to the burden. There'll come a time when you'll want your own plot of ground, and your four walls, and your roof, and somewhere to lay your poor tired bones."

"The whole country belongs to me, Mary, if it comes to that, with the sky for a roof and the earth for a bed. You don't understand. You're a woman, and your home is your kingdom, and all the little familar things of day to day. I've never lived like that and never shall. I'll sleep on the hills one night, and in a city the next. I like to seek my fortune here and there and everywhere, with strangers for company and passers-by for friends. Today I meet a man upon the road and journey with him for an hour or for a year; and tomorrow he is gone again. We speak a different language, you and I."

Mary went on with her patting of the horse, the good flesh warm and damp beneath her hand, and Jem watched her, the ghost of a smile on his lips.

"Which way will you go?" she said.

"Somewhere east of Tamar, it doesn't matter to me," he said. "I'll never come west again, not until I'm old and grey, and have forgotten a lot of things. I thought of striking north after Gunnislake and making for the midlands. They're rich up there and ahead of everyone; there'll be fortune there for a man who goes to find it. Perhaps I'll have money in my pockets one day and buy horses for pleasure instead of stealing them."

"It's an ugly black country in the midlands," said Mary.

"I don't bother about the colour of the soil," he answered. "Moorland peat is black, isn't it? And so's the rain when it falls into your pigsties down at Helford. What's the difference?"

"You just talk for argument, Jem; there's no sense in what you say."

"How can I be sensible when you lean against my horse, with your wild daft hair entangled in his mane, and I know that in five or ten minutes time I shall be over the hill yonder without you, my face turned towards the Tamar and you walking back to North Hill to drink tea with Squire Bassat?"

"Delay your journey, then, and come to North Hill, too."

"Don't be a damned fool, Mary. Can you see me drinking tea with the squire, and dancing his children on my knee? I don't belong to his class, neither do you."

"I know that. And I am going back to Helford because of it. I'm homesick, Jem; I want to smell the river again and walk in my own country."

"Go on, then; turn your back on me and start walking now. You'll come to a road after ten miles or so that will take you to Bodmin, and from Bodmin to Truro, and from Truro to Helston. Once in Helston you will find your friends and make a home with them until your farm is ready for you."

"You are very harsh today, and cruel."

"I'm harsh to my horses when they're obstinate and out of hand; but it doesn't mean I love them any the less."

"You've never loved anything in your life," said Mary.

"I haven't had much use for the word, that's why," he told her.

He went round to the back of the cart and kicked the stone away from the wheel.

"What are you doing?" said Mary.

"It's past noon already, and I ought to be on the road. I've havered here long enough," he said. "If you were a man I'd ask you to come with me, and you'd fling your legs over the seat and stick your hands in your pockets and rub shoulders with me for as long as it pleased you."

"I'd do that now if you'd take me south," she said.

"Yes, but I'm bound north, and you're not a man, you're only a woman, as you'd know to your cost if you came with me. Move off from the trace there, Mary, and don't twist the rein. I'm going now. Good-bye."

He took her face in his hands and kissed it, and she saw that he was laughing. "When you're an old maid in mittens down at Helford, you'll remember that," he said, "and it will have to last you to the end of your days. 'He stole horses,' you'll say to yourself, 'and he didn't care for women; and but for my pride I'd have been with him now.' "

He climbed into the cart and looked down upon her, flicking his whip and yawning. "I'll do fifty miles before tonight," he said, "and sleep like a puppy at the end of it, in a tent by the side of the road. I'll kindle a fire and cook bacon for my supper. Will you think of me or not?" She did not listen, though; she stood with her face towards the south, hesitating and twisting her hands. Beyond those hills the bleak moors turned to pasture, and the pasture to valleys and to streams. The peace and quiet of Helford waited for her beside the running water.

"It's not pride," she told him; "you know that it's not pride; there's a sickness in my heart for home and all the things I've lost."

He said nothing, but drew the reins into his hands and whistled to the horse. "Wait," said Mary, "wait, and hold him still, and give me your hand."

He laid the whip aside and reached down to her and swung her beside him on the driver's seat.

"What now?" he said. "And where do you want me to take you? You have your back to Helford, do you know that?"

"Yes, I know," she said.

"If you come with me it will be a hard life, and a wild one at times, Mary, with no biding anywhere, and little rest and comfort. Men are ill companions when the mood takes them, and I, God knows, the worst of them. You'll get a poor exchange for your farm, and small prospect of the peace you crave."

"I'll take the risk, Jem, and chance your moods."

"Do you love me, Mary?"

"I believe so, Jem."

"Better than Helford?"

"I can't ever answer that."

"Why are you sitting here beside me, then?"

"Because I want to; because I must; because now and forever more this is where I belong to be," said Mary.

He laughed then and took her hand and gave her the reins; and she did not look back over her shoulder again, but set her face towards the Tamar.

HURRAY FOR ME
A nostalgic novel of childhood

"...one of the most moving novels
of childhood yet to appear on the American
scene. The total effect is powerful and unforgettable..."
—ST. LOUIS POST-DISPATCH

S. J. Wilson

75090/75¢

PUBLISHED BY
POCKET BOOKS, INC.